DIRTY BOSS

VOLUME ONE

K.M. SCOTT

SWEET THINGS

From the moment I met Maddie, I wanted her. I can have any woman I want, but she's all I can think of. She's supposed to be my in-house cook, except for the fact that I rarely eat at home.

So why do I have a cook at all? That's Louis DeVille's fault. I don't know how he did it, but the owner of DeVille Staffing somehow convinced me to hire a cook, despite the fact that I don't need or want one.

What I do want is Maddie. From the moment I met her, I haven't been able to think of anything but her. It's like I'm under a spell and I won't be normal again until I have her.

PRIVATE SECRETARY

No matter what it took—sixteen-hour workdays, no social life—I worked day and night and it paid off.

My tech company is what I always dreamed it could be and growing more each day.

My business partner thinks that means I need an assistant, so he had DeVille Staffing help out. Louis DeVille promised he would send over the perfect secretary to help me around the office.

The second I see Emma at my door, I'm sure that DeVille guy has made a mistake. Young, beautiful, and smart, she's a distraction I don't need in my work life.

The problem is what I need isn't the same as what I want.

PLAY DATE

The last thing I wanted was a five year old girl living in my house. Do they all cry this much or just my niece?

Thankfully, I'd heard about DeVille Staffing, so I called Louis DeVille and ordered up a nanny to solve my problem. I didn't care who he sent, as long as she could get my niece to stop all that noise.

Tia is only supposed to be here to take care of the little girl, but with every day she's living in my house, I can't think of anything but her. She's an even bigger distraction than my niece.

I usually hate losing my focus, but for Tia, I'm willing to change.

SWEET THINGS

K.M. SCOTT

addie

MY FRIENDS AND I GATHERED FOR OUR WEEKLY GET-together at Cat's apartment to drink wine and try to forget our troubles. Inevitably, though, reality snuck into our fun, and the fact that we all needed new jobs became the focus.

I poured myself another glass of wine and announced something I'd been thinking about for a while. "I think we need to strike out on our own. We have skills. We all do. So why not?" I said to my friends, Tia, Cat, and Emma, all four of us unemployed and not liking it one bit.

"Strike out on our own? What does that mean? And what kind of skills do we have?" Tia asked. She'd always been the timid one of the bunch, but I needed her to get on board with this plan if it was going to work.

Before I could answer her, Cat piped up with an even better answer than I had to give her. "Lots of things! I, for one, am a damn good driver. That doesn't seem like a big thing, but to people who can't or don't want to drive, I'm like some kind of magical being. You just have to think about what you do well. Maddie, you may not be a chef, but you're a damn good cook. And Tia, you're great with kids. Do you know how many people in this world have kids and need help with them? Millions. Maybe even billions."

She turned toward Emma and smiled. "And you're as organized as they come. Do you know how many people aren't in this world? People seek out that skill, as well as the ones the rest of us have."

"Exactly!" I said, jumping up from my chair as Cat's enthusiasm overcame me. "We just need to market ourselves. I say we start posting around on any site that will let us that we're here and ready to work. I know none of us have college degrees, but we can do this. We're young and full of ingenuity. That's a winning combination, in my opinion. What's the alternative? Low paying jobs don't pay the bills. I think we can all agree that's not going to work."

Although Emma and Tia didn't look completely convinced by my idea, they nodded their heads in agreement with Cat and me. This could work. I knew it. It had to because at the rate we were going, the four of us would be in real dire straits if it didn't.

Cat stood to join me. "Okay, then that's what we'll

do. We'll spend the day writing up ads we can post so the people who need our skills out there can find us. Time to sell ourselves, ladies!"

Emma's eyes opened wide. "Sell ourselves? What are we talking about here, Cat?"

I quickly moved to calm her. "Don't worry. We're not saying we're going to sell our bodies. What Cat means is we're going to create killer write-ups so people will be getting in line to pay us to do what we do especially well. Like with you, for example, your write up has to say how organized you are and how efficient you are as a worker. People who lack the ability to get their shit together love those kinds of things. Trust me. I'm one of them, and just hearing someone is organized and efficient makes them instantly impressive to people like me. Trust me, Em. This is going to work."

She took a deep breath and looked over at Cat and Tia. "Okay. Let's do this!"

Four hours later, we'd finished off the last three bottles of wine Cat had on hand and each of us had our ads. We'd written and rewritten them a dozen times, but finally, we liked what we had down on paper.

Each one of us had our skills highlighted, what tasks we could perform, and any other special things of interest we wanted potential employers to know. I made sure to include that I could be a live-in cook, if necessary, since I had no problem living somewhere else for a while.

"Remember, when you're posting on whatever site

you're on, be sure to check the Help Wanted section too. Your perfect employer-employee match might be lurking in there."

Cat added, "And if you're unsure what to say in reply to one of them, just type out what we wrote today. Now let's go post and get ourselves some good paying jobs!"

Two days of working every site that would take posts like ours had produced nothing for me, but I didn't lose hope. Sometimes these things took a little while. I just hoped they didn't take too long because I needed money and I needed it soon. My friend Candy had been nice enough to let me crash at her place for the past few months, but I knew that couldn't last forever.

Scrolling through the Help Wanted ads on the site I felt sure would produce some results, I came upon something I thought might be perfect for me.

Cook Needed for Private Residence

Position will require person to live on premises and work irregular hours. Additional requirements: ability to work well with others, clean criminal background, clean drug test, flexibility, interest in learning new things. Position will be rewarding to the right candidate.

I had experience in my uncle's restaurant all through high school doing everything from dishwashing to waitressing and then cooking on the line, and I had the ability to live wherever I wanted to and strange work hours didn't bother me in the least.

I'd always been told I worked well with others, and I was as clean as they came. Plus, I possessed an urge to learn new things, so it felt like the ad had been written just for me.

But did this would-be employer want someone with real training in cooking? I had the experience, but I was no professional chef. I'd worked at my uncle's restaurant all through school, but college had never appealed to me, so I instead decided to enter the workplace and make some money. The problem was I lived in what may have been the smallest town in the whole country, so there wasn't a lot of money to be made in Castine, Maine, a place that could boast having some very nice people and little else.

My uncle had offered to let me continue to work at his restaurant, but I wanted to try new things and see new places, so I set out on my own and headed toward New York City to visit my friend Candy, a childhood friend who had left our hometown the minute they handed her the diploma.

While I'd had some fun, after two months all my money was gone. I'd had some luck in finding odd jobs, but minimum wage paydays didn't go very far, so it was time to find a job that would pay more.

I looked at the bottom of the job listing and saw a name. DeVille Staffing. Below that was a number and a website address to apply for the job. My heart raced at the thought that I might have found something so quickly. My hands shaking, I clicked on the link and copied what my friends and I had written to sell me to potential employers.

Then I sent it off to DeVille Staffing and sat back, excited by the possibility that I'd soon hear something. I couldn't give up searching, though. I had a good feeling about that position, but I couldn't sit back and wait for them. My dwindling bank account demanded I keep looking.

But twenty minutes later, my phone let me know I had an email, and there in my inbox was a request to come in for an interview that afternoon at two. I quickly emailed back to say I'd be there, and then realized I had no idea of where DeVille Staffing was located.

No matter. I'd search for that later. First, I had to text my friends about my good luck.

I found something in the Help Wanted section of EmployWe this morning. I just got an email from a staffing agency to come in for an interview this afternoon. I'll let you know how it goes. Wish me luck!

"MADDIE THOMPSON!" SOMEONE YELLED FROM THE front of the waiting room of DeVille Staffing, and I looked up to see a pretty blond woman waving at me.

I gathered up my purse and my references and hurried to where she stood. "I'm Maddie."

"It's nice to meet you. Come with me."

"Okay. Thanks!" I answered enthusiastically, trying to show how eager I was to find a position, hopefully the one I'd applied for.

As we walked back toward an interview room past a line of people waiting to be called, the woman turned around and looked me up and down, making me doubt my choice of the black skirt and pink blouse. I should have gone with my favorite navy blue and white polka dot dress, but after a party at Candy's last week, I forgot to wash it, so business boring was the only choice available.

"Mondays really are busy days here, aren't they?" I asked, needing to fill the empty space in the conversation before my insecurity did as we entered a small room at the end of the hallway.

She nodded and smiled before offering me a seat at the table in the center of the room. "It definitely is. Take a seat and Mr. DeVille will be in shortly. Good luck!"

Before I could say a word, she disappeared, leaving me sitting there with my sweaty palms and butterflies in my stomach. Thankfully, I didn't have to wait too long before a very attractive man with jet black hair and sparkling blue eyes walked into the room. He wore a goatee that gave him a sinister look that intimidated me, but then he smiled and my fears melted away.

Closing the door behind him, he sat down and looked across the table at me, his blue eyes scanning my face for a moment before he said, "Welcome to DeVille Staffing, Maddie. I'm the owner, Mr. Louis DeVille. I've looked at your application and believe you're a perfect match with one of our best clients. If you can start today, we can get you together with your new employer, Mr. Eric Pierce, as his personal cook."

My heart leapt with joy! "Oh, that's wonderful. Thank you! I can start today, of course. Just tell me what I have to do and I'll do it."

Mr. DeVille jotted down a few notes on the application I'd filled out online and then looked up at me. A sly smile spread across his mouth.

"I like to hear an applicant say they'll do whatever they have to in order to make a client happy. I think you're going to be a perfect match for this position. Mr. Pierce is eager to get started immediately. Do you have any details to wrap up before heading out to his house?"

I quickly ran through anything that I might have to do before starting my new job and shook my head. "No, sir. I'm ready to go right now."

His gaze slid down to my breasts, and he arched a single dark eyebrow. "Excellent. I'll arrange transportation for you immediately, and you'll be at your new job in no time."

He stood to leave, but suddenly I began to question everything. Who was this Eric Pierce? Would I be working for just him, or was there an entire family living there that I'd be cooking for? I didn't doubt I could do the job, but I wanted to know what I was getting into.

"Excuse me, Mr. DeVille, but I was wondering if you could tell me a little about the position. How many people live in Mr. Pierce's home? Will I be required to prepare any menus to adhere to any special diets anyone must follow? I want to make sure I do the best job I possibly can."

The owner of DeVille Staffing looked down at me and smiled. "Very good questions. I like that you're so attentive, Maddie. I have a feeling Mr. Pierce will appreciate that too. To answer your questions, Mr. Pierce lives alone, except for other members of his staff. He will instruct you on what he will want you to prepare for him. Do you have any other questions?"

It felt like I should have a million other questions, but as I sat there looking up at Mr. DeVille and getting lost in those gorgeous blue eyes of his, I couldn't think of any others. "No, I guess not," I said quietly.

I needed a job badly, but something felt off about all of this. I couldn't put my finger on what, though.

"Is something wrong?" Mr. DeVille asked.

Hesitating because I didn't want to insult him, I finally squeaked out, "You run checks on clients, don't you? I mean, I know you run checks on those of us who are looking for jobs, but do you do the same for prospective employers? I only ask because I'm going to live there, so I feel like I should know."

As I spoke, his expression softened until he finally smiled when I finished. "That's a good question to ask, and you have every right to do so. I can assure you that we investigate all our employers, and Mr. Pierce is an upstanding citizen. You'll be in good hands with him."

I let out a heavy sigh. "Okay. Thank you."

"Good. You can go outside to the receptionist and

she'll instruct you on where to wait for your escort to Mr. Pierce's house. Good luck, Maddie, and remember that your job is to do exactly as your new employer demands. Do that, and I have no doubt you'll find your new position more than satisfactory."

And with that, he walked out, leaving me sitting there wondering if I'd gotten myself into more than I could handle. I didn't know who this Mr. Pierce was and now I was moving out to his home where he lived alone, except for his staff. I didn't even know where his house was located.

But I didn't have much of a choice. I needed money and I'd succeeded in getting hired, even though as I walked out to speak to the receptionist, I realized I hadn't asked one of the most important questions of all.

How much was I going to be paid for being Eric Pierce's cook?

JUST ABOUT AN HOUR LATER, THE CAR PULLED UP TO an enormous home with a grey stone façade and what looked like enough bedrooms to make the place a hotel. I stared out the backseat window as my mouth dropped open at my new home. Even though I'd likely be living in some small room in the servants' quarters at the rear of the home, I assumed, it still was the nicest place I'd ever been to.

"This is the place, miss," the driver said while he looked back at me in the rear view mirror.

I smiled and thanked him for the ride before I stepped out onto the circular driveway. I had no bags, which made me feel like I was missing something or homeless, and I watched as the car rolled away, leaving me standing there at this strange house and wondering if I'd made the biggest mistake of my life.

You need money, Maddie, so just suck it up and get in there.

"Can I help you?" a soft voice asked from behind me.

I turned around and saw a beautiful young woman with braided black hair down to her waist looking at me with a curious gaze. She had an exotic feel to her that I instantly wished I possessed, and for a moment, I was struck by how shiny her hair looked. Mine never looked like that, no matter what shampoo and conditioner I used.

Nervously tugging on my brown hair that barely reached my shoulders, I moved toward her and explained, "I'm here from DeVille Staffing. Mr. Pierce advertised for a cook, and they sent me."

God, that sounded sad, like I was some kind of consolation prize. I didn't think of myself like that, so why had the words come out so pathetic?

The woman didn't seem to pick up on it, though, and waved me toward her. "Okay. Come in and I'll let Mr. Pierce know you're here."

I followed her in through the massive front doors into a two-story grey stone entryway that matched the stone on the outside of the house and gave the place a ski lodge feel. She stopped me as she moved toward a room off to the right.

"Stay here, please. When he's ready, Mr. Pierce will call you in."

"Okay."

Standing there, I again felt out of place like I had outside after the driver dropped me off. I needed to get myself together before the man of the house came out and immediately wondered if Mr. DeVille had made a mistake choosing me to fill the position. So I took a deep breath and closed my eyes to steady myself.

It was, after all, just a cook job.

Except that it seemed to be at the finest house in all of New York State and the person I'd be working for might have more money than every man, woman, and child I'd ever met combined and times by ten.

"Miss Thompson?"

My eyes flew open, and I saw a man standing in front of me. At least six foot two, he wore a suit just like a man should, filling it out in all the right places. My gaze settled on his chiseled features, beautiful mouth, and deep blue eyes as they studied me. He was nothing less than stunning.

"Yes, I'm Maddie. Maddie Thompson, sir," I answered quickly, instantly nervous around him.

"No need for sir, Maddie. Please feel free to call me Eric. Follow me into my office so we can talk."

He turned around and began walking away, so I followed him and couldn't take my eyes off his perfect ass. It looked like you could bounce a quarter off it. I normally wasn't an ass woman, preferring a great set of washboard abs and what sat below, but Eric Pierce's ass could change my mind.

What that ass would feel like in my hands as he pumped into me...

I shook my head to push away the sexual fantasy playing in my mind and sat down in front of his desk when he offered me a seat. If I didn't learn to control myself around him, I wasn't going to make it through the first week without getting fired. I needed this job too much to let my overactive imagination get the best of me.

Eric leaned back in his chair and folded his arms behind his head in a way that made me feel like he knew how incredibly sexy he was and enjoyed lording it over others. With a sly grin, he said, "So tell me about yourself, Maddie. Why did you want to be my cook?"

Every professional answer I possessed seemed to disappear from my brain, leaving me staring at him and wondering what he looked like under that thousand dollar dark grey suit, tailored white dress shirt, and red power tie. Christ, this guy was like one huge walking aphrodisiac.

So without any clever answers to give, I chose to go with the truth and hoped he'd appreciate honesty. "I need a job and I've been a pastry chef before. It was in my uncle's restaurant, but the job was still the same as it would be at any other restaurant. I saw the DeVille Staffing ad online and decided to give it a try.

The worst that could happen was I didn't get the job and I was no worse off than before."

For a moment, Eric didn't say anything but just sat there staring at me like he was studying me to see if I was telling the truth. I waited for him to respond, hoping I hadn't blown my chance at the job even before I started.

Finally, he pursed his lips and made a smacking noise like he had just tasted something he liked. "Honesty. I love that in the people who work for me. You're going to fit in here just fine. You don't have any issues with the requirement that you live here? Won't your boyfriend or husband mind that he only gets to see you once a week on your only day off?"

I shook my head. "I don't have a boyfriend or husband, so there's no one to miss me at all, other than my friends, and they'll be fine seeing me only once a week," I said with a smile.

He lowered his arms and sat forward in his chair. "You sound perfect for the job. I'll let you get settled and tomorrow we'll start. Do you need any help with your things?"

I sheepishly looked around me at my non-existent bags. "I didn't really have time to pack anything. Mr. DeVille told me I had the job, and the next thing I knew I was sitting in the back of a car on my way here. I sort of assumed his driver would let me stop at my place to grab a few things, but he didn't."

My continued honesty seemed to make him happy, and he smiled at my answer. "Well, I'll have my driver take you to your apartment so you can get what you need. How does that sound?"

How it sounded was more than nice. Eric Pierce was not only incredibly sexy and gorgeous, but he was also more thoughtful than any boss I'd ever had before, even my uncle. If he was anywhere as considerate once I began actually cooking for him, I was going to love this job.

"Thank you so much. That's very nice of you. I have to admit I was wondering what I was going to do for clothes and a toothbrush."

My answer made him laugh out loud, and he threw his head back. "You have a wonderful way of cutting right to the nub of the issue. Well, take the rest of the day to go get your things and we'll start working tomorrow. I have a few events coming up, so I'll need you to plan some menus for me. I'm looking forward to seeing what you come up with."

Hearing he had events I'd have to design menus for made me doubt myself for a moment, but I'd just have to fall back on my experience at my uncle's restaurant. More than once, I'd helped him and my aunt with the catering for parties, so hopefully, this wouldn't be too different.

Eric reached across his desk to shake my hand, and just the touch of his skin on mine made something come alive inside me. His grip was strong and commanding, like a natural leader. I had no idea what he did for a living, but something told me as I looked into his dark blue eyes that he was definitely more than just some middle management type.

My curiosity about him took over, and before I knew it, I asked, "What do you do, Eric?"

Worried I'd overstepped my bounds, I took back my hand and shook my head. "I'm sorry. That was rude of me."

He smiled and shrugged like my intrusive question had been perfectly okay. "I'm the owner of The Cask Room in town."

"Oh. What's The Cask Room?" I asked, thinking his business might be a distillery.

"It's a restaurant. I've owned it for the past two years, and I'm very proud to say it's become a very popular destination for people coming from the city."

A restaurant? My new boss owned a restaurant and went to DeVille Staffing for a cook? That didn't make any sense at all.

I considered asking why he didn't just find a cook on his own since he likely could find a great one with little trouble as he was a restaurant owner, but I didn't say a thing and instead just smiled.

Nothing like having to prove yourself to a man who likely knows your job better than you ever could.

Eric stood from behind his desk and walked around to where I sat. Looking down at me, he smiled. "I'll have Magda show you to your room and then just let her know when you're ready to go and Clyde will drive you wherever you need to go. Magda can also tell you about the house and answer any questions you have about the place."

I stared up at him and felt myself become practically intoxicated by the sight of him. Those blue eyes looking down at me made me feel like he was looking directly into my soul, and his being so close to me made me unsure if my legs would hold me when I stood from my chair.

"Okay, thank you," I mumbled as I got up and prayed to God my knees didn't buckle.

Eric pressed his hand to my lower back and guided me toward the door. "I think you're going to work out perfectly, Maddie. I hope you like it here."

The feel of his palm against my body made an ache form in the pit of my stomach, and I clenched my thighs together to feel the sweet twinge of need settle in between my legs. If just his touch made me want him this much, I could only imagine what effect he'd have on me if we ever got to do anything like I'd fantasized about as I sat there in his office.

I turned around to face him and forced myself to say something intelligent. "I'm sure I will, Eric. I just hope you're happy with what I can do."

A slow smile spread across his perfectly full lips. "I'm sure I'll be more than pleased with you, Maddie."

If I didn't know better, I would have said Eric wanted me as much as I wanted him. But I must have been reading all the signs wrong. He was gorgeous and wealthy, a man who could have any woman he wanted.

What would he want with someone like me?

CHAPTER 2

ric

I WALKED BESIDE MADDIE AS I TOOK HER TO Magda's office in the back of the house and couldn't deny how gorgeous she was, even though she wasn't anywhere as polished as the women I usually preferred. That I even wanted to show her where to go was out of character for me. Normally, I would have pointed toward the hallway and sent her on her way.

But something in the way she seemed so candid intrigued me. Again, that was unlike the women I usually spent my time with. I'd gotten used to hearing lie after lie coming from the lips of beautiful women, so when Maddie answered my questions honestly, something inside me came alive.

As we approached Magda's office, I stopped so I could get a look of Maddie from behind. The view didn't disappoint. My cock strained against my boxers at the sight of her perfectly round ass and shapely legs making that boring business skirt look better than I had ever seen it look on any other woman.

She turned around when she realized I wasn't beside her anymore and caught me checking her out. Lifting my gaze from her beautiful ass, I smiled.

"You'll find Magda right in there. Come find me if you need anything today. I'll meet with you tomorrow morning bright and early before I leave for the restaurant to tell you what I want. Enjoy your night, Maddie."

"Thanks, Eric. I appreciate how welcoming you've been. I won't let you down," she said with an earnest look in her eyes I believed was real.

I headed back to my office to get ready to go to work with that gorgeous ass of Maddie's on my mind. I hadn't even wanted a cook, but now that she was here, I was happy Louis DeVille had talked me into hiring a cook for my personal use here at the house.

It was like the man knew what I needed even before I did.

WALKING THROUGH THE MAIN DINING ROOM OF THE Cask Room, I smiled at the last of the night's guests as they began to walk toward the exit. It had been a good day of business for the restaurant, much like every other day since opening a few years ago, and after glad-handing customers for hours, all I wanted to do was relax with a glass of scotch and soda with my friend and business partner.

I had the bartender Sheila pour me my drink and settled into a comfortable leather chair in one of the private rooms where Jack was already a full glass of whisky ahead of me. With his feet up on one of the coffee tables in the middle of two chairs, he grinned wide and gave me one of those Irish smiles that never failed to make women fall at his feet.

He tilted his glass up until the last drop of alcohol slid into his mouth. Running his hand through his dark hair, he groaned. "Man, this day has been a bitch. I needed this night to end about twelve hours ago."

"It wasn't too bad," I said as I took my first drink of scotch since the day before.

Jack set his glass down on the table and leaned back in his chair. "What's with you today? You've been like some motherfucking Pollyanna, all happy and shit. Even when that party of eight wanted to argue over every fucking thing they ordered, that damn smile never left your face. What's going on? You want to share with class, Eric?"

"What are you talking about? Just because I don't chew customers out when they have a problem doesn't mean I'm a fucking Pollyanna. Man, a guy is anything but miserable one goddamn day and he gets this kind of grief."

I tipped my glass up and let the scotch slide into my mouth before it went on its way down my throat. Jack wasn't the type of guy to just let something go, though, so I waited for him to continue to pry into why I seemed happier tonight.

A few seconds later, he leaned forward and stared at me, narrowing his eyes like he was studying my behavior. "What's with all the damn smiling tonight? Something is definitely up with you."

I realized I was smiling and pressed my lips together for a moment to stop my grinning. "Why does something have to be up for me to be happy? Fuck. Nothing like working all day and then being subjected to an interrogation. Just get yourself another drink and stop worrying about my mood."

"You've been downright pleasant, Eric. That's not your style. Did you get a blowjob on your way into work today? At least that would explain you being in a good mood, although I'd need about five blowjobs to be as happy as you are today. Let me guess. That blond who came in last week to talk about going with that produce company she works for. Fuck, I'd do her."

I thought back to the woman he was talking about and had to admit I had liked her. Halfway through our discussion about produce, all I could think about was bending her over the desk in my office and burying myself balls deep inside her. That I didn't make a move on her was only because our meeting got interrupted by half a dozen problems that suddenly cropped up just as she and I were getting friendly.

Fucking servers and their issues.

But the sexy produce saleswoman wasn't the

reason my mood had taken a turn for the better that day.

"She was hot, wasn't she? A hell of a lot better than the usual produce salesmen we get here."

Jack laughed, throwing his head back. "So is that why you're so fucking happy today? Did you get with her last night?"

I shook my head and smiled. "No. Didn't even make a move."

His eyebrows shot up into his forehead and his eyes grew wide to show his disbelief. "You're crazy, man. If you aren't planning on going after her, I will the next time she comes in to talk celery stalks and melons. Hey, that sounds like code for sex. I'm going to fuck her wild with my stalk and come on her melons."

Sometimes Jack acted like a sixteen year old with a perpetual hard on. Well, most of the time. And at the moment, he looked like he was about to come all over himself.

"Settle down. You might want to try to make yourself sound older than an adolescent if you want to get into that woman's pants."

He pointed at me and grinned. "Now there's the curmudgeon we all know and love. But I still want to know what was making you all happy and mellow tonight. If it's not the melon lady, was it that bartender you used to sleep with? Is she back in town? I thought she got married, though."

"Dude, that was like three years ago when Casey

and I were together. And I don't do married women. Ever. It's a hard and fast rule."

Frustrated with my refusal to just spill the beans about what had caused my good mood, he rolled his eyes and poured himself another glass of whisky. He took a drink and then got right back to his interrogation.

"Fine. So if it isn't melon girl or Casey, who put that smile on your face today?"

"I do see other women than ex-girlfriends I haven't been with in years and the produce saleswoman, Jack."

His eyes grew wide and he barked, "For fuck's sake, will you just tell me what the fuck is making you so happy today, Eric? I'm sick of this cat and mouse game, and I'm not drunk enough to not care, so put me out of my fucking misery already, will you?"

As much as I enjoyed busting Jack's balls, I did sort of want to tell someone about Maddie. Since he was the closest thing I had to a best friend, I figured why not? Maybe talking about it would help me figure out why I couldn't get her off my mind.

"Okay, but I can't explain this whole thing, so don't ask me to."

He arched one eyebrow and leveled his gaze on me. "I'm intrigued. What can't you explain?"

After I took a sip of scotch, I tried to put together what I wanted to say and finally just said what was on my mind. Even if it sounded bat shit crazy.

"Do you remember that guy who came into the restaurant a week or so ago? The one with the jet black hair and goatee? He owns the employment agency DeVille Staffing."

Jack thought about what I said for a moment and nodded. "Yeah, I think so. He drank a shit ton of cognac, didn't he?"

"Yeah," I said, remembering how much Louis DeVille liked his drink of choice.

"Okay. So you're happy because of him?" Jack asked, completely missing the point.

"No. But I was talking to him that night and mentioned I needed a maid. He told me to come in and talk to him, so I did. By the time I left his office that day, he had me convinced I needed a cook for the house."

"Dude, you live alone. You eat most of your meals here, for fuck's sake. What do you need a cook for?" Jack asked, shaking his head in disbelief.

"I didn't think I did. I walked into his office wanting a maid, and I walked out with his promise that he'd send me the perfect cook."

"Sounds like a quack to me. You, better than anyone else, would know where to find a great cook. Hell, if I wanted to hire someone like that, I'd ask you for help. What makes this guy think he knows better than you?"

I shook my head, still not quite understanding why the owner of DeVille Staffing had been able to convince me that I needed to hire a cook. "I have no idea, and to be honest, I'm not sure how he made me agree to it, but I did and she showed up at my house this afternoon to start as my live-in cook."

Jack smiled broadly and excitedly smacked his leg. "Now we're getting somewhere! I knew it was a woman. You had that look on your face. So what happened? What's she like?"

Everything I knew about Maddie raced through my mind. "Hot. Like fucking hot. Brunette with big brown eyes hot."

Wincing like he was in pain, Jack leaned back in his seat. "I love that look. That big brown eye thing never fails to make me want a woman. How's the body?"

"Gorgeous. Big tits, great legs, and an ass I can't wait to have in my hands."

"Damn. She doesn't sound like any cook I've ever seen, and we've had a lot come through these doors. Where's she from?"

I shook my head. "I have no idea. I didn't ask. DeVille said he'd check out all the applicants and send out the best one, so I left everything up to him. I don't even know what kind of experience she has. All I know is she showed up today and I couldn't take my eyes off her. Hell, thank God for my desk because I had a hard on the whole time I was sitting there talking to her."

"So now you have a cook you don't need and no maid that you do need. This DeVille guy doesn't sound very good at his only job of filling positions. At least she's hot. There's that."

"Yeah, I guess. It's just weird. She's not like any woman I've ever been interested in, but from the minute I saw her, I couldn't take my eyes off her."

"Well, what's the name of this super-hot woman who's got your head all turned around?" he asked, chuckling.

"Maddie Thompson."

"So now you have a gorgeous woman working for you as practically a servant. I think this might be a fantasy come true. Why do great things always happen to you?" Jack asked, practically sulking.

He wasn't wrong. Having Maddie living with me did seem to be an opportunity for something pretty great. I'd be a fool not to take advantage of that practically dropping in my lap.

"So have you made your move yet?"

"No. I haven't done anything yet. I had Clyde take her back to her apartment to get her things so she can start work tomorrow."

Jack laughed. "And what will she be doing since you don't eat at your house ninety percent of the time?"

"I guess maybe I'll start eating there from now on. I lied and told her I was going to be having a few parties soon that she'd have to create menus for. I could do that too."

"Cool. Make sure to invite me because I want to get a look at this sexy cook who should have been a maid," Jack joked.

"You're the last person I'm having to a party, man. You'll be all over her two minutes after you walk through the door. You're a dog, dude."

He winced like what I said hurt him. "You cut me deep, Eric. Do you actually think I'd swoop in on a girl you had your eyes on? What kind of friend and business partner do you think I am?"

"The kind who would do exactly that. Do you remember when I told you I liked Casey? Not a day later, I caught you trying to ask her out in the stockroom."

Narrowing his eyes, he hummed. "That's right. I am a dog. Damn. What if I promise to not make a move on your cook? Can I still come to the party?"

I blew the air out of my lungs slowly, already sure I didn't want to have any parties. "If I decide to do anything, I'll let you know."

"So how much are you paying this woman to basically appear in your fantasies until you sleep with her since you don't need a cook?"

There was no way in hell I was going to tell Jack I'd agreed to pay a full time salary for a cook I didn't need. Drinking the last of my scotch, I stood up and headed toward the door.

"Night, Jack. See you tomorrow."

CHAPTER 3

M addie

BRIGHT AND EARLY THE NEXT MORNING, I STOOD beside the butcher-block topped center island and marveled that a man who lived alone and who Magda had warned me rarely ate his meals at the house had what was nothing less than a chef's kitchen.

White quartz and stainless steel filled the room. To my left was another island, and on the back wall a built-in restaurant grade refrigerator and freezer. On the other side of the kitchen stood a gas range with a grill and griddle and two ovens.

What on earth could a man who liked to eat at restaurants all the time want with a kitchen like this?

"It's gorgeous, isn't it?" he said as he walked up behind me.

I turned around to see him standing there at eight

28

o'clock in the morning looking stunning in his black suit and a sapphire blue dress shirt that made the blue of his eyes pop. The man knew how to wear a suit, no doubt.

Just being next to him made me forget everything about the incredible kitchen I stood in, and my mind drifted to the erotic fantasies I'd had the night before lying in bed in my new room at the back of the house. The smell of his masculine cologne wafted toward me, and I found myself taking a deep breath in to savor it. Woodsy with hints of lavender and vanilla, the scent was intoxicating. I wanted to press my nose to his neck and lose myself in the delicious smell and him.

"Definitely gorgeous," I answered, meaning more than one thing in that room could be described that way.

"I don't think I've eaten food cooked here more than a handful of times. I'm looking forward to you changing that, though," he said with a sexy smile that showed off his straight white teeth.

Unable to take my eyes off him, I tried to keep my mind on my work, as hard as that was. "About that. What kind of meals are you looking for?"

He hesitated, and it seemed like he wasn't sure how to answer my very simple question. I didn't necessarily need specific details, but I hoped he would tell me what he liked, at least.

Before he answered, I tried to explain what I needed from him. "I mean, is there anything you don't like? Like liver? Nobody seems to like liver, so unless you tell me you want liver, I won't be making that for you."

Eric pursed his lips and groaned. "No, I have no interest in liver. You can also forget meatloaf and anything called a pot pie."

I chuckled at his swipe at the common meals I'd grown up with back home. "Got it. Is there anything you'd like? I want to make you happy, and the best way to do that is to know what you want as much as what you don't want."

He ran his tongue along his perfect bottom lip and smiled. "I think you might be the only person in the world at this moment that wants to make me happy. I like that. I also like pork. It's mundane, but there it is."

"Now we're getting somewhere. Pork. Okay. How about Italian food? Yay or nay?" I asked as I scanned the room for a pen and paper.

Handing me a pen from his pocket, he answered, "I love Italian. Lasagna is my favorite, but I can do manicotti or stuffed shells."

I found a sheet of paper in a drawer nearby and scribbled down what he said. Looking up, I saw him smiling. He looked happy and relaxed, but I had the sense he didn't usually feel that way.

"Okay. I have something to go on. Now how many meals a day will you be eating here? Since you own a restaurant, I'm guessing you won't be eating at least one here each day."

He took a few steps toward me and stopped just a few feet away. "I haven't eaten breakfast since I was in

high school and I needed the strength for practice, so
let's say dinner only for now."

The scent of his cologne began to make me think
impure thoughts about him again, so I shook my head
slightly to clear my mind and quickly wrote down the
word dinner. Without looking up, I asked, "And what
time do you expect dinner to be served?"

"I've been planning on changing my schedule for
months, so this will give me a good reason to be out of
the restaurant by eight. Let's say nine o'clock. I won't
be able to be back here tonight or tomorrow night by
then, but let's aim for Thursday, okay Maddie?"

The way my name left his lips like some sexy
whisper made me look up, and instantly my stomach
dropped when I saw him staring at me with a look of
want in his eyes. I hadn't been wrong yesterday. I
didn't know how I could honestly think it, but I did.

He wanted me like I wanted him.

The only problem was I would have to be crazy to
sleep with my boss. Anyone with half a brain knew
that was a road to nowhere but unemployment. I
needed this job and the money it offered too much to
risk getting fired because I couldn't keep my hands off
the hottest man I'd ever met.

A man with a mouth I was sure could take my
body to heights it had never experienced before.

"Nine o'clock it is, Mr. Pierce."

"Please call me Eric. We're going to be living here
together, so we might as well be friendly."

Something in the way he said the word friendly
and the way his eyes sparkled when he told me to call

him by his first name made me wonder just how long we'd be able to keep up this employer-employee business relationship.

If only I didn't need this job so badly.

AFTER TALKING TO MAGDA AND FINDING OUT ERIC had an account at Canton's store in town, I had his driver take me there so I could buy ingredients I needed to make some meals to practice before Thursday. A few hours later, I'd gotten enough groceries for what I had planned and was ready to start cooking.

But who would be my guinea pigs?

As I shuffled around the kitchen whipping up Calabrian Pork, I saw Magda and Chloe, another member of the household staff, pass by the doorway. They would be perfect!

"Excuse me," I called out as I finished deglazing the pan with some white wine. "Could you help me with something? Both of you, if you don't mind."

The two women stopped and exchanged a shared look of what I imagined was confusion before nodding hesitantly. Magda and Chloe could best be described as polar opposites. Compared to Magda's dark and exotic looks, Chloe's pale blond hair cut short into a pixie style and fair skin seemed almost Nordic. For all I knew, she may have been that.

"What do you need from us?" Magda asked as they stepped into the kitchen.

I added the sliced potatoes and red peppers to the

oil in the skillet and set the heat to medium. Wiping my hands on my apron, I smiled and hoped the two of them would be willing to be part of my experiment.

"I'm making a few meals before Mr. Pierce has his first meal on Thursday, and it would be so helpful if you'd try them out. Today I'm cooking Calabrian Pork. Would you two eat some for lunch and let me know what you think?"

Neither one seemed thrilled by my offer. Magda's expression still showed her confusion about this whole thing, and I had a feeling Chloe would at any moment just turn on her heels and walk out.

Before they could say no, I moved to my next plan. Begging.

"Please. I really need this job, and I don't want to disappoint Mr. Pierce. I know you don't know me from a can of paint, so if you don't want to do this to help me, do it to help him. Pretty please."

That seemed to melt their resistance to my offer, and they nodded in unison. "Okay. My mother used to make that exact dish when I was a kid, so it'll be nice to have it again," Chloe said with a tiny smile.

"Excellent! Thank you so much. I really appreciate this," I gushed as I backed up toward the stove where my potatoes and peppers cooked. "I just have to finish, so give me about twenty minutes and lunch will be served."

The two women smiled and left as I began to complete the final steps in the recipe. This would be good. They seemed to be nice people, but I had the sense that neither one of them cared much about hurting my feelings, so they'd be honest about how the dish tasted.

I just didn't want to mess this up.

A half hour later, the three of us sat around the kitchen table with my Calabrian Pork meal waiting to be enjoyed. I watched, holding my breath, as they both lifted their forks to their mouths and tasted the dish for the first time.

It felt like forever before one of them spoke, but finally Chloe said, "This is the tenderest pork I've ever had in my life. This puts my mother's to shame. This is really good, Maddie."

Magda agreed, and after taking another forkful of pork and potato, she sighed. "I love the spices you used. Oregano and basil? And garlic, of course. But it's not too strong. Just right. If all your meals are like this, Mr. Pierce is going to love you."

I felt my cheeks heat at the mention of Eric feeling anything for me, but I knew she meant my cooking and the food, not me, necessarily. Nervous, I hurriedly replied, "That's what I'm hoping for. That he loves the food I make, I mean."

My stomach dropped as Chloe stopped chewing and gave me a look like she saw exactly how attracted I was to our boss. "What I don't understand is why he hired you to cook. I don't mean to be rude, but Mr. Pierce rarely eats any of his meals here."

"I know. He told me that, and I'm not sure I know the answer. Maybe he's tired of restaurant food?" I answered, still confused about why a man who clearly could find his own top-rate chef would use DeVille Staffing to find someone like me.

"Maybe. It still seems odd to me," Chloe mumbled before taking another bite of pork. Then a second later, she turned to look at Magda. "You don't think he's selling his share of the restaurant, do you?"

Magna simply shook her head until she finished her food and then said, "Even if he was, it still doesn't mean he'd suddenly start eating at home enough to warrant hiring a cook."

I was beginning to feel out of place, so I turned to my lunch and started eating, hating how unnecessary I truly was here. At least the Calabrian Pork had turned out right. Just enough garlic and I didn't dry out the pork.

As they talked between themselves, Chloe dropped her fork onto her plate and exclaimed, "Oh my God! He's hired Maddie here because he's worried someone's not doing their job. That's it! He's going to be around much more to see who's slacking off, and then that person is going to be fired. I know it."

Magda tried to talk her out of spiraling out of control, but I saw in her expression she worried about that exact thing too. When I finished my mouthful of food, I said, "Not to put a damper on this wild speculation, but he didn't have to hire a cook to stay home more and eat. I'm sure he could just have someone from his own restaurant deliver food every day, or he could get any other restaurant within a ten mile radius to bring him food."

The both of them stopped their fretting and looked

across the table at me with relief. "That's true," Magda said, smiling. "It makes sense he could just get food from anywhere."

Chloe's eyes lit up. "That's true. I mean, it's not like we're out in the wilderness where he can't find food anywhere he wants. I guess that does make sense. Maybe he just wants home cooked meals. If that's the case, I bet he's going to love this pork and potatoes meal. Assuming he likes pork, of course."

"Oh, he does," I said proudly, happy to hear she thought he'd love my cooking. "He made a point of telling me he loves pork. That and Italian food, so I'm going to make him lasagna for Thursday's dinner."

Magda and Chloe cooed at the mention of lasagna. "Oooooh, any chance you'll make enough for there to be leftovers and then we can sneak some?" Chloe asked.

"I'll make sure to make enough, I promise."

CHAPTER 4

*M*addie

BY THURSDAY, I'D COOKED MAGDA AND CHLOE Calabrian Pork and Chicken Orzo as I eased into the lasagna meal I planned for Eric. They'd loved both dishes, so I felt pretty sure tonight's dinner would be a hit. I wanted to impress him and let him know that he hadn't made a mistake by hiring me, despite my complete lack of experience as a personal chef.

There was just one problem.

I'd never made lasagna before in my life. I'd never even eaten lasagna. Not even once. My uncle's restaurant hadn't featured it on the menu and my mother had an irrational hatred of anything with noodles, so I'd never gotten a single chance at experience with it.

Thank God for the internet. Two dozen YouTube

videos later, I had a good sense of what a pan of lasagna should look like and exact instructions on how to make it.

Around seven, I set about cooking the lasagna noodles in a pot of boiling water and turned my attention to browning the hamburger meat in a pan on the most impressive gas stove I'd ever seen. Then I put that off to the side and cooked bell pepper, onion, and fresh garlic together before adding the meat to that skillet.

So far, so good.

Next came the crushed tomatoes, tomato sauce, and tomato paste, along with parsley, oregano, and even more garlic. As the kitchen began to smell of the delicious lasagna sauce, I let it simmer for the time the recipe called for and turned back to making sure the pasta didn't overcook to soggy sheets of droopy noodles.

By the time I was done layering the drained noodles and sauce mixture three times until it all reached the top of the dish, I'd convinced myself I was quite the lasagna wiz. Forty-five minutes in the oven and Eric's favorite Italian meal was ready.

I excitedly cut into the dish and scooped out a piece onto a plate for him as I heard him arrive just before nine. Setting out a basket of bread and a dish of butter, I had everything ready for him when he sat down.

"This looks incredible, Maddie," he said as he picked up his fork. "I'm starving, so this is perfect."

He took a bite and began chewing, but the look on

his face said my wonderful lasagna wasn't a hit in his mind. Smiling as he swallowed the forkful, he looked up at me and I instantly knew what I'd done wrong.

The cheese! I'd forgotten to add the ricotta cheese!

"Um, this is different. I've never had lasagna that tastes like this."

I felt like I wanted to fade into the blue dining room wall behind me. My first meal made for him and I'd ruined it.

"I'm so sorry. I forgot the cheese. I can't believe I messed this up. I'm so, so sorry."

Looking down at the floor because I couldn't bear to face him after making such a stupid mistake, I waited for him to tell me I was fired. I deserved it. I'd had a chance to impress him with a meal any idiot could make, and I hadn't been able to do it.

And now I'd lose my position, just as I should.

He said nothing for a few moments, which only made the inevitable all the worse. Too afraid to look up, I stood there waiting to hear him say the words that I hadn't even made it a full meal into my job cooking for him before messing up.

Whatever he chose to say to me, I had it coming.

"It's okay, Maddie," he said in a low voice. "Maybe lasagna isn't your specialty."

Embarrassed, I avoided his gaze and quickly left the room as my emotions threatened to overwhelm me. I didn't need to wait around for him to fire me.

I headed toward my room and quickly began packing my things I'd just put away a few nights before. I couldn't believe how stupid I'd been. This job had never been a good fit for me. Why did I let that DeVille man convince me that I could do this? I wasn't a personal cook. All I'd ever really done at my uncle's restaurant was make desserts.

Whatever I'd wanted to believe, I wasn't the right woman for this position.

After packing my suitcase until it couldn't hold any more clothes, I turned around and saw Eric standing in the doorway. "I'll just send someone to get the rest of my things if you don't want to have your driver bring them to me. Whichever way you want to do it."

He didn't say a word and instead just stared at me as he loosened his tie and unbuttoned the top button on his shirt. I waited for him to speak, and when he didn't, I moved to push past him so I could escape the awkwardness of standing there not knowing what to say or do.

As I reached him, he slid his arm around my waist and stopped me. "Where are you going?"

I looked up and saw not anger or disappointment in his eyes but something else. Something I'd seen in them that morning in the kitchen.

"I thought I should go. I made a mess of the lasagna, and I figured you were just going to fire me anyway, so I thought I'd make it easy on both of us."

"People make mistakes. Things happen. I know you can cook, Maddie. I had some of that pork you made the other day and that was great, and yesterday's chicken and orzo I found in the refrigerator was delicious."

"I didn't realize you had any of those."

He shook his head and smiled. "Well, I did, and that's why I wasn't going to fire you, Maddie. Put your suitcase down."

I did as he ordered, dropping my heavy suitcase onto the floor with a thud, as I stared up into those blue eyes staring down at me. "You're not firing me?"

"No," he answered in a husky voice that hit me deep inside and made my body ache. "I want you to stay. Do you want to stay?"

My mind swam with a single word as I watched him lick his lips. "Yes."

He didn't say anything else but leaned down and brushed his mouth against mine, teasing me and making me whimper in need. I wanted him to kiss me with those perfect lips. I wanted to feel his body against mine, and I didn't care if I had a job afterward.

I just wanted him.

Lifting my arms, I encircled his neck and trailed my fingertips across where his hair hit his collar. It felt silky against my skin. I leaned in toward him and inhaled deeply the scent of his cologne that had excited me every time he was nearby.

As I reveled in the sensations he created in me, Eric slid his hands down to my ass and squeezed hard, sending strings of desire through me. I moaned and pressed my face to his neck, loving how he felt against my lips.

"I want to be inside you so fucking bad, Maddie," he whispered, tilting his hips so his rock hard cock pressed against the front of my pants.

Before I could say I wanted him too, he kissed me

hard on the lips, taking my breath away. He unbuttoned my pants and roughly thrust his hand inside them and between my legs, sliding his fingers through my already wet pussy.

I kissed him like everything I ever wanted in the world existed in that beautiful mouth of his. My tongue teased his as his fingers slid inside me and he began to fuck me with one and then two as his thumb pressed against my tender clit. Ribbons of desire rushed through me, and with every thrust into me, I silently begged for the thing I truly wanted.

My fingers fumbled with his belt and then his zipper before I finally got where I wanted to be. Palming his thick cock, I wrapped my hand around it and stroked from the base to the tip.

Eric moaned a needy, throaty sound into my mouth as he stuffed his hand into my hair and tugged my head back. Looking down into my eyes, he smiled sinfully.

"Take off your pants."

I did as he ordered while he stripped out of his shirt and tie to reveal the kind of body most women only dream of seeing on a man who wants to fuck them. Muscular shoulders and pecs sat above abs that I could have washed clothes on. Licking my lips, I yearned to run my hands over the peaks and valleys of his hard body and feel it against mine as he buried his cock inside me.

He pulled my shirt over my head, leaving me in just my bra and panties and him still wearing his pants. I needed to change that, so I slid them down his legs and then did the same with his boxers, setting his cock free so it stood proudly against his stomach, hard and ready for everything I wanted to give him.

Eric grinned, and I dropped to my knees. Looking up at him, I gripped the base of his cock and slowly slid my hand up the full length of him, loving the softness of his skin on top of that masculine hardness. He watched like my every move thrilled him, his blue eyes hooded with need but completely focused on my mouth as I flicked the tip of my tongue over the head of his cock.

"Oh, baby...that's it," he moaned. "Take it all."

Closing my eyes, I slid my mouth down every delicious inch of him, loving the feel of his hands holding my head and guiding me exactly where he wanted me to go. As much as I held him in the palm of my hand, he controlled everything about our time together.

And I loved it.

As the head of his cock nudged up against the back of my throat, he sighed and said, "Look up at me. I want to watch you as I fuck that mouth of yours."

I did as he told me to, and he tightened his grip on my hair. A second later, he began pumping into my mouth as he held my head so I couldn't move, literally fucking my mouth. My pussy grew wetter by the second, and with every plunge of his cock, I imagined how incredible it would feel when he moved down to between my legs.

Eric pulled hard on my hair, and I sensed he was close, so I tightened my grip on him and began stroking him. In moments, he groaned low and deep and came, shooting hot cum down my throat. I sucked him hard into my mouth, taking every last drop of him until I felt his hands loosen their hold on my hair.

I stood up and licked my lips, reveling in the taste of this beautiful man. "Does that make up for the mess I made of the lasagna?"

"Not yet. I think you need to do a little more making up first," he said, nuzzling my neck as he unhooked my bra.

Stepping out of his pants and boxers, he tugged my panties down my legs until I stepped out of them and kicked them across the room. His cock at the ready, he lifted me up and held me against the wall next to the door before he slid into me until I was completely filled by him.

Kissing me, he moaned against my lips, "So fucking tight. God, you feel good, Maddie."

I bit his lower lip and scratched my fingernails down over his shoulder blades as he slowly began to move in and out of my pussy. Pressing my mouth to his ear, I begged him for what I'd wanted from the moment I met him.

"Fuck me...God, fuck me hard."

My pleading excited him, and he began stroking into me faster and faster until his cock was like a piston sliding in and out of my body. Even more, as Eric inched closer to coming, he revealed his penchant for dirty talking that made my body feel like it was on fire.

In my ear, he groaned, "Fuck...your cunt is so

tight, baby. You're going to make me come so fucking hard for a second time."

I arched my back and tilted my hips to feel more of him on my clit every time he slammed into me. I desperately wanted to come and to feel him fill me up.

My thighs began to quiver against his sides as my orgasm raced through me. Eric continued to pump into me, stretching me to take all of him as my body began to surrender. Suddenly, I closed my eyes and bright colors exploded in the darkness as I came harder than I had ever come in my life. I dug my heels into his back while everything in me focused on my pussy and the incredible sensations his cock created in me.

As I got lost in my ecstasy, Eric thrust his hips one final time until he was balls deep and a second later, he stilled inside me. I felt his cock twitch, and then he flooded my body until his release trickled down between us and he sagged against me and the wall.

Exhausted and more satisfied than I'd ever been with a man, I slowly trailed my fingers along his shoulders. A thin sheen of perspiration sat on his skin after our time together, and when I touched the bottom of his hair, I felt it damp against my fingers.

"Fuck...that was incredible," he groaned softly next to my ear. "I don't know if I can move after that."

I clung to him, hoping if he did move that he didn't drop me. "Maybe we should see if we can move toward the bed."

He leaned back and smiled. "The bed might be too far."

"Just don't drop me on the floor."

Easing out of me, he turned toward the bed and took a step, and that was it. We fell onto the bed, still in each other's arms, neither of us able to move after our time together.

Eric looked over at me and chuckled. "I was hungry before, but now I think I'm starving."

"Sorry about the lasagna. I guess that's probably why you're starving now."

He kissed me softly on the lips and nodded. "Probably, but this was better than any food I've ever eaten in my life."

I had no idea what would happen next. He hadn't fired me before we hooked up, so I was still technically his personal cook. But now that we'd slept together, would I still have my job, and even more, would fucking my boss be part of my new duties?

As much as I didn't usually like extra responsibilities heaped on me at work, I think I could handle that.

Yeah, I could definitely handle that.

CHAPTER 5

ric

THE NEXT MORNING, I WOKE UP HUNGRY. NOT FOR food, though.

For Maddie.

One taste of her, one time dipping my cock into that beautiful cunt, and I wanted her again and again. For a fleeting moment, the thought crossed my mind that I shouldn't be sleeping with my employee, but I'd never wanted to hire someone to cook for me anyway. That DeVille guy had just made me think I did.

No, I had no intention of staying away from Maddie. What I needed to figure out was what to do with her as my employee. Paying a woman to fuck your brains out wasn't illegal. Hell, every married man I'd ever met did exactly that on a daily basis and rarely got equal trade in return. But Maddie and I weren't married, and the four thousand dollars a month I was paying her to be my cook seemed like a hefty price for what she could give me.

Then again, having a woman at my beck and call to do whatever I wanted with might be a priceless thing.

I stretched my legs and felt the familiar ache in my thighs I always got after a night of great sex. There was something that happened with my muscles because of an incredible fuck that left me sore, but the pain only served to remind me that I couldn't wait until the next time I had the chance to be inside Maddie.

My morning hard-on turned into a real one as the memory of her tight cunt rolled through my mind, making me wish she was lying next to me so I could have her again and start my day off right. Since she wasn't, I'd have to suffer.

But not for long. I didn't plan on letting more than a day pass before she was beneath me and I was buried to my balls inside her.

After showering and getting ready for what was going to be a long day at work if I couldn't get my mind off Maddie, I headed toward the kitchen to get a cup of coffee and found her already back to her job and up to her wrists in French toast batter.

"Good morning?" I said, making it a question as I wondered what the hell she would be making breakfast for since I never ate anything before noon.

She looked up from the bowl of egg mixture and smiled. "Hi! Did you sleep well?"

After the sex we'd had together, I couldn't imagine not sleeping well. "Yeah. What are you doing?"

Maddie looked down at the bowl and then back up at me with a confused expression. Admittedly, it wasn't exactly a question that had to be asked considering the answer was obvious.

"I'm making French toast."

She returned to dunking the slices of bread and didn't offer to give me any, which I found as interesting as her standing there making breakfast for her employer who never ate the meal. "I can see that. My question is why."

"Because I'm the cook," she answered matter-of-factly with a smile.

"But you're supposed to cook only for me, and I don't eat breakfast or French toast."

"Never?" she asked in a tone of complete disbelief.

"Never."

Her hands stilled again and she looked up at me. "Really? I've never met anyone who never eats French toast. I mean, it's like dessert for the first meal of the day. Who doesn't like that?"

"Me."

"Well, okay. You don't have to eat it then."

"Doesn't that go against the idea of what your entire job is about?" I asked with a chuckle as I thought about expanding Maddie's job description to include what we'd done last night.

"Are you saying that I can only make food in this kitchen that will pass your lips, Mr. Pierce?" she asked as she arched one eyebrow.

I couldn't help but smile. She really was unlike any other woman I'd ever spent time around. "I think we've moved past the Mr. Pierce thing, haven't we?"

She twisted her face and shrugged. "I guess we have, Eric."

"Good. Now can you explain to me what the French toast making is about?"

Maddie hung her head and didn't say anything for a minute. Finally, she sighed and turned to walk over to the sink to wash her hands. I waited for her to begin talking, but she didn't until she dried them and turned back around to face me.

"I've never been a cook. Well, that's not exactly one hundred percent true. I worked at my uncle's restaurant in high school as everything from a dishwasher to a server and even did some time on the grill. I don't know if I can honestly say I was good at that, but I'm especially good with anything that comes close to a dessert. Other things not so much."

"Okay," I answered, still confused why a bowl of French toast mixture and a soggy piece of bread sat on the counter.

"I really need this job, Eric. I moved from my hometown to the city and this is the first time since I left home that I've had a job I wanted. I just figured if I could show you that I had some purpose, you'd keep me on staff for at least a little while so I could save up some money. I know you don't need a cook. What on earth would a man who rarely eats at home need a cook for? But I thought that maybe you like sweet things, which I'm pretty damn good at making, if I do say so myself."

When she finished speaking, she opened her eyes wide with an innocent look that only a bastard could see and still want to fire her. I didn't want her to leave, but just like I didn't need a personal cook, I didn't need a dessert chef either.

But the way she looked at me with that hope in her eyes made me want to see her happy.

"Well, you can make whatever you want. How's that sound?"

She smiled broadly and nodded. "It sounds great. You're going to love what I make. I mean, you'll have to eat your meals somewhere else, but there will always be a sweet treat here when you come home."

I wasn't sure if she had an inkling about what kind of sweet thing I'd prefer from her, but for the time being, this would work. I wanted her to stay at the house for my own wicked and selfish reasons, and making her happy made me happy.

Later that night, I planned on showing her just how I planned to change that job description of hers, but now I had to go to work. "Enjoy your day. I'll be back by nine o'clock tonight. I'm going to want to see you when I get here, Maddie. Do you understand?"

For a moment, she looked at me like she'd missed my intention, but then she simply smiled. "I understand."

And with that, I left for work without even getting the cup of coffee I'd originally went into the kitchen for. Maddie had that kind of effect on me. If I didn't know better, I would have thought she'd somehow put me under some kind of spell.

I knew better though. There was nothing supernatural about what we wanted from each other. That was purely physical.

AFTER A LONG, FRUSTRATING DAY OF DEALING WITH people who seemed to want to complain about every fucking thing that ended up on their plates and managers who couldn't figure out how to make them happy, all I wanted to do was get lost in Maddie and forget that life existed outside the walls of my home. I opened the front door and instantly the scent of sugar hit my nose. Never much for sweets, I had to admit whatever she had made smelled delicious.

I pushed open the door to the kitchen and found her in the same place as when I left that morning in front of the center island. She looked different now, though. Wearing a tiny black dress and three inch fuck-me heels, Maddie seemed more like something from one of my teenage fantasies than a mere cook in my home.

"Did you have a good day?" she asked with a smile as she held up a plate of cookies for me to see.

"No, but it looks like things are definitely improving," I answered, licking my lips at the thought of trying one of those cookies and then getting her out of that dress.

The shoes could stay, though. I liked the idea of

her wrapping her legs around me as I fucked her in them.

Maddie held the plate out for me to take a sample of what she'd made, and I picked what looked like a sugar cookie dusted with pink sugar crystals. One bite and I knew she hadn't lied about being able to make sweet things. It may have been the most incredible cookie I'd ever tasted.

"This is great. What is it?"

"Just a sugar cookie with some special ingredients," she said with a big smile.

"Special ingredients?" I asked before taking another bite. "Like what?"

Shaking her head, she placed the dish on the counter. "I can't tell. Old family secret. I'm glad you like them."

"I do. You look nice. Why are you dressed like that?" I asked, not really caring before but suddenly wondering if she was planning to leave tonight. For some reason, the thought truly bothered me.

Maddie looked down at her dress and then back up at me. "Just something I felt like putting on tonight."

"So you aren't going anywhere?"

She shook her head. "I didn't think I was allowed to."

"You're not a prisoner here, Maddie. You work for me. You aren't a slave."

She took a step toward me and looked up. "I thought I was supposed to be here whenever you're here in case you need anything."

"I never thought of it that way."

"Well, then I guess I could go out. I'm dressed for it, don't you think?"

The twinkle in her eye told me she knew exactly what she was dressed for, but she wasn't going anywhere except to my bed. I snaked my arm around her and pulled her body to mine before kissing her.

"No going out tonight. I want you here with me."

"Do you have something you want me to do tonight?" she asked with a look of innocence that made my cock harden like steel.

She was no more innocent than I was, but that look in her eyes made me want to corrupt her.

Sliding my arm around her waist, I pulled her to me so her breasts pushed against my chest. Looking down into her still wide eyes, I thought about what I wanted her to do and smiled.

"I have a few things in mind. Let me have another of those cookies and then we'll go upstairs so we can get comfortable."

"So you like the cookies?" she asked sweetly as she fed me a second one.

I nodded and finished the last bite of the delicious dessert. "Even though I don't usually like sweet things, I think I do like these. I'm curious about this secret ingredient. Are you going to tell me what's in them?"

Maddie licked her lips, and the smile that spread across them was nothing less than naughty. "Just tender loving care. That's it."

Something told me that wasn't her secret ingredient, but I had other things I wanted to do than interrogate her on what went into her sugar cookies. Taking her hand, I led her to my bedroom, and closing the door behind us, I slid my hands up underneath that dress of hers to find that she wasn't wearing anything beneath it.

"Mmmm...I like a woman who plans ahead."

She reached out and began to unbuckle my belt. Slowly, she slid it through each belt loop until she held the long strip of black leather up in front of her. "Maybe we can use this somehow?"

I took it out of her hand and threw it on the bed behind her. Hooking my fingers along the hem of her dress, I said, "Maybe. First, I want you out of this. Then I'll decide what I want to do with you."

It slid over her head easily, and then she was simply nude and there for the taking. I tossed that black dress across the room so it landed on a chair and turned my attention to the perfect woman standing in front of me ready to give me whatever I wanted.

And what I wanted tonight was to forget anything else existed but her.

I slid my hands over her shoulders down to her breasts and cupped them in my palms. Full and perfect, they begged to be fondled. Dipping my head, I flicked my tongue over her left nipple and heard her moan. She stuffed her hands into my hair and tugged hard to hold me there, so I sucked hard as she begged me not to stop.

"Harder...God, that feels good. Suck harder...let me feel your teeth on me."

So she liked it a little rougher? Good. I was in the mood to leave my mark on her.

I bit down on her nipple and she moaned low in a way that made my cock desperate to be inside her. As if she was reading my mind, she slipped her hand into my pants and wrapped it around me, squeezing hard as she began to stroke me from base to tip.

"Oh, God...I want you inside me," she whimpered above me.

Letting her nipple pop out of my mouth, I titled my head back and smiled up at her. "All in good time. First, I plan to get a taste of that beautiful cunt."

I slid my mouth down her body, licking over her abdomen and hips until I came to her bare pussy. Sitting back on my haunches, I gazed at it, my mouth watering at the thought of finally tasting her on my tongue.

With my fingers, I spread her open to reveal her clit swollen with need. I wanted to suck that pretty thing between my lips and feel her body beg for more as she moaned for me to make her come.

Looking up, I saw her staring down at me with a glazed over look and biting her lip in anticipation of what I'd do next. There was nothing sexier than seeing that expression of pure need in a woman's eyes.

I leaned forward and slowly dragged the tip of my tongue over her exposed clit. Her whimpers turned to sensual groans as I licked her pussy and then sucked that beautiful nub into my mouth and gently bit down.

"Oh, God! That feels so fucking good. Stick your

fingers inside me. I want to feel you filling me when I come."

I hummed against her supple skin, sending vibrations out from her clit. Her knees buckled, but I caught her as she began to fall back and pulled her down to the floor with me. She collapsed against my chest for a moment, but it didn't take long for her to regain her strength.

Her hand wrapped around my cock again, and looking up at me, she said, "Enough with the foreplay. Fuck me."

"Not so fast. I still want you on my tongue. After that, I've give you what you want."

She turned her mouth down into a cute pout, but I wasn't going to be put off. I'd wanted to eat her pussy since the moment I set eyes on her, and now I'd finally have that and get her off too.

Nothing like a win-win to start the night.

With one movement, I put her onto the bed and buried my face between her legs, lapping her cunt like a starving man. I sucked her clit between my lips and slid two fingers inside her as she cried out in ecstasy with every flick of my tongue over her sensitive skin.

It didn't take long before her body began surrendering to me, squeezing my fingers even as she spread her legs wider so I could taste every beautiful inch of her pussy. With one final flick of my tongue, she came and convulsed against my fingers as her cunt milked them like it would do to my cock in just a few moments.

"Oh, God! I'm coming...don't stop...that feels so

fucking good!" she wailed as wave after wave of her orgasm raced over her and I continued to eat her out.

When she finally stopped trembling, I slid up her body and kissed her hard on the lips so she could know how delicious she tasted. "Ready for more?"

Nodding, she smiled. "Yep."

"Good."

I flipped her over onto her stomach and pulled her up onto her knees. Leaning forward, I slid my cock through her pussy and wrapped my hand around her throat.

"You should be careful what you wish for, little girl. Now you're going to get it."

She turned her head and looked back at me with nothing but desire in her eyes. "Good."

Without another word, I reared back and rammed into her body until we joined completely. She cried out for a moment but immediately pushed back when I began to move out of her. We quickly found our rhythm. I plunged into her, and she moved back to receive every inch of me. Over and over, we fucked like wild animals until I felt her cunt begin to squeeze my cock, and I knew she was close.

I squeezed my hand, closing it around her neck, as I began to jackhammer into her with the dual goals of filling her up and making her come. We raced toward release, the two of us slamming our bodies together as her cunt and my cock joined to produce pleasure like I'd never felt before.

"Oh, Eric...don't stop...I'm close...harder...God,

don't stop!" she croaked out as she tightly gripped the sheets in her hands.

One last thrust and she came apart around me, her cunt greedily milking my cock like it had milked my fingers before. Her thighs quivered as I continued to fuck her through her orgasm, and seconds later, cum rushed out of me, filling her until it began to ooze out past my cock.

I released my hold on Maddie's throat, and she collapsed onto the bed beneath me. I sat back on my heels and stared down at how beautiful she looked lying there, exhausted by our fucking. Her hair lay fanned out around her head, and as I watched, a trickle of sweat slowly ran down her back toward her perfectly round ass. There was nothing better than knowing you'd satisfied the woman who'd just begged for your cock.

CHAPTER 6

*M*addie

MY BODY FELT LIKE I'D LITERALLY BEEN FUCKED INTO submission. I couldn't move, and the most complete feeling of exhaustion made every muscle exquisitely ache. With my head buried in the pillow, I listened to Eric ease himself off the bed and then lean down next to me.

"Maddie?" he whispered, sounding like he was worried he might have been too much for me.

But nothing about our time together had been too much. Most men I'd been with tended to be too gentle, too timid when they got me into bed. It was the reason I stopped dating them because I couldn't imagine a possible future with any man who couldn't rule me in the bedroom.

Eric definitely didn't have that problem. His every

touch and movement held me captive and made me want more of him. Every time he rammed his cock into me made my body come alive more and more, and for one of the first times in my life, I could imagine a future with a man like him.

Not that I'd thought about anything like that yet. I'd only been working for him for a few days, and I wasn't a fool. I knew what was happening between us was nothing more than physical. Eric Pierce could have any woman he wanted. He had the looks, the brains, the reputation, and the money.

And I had no doubt that he'd had lots of women before me lying next to him in this very bed.

So no matter how much my mind might want to entertain ideas of us doing this forever, I knew it was more likely that this was only temporary.

Very temporary.

"Maddie? You okay?"

I looked at him through a veil of my hair and saw real concern in his eyes. It made me feel wanted more than just for my body.

Pushing my hair off my face, I smiled. "I'm good. What about you?"

He blew the air out of his lungs and grinned. "I'm definitely good. That was incredible."

"We're pretty good together," I said, instantly hating that I'd said it that way.

We weren't together in any real way, so why had I phrased it like that? Damnit! I shouldn't have said something so ridiculous.

Eric's expression darkened, but then he forced a smile. "Not too shabby at all."

Great.

People said that when they had a decent slice of pie or someone did an okay job on hemming a pair of pants. To hear sex described like that was like the kiss of death. And here I'd thought it had been life-changing.

What a fool I could be sometimes.

I closed my eyes and let my hair fall back over my face to hide my disappointment. I needed to remember that ridiculous girlish fantasies had no place between us. I was his employee, and no matter how much he seemed into me when we were naked together, that's all I was.

"As soon as I can move my legs, I'll go to my room."

The way those words came out made it sound like I was sulking. Christ, I should just shut my mouth and slink away before I made a complete fool of myself.

"It's okay, Maddie. You can stay as long as you want."

More tepid words. How could two people who were so incredibly hot together when they were naked be so awful after the sex was over?

I lay there silently counting the minutes before I could leave and not look like I was running away. I could almost feel the awkwardness growing between us, like someone placing brick upon brick as they built a wall right there in the center of the bed. When I finally did leave, Eric and I exchanged strained pleasantries and I quickly dressed before I hurried to my room at the back of the house.

The place where I belonged.

Throwing myself onto my twin bed that suddenly seemed so tiny after my time in Eric's king-size bed, I covered my eyes and tried to forget the entire episode with him. What was I thinking? We're pretty good together? Why didn't I just ask him how long it would be before he planned to ask for my hand?

It would have had the same effect.

Nothing like saying the exact thing that would terrify a single man, Maddie. Way to go. For an encore, do you plan to start picking out new furniture and showing him your paint choices for when you redecorate his home to your liking too?

Disgusted, I grabbed my cell and called Cat. Anything to get my mind off how I'd ruined things.

"Hey, Maddie! How's the new job going?"

"It's okay."

The phone fell silent and then she asked, "Is something wrong? You sound strange, like that time when you called me after you and that guy broke up."

Jesus, now even people who couldn't see my expression knew something bad had happened.

"No, nothing's wrong. I'm fine. The job's fine. It's only been a couple days, but things are…"

I couldn't think of another word to describe the lie I was trying to push on Cat, so I just let my sentence fade away. She knew me too well to just let it drop, though.

"Okay, so now that we've established that everything's fine, tell me the truth. You aren't in trouble, are you? I thought something strange might be going on with that job. I mean, it's not that I didn't think you could be a personal chef, or whatever they're calling it, but it does seem odd that you'd be hired right on the spot."

I didn't answer her because everything she said was right. Maybe Eric had told the man at DeVille Staffing that he wanted an in-house sex slave but they'd decided that personal cook sounded better and more legal. Or maybe Mr. DeVille had given me more credit than I deserved.

"Not in trouble. Just feeling a little weird and wanted to talk."

"So tell me what your new boss is like. I'm imagining he's like a hundred years old and a recluse who never leaves his house and makes you spoon-feed him soft foods because he's ancient. Am I right? He's got like three long grey hairs the nurse combs over his bald head, doesn't he? And liver spots," she said with a giggle.

Cat always knew how to make me laugh. I chuckled out loud and rolled my eyes at her description of Eric. If only he was like she thought I wouldn't be in the jam I was in.

"Not exactly. Where do you get this stuff from anyway?"

She laughed at my question. "I was watching a show on that Anna Nicole woman last night. Sorry. So what's the new boss like? How do you like living in his house? Are we talking mansion here or what?"

I thought about how to answer her questions and

figured honestly was the best way to go. "He's nice. He doesn't seem to eat at home much, so I don't do much cooking. He does like me to make desserts, though."

Okay, so that wasn't entirely truthful. I had no idea how Eric felt about my interest in sweets. He seemed to tolerate it so far, but I shouldn't have said he liked it. What he liked was me dressed up to fuck him and feeding him sugar cookies.

"That sounds weird since your job is personal cook, but if he's still paying you, I say good for you. The less you have to actually work, the better, right?"

Suddenly, what Eric and I had been up to felt wrong. I had a feeling if I told Cat that what I'd primarily been doing since I entered the house was sleeping with my boss that she'd tell me how wrong it was. The thought had already crossed my mind, but every time I considered telling him no, I remembered how incredible it felt when we were together.

How incredible every moment felt with him.

"Maddie, you still there? Did I say something wrong?"

"No. I was just thinking. Can I ask you a question, Cat?"

"Sure! Ask away!"

I thought about how I could phrase what I wanted to ask her and realized no matter how I said it, what I'd been doing sounded bad. Nobody was getting hurt, so why did it feel so wrong?

"Is it ever okay to do something just because it

feels good? I mean, is it a bad thing to do something just because you like it?"

She didn't say anything for a few seconds, but then she finally answered, "I don't think so. Unless you're selling your body, of course. Then the lines get a little blurred. You're not selling your body, are you?"

Her question was meant as a joke, but I didn't think it was funny because it felt like that was exactly what I was doing. I'd been hired to cook for Eric Pierce, but he no more needed a cook than he needed someone to fly him to Mars. So instead of actually working at cooking meals for him, what I'd basically done in the time since I arrived at his house was have sex with him.

God, I was selling my body for four grand a month!

My mind drifted off to thoughts of how much prostitutes made a year. How much did they charge per hour, I wondered. Or maybe they charged by the act. I had a vague sense that I'd seen that happen in a movie one time. Was four grand a month good for a hooker?

Oh, God! That made me feel even worse.

"Maddie, it sounds like something's wrong. What's going on?"

I took a deep breath and let it out in a whoosh before I told her the truth. "My new boss isn't an old guy but a young guy who's incredibly hot and wealthy and everything any woman would want. And since I got here, all I've really done is fuck him because every time we're together we can't seem to keep our hands off each other. But now I'm feeling like I'm some kind of prostitute because he's paying me. Not that he's paying me to have sex with him, but maybe he is since I don't seem to be doing much else here."

"Wow! That's a lot of New England small town guilt you've got going on there, Maddie. You're an adult, so if you want to have sex with someone for whatever reason, then so be it. It's definitely not the kind of arrangement you run into every day, but maybe he's the kind of guy who doesn't like to date or he's too busy with his career and doesn't have time to go out and find women. If he likes you and you like him, I don't see the problem. This job was never supposed to be permanent anyway, so you might as well enjoy yourself for the time you're there."

"I guess. It wasn't meant to be permanent, so you're right about that."

"Honey, I hear something else in your voice, though. Are you falling for this guy? That might be a problem because this is just temporary. Don't lie to yourself about things. Trust me. It never works out when you do."

She wasn't wrong. Falling for Eric would be the biggest mistake I could make.

"I don't know what I'm thinking, to be honest. I didn't think anything until tonight, and now I feel terrible. I just don't know why."

"I think if you're having a good time, then enjoy yourself. If you aren't, don't do anything else with him. You were hired to be a cook, so if he doesn't need one, maybe the job will just be over and you can find another one."

"Yeah. You're right."

The problem was everything Cat said was the truth. It was also the truth that I should have known better than to let myself develop feelings for Eric. I had thought I could just sleep with him and that would be that, but everything I felt after his reaction to my innocent statement about us being together told me another truth.

I'd let real feelings creep in to what I was doing with him.

"Are you going to be okay?" Cat asked in that older sister way she had of worrying about me.

"Oh, yeah. It's all good. I'm a big girl. I can handle myself. You know that."

She chuckled at my attempt at bravado. "I know, but you're still that small town girl from Maine underneath all that big girl, so I worry."

"I'll be okay, Cat. Thanks for letting me bounce all this off you. How are things going in your life since I left?"

"You've been gone less than a week, so it isn't like much could have changed. I still haven't found a position, but I have to admit, at this point, I wouldn't mind finding one like you have. Other than that, I don't do a whole lot, which I think makes me the most boring person in the world now that I'm saying it out loud."

"Well, even if you are a boring person, which you're not, I still love you for listening to me talk about my stupid problems. I'll call you next week and we can talk, okay? And don't worry about working. Something will come along. I know it."

"Thanks, Maddie. Stay safe and only do what makes you happy. That's the best advice I can give you."

"Thanks, Cat. I'll talk to you later."

I ended the call and tossed the phone on the bed behind me before flopping back onto the pillow. She was right. Whatever I did, I needed to at least be happy doing it. Now I just had to figure out what that would be.

BY THE TIME I GOT TO THE KITCHEN THE NEXT morning, Eric had already left for work. I had the feeling he was avoiding me, which only made me feel even worse. But maybe that could be a good thing. If we never got together again, at least I wouldn't have to wonder what I was getting paid to do at the house.

The plate of sugar cookies sat on the counter, but I noticed that someone had eaten three more after Eric had the first two. Maybe Magda or Chloe had taken them. If I saw them today, I'd be sure to ask if they liked them.

At least someone might enjoy my treats.

My mood made creating anything sweet difficult, so I headed outside to walk around the grounds for a little while to get some fresh air and clear my head. I couldn't afford to lose this job before I even got paid, so I had to find a way to get past what happened with Eric and do the job I'd been hired for.

Or at least a similar job he might want to let me continue doing.

The bright morning sun hit me as soon as I walked outside, and I instantly wished I had my sunglasses with me. I didn't really feel like going back into the house yet, so I shielded my eyes with my hand and started on my walk down the driveway toward the garage where someone stood next to one of Eric's cars. It wasn't Clyde, the driver who had taken me to get my things right after I was hired, and I didn't recognize the man as I walked closer.

He turned to face me and I couldn't help but be struck by how good looking he was. Black hair hung ever so slightly too long in front of his eyes, but when he pushed it back, I saw the darkest brown eyes I'd ever seen framed by eyelashes women would kill for. My gaze slid down to his body as he stood there in a dark suit and tie, and I wondered who he could be hanging out in Eric's garage and where Clyde could be.

"Good morning! You look like you were expecting to see someone else. Sorry to disappoint," he said in a deep voice that slid over me like silk.

The stranger smiled a wicked grin that told me he wasn't offended by my confusion, so I shook my head and returned his smile with one of my own. "No, not disappointed at all. I thought Clyde was the only driver for Mr. Pierce."

"Clyde called in sick. I think he has the flu."

Extending his hand to shake mine, the man said, "I'm Antonio. Nice to meet you."

Antonio. He looked like someone who would be called Antonio. I shook his hand and liked how strong his fingers felt against mine when he lingered a moment too long on my skin before slowly removing his hand.

"I'm Maddie. Nice to meet you too. So how long are you here for, Antonio?" I asked as he stared directly into my eyes like he was searching for something in them.

"As long as Clyde's sick, you're stuck with me. But I'll give you a ride whenever you want. All you have to do is ask."

God, the way he said that sounded so sexual that I nearly forgot that he meant he'd give me a ride to the store or wherever I needed to go. Something about this man made me think about nothing but sex.

Or maybe it was this house. Since I arrived, I practically jumped into bed with Eric mere days after he hired me, and now I hadn't said a hundred words to Antonio and already I was imagining what it would be like to have him between my legs.

I'd never been this oversexed before. At this rate, I'd have trouble defending my actions to even myself the next time I looked in the mirror.

It must be something about this house. That had to be it. What, I had no idea, but this place was turning me into a nymphomaniac!

"Oh...oh...okay," I stammered out, secretly embarrassed at my thoughts. "I might have to go to the grocery store sometime today for some things to make tonight's dessert."

I had no idea if I'd have to get any ingredients or even what I would make today, but I felt like I needed to say something just in case the lust in my mind was written all over my face.

"Just give me the word and I'll take care of you," he said in that deep voice that made me want to close my eyes and let my brain slide into fantasy mode.

"I definitely will. Thanks!"

Turning to leave, I heard him say, "Hey! You never told me what you do here, Maddie."

His question stopped me in my tracks, and I looked around to see him smiling at me in a way that made me wonder if he already knew exactly what I did with Eric. Had he told him?

My brain quickly began to spin the possibilities that Eric had actually done the locker room talk thing with this guy who was temporarily taking his driver's place. For a second, I felt defensive at the mere thought that he'd shared that information with this person, but then common sense took over and I decided there was no way Eric would ever do that. I might not have known him very well any way other than physically, but I hadn't gotten the vibe that he was the type of man who would kiss and tell.

"I'm Mr. Pierce's cook. Well, his dessert chef, to be precise."

Antonio raised his eyebrows. "Dessert chef? I've never heard of anything like that. Does that mean you spend all your time making Mr. Pierce sweet stuff?"

I nodded. "I guess, yeah. So far, I've only made sugar cookies, but I'll be making something new today."

Antonio licked his lips and winced. "Mmmm, I love sugar cookies. Mr. Pierce is a very lucky man to have someone like you devoted to making him sweets. What will you make today?"

"I don't know yet," I admitted with a chuckle. "Any suggestions?"

He took a step toward me and leaned down so his lips were next to my ear. "You look like the kind of woman who could make even the most wholesome apple pie sinful."

Oh my... He smelled exactly like a man should. I wanted to bury my face in his neck and inhale that delicious scent as he slid inside me and...

What was I thinking? I wasn't exactly a Vestal virgin, but I wasn't the town whore either. I needed to get back into the house and get my mind on work immediately before I did something I'd no doubt regret. Good God, I needed to get my thoughts out of the gutter or I'd end up sleeping with Antonio too.

I took one last look at him and began backing away. "I have to go. Thanks for the suggestion. Bye!"

CHAPTER 7

ric

I STOOD WATCHING THE MAN WHO'D BEEN SENT TO replace my driver until his forty-eight hour flu ran its course and didn't like how close he stood to Maddie instead of doing his fucking job. He smiled at her like he planned to be fucking her before the day was over. Who the hell was this guy anyway?

At my sides, my hands balled into fists. Anger coursed through me as each second ticked by and she just continued chatting him up. She looked far too happy as he spoke to her, smiling and laughing at whatever he was saying as she stood there looking beautiful in her pink sundress, and I watched in horror as he leaned in to whisper something in her ear. Did she know this guy? Fuck, I didn't even know this guy. He was just someone sent by that employment service to fill in for Clyde while he was sick.

Maybe she did know him since he'd been referred to me by that DeVille guy, but that didn't make what I was seeing any easier to handle. They looked way too cozy together there next to the town car, him leaning on it while he smiled like some kind of fucking Cheshire cat and checked her out and she giggled at whatever he was saying.

If I hadn't had to come back to the house because I forgot those damn papers for Jack this morning, who knows what they'd be up to. Not that either one of them noticed I was watching their little meeting. They both seemed too interested in one another to notice much of anything going on around them.

Jealousy made my stomach twist into knots, and by the time Maddie turned to walk away from Mr. Loverboy Fill-In Replacement Driver, I had to fight back the urge to march over there and tell both of them they were fired. She made her way toward me and smiled but said nothing as she passed me on her way into the house. I looked back at him still leaning against my car and saw him checking her ass out as she walked away. Likely lost in some fantasy about fucking her, he didn't even notice me heading toward him.

"Enjoying the sights?" I asked, not bothering to curb the sharpness in my tone.

He nodded and gave me a knowing smile, like we shared something in common when it came to Maddie. "You do have a very nice set-up here."

"What is your name?" I asked, unsure why I wanted to know since every fiber of my being wanted to throw him off my property.

"Antonio," he answered, smirking like some kind of punk.

"Antonio what?"

"Antonio Lucero."

His name sounded like a dick's name. Between the dark hair and the whole Mediterranean swarthy look he had going on, he was giving off a gigolo vibe I hated more and more with each passing second.

Even worse, Maddie seemed to have liked him and his whole thing he had going on.

"Well, Antonio, you're here to drive, not hit on my staff. Do you understand me?"

For a second, he seemed to be irritated by my reprimand, arching one dark eyebrow and leveling his gaze on me, but then he just shrugged and smiled. "As you wish, sir. You're the boss. I was just sharing a little conversation with your dessert chef. I didn't realize that was off limits."

"What? What was off limits?"

"Talking, sir. I didn't realize talking was off limits. But now that I know it is, you don't have to worry about me trying to talk to her again."

Happy he understood how things worked, I turned around to head back to the house, relieved Antonio wouldn't be an issue from now on. As I walked away, he said something else, though.

"You might want to tell her that, though, sir. She's a chatty one. I suspect she doesn't know the rules about not being able to talk to anyone here, so she'll be back to see me by lunch."

I spun around to face him and saw that fucking smile again that told me he knew the effect he had on women with that suave way about him. The question was if he had that effect on Maddie.

"Remember the rules or you're going to find yourself replaced before you know it. I have no problem with calling your boss and telling him to send someone else."

Antonio said nothing in response to my threat, and I continued into the house to talk to Maddie, completely forgetting what I had come home for in the first place. I didn't know if I had any right to be so possessive of her. If she was just my dessert chef, whatever the fuck that was supposed to be, I wouldn't have given a damn about her talking to Mr. Suave Gigolo out there. Hell, I wouldn't care what she did if she was just one of my employees.

But she wasn't.

Maddie hadn't been merely an employee from the moment I hired her. She hadn't been in the house for half an hour before all I could think of was being inside her. I thought she wanted me like I wanted her. The way she was when we were together said she did, but after seeing her talking to the driver, I wasn't so sure.

I planned on finding out, though.

She stood at the center island kneading a ball of dough in front of her on a cutting board that had never been used before she arrived here. A frilly apron covered her sun dress, making her look like some housewife straight out of the 1950s. Even with jealousy and anger raging inside me, I couldn't help but admit she looked so cute like that.

I stopped in the doorway to the kitchen and cleared my throat. "Maddie, I want to talk to you."

She looked up and smiled, but I noticed it wasn't as enthusiastic as the smile she'd given Antonio. "Okay. Just give me a second."

Wiping her hands on a dishcloth, she cleaned herself up and then turned her attention to me. "All right. What's up?"

Nothing in her sweet way said she knew what was about to come out of my mouth, so maybe she hadn't been out there flirting with Mr. Rico Suave, but I still needed to say what I came to say. Folding my arms across my chest, I said, "You're here to be my dessert chef. You're not here to socialize with other people on my staff. Do you understand me?"

She scrunched up her face in a look of confusion and shook her head. No, she definitely didn't understand.

"What do you mean? I've been talking to Magda since the day I got here, Eric. Chloe too. Are you saying I can't be friendly with them?"

"Magda and Chloe are different. They're part of the household staff, so it's only right that you'd speak to them since it's necessary for your job."

Maddie took a step toward me and tilted her head to the side. "Then just who can't I socialize with? Other than you, I've only really spoken to Magda,

Chloe, and Darnell while he was pruning the rose bushes outside. Did he complain about me talking to him while he was working? I didn't mean to distract him from his job. I hope you know that."

"I'm not talking about the damn gardener, Maddie. I just saw you outside talking to the guy who's filling in for Clyde."

She leveled her gaze on me and smiled. "So it's him I can't socialize with. Okay. What am I to do if I need to go to the store? I'd normally ask Clyde to drive me there. Are you saying I can't even ask Antonio for a ride to the grocery store if I need ingredients to make you something like an apple pie?"

Her questions told me she knew why I didn't like her talking to him. She was enjoying seeing me jealous.

I stepped toward her and looked down into her dark eyes. "I don't like apple pie, so you won't have to go anywhere today. I'm sure everything you need you can find right here in the cupboards."

"But what if I can't? Am I supposed to walk all the way to the store? That seems like a huge waste of time. I mean, it's bad enough you're paying me to be a dessert chef since you don't need a personal cook because you rarely eat at home. Now you're going to be paying me to walk for miles, basically employing me to keep in shape?"

"I don't want you to walk, Maddie. Just stay here today. Make me something from the ingredients you have on hand."

She shrugged. "Fine. I'll make you a dough ball.

Maybe I'll throw some sprinkles on it. Or thyme since whoever stocked this kitchen seems to have thought five containers of thyme was necessary."

"That sounds disgusting, but I trust you to make me something I'll like."

Her lower lip jutted out into a pout. "I don't know why you say you trust me. You don't even trust me to talk to the driver and go to the store, Eric. Trust isn't exactly what's going on here."

She frowned, and for a moment, I hated myself for being so fucking jealous. I'd never been this jealous in my life, and I'd only known her for a few days.

"What's going on here then, Maddie?"

"I could ask you the same question, Eric. I thought we were having a good time, but you gave me the cold shoulder last night and since then you've been downright chilly toward me. Now you see me talk to that Antonio guy for a few minutes and you're all ugly green monsterish and telling me I can't even leave the house today. So you tell me what's going on here."

"Ugly green monsterish? What the hell does that mean?"

Tilting her chin up, she put her hands on her hips. "It means you're jealous of me talking to that guy, even though you couldn't even be bothered to speak to me after I said that thing last night and you got all ice cold. That's what it means."

"I have no idea what you're talking about. I am not jealous, and I don't know what you said that supposedly made me cold, which I'm not."

"Yes, you do. I said we were pretty good together,

and from that moment on, you've been distant. You basically couldn't wait until I left your bed last night. And now you want to be all jealous about me talking to some other guy. Well, at least he probably wouldn't just kick me out of bed because I said the wrong thing."

The image of Maddie anywhere near that guy's bed made my head feel like the top of it was going to explode. Even hearing her refer to him that way enraged me.

Trying to keep my temper under control, I said through gritted teeth, "Maddie, I don't know what you're talking about. Just don't talk to the driver. Understand?"

"What I understand is that you think I am some kind of property of yours that you can be nice to one minute and dictate what I can do the next. Well, forget it. I quit!"

She pushed past me out of the kitchen, and as watched, she tossed the apron behind her and stormed down the hallway toward the wing that contained the staff's bedrooms. All the jealousy and anger I'd felt from watching her talk to that guy disappeared, replaced by a feeling of emptiness at the idea that she had just quit and would be leaving this house.

Leaving me.

I followed her and found her packing her bag to leave. My chest felt like someone had placed a lead weight on it as I watched her getting ready to walk out of my life forever. I barely knew her, and I knew how crazy it was to say I'd miss her more than I'd ever missed anyone, but that's exactly what I felt as I stood in the doorway of her bedroom.

For years, I'd had whatever woman I wanted and for as long as I wanted, but now that I'd met Maddie, I couldn't imagine my life without her in it. After just a few days, she'd somehow imprinted on my heart so much that I couldn't let her go.

"Stop doing that, Maddie. You're not going anywhere," I said quietly.

She turned her head to look back at me and then returned to what she was going. "Yes, I am. I didn't like how I felt last night, and I don't want to feel that way anymore."

"Then stay."

As she folded a shirt and stuffed it into her bag, she said, "That's what made me feel that way in the first place, Eric. Well, you made me feel that way. I didn't like it, so I think it's time for me to go. You don't need a dessert chef or whatever I was supposed to be pretending to be anyway, so you won't miss me."

Her words cut me to the bone. I didn't mean to make her feel like she'd said or done anything wrong last night. That's just the way I'd always been with women.

"I'm sorry, Maddie. I never meant to make you feel bad. I don't even know exactly what I did to do that."

She stilled her folding for a moment and turned around to face me. Her frown, deeper now than before, made me hate myself because I was the one responsible for putting it there on her beautiful face.

"I said we were pretty good together, and you

pulled away. I guess I can understand why. I mean, this was never supposed to be anything permanent. I get that. I just thought we were good together, but as soon as I said that word together, you iced over."

I walked around the bed and took the shirt out of her hands. Placing it back into the dresser behind me, I looked at her and for the first time in my life, I told a woman the truth.

"Nothing you said bothered me. Well, not consciously anyway. I guess I'm just used to being single and deciding when things end."

Maddie hung her head and quietly said, "And you decided last night things were going to end. Fine. Just let me pack and I'll be out of your hair so you can go back to your single life and I can go back to mine. I'll have the driver take me to my house, and you'll never see me again."

Just the thought of her alone with that guy made my jealousy rear its ugly head once more. Grabbing her wrists, I held her so she couldn't move. "You're not going anywhere with him."

She looked down at where I clutched her arms in my hands and then looked up at me with confusion written all over her face. "Why do you care what I do? You just told me you're used to being single and deciding when things end. I get it. You decided it wasn't going to go any further last night. So why would it bother you that your driver is going to give me a ride home? Do you plan to have me walk all that way too, suitcases in hand like some poor refugee forced to leave her homeland?"

For a moment, I couldn't form the words to explain why everything she thought was so wrong. I hadn't decided things were over between us the night before. How I reacted had just been my normal way of dealing with women when I began to feel something for them.

But I didn't want that to be the way I dealt with Maddie. I couldn't explain it, but I didn't want to push her away like I had with everyone else.

"That isn't what I meant. I don't want this thing between us to be over. I'm sorry that the word together made my subconscious freak out. I'm just so used to pushing people away when they get close that I guess I did that to you too. But I don't want to push you away."

She didn't say anything for a long moment, and I wondered if any of my words had made a difference. Then she looked up at me and asked a valid question, even if it was an impossible question to answer.

"What are we doing, Eric? You have me working for you as some ridiculous dessert chef when you don't even seem to like sweet things much. In truth, you're paying me to have sex with you. I don't think I like that. I don't want to be some guy's concubine."

I blew the air out of my lungs slowly until there wasn't any left inside them and I had to answer her question. Not that I knew what to say. I didn't. But I had to at least try.

"I don't know. I never planned on any of this. I just wanted a maid to clean my house, to help Magda, but that DeVille guy convinced me I needed a cook more.

Then he sent you here knowing you aren't a cook but could make desserts, which I don't really eat. All of that aside, I just know that from the minute I laid eyes on you, I couldn't imagine you not being mine. That's the honest to God truth. I wanted you from the second I met you, and I've never felt that for any women ever before. And you're not my concubine."

Maddie smiled, and I released my hold on her wrists. "That's the most I think I've heard you say since I met you, Eric."

"Sometimes I have things to say. Most of the time I don't, though. I don't want you to leave. I can't tell you what's going to happen, but I want you to stay here with me. You don't have to bake another thing for me. I'm fine if you just want to lay out in the sun all day, just as long as you're not hanging out with whoever that guy is who's driving while Clyde's out, okay?"

She cradled my face in her hands and kissed me. "His name's Antonio, and you don't have to worry. I don't want him. I want you. But I don't want to just be some leech who hangs out here all day. I wouldn't feel right about that, so I'm going to keep making sweets, and if you don't eat them, then I guess Magda and the rest of the staff are going to have treats for as long as I'm here. If you're okay with that, I'll stay."

I kissed her long and deep, loving the feel of her lips on mine and happier than I thought I could ever be at hearing her say she'd stay. I couldn't explain why after just a few days of having her around she meant so much to me, but I didn't care. All I knew was for the first time in my life, I felt something for a woman. More than the desire to just get between her legs and fuck her.

And whatever this was I felt, I didn't want it to end.

CHAPTER 8

*M*addie

ROLLING OVER, I LOOKED AT THE ALARM CLOCK ON the nightstand and saw the time. Nearly one o'clock in the afternoon!

I nudged Eric's shoulder. "Hey, do you know we've been lying here for nearly two hours? Don't you have to go to work?"

He slid his arm around me and pulled me close to him so my cheek rested on his shoulder. "I figure I don't take too many days off, so one won't kill me."

"Okay. I just thought I should mention it," I said as I traced my fingertip along his collarbone.

"And by the way, we haven't been lying here for all that time. I vividly remember doing something far more active than just lying in bed at least twice."

I felt my skin warm as a blush raced over my

cheeks. We had done way more than just lie around since he came in to ask me not to leave. Two sessions of incredible, mind-blowing lovemaking and one wild attempt at sixty-nining that resulted in my almost falling off the bed as I came and the near spraining of Eric's cock as I attempted to hang on to him had definitely been more than just lazily lying around.

Sliding my hand down his chest, I stopped just near his hip. "Are you feeling any better now?"

He nodded. "He's pretty resilient. Considering what the average guy does to his cock, they have to be. We give them a beating."

I couldn't help but cringe at his description of what men do during masturbation. "That doesn't sound good at all."

Eric pushed at the base of his cock so it stood straight up off his body. "It feels good, so that's all that matters. See, he doesn't mind. Just talking about sex makes him want to go again."

Nuzzling his neck, I giggled at his way of making it sound like his cock had opinions and a personality. "You're cute when you're like this. I think if you tell me you have a name for it, I'm going to laugh out loud, though."

He looked down at me like he couldn't believe his ears. "Of course I have a name for my dick. Every guy does. Let me introduce you to Dirk."

I looked down his body and saw him wiggling his cock at me, as if to make it look like it was saying hello. "Dirk? Dirk Dick? It doesn't flow trippingly off the tongue, that's for sure."

"That's not what he likes to do with tongues, to be honest. And he prefers to be called Dirk Cock, thank you."

Damn, he could be so sexy when he was being silly.

"Well, I guess Dirk Cock sounds a little better. Dirk is a strange name for a body part, though."

Eric let his cock slip from his hold, and it slapped against his lower stomach. "I don't think it's that strange. What would be strange would be if he had a girl's name. Imagine if I named it Bertha or something like that. That would be strange."

I rolled my eyes and threw a leg across his body to sit on top of him. Staring down into his face, I smiled. "I don't think I can ever have sex with you again if I think of you calling it Bertha. As far as mojo killers go, that's a pretty big one."

He pulled me down to kiss me hard on the mouth as he lifted his hips off the bed to slide his cock through my already wet pussy. "Then never think about it again since I plan on us having sex many more times."

I didn't know what that meant or how long we'd be together, but after our discussion earlier, at least I knew that whatever I was feeling, I wasn't alone. I'd never believed in love at first sight before, but maybe that's what this was. Even if it wasn't love, it felt right, so for now, I planned on enjoying myself and Eric for as long as I could.

"Ready for Round Three?" he asked before easing into me in a slow thrust.

"Mmmm..." I moaned as I rolled my hips to take him as deeply as I could. He filled me like our bodies were meant for one another, and I reveled in the feel of his cock touching that part of me no other man ever had.

Eric stuffed his hands into my hair and tugged hard so I had no choice but to sit up on him. When I straddled him like that, it made my swollen clit brush against his body with every time he pushed into me, sending waves of pleasure racing through every part of me.

He rested his hands on my hips and held me there as he groaned, "Let me see you ride me, baby. I want to watch you ride my cock."

I looked down into his heavily lidded eyes and watched as he winced in ecstasy with every slow and sensual roll of my hips. Lifting myself off him, I kept only the head of his cock inside me for a moment and then leisurely lowered back down so every delicious inch of him was buried inside me. He kept his gaze on my face, never moving his attention as I rode his cock, fucking him until I knew he was close to the edge.

Just as he looked like he might come, I rolled off him onto my stomach and teasing him, wiggled my ass at him. "What do you say to a change of position?"

Eric didn't bother to answer, and in seconds, he knelt behind me with his cock pressed to my ass. "I love this idea."

He covered my back and with his face next to mine, sunk his teeth into my earlobe. "Doggy it is, but I'm thinking something extra this time. You game?"

What that something extra could be I had no idea, but nothing he'd ever done to me sexually had been anything less than incredible, so I bit my lip and nodded, even as I wondered if extra would be too much for me.

Sliding his hand around my throat, he squeezed ever so slightly, and I sensed his control over me settle in. One hard thrust buried him inside my pussy to his balls. He moaned and then began pushing his hips forward, fucking me slow and easy and making me want to beg him to move faster to get me to my orgasm I so desperately wanted.

I dropped my head and steadied my weight on the bed so I could push back against him when he thrust into me, but then suddenly I felt something new in our fucking. My eyes flew open at the feeling of electricity tearing through my pussy straight to my clit as I realized it was his fingertip massaging my asshole.

"Oh, God...that feels so good..." I moaned.

Then as he began to fuck me faster, he slid a single finger into my ass and everything felt like my body began to unravel. He finger fucked me there as his cock filled my pussy, and every thrust into each hole made me race toward my orgasm that much faster.

Finally, I couldn't take it anymore and began playing with my clit. Ignored so far during this session of fucking, it practically begged for attention, and within seconds of me starting to rub it, I felt my release begin and Eric groan behind me.

"Come for me, baby. I want to feel your cunt milk my cock dry," he said low and deep as he slid his finger from ass and held onto my hips tightly to keep himself inside me as I writhed in ecstasy.

My body did just as he ordered, my pussy contracting around his thick cock with each wave of pleasure rolling over me. I gripped the sheets in my hands and screamed into the pillow with every single thrust of his cock into my body.

Seconds later, Eric stilled behind me and sighed as he came hard, filling me until I couldn't take anymore and collapsed onto the bed beneath me. Eric fell down beside me and groaned as he closed his eyes.

"That was fucking incredible."

Barely able to speak, I smiled at how exhausted he looked after our most recent round of sex. "Yeah, that was unbelievable."

He opened his eyes and turned to look at me. With a smile, he said, "I'm not sure I would be alive if my cock was in your ass, you know that? When you started coming, my finger barely fit."

"Aren't you the romantic?" I teased, poking him in the shoulder. "I could have told you that. One look and I knew I wasn't going to be able to take you that way."

With a sigh, he shrugged. "Maybe someday. It's something we can ease into."

I giggled at his unintended pun. "Literally."

Eric pulled me to him and wrapped his arm around me. I laid my head on his shoulder, loving how romantic he truly could be. Well, not when he was talking about sticking things into my ass, but otherwise. Nothing had really changed between us between last night and now, but it felt different.

Sexier yet more comfortable.

I didn't know how long we would last or what would happen next, but I knew he cared about me and I cared about him. Nothing else really mattered.

"MADDIE, TIME TO WAKE UP."

I opened my eyes and saw Eric sitting next to me on the bed and smiling. He looked fresh and clean, like he'd already showered after our last sex session. Scrubbing the sleep from my face, I hoped I didn't look like the walking dead. This was the first time we'd ever slept together after having sex, so he was likely seeing me at my least appealing. Nothing like looking like a raccoon with mascara an inch beneath your eyes as the man you're falling for is sitting next to you looking like he just stepped off the cover of GQ.

"Please tell me I don't resemble the train wreck I think I do," I said as I covered my face and insecurity rolled over me.

"You look beautiful, like always. It's nearly four o'clock in the afternoon. We need to get out of this house and get something to eat."

"I need to get a shower so you don't look like you're walking around with a pile of trash if we're going anywhere."

Just as I rolled over to get out of bed, he gently pushed my shoulders back down onto the bed and kissed me softly on the lips. "You look fine, although that whole dusky eye thing might be a little extreme. But you look beautiful, like always."

I squeezed my eyes shut and wished I could disappear at that moment. I must have looked even worse than I thought if he was mentioning the dusky eye look, which was not exactly a common thing for most men to talk about.

"Let me get a quick shower and fix myself up. Give me a few minutes and I'll be ready to go."

Eric kissed me again and chuckled. "You've got thirty minutes. Go work your magic and meet me in the kitchen."

I hurried out of the bedroom as I yelled back at him, "You're pretty bossy there."

"I'm your boss!" he teased as I closed the bathroom door behind me.

Twenty minutes later, I appeared in the kitchen doorway in a navy blue and white polka dot sundress and white sandals looking a million times better than I had a short while before. Twirling to show off my look, I smiled at Eric as he stood at the counter eating one of my sugar cookies.

"Better?"

"You clean up nice, Maddie," he joked as he took the last bite of cookie into his mouth.

"I thought you didn't like sweets."

Eric looked at the nearly empty plate of cookies and shrugged before looking back at me. "I never have. It's strange. Your creations make me want to eat more too."

"Good. It's the secret ingredient, you know."

He walked up to me and kissed me sweetly on the lips. "Tender loving care, right?"

"Uh-huh. That's it."

"Ready to go get something to eat?"

"Sure, but you've already had dessert. Where are we going?" I asked as he took my hand and began pulling me toward the front door.

"I thought I'd take you to the restaurant. We don't open until five tonight, so we'll have a quiet dinner alone, just the two of us, and you'll get to see my business."

Taking me to his workplace seemed like a big step, and even though I wasn't sure we were ready for that, I simply smiled and followed him out to his car, a red Porsche waiting for us in the driveway.

"Nice car. I guess the house isn't the only stunning thing you have," I mumbled as he opened the passenger door for me.

"No, it's not. I like surrounding myself with beautiful things," he answered with a sexy smile.

As I waited for him to come around the back of the car and get in, I wondered if I was one of those beautiful things he surrounded himself with.

ERIC'S RESTAURANT, THE CASK ROOM, WAS located just a few miles from his house. He'd mentioned on the drive there that the building used to be a saloon before Prohibition and was turned into a restaurant while alcohol was illegal, even though the back room with its hidden door to a separate secret room showed that the owners hadn't been the most lawful and upstanding citizens. The restaurant closed sometime in the 1970s, and the building stayed vacant until he and his friend Jack bought it for next to nothing and set about entirely redecorating the place so it could be an upscale restaurant.

As soon as we walked through the front door, my mouth dropped open at how impressive the inside was compared to the very ordinary brick outside of the building. Decorated in art deco style with its large geometric designs and lots of glass and stainless steel, The Cask Room looked like something straight out of a Hollywood movie set.

He turned to look at me and smiled. "It's pretty nice, isn't it? Jack and I couldn't agree on anything the designer suggested until she showed us this. I don't know if I'd want a whole house in art deco, but it works here."

I swiveled my head back and forth looking at the gold and crystal chandelier on the ceiling and the enormous light sculpture in the corner of the room that reminded me of the Chrysler building.

"It's stunning. I feel underdressed for this, though," I sheepishly admitted, even though he only wore black dress pants and a forest green button down shirt with no tie.

"Let's go to the back room. I told my staff that's where we'll have our meal so when the restaurant opens, we'll still have privacy."

He took my hand in his again and led me through the restaurant as I tried to see everything going by so quickly. We walked through a doorway to a small hallway and then the art deco style disappeared and we were standing in a much smaller room. Gone were the glass and stainless steel, and in their place were dark wood floors and walls with dimmed lights scattered around the room to give the place a secluded feel.

"The bootleggers supposedly did their illegal business right out of this part of the building," he explained as he led me to one of the four tables in the room.

"What do you use this room for now, other than intimate dinners?" I asked, impressed by how different this part of the restaurant looked compared to the other room.

"We do private parties here, and when it's not in use, it's where Jack and I sit at the end of the night and relax after a long day of the restaurant business."

Eric waved to a woman standing near the door, and moments later, two males began to serve us our meals. First came a salad with a dressing like I'd never tasted before. I didn't want to ask what it was and look stupid, but I was sure I tasted citrus and maybe sage. Eric and I said little as we ate, and I saw that what he said about himself was true. He didn't talk much, but I liked just sitting there with him.

A short time later, the servers brought out our meals of steak medallions with mushrooms, grilled lemon asparagus, and roasted garlic potatoes along with a cabernet better than any wine I'd ever had before. One bite of the meal and I thought I'd died and had been transported to heaven. The food tasted like nothing I'd ever eaten. No wonder he rarely ate at home. I wouldn't have eaten anywhere but the restaurant with food like this.

As I enjoyed the superb meal, I secretly felt a twinge of embarrassment. Eric was used to the finest food available, and I'd screwed up the very basic lasagna I'd tried to make. Even my desserts were nothing compared to what they probably had there.

"Is everything okay? You don't look like you're enjoying your meal, Maddie."

The look of concern in his eyes told me he likely hadn't thought about how inadequate my culinary offerings were, so I forced myself to smile. "No, it's wonderful. I can't say when I've had a more delicious meal. It's all wonderful. Thank you."

"The only thing that would make it better would be one of your sugar cookies to top it all off," he said with a smile that seemed to be genuine.

But how could he mean that when my cookies were nothing compared to the meal we had in front of us?

"You don't have to say things like that. I know the difference between a tasty snack and fine food. My sugar cookies don't belong anywhere near this meal."

He drew his eyebrows in and shook his head like he disapproved of what I said. "That's not true, Maddie. I love those cookies. Who do you think has been eating them?"

Stunned by his admission, I said, "I thought it was

Magda or someone else on the staff. It's you who ate all those cookies?"

Nodding, he smiled and his face brightened again. "Yeah, I'm the one."

"I didn't even think you liked them much, and now that I'm here and see what you eat all the time, I felt a little ashamed at what I made. I imagine the desserts here are masterpieces. Certainly better than some cookies."

"I wouldn't know. I've never eaten anything here for dessert. I mostly just grab a quick bite every night I'm at work and have a drink after my day is done."

"So you don't eat all this great food all the time?" I asked, confused why anyone wouldn't take advantage of having the finest meals available to them any day of the week.

He shook his head. "No. Just a bite here and there. I think this might be the first time I've ever sat down and eaten an entire meal in my own restaurant."

Before I could stop myself, I let my curiosity come tumbling out of my mouth in a question I shouldn't have asked not only because it made me sound insecure but also because I didn't know if I would like the answer.

"Don't you bring dates here for dinner?"

I inwardly cringed as the words left my mouth, but Eric didn't seem bothered by the question and answered, "No, I generally don't bring women here to the restaurant. It never felt like someplace I'd want them to be."

"But you brought me."

"You're different."

Part of me wanted to know how I was different, but I didn't ask because I knew what he meant in a way. I'd never experienced a whirlwind relationship like we'd had so far. Eric was the first man I'd ever slept with so soon after meeting him. In fact, nothing about what we'd become so quickly had ever happened to me before.

As much as I enjoyed sitting there talking to him, he didn't seem to want to stay long after we finished our meal. Not five minutes after the last bite, he finished his wine and stood up from the table.

"Let's go. How does a drive sound?" he asked as he extended his hand to take mine.

"Okay, I guess. You don't want to stay here for a little while?"

A sly smile spread across his lips. "Not really. I just wanted to impress you. Was I successful?"

God, he could be so cute. "Yes, definitely."

"Good. Now let's go before Jack shows up and makes a move on you. I'd hate to have to go all caveman on someone twice in one day."

He held my hand and began to walk toward the secret door bootleggers had used all those years ago. As I followed him, I asked, "Why would you have to go all caveman on him?"

Eric turned around and chuckled. "Because my partner is the kind of guy who has no problems hitting on a woman while she's with a man. Even me. Since I had to hold myself back from pounding that new driver this morning, I have a feeling one wrong word from Jack and my fist would be meeting his jaw. Since I have to work with the guy, I figure it's better to just whisk you away and avoid all that."

I had to smile at his honestly. Under his icy coolness and all-business attitude, Eric was very much a typical Alpha male. No wonder I'd wanted him from the minute I met him.

ric

CLOSING THE FRONT DOOR BEHIND ME, I SAW Maddie walk toward the kitchen and wondered what she could be doing going there after the meal we'd enjoyed at the restaurant not two hours ago. I followed her and stopped in the doorway when I saw her slipping the apron over her head.

"What are you doing?"

She looked over toward me with resolution in her eyes. "I feel like making you something."

"I'm not really hungry. At least not for food," I explained, smiling so she could know exactly what I wanted.

"I told you I didn't want to be your concubine, Eric. I bet everyone in this house thinks I'm some kind of prostitute or something. I was hired to cook, so cooking is what I plan to do tonight."

Stepping into the kitchen, I watched her assemble a mixing bowl, mixing spoon, and measuring cups. "A prostitute who cooks? I don't think I've ever heard of that."

She stopped and frowned at me. "I'm not kidding, Eric. You're making fun of me."

I tried to stop myself from laughing, but a chuckle slipped out. "I'm not. I swear. It just sounded funny when you mentioned anyone thinking you're a prostitute because even though I don't have experience with them, I'm relatively sure they don't stay in your house or bake you cookies, Maddie."

"You're not taking this seriously at all, are you?"

"It's hard to take seriously since I already told you that I didn't need you to do anything for me. Nothing at all."

"Except sleep with you," she said like it was some kind of punishment.

"Is there something wrong with that?"

Her lower lip jutted out into the most adorable pout. "You're paying me to sleep with you. I think that's the exact definition of prostitute in the dictionary."

The way she looked so upset about this made me want to take her into my arms and kiss her, so I pulled her to me and did just that. She didn't respond at first, refusing to enjoy it since she'd gotten it into her head that she should fight whatever this was between us — why I had no idea after the great time we'd had that day—but I planned to change her mind for good tonight.

When she finally relaxed in my hold and kissed me back, I leaned back from her and smiled. "Now that wasn't so bad, was it?"

"I don't want to be a prostitute, Eric. Or a concubine," she answered, her eyes wide with concern.

Did she honestly believe that's what she was?

Cradling her face, I kissed her softly on the lips and tried to reassure her she was neither of those things. "Maddie, you're my girlfriend. You're also the woman I enjoy fucking. You're not a prostitute, and you know why? Because I don't pay you. DeVille Staffing does. I pay them, so you're not being paid for sex."

"That's the most convoluted thing I've ever heard. I'm still being paid to have sex with you. Now you've just made that owner guy, Mr. DeVille, my pimp."

She was infuriating! There had to be some way to convince her I wasn't paying for her to have sex with me. Maybe I just needed to turn the tables on her.

Pulling away, I folded my arms over my chest. "You know, it's sort of insulting that you think I have to pay beautiful women to spend time with me."

Maddie's mouth dropped open and her dark eyes grew as big as saucers. "What? I never said that. That's not what I meant at all."

"Well, that's what it sounds like. If you're a prostitute and I'm paying you, then you must think I have to pay women to spend time with me and sleep with me."

She pressed her lips together and groaned. "You're putting words in my mouth, and you know it."

"I'm just taking your argument to its logical end. If I'm paying you to have sex with me, then I must have to so I can have sex."

She scrunched up her face in that cute way she did when she didn't have an answer to something and let out a heavy sigh. "Fine. I'm not a prostitute or a concubine. Happy now?"

I smiled at how sweet she could be and wrapped my arms around her again. "I never said you weren't my concubine. They don't get paid, so you still could be one of those."

Maddie narrowed her eyes to angry slits and pushed against my chest to let her go, but there was no way I wanted to do that. "I don't much like the concubine idea either, Eric. And I'm no fool. I don't think I could be called your girlfriend either. In fact, I'm pretty sure I have no role whatsoever in this house, except to sleep with you, which brings me back to the whole prostitute thing."

Smoothing her hair back off her face, I placed a tiny kiss on her forehead and smiled. "Concubine sounds so much better. It's got a much older, more impressive sound to it, don't you think?"

Maddie looked up at me with a pleading expression in her eyes. "Why won't you take this seriously?"

"Because it's not serious. Why do we have to explain what you are to me or what I am to you? We've been crazy about either other since about twenty seconds after you walked into my office, so who the fuck cares what my gardener thinks your job is? You make me happy, and I think I make you happy, don't I?"

"Yes," she answered sheepishly.

"Then who cares what anyone thinks? Don't spend another minute trying to figure out what this is between us. Just enjoy it. I know I've never been this happy with anyone, Maddie. Are you happy?"

"I am, but I worry that it's too good to be true, so I keep trying to find some way to explain it."

Shaking my head at her stubbornness, I leaned down and kissed her. "Maybe there is no explanation for it," I whispered against her lips. "Maybe it's just the way we're supposed to be. No point in questioning happiness."

She lay her head on my chest and sighed. "Okay, I'll try not to worry about things. I won't worry about whatever job I'm supposed to be doing or where I'm going to get money when this ends."

I pressed my lips to the top of her head and let myself enjoy the feel of her soft hair. In truth, I knew I should care more about the fact that she was my employee, but I didn't. Maddie had walked into my life and made things inside me come alive that I never knew existed before her. I wanted to spend every waking moment with her enjoying that feeling of being alive.

Truly alive.

And I didn't give a fuck if I had to pay that DeVille guy an entire year's salary for it. I wasn't paying for her to be here or even to have sex with her. If he broke the contract tomorrow, I wouldn't care. I'd just ask Maddie to stay with me. Not as a cook or anyone else who worked for me.

Just stay with me as my girlfriend.

"So what do you want to do tonight, man who isn't my boss?" she asked with a giggle.

As much as I wanted to take her to my bed and bury my cock inside that beautiful cunt of hers, I knew she'd just think I wanted her only for sex and that wasn't the truth. I loved fucking her, but just being around her made me happy. I wanted her to know that.

"What do you say to going out to a movie?"

I hadn't been to see a movie in nearly five years. Christ, I hadn't taken a woman to the movies since I left high school.

"A movie? What movie do you want to see?"

With no clue what movies were even playing, I drew a blank. "The new Star Wars movie?" I suggested, sure I'd heard some people at the restaurant talking about some new movie in that famous series.

Maddie raised her eyebrows and stared up at me with a look of surprise in her eyes. "You like Star Wars?"

"Sure. Doesn't everyone?"

"I have a better idea. Why don't we have a drink and relax right here at the house? We can even watch TV, if you want," she said with a smile.

"Great idea! I'll pour the drinks and you pick something to watch."

Taking my hand, she tugged me toward the hallway. She looked back at me and smiled. "Good plan. I'll have whatever you're drinking, unless it's tequila, which means I'll have red wine."

"I'd planned on having a bourbon."

"Good. Make it two and I'll find us something interested to watch."

MADDIE SAT CURLED UP NEXT TO ME ON THE COUCH in my living room, and I wrapped my arm around her, squeezing her to my body as we finished watching some movie about robots or space aliens. I stopped paying attention about ten minutes into it when she leaned her head on my shoulder and sighed contentedly. From that moment on, I couldn't think of anything but how genuinely happy I was just sitting there with her watching some stupid movie.

I looked down at her head resting on my shoulder and saw her eyelids flutter closed. She looked so sweet and so innocent lying there. No matter how much I wanted to take her into my arms and carry her to my bed for another marathon round of incredible sex, I couldn't disturb her looking so angelic at that moment.

As the credits rolled on the screen, my phone began to ring. Hoping it wouldn't wake Maddie, I reached over her to hurriedly grab it off the end table.

I didn't recognize the number, but since I'd made all that effort, I answered it anyway. "Hello?"

"Mr. Pierce? It's Louis DeVille from DeVille Staffing. How are you tonight?"

"I'm fine, thank you. I'm a little surprised to hear from you though."

He chuckled in a way that sounded nothing less than devilish. "I often surprise people. I'm not interrupting anything, am I?"

His question gave me the impression he didn't care if he was interrupting. "No. Not at all. What can I do for you?"

"I was just calling to see how things are working out with Maddie. She's the young woman I sent over about the cook job. Has that worked out well?"

Looking down at Maddie resting against my side, I smiled. "Very well. Thank you."

"Well, I'd like to speak to you a bit more in depth about her work. First, have you found her to be easy to get along with? Oftentimes, in-house help aren't a great fit, and here at DeVille Staffing, we always strive for as perfect a fit as possible."

"Is it possible we could do this tomorrow sometime, Mr. DeVille?" I asked as Maddie began to stir.

"Unfortunately, it must be done tonight. I promise this will only take a few minutes, Mr. Pierce."

Not wanting to have this discussion in front of Maddie, I gently eased her off me and laid her down on the couch before taking the call out in the hallway.

Closing the door behind me, I quietly said, "Okay, what can I do for you?"

"Just a few questions, I promise. Can you tell me about how she's fit into the household? We always hope for our staff to be as unobtrusive as possible so as not to disturb the day-to-day goings-on at the employer's home."

The thought of Maddie being inconspicuous anywhere made a chuckle escape from my throat. "She's been fine. I wouldn't called her unobtrusive, but she's fit in just fine."

Mr. DeVille hummed into the phone. "Hmmm. Okay. Next question then. Have you been satisfied with her performance?"

As much as I didn't think of myself as paying Maddie to sleep with me, DeVille's question about her performance made me smile. Her performance, as he termed it, had been nothing less than fantastic, and that included her delicious sugar cookies.

"Very satisfied. She's been wonderful in every way."

"Very good!" he said, clearly pleased with my answer. "I'm very happy to hear that. Next, her trial period will be over in a few days. How would you rate her work so far during this period?"

"I think she's been a wonderful addition to the household. I would give her an exemplary review, Mr. DeVille."

"Wonderful! Just one more question and I'll let you go enjoy your night. Do you plan to keep Maddie on permanently?"

The rest of his questions had been easy to answer, but this one seemed harder. I loved having Maddie around, and I'd never been happier. But I didn't want her to stay in my life as my dessert cook who never really had to do anything. If she stayed, I wanted her to be with me as the woman I loved, not as one of my staff.

"I don't know if I'll need a cook permanently, Mr. DeVille. I'll make my mind up about that soon, though."

"Hmmm. Okay. Thank you so much for answering my questions honestly, Mr. Pierce. Have a good night."

"Thank you. You too," I said before ending the call.

Louis DeVille always struck me as odd, and tonight was no different. Ten o'clock at night seemed a strange time to be calling clients. His staffing service did offer round the clock assistance, though, so maybe this was one of those times when he worked nights.

I pushed any thoughts of the DeVille Staffing owner and his oddness out of my mind and returned to the living room to find Maddie still curled up on the couch and making tiny snoring noises. As much as I didn't want to disturb her, I didn't want to leave her there while I went to my room, so I scooped her up into my arms and turned off the TV.

She opened her eyes and looked around, confused about what was going on. "What time is it?"

"It's around ten. You fell asleep while the movie was still on," I answered as I eased the two of us through the doorway.

K.M. SCOTT

"Oh. Did the robots win?"

I walked to my bedroom and gently placed her on the bed. "I think so. The story got a little muddled after a while, so I'm not sure."

Maddie looked up at me and smiled. "Did you fall asleep too?"

"No. I just lost the story pretty quickly," I admitted with a smile.

As I stripped out of my clothes, she watched me, and when I climbed into bed, she cozied up next to my side. "Are you tired?"

Even if I was, my cock had different ideas and was nearly stiff as a board already. "No. Are you?"

She smiled and ran her hand over my chest and down my stomach. "I think I got my second wind from that nap."

Pulling her to me, I kissed her long and deep, loving the feel of her mouth on mine. She slid her tongue past my lips, teasing me with gentle flicks against my tongue and sending my need to be inside her into overdrive.

"I want you so fucking bad, Maddie," I murmured as I rolled her onto her back and crawled on top of her.

She opened her legs and slid her hands down to grab my ass and pull me into her. "Don't make me wait."

Her cunt was wet and ready for me, so I flexed my hips and pushed into her until my balls pressed against her body. She felt warm and tight and made perfectly just for me.

Digging her heels into my lower back, she urged me to fuck her, and I happily obliged. "Fill me up. I love how it feels when you're inside me, Eric."

I fucked her slow and easy, taking my time to enjoy the taste, sound, smell, and feel of her like I never had before. She met my thrusts with her own and we joined together to find a sexual rhythm that felt better than anything I'd ever felt with a woman.

And when I felt her cunt tighten around my cock and begin to milk me to my own release, I couldn't imagine life without Maddie.

I didn't know how or when, but I'd fallen in love with her and didn't want to ever be without her again.

CHAPTER 10

ric

MY PHONE RANG JUST AS I PULLED INTO MY parking space at the restaurant. I recognized the number from the night before. It was the owner of DeVille Staffing calling again, but why now?

"Hello, Mr. DeVille. What can I do for you this morning?"

"I need to meet with you today, Mr. Pierce. How does eleven-thirty sound?" he asked in a tone that said he expected me to make room in my schedule for him.

Why was this guy so interested in talking to me all of a sudden? Had someone reported Maddie to him for what she and I had been doing? Instantly, I hated that damn Antonio even more. That fucker had said something, hadn't he?

Glancing down at my watch, I saw it was almost

quarter after eleven already. Whatever he had to say, he sure was in a hurry to get it out.

"Okay. I'll be at my restaurant. Feel free to stop by anytime."

In a serious voice, he said, "I'll be there at eleven-thirty sharp."

Fifteen minutes later, I looked up from my desk and saw him standing in my office doorway looking even more somber than the first time I'd met with him. His steely eyes stared directly at me, and something about that goatee he wore made him appear menacing.

I stood and extended my arm to welcome him in. "Mr. DeVille, please take a seat. What can I help you with?"

"I'm afraid I have some bad news," he began as he sat down in front of my desk. "I thought it would be best to tell you in person as telling someone this kind of thing over the phone seems far too impersonal. We at DeVille Staffing strive to offer the most personal service around."

"Bad news?" I asked.

Now I was sure someone had reported Maddie to him. Fucking driver! Well, I had no intentions of letting her be reprimanded for being with me. If there was blame to be assigned, I had to take at least half of it, but I wasn't ashamed of what had happened between us, so if he was there to say we'd done something wrong, he'd get an earful from me.

He drew in his dark eyebrows so they looked like angry black slashes. "I'm afraid Maddie is going to have to end her time as your cook, Mr. Pierce. I'll be calling her right after we finish here and letting her know. I'm sorry things didn't work out, but I can assure you that we'll have a replacement out to your house by tomorrow at the latest."

I sat there stunned at his words, and before I could respond, he stood to leave. "Thank you for meeting with me, Mr. Pierce, and again, I do apologize."

He began to walk away, but I needed answers about this whole thing. "Wait! Why are you forcing her to leave? She's done a fine job, so what's the problem?"

Frowning, he shook his head. "I'm afraid I can't divulge that information, Mr. Pierce. I assure you that we will have a new cook for you no later than tomorrow, so you won't suffer much inconvenience. I appreciate that this might seem like a bit of an upheaval in your household, but your patience will be rewarded, I assure you."

"Why won't you at least give me a chance to explain? Maddie isn't the only one to blame here. We did nothing wrong, but I think I deserve the chance to put everything in context," I said, practically pleading with him as he continued on his way out of my office.

He didn't answer, and by the time I caught up to him in the hallway leading to the front door, he was speaking to someone on the phone. Grabbing the sleeve of his black suit coat, I stopped him, but he waved me away.

"I'm sorry, but I have to take this call, Mr. Pierce."

"I don't want Maddie to leave, Mr. DeVille. I'm quite happy with her as my cook, so whatever's happened, I'm sure it can all be cleared up and she can stay."

"I'm sorry, but it's been decided. As I said, it won't be too much of an inconvenience since we'll make sure to have someone to replace her at your house by tomorrow. It's only a cook, Mr. Pierce."

He walked out of the building as I stood there in shock. Maddie wasn't only a cook. In fact, she wasn't a cook at all, but that didn't matter. I didn't want her to leave.

I raced back to my office and called the house, but Magda didn't know where Maddie was and hadn't seen her all morning. Frustrated, I stared at my cell phone in disgust that I didn't even have her number. Then again, since we'd only known each other for a week and she lived at my house, I never thought to ask for it.

"Ancho just called and said he might be late for his shift tonight. Something about his car needing new tires. Or maybe he said someone stole his tires. I'm not really sure. I wasn't paying a whole lot of attention."

Lifting my head, I saw Jack standing in the doorway to my office. "What are you talking about?"

"Our sous chef Ancho? You remember him? He might be late for work tonight. What's up with you, Eric? You look like you just got the news someone died. Did someone die?"

It felt like someone died. My body ached as if I'd been punched in the gut. "Nobody died."

"Then what the fuck is wrong? Should I be worried? You look pretty bad, man."

I stood from my chair and grabbed my phone and my car keys. "Hold down the fort for a while, okay? I'll be back. I have something I have to do."

Jack stepped aside as I brushed past him on my way out and called after me as I left, "Okay, I got things here. You take care of what you need to do."

I jumped into my car and floored it the five miles back to the house faster than I'd ever gotten the Porsche to go. Slamming my foot on the brake, I barely stopped the car before jumping out and running up to the front door. I wasn't sure what I would say to Mr. DeVille to change his mind, but I had to do something.

But first I needed to speak to Maddie.

It wasn't just that she wasn't going to be my cook anymore. I had a feeling if I didn't stop her from leaving, I'd never see her again.

"Maddie! Are you here?" I yelled as I tore down the hallway toward the kitchen only to find it empty.

I hurried to her room and found it empty. Checking the dressers and closet, I found them empty too. Everything about her was missing from her room. Had DeVille already taken her away?

My mind whirled with uncertainty. What had been so bad that she had to be removed from here and why so quickly? Why had the owner of DeVille Staffing refused to tell me anything about what had happened?

Nothing Maddie could do warranted this kind of reaction. I refused to believe she could ever be guilty of any kind of wrongdoing. And if that wasn't the reason why she had to leave, then why wouldn't he tell me the truth about why she was being taken away from me?

After I'd checked every room and every inch of the property, I walked back to the house and found my way to my office. I opened the door and looked around, remembering how she had sat in the chair a few feet away and how she'd enchanted me from the moment we met.

Now that she was gone, everything felt empty. What once was a house I thought of as a place to sleep and do some work in now seemed lonely. Without Maddie, it was merely a house.

Nothing more.

Gone was the sweetness I'd grown to love in the short time she was there with me. Before she came along, I never realized how much I wanted to have someone in my life who made me smile and look forward to the next time I'd see them.

Now that I'd lost her, I knew all that had been taken away with her too.

There had to be some way to fix this. Some way to make DeVille understand that Maddie couldn't be replaced by some other person in less than twenty-four hours. That inconvenience wasn't what I'd suffer because he'd forced her to leave.

I quickly found his number and called him, prepared to drive to his office if I had to and demand he give me Maddie's number so I could find her and tell her I wanted her back with me forever.

"Mr. Pierce, I'm surprised to hear from you. I did say we would have someone to your house by tomorrow," he said with a happiness in his voice that bothered me.

"I don't want another cook or anything else but Maddie's number. Just give me that and I won't bother you again."

"I'm afraid I can't divulge an employee's personal information like that. I'm sorry."

"Why are you doing this? Why did she have to leave immediately? Whatever she did, tell me. If it's a matter of money, I have more than enough. I can pay for whatever she did. Just tell me."

He said nothing for a long moment, and then just as I worried he'd ended the call, he asked, "Why would you bother to do anything like that for someone who's only worked for you for a week?"

I knew my answer would sound crazy, but I didn't care anymore. I had to get Maddie back. "I just need her to come back to the house. Not as a cook or one of my staff, but just her back here with me."

"Why? You didn't even eat the single meal she cooked for you," he said in a tone of disbelief.

"What? How do you know that?"

He said nothing in response to my question. What was happening here?

I didn't want to tell him everything we'd done together. He didn't need to know about our personal lives. But I needed to convince him to at least tell me where I could find her so I could let her know I wanted her to come live with me.

"I never needed a cook. I didn't know I needed someone to love, but that's what I found in her. I know it sounds insane to say I'm in love with a woman I just met a week ago, but that's the truth. I love her and now that she's gone, nothing's the same. Everything feels empty now. The house. My office. Everything. I just want to find her and bring her home."

"Hmmm. It sounds like you truly love her, Mr. Pierce. But does she feel the same way about you?"

I wanted to believe Maddie loved me like I loved her. I knew she wasn't the closed-off person I was, so maybe everything in her life didn't feel empty now. But I had to think that what we'd been together meant something to her.

"Ask her. If she says she doesn't, then I won't bother you about this ever again. But if she says she loves me too, then you won't stop her from coming back to me. Deal?"

"Now we're making deals, Mr. Pierce? Okay, it sounds fair to me. I'll ask her and if she loves you like you love her, then she's yours. If not, you must forget her. No trying to find her. No calling me to badger me for a way to contact her. Those are my terms. Do you agree to them?"

I swallowed hard to get rid of the lump in my throat and answered him as all the air felt like it was being sucked out of the room. "I agree. Ask her."

"Good luck, Mr. Pierce. I hope you find the happiness you so want."

His words sounded so final. When I went to ask him what that meant, he ended the call. Was she sitting there listening to the entire conversation and told him she didn't love me?

$\mathcal{M}$addie

CAT SAT CROSS-LEGGED LISTENING TO MY STORY, her eyes wide and her mouth hanging open. I had to admit that what I'd told her was pretty amazing. I'd gone to DeVille Staffing to get a job, and in less than a week, I'd found everything I could ever want in the world.

"So what are you doing here hanging out with me? Why aren't you at that gorgeous house with the man of your dreams?" she asked with a silly smile.

"Because he has to work and I went to see the man who runs the staffing agency this morning to tell him that I wasn't going to be able to work for him anymore. I figured I'd stop over and see you while I was in the city."

She made a funny face and pursed her lips.

"Maybe I should sign up for a temp job with this DeVille Staffing place. I'd like a man of my dreams all of my own too."

"That's not what he does, Cat. This whole thing with Eric is a total coincidence. I guess it was just meant to be."

Standing up, she walked into the kitchen to pour us both a drink. As she handed me my glass, she said, "I guess, but it's a pretty incredible coincidence. So what are you going to do now?"

"Well, Mr. DeVille told me he had some business to finish up on my file, so I have to go back to see him in about an hour and probably sign some papers. Then I'm going to go back to the house and when Eric comes home, I'm going to tell him I'm not longer with the agency and just hope he still feels the same way about me as he said he did last night."

"Hope?" Cat asked like I said something bizarre. "From what you told me, he's crazy about you. I don't think you have anything to worry about."

"Just in case I do, I took all my things out of the house when I left this morning. I want a clean slate. If it doesn't work, I'll be back to searching. Have you found anything yet?" I asked, quietly terrified that I'd have to do just that and start over.

Without Eric.

"No, but I'm still hoping."

I knew I was taking a chance quitting my work with the DeVille agency, but something told me I'd be okay. If worst came to worst, there were always lots of waitressing jobs out there in the world and I'd just get one of them. Maybe my roommate would let me slide on the full rent for a while. Or maybe I could move in with Cat.

Replacing Eric in my life wouldn't be anywhere as easy, but I didn't think I'd have to. True, we'd moved at warp speed in our relationship, but I'd heard of stranger things happening.

When it was right, nothing else mattered. At least I hoped that was true.

"Well, you got the dream guy to go back to, so you better get going," Cat said.

I couldn't help but smile when I thought about that very idea. I'd met a great guy who owned his own business and a gorgeous house, and he was crazy about me. It's all I'd ever dreamed of, and now all those dreams were coming true.

"Well, I hope you're right. I have to meet Mr. DeVille soon. I want to get together with you, Tia, and Emma this week. I'll call you so we can set things up."

I stood up to leave and Cat hugged me tightly to her. "I'm so happy for you, Maddie. Take care of yourself."

Leaning away from her, I smiled at my friend who always supported me from the day I met her right after getting to the city. I hadn't reached many of my goals yet, but I had found someone to love, and that was the most important goal of them all.

"I will, and you take care of yourself too. Be good."

Cat grinned wickedly. "I'll be careful, but I can't promise I'll be good."

I rolled my eyes. "Then be careful. I'll talk to you

in a few days and we'll make plans. Tell Tia and Emma I said hello."

"It's a date."

My phone rang just as I got down to the street, and I saw it was the owner of the staffing agency. "Hi, Mr. DeVille. I'm on my way to your office right now. I should be there in no more than twenty minutes."

"No need, Maddie. I got everything straightened out, so you don't have to return to the office today. I'm always sorry to lose an employee, but I wish you luck in your future."

"Thank you, Mr. DeVille. I appreciate that. And thank you for being the person who introduced me to Eric Pierce. You don't know how much help you've been."

He chuckled. "Oh, I'm happy to help. It's what I do, after all. We here at DeVille Staffing are so pleased things worked out for you. Good luck, Maddie."

"Thanks!"

And with that, I began to make my way to the train to take me back to Eric's house.

MAGDA STOOD AT THE COUNTER IN THE KITCHEN finishing her lunch when I came through the side door. Her eyes opened wide, like she was surprised to see me.

"Where did you go, Maddie?"

Placing my purse on the center island, I smiled. "I had to run into the city for a few hours. I hope it wasn't a problem."

She didn't return my smile, though, and instead turned to wash her plate in the sink. "Mr. Pierce is in his office. I think he's waiting to speak to you."

Eric shouldn't have been home in the middle of the day. He hadn't mentioned anything about taking the day off. And why would he be waiting to speak to me?

"Okay. I'll go see him right now."

"Maddie, wait. I want to say something to you."

I stopped and turned to see her drying her hands on a dish cloth and frowning. What was wrong? Had something happened?

She walked toward me and stopped in front of me, taking my hands in hers. For the first time since I came into the house, she smiled.

"You've never really been a cook here, even though I loved those dishes you made and your sugar cookies are delicious, but I've never seen Mr. Pierce happier in all the years I've known him. I just wanted you to know that."

I didn't know what to say. Suddenly, I worried something bad had happened to Eric.

"Okay, thanks. I'm glad you liked the cookies. Is everything okay?"

She forced a smile but said nothing else, so I hurried to Eric's office and hoped he hadn't gotten hurt. I looked into the room and saw him sitting at his desk, his eyes closed, and he wore an expression like he'd lost his best friend.

Had something happened at the restaurant?

My mind whirled with ideas. Had there been a fire? Had his partner been hurt, or worse, killed?

I wanted to reach out and take him into my arms to make him feel better about whatever had happened.

Poking my head in, I quietly said, "Eric, I heard you wanted to speak to me."

His head snapped around and he looked at me with surprise in his eyes. "Maddie? You're here."

"Of course, I'm here. I did go out for a little while, and no, I didn't ask your driver to take me anywhere, but I'm back now. What's wrong? You look like you're having the worst day of your life."

He stood from behind his desk and rushed over to take me in his arms. "I thought when he didn't call back that you didn't..."

His words trailed off, and he squeezed me to him. "What are you talking about? Who didn't call back?"

"Nobody. It doesn't matter. All that matters is you came back."

I pulled away from him, unsure what had happened while I was out. Studying his face, I couldn't make out why he thought I wouldn't come back here.

"Eric, what's going on? Why would you think I wouldn't come back here today? Didn't Mr. DeVille explain that I was leaving the agency, not you?"

"What are you talking about, Maddie?"

"I told him that I wasn't going to be working as your cook anymore. I know I didn't discuss it with you, but after you said you didn't want me to work for you at all and that I could still stay here, I wanted to make it official. I know you never cared what anyone else thought, but I do. I don't expect to just freeload off you or anything like that, so I hope you don't think I'm being presumptuous."

Eric stared at me for a moment and then shook his head. "I don't care about any of that. I have more than enough for both of us, but if you want to get a job somewhere, that's fine too. As long as you're here with me and every night you're in the bed beside me, I don't care what happens."

He seemed relieved by my explanation and didn't even care that I had resigned from DeVille Staffing without telling him. I wasn't sure why he thought I would leave him, but the happiness I saw in him now made me not want to push any further for details.

"Magda told me you wanted to speak to me. What's up?"

A big smile spread across his lips. "I just wanted to tell you I love you and I'm happy you're here."

The way he said those words — I love you — so easily, like he'd said them a thousand times before, surprised me. We'd never said that to one another, and even though I'd only known him for about a week, I loved him as much as I could any man.

"You love me?"

He nodded. "I do love you, Maddie. I didn't realize it until this morning when I thought I might lose you. All of a sudden, life felt empty without you, and I knew it wasn't just your sugar cookies."

"I love you too, Eric. I know this whole thing has happened at warp speed and I know most people would say we're not in love, but — "

Pulling me to him, he stopped my talking with a

kiss that nearly took my breath away. "I don't care what anyone thinks or says, Maddie. You make me happy, and if I do the same for you, then that's all that matters."

I looked up into his beautiful blue eyes gazing down at me like I was the most important thing in the world to him and I felt loved. He was right. That's all that mattered.

"You do make me happy. I guess there is such a thing as love at first sight," I said with a smile.

"I never believed it before, but I guess there is. What do you say to me telling Jack to run the restaurant again today and you and I spend the day together?"

"Can you do that?"

He smiled. "Of course I can. I'm one of the owners. And Jack has left me alone dozens of times for far less."

"What are you going to tell him is the reason why you aren't coming back today?" I asked as he took my hand in his and began to lead me down the hall to his bedroom.

Eric stopped and kissed me softly on the lips. "I'm going to tell him to mind his own business, and if he asks again, I'll tell him the truth. I've fallen in love with the woman who was supposed to be a cook for a man who never eats at home. He won't understand, but he probably won't ask again."

As strange as that answer sounded, it wasn't wrong. I'd been sent to Eric's home to cook for him, even though he never needed a cook. For whatever reason, Mr. DeVille had gotten this job wrong. I didn't hold it against him, though. He couldn't be right all the time.

So Eric Pierce, a man who came to me looking for a maid, got what he truly needed. He thought if he could have someone keep things tidy in his home that would make him happy, but as always, I knew better. You see, the human soul isn't a difficult thing to understand. Not for me, at least. I knew the moment I met him what he truly needed was someone to make him understand that all work and no play makes for a very dull life.

Maddie was just that someone. No, she couldn't cook, but I hadn't convinced him to hire a cook so he would eat at home. One glance at her and her sweet nature, and I knew she'd be perfect for him. Then it was just a matter of making him jealous and then making him think he'd lost her to nudge him to the realization that what he needed was her.

As I said, the human soul isn't difficult to read. You all want the same thing. I just do what I can to supply it. And in return, I ask for nothing. Well, that's not true, but I ask for nothing most won't willingly give up.

Love is worth it, right?

PRIVATE SECRETARY

K.M. SCOTT

CHAPTER 1

mma

I TOOK A DEEP BREATH TO STEADY MYSELF AND stared up at the sign on the building that said DeVille Staffing as the traffic raced by on the busy street behind me. It wasn't my first choice to come to the hiring service, but times got tough, and I needed to make money. I didn't like that either, but I had to face reality and do something.

So much for the life I planned. I got accustomed to living in my beautiful little apartment, and I wasn't interested in moving in with other people. Not after finally getting the place to myself after my ex-boyfriend Kyle bailed on me. I had to do this or I was about to come to the point of having to move to cheaper place or finding roommates.

Neither one of those was an option.

I'd lived there since I moved to the city with that good-for-nothing ex, the substantial savings account I had acquired from working every night in high school, and a lot of help from my family. I'd been so happy when Kyle finally left since I didn't even like him much but we'd both wanted to move to New York.

He was a Minnesota eight but a New York two, and that was being generous.

I busted my ass through high school and saved up enough to keep me going for a while afterward, but after spending two years making the mistake of trying to keep a guy happy, which hadn't put anything in my bank account, I lost my job a few months ago and now was in danger of losing everything.

Nope. That wasn't going to happen. So that's why after Maddie found such success with this DeVille Staffing place, I figured I should go for it. I didn't expect to find what she found. I just needed a paying job.

Not that I would ever turn up my nose at what Maddie got from her placement. I just didn't have my hopes up. This was about making money and paying my rent. Love had nothing to do with it.

I always figured that getting a job was done the old fashioned way, but not anymore, it seemed. At least not in New York. For three months, I applied to places online and went to businesses in person hoping that I could get a job the same way I had in high school.

With a friendly smile and what my parents called a go-getter attitude.

But I wasn't back home in small-town Minnesota anymore, first of all. Also, everywhere I went either turned me down, wasn't hiring, or wanted someone with qualifications that no twenty-one-year-old would have unless they'd finished college at the age of fourteen. I was at my wit's end, but something about going to a hiring service felt like giving up to me.

Still, a job was a job and if I did it well, what did it matter who helped me get the job in the first place?

Since deliberating by the door wasn't going to change my circumstances at all, I pushed it open and plastered my best smile on my face as I walked up to the reception desk. "Hello," I said in my most positive voice to the perky woman with big blue eyes that sat looking at me.

"Good afternoon, how may I help you?" she asked in a chipper voice.

She was exceptionally tan and platinum blonde, and her smile showed off teeth so bright she could have gotten a job doing toothpaste commercials. Whoever she was, she could have been a model, so what on earth was she doing as the welcome receptionist at DeVille Staffing?

I set my bag down next to me and pulled out the paperwork I'd been told to print out and bring with me today. Handing it to her as I forced myself to smile even bigger, almost like we were having a competition to see who could smile more, I said, "My name is Emma Cooper, and I have an appointment with Mr. DeVille today at three o'clock."

She extended her gold jewelry clad hand to take

the papers and nodded before replying in a soft, almost husky voice, "Okay, I'll file all of this and Mr. DeVille will be with you in just a moment. If you'll have a seat over there." She gestured across the room to some nice looking leather seats surrounded by tables with magazines and added, "Do you have any questions before Mr. DeVille sees you?"

"No, no. I'm fine, thank you," I said, smiling wide before I grabbed my bag and went to sit down.

I looked around the office and had to admit that the meager façade offered by the outside of the building did not measure up to what the inside was showing me. Everything was not only pristine but looked classy and expensive. I'd worried I was walking into some dingy New York hiring agency like people had told me horror stories about, but this was nice.

Before long, a large oak door behind where the receptionist was sitting opened, and a tall and lean man in an impeccable dark suit walked out. The receptionist said something to him that I couldn't hear and the man smiled before looking up and walking over to me as he extended his hand to shake mine.

"Miss Cooper, a pleasure to meet you. What good timing you have. I hope the commute here wasn't a problem. They aren't calling it the summer of Hell for nothing with all those broken down trains and this heat."

I shook his hand and found myself staring up into his stunning blue eyes fixed on me. "No, it was no problem at all, thank you."

In all honesty, it had been a nightmare getting to his office, and I had been stuck next to some seriously sweaty individuals in too little clothing, but that wasn't something I was about to tell Mr. DeVille. Instead, I continued with something a bit more classic and tasteful. "Please, call me Emma. It's so nice—"

"Well, Emma, let's go into my office and talk about what we can find you. I think I have the perfect position for you."

"Oh?" I said, cocking my head.

Unlike in Maddie's case, I hadn't applied for any particular position with DeVille Staffing and had instead just presented my work experience and abilities and hoped they would fit with something Mr. DeVille had available. That he had something he thought would be perfect for me intrigued me while at the same time made me even more nervous about all of this.

He turned his head to smile at the receptionist and beckoned me to come with him. I wasn't sure how I was supposed to respond to what he said and was taken aback by him cutting me off, so I opted for silence. I waited for a moment for him to continue, but he turned his back to me and strode away. Confused by his abruptness, I hurried to follow him to an office across the room.

He took a seat in the plush, black leather office chair behind his wood desk and gestured for me to take a seat in a chair in front of it. The room was sparsely decorated but still exuded the same class that I had found in the waiting area. Everything about the place made me feel like I had made the right choice following Maddie's advice.

At least I hoped I had.

"So, do you have any questions for me, Miss Cooper?"

I shook my head and sat quietly before remembering what Maddie had told me. "Be honest with him, Em. He's a strange kind of man, but he seems to have a knack for things. Eric can't say enough great things about him."

So I did as she said and told the truth. "Yes, actually I do. I understand that this is a hiring service, but I was wondering if I could make a request."

He smiled a wide grin and sat back in his chair, arms folded across his chest, before replying in a very serious voice, "You're perfectly welcome to make a request, Miss Cooper. Whether or not I can fulfill that request is another story entirely. I'll do my best, though."

I sat perfectly still, not knowing what to say until Mr. DeVille chuckled. "Relax, Miss Cooper. Just tell me what it is you want. I'm here to help."

"Well, it's more of what I don't want, really."

He leaned forward and steepled his hands in front of him. "Oh, now I'm intrigued. Go on. I so rarely get these kinds of requests."

"I hope this isn't too much to ask, but I think I would be well suited for something that doesn't involve children. It's not that I have any serious issue with them. In fact, it's usually them who don't like me, but I do think I would work much better in a field that doesn't involve a lot of one-on-one contact with children," I said, hoping I hadn't ruined my chances at a job.

I didn't hate children, but I'd never had much luck with them. I didn't know why, but they never warmed up to me. I looked over at Mr. DeVille, nervously, and asked, "Is that okay?"

"That's no problem at all. If you don't like something, you won't do it well and we don't want the people finding jobs through us here at DeVille Staffing giving us a bad name, after all. Your request is granted. No children for you. I find the little rug rats annoying myself. Always shrieking and drooling. It's too much. Now your paperwork says you're available immediately. Is that true?"

"Yes, sir. I can start today at a job, if you have one ready for me."

Ordinarily, I wouldn't have sounded so eager, but I needed to start making money and quick.

"Good, good. Well, Emma, I looked around and given your skills and past employment history, I think I've found a place that'll work for you. Am I correct in assuming that you're familiar with the basics that go into being a secretary? That includes being able to set appointments, computer work, get what the boss needs, those kinds of things? Nothing too physically intensive, mostly desk work. The prospective employer I'm looking at for you might send you out to get lunch, but nothing more major than that. What do you think?"

"Yes, I can do all of that," I said, my heart racing at

the idea of getting such a cushy position right off the bat.

My friends had been worried that I was going to get some awful job cleaning toilets or something equally as gross. Desperate times called for desperate measures, but I had secretly hoped for something less disgusting.

"Good. Well this will be a short meeting then. Tomorrow you'll go to this address and start. The man in charge there is named Mark Tanchen. He's a CEO of a tech company that's experiencing tremendous growth, and as his business is expanding, he needs a secretary. Tina will email you all the details, such as where his office is located, the hours, and other pertinent information. I would suggest wearing something professional, of course, but you don't seem to have an issue with that," he said, gesturing at my outfit and making me smile.

I had taken extra care to ensure I looked the very picture of a professional in my black skirt, red silk blouse, and sensible heels my mother suggested I wear. As usual, she'd been right.

"Does everything about that sound good to you?" Mr. DeVille asked, typing something into his computer as he waited for me to reply.

"Yes, thank you so much, Mr. DeVille. Is there anything else you need from me?"

He looked across the desk at me and pursed his lips. "No, if we need anything, Tina will be in touch with you. If you've signed all the paperwork you gave her, then go enjoy your night off before you start tomorrow. He's a busy man, so I suggest getting there a little early on your first day."

"Thank you so much, sir. I really appreciate this."

"It's what I do," he said with a chuckle.

I smiled once more at him before standing to leave. When I reached the door, I remembered I hadn't asked one important question. I turned and said, "Mr. DeVille, as for my salary…"

"Your new boss will go over all of that. Again, any issue and we're here. That being said, we work with excellent clients, and none of them are the kind of people who expect superior work without paying superior money."

Not exactly the answer I wanted, but he did say superior money. "Okay. Thank you, sir," I squeaked out before leaving.

When I walked outside, I beamed about my success. I had to remind myself that jumping around in celebration was something I could save for when I was back in my apartment and wouldn't look like a lunatic on the street. That hadn't been bad at all and faster than I could have ever imagined.

I had a job.

Oh, God! In my excitement, I didn't ask him where Mr. Tanchen's business was located. No matter. I didn't care how far I had to travel each day. I had a job, and if it paid a superior salary like Mr. DeVille said, it would all be fine.

On my way to the train, I quickly called Maddie to share my good news. Without even saying hello, I jumped right in. "Hey! I just left DeVille Staffing, and I have a job starting tomorrow!" I squealed.

"That's great! Didn't I tell you that place was good? What did you think of that DeVille guy? He's sort of sexy in a scary kind of way, isn't he?" she asked with a giggle.

I thought back to my very brief meeting with him and had to agree. "Yeah, he is. But like you said, he seems to be good at this thing. He had a job lined up for me when I got there this afternoon."

"Maybe it will end up like mine did," she said in a singsong voice.

"I'd just be happy if it ended up with me making some good money. True love and great sex are nice, but money is what this girl needs to make her world go round."

"So what's the job? He didn't give you anything with kids, did he? I know how you feel about them," Maddie said in a voice that told me she was genuinely worried. God, was I really that bad with kids?

"No. I actually mentioned to him that I would prefer nothing having to do with children, and he seemed okay with that. My position is as a secretary. I didn't even realize people actually used that term anymore. I mean, it's kind of old-fashioned, isn't it?"

As I said that, I thought about the type of person who would use the word secretary. My new boss was probably an old geezer. A small part of me felt disappointed as the possibility of having what happened to Maddie faded away in my mind.

"I don't know. They still use the title Secretary of

State, and that's not usually a woman. I think it sounds distinguished. Let's say you're someone's private secretary. That sounds even better. So who's your new boss?"

"A man named Mr. Tanchen. He's probably a dinosaur, but I'm fine with whatever as long as I'm making money and don't have to leave my apartment."

That sounded more pathetic than I wanted it to, but I didn't care. A job meant money. That's all. Anything else I could find on my own after work hours.

"Well, I'm just happy you got a position. Let me know how it goes. I'm dying to know, okay?" Maddie said sweetly, even as a hint of sympathy crept into her words.

"Okay, I'll let you know. Thanks, Maddie!"

So I wouldn't have a hot boss who falls madly in love with me. At least I had a job and some money coming in.

I WOKE THE NEXT MORNING FAR EARLIER THAN I normally would have and made sure I looked as perfect as possible for my new secretary position before grabbing the train and making my way to the Upper East Side. When I arrived, I was surprised to see that the building where I was to work wasn't an office building at all, but a home. Mr. DeVille hadn't mentioned that Mr. Tanchen worked out of his house.

Mr. Tanchen's home was a brownstone so common

to Brooklyn mostly, but anyone who'd ever watched Sex in the City knew they existed outside of that section of New York. As I stared up at the gorgeous place in front of me, I had a feeling this was what DeVille had meant by superior clients. Mr. Tanchen clearly had money.

I was a little early, even by first day standards, but I couldn't bear standing outside and waiting. I was far too excited. I hurried up the stairs and rang the doorbell. Nervous, I looked up and down the street and watched people leaving their homes to begin their workday on this warm morning.

I'd tried to find a picture of my new boss online after my interview with Mr. DeVille, but it seemed Mr. Tanchen didn't appear in any. He had no Facebook profile, which meant he was likely quite old. But I didn't want to let disappointment that I wouldn't have what Maddie got get in the way of making money, which was far more important than anything else.

After enough time that I was actually considering ringing the bell again, a man appeared on the other side of the glass door. A stunning man with dark brown hair and deep brown eyes like melted chocolate, he wore a black suit with a pale blue shirt and tie that matched almost perfectly and highlighted how well-built he was underneath those expensive clothes. I felt my eyes roam over him and then caught myself. This couldn't be my new boss.

Could it be? No. Maybe it was his son?

While my mind imagined what this man looked like under that perfect fitting suit, he opened the door

143

and in a deep voice that rolled over me like silk, he said, "Hello? Do you have an appointment?"

My voice seemed to disappear as I caught my breath at how beautiful this man was. "Hi. I mean, good morning. I'm looking for Mr. Tanchen. My name is Emma Cooper, and I was sent from DeVille Staffing to…"

He stared at me for a long moment and then a slow smile lit up his dark expression. "Oh, you're the secretary. Come in, and we'll get you set up. I'm sorry it took so long for me to get to the door, but as you know, we didn't have a secretary until now. I'm Mark Tanchen."

This was Mr. Tanchen?

My new boss beckoned me in, and I looked around the beautiful, albeit bare, home. As we walked through the living room, I noticed it had been converted into an empty space with a nice desk and chair.

He saw me looking in the room and smiled in a way that made him look very friendly. "That's going to be your office. People call, you answer. People knock, you answer and help them before they come to meet with me. Granted, we don't get too many people coming by, but it does happen from time to time. Sound like something you can do?"

I looked away from the office and returned his smile with one of my own. "Absolutely, Mr. Tanchen. I'll have no trouble at all."

With a curt nod, he continued walking toward the kitchen that had been left as a kitchen after the business took over. When he got there, he opened the refrigerator and said, "This is where you can keep any food or drink that you might want to bring in. Most of the time it'll just be the two of us here. I keep sodas in here for myself and people who might come in for meetings, but feel free to take one whenever you like."

"Okay. Thank you, sir," I said, not knowing what to call him.

His expression twisted, showing he didn't like what I'd chosen. As he handed me a can of soda, he said, "You don't have to call me sir. Mr. Tanchen is fine. Sir makes me sound old and boring, and I'm only one of those things."

As he opened his own soda, I looked at him and took stock of the person I would be employed by for the foreseeable future. Old was not the adjective I would have used to describe him at all, though he was clearly older than me. He was tall and built, and I suspected his work clothes hid a great body. His dark brown hair clearly enjoyed trying to get into his deep brown eyes, and there was something about his chiseled cheekbones that made him look rugged.

Whatever I'd thought yesterday, I'd been wrong. I had a hot boss. He had a bit of a nerdy vibe to him, but it was a sexy, smart kind of nerdy that I found intriguing. I'd had my fill of bad boys and jocks. Nerdy was appealing now.

As soon these thoughts entered my head, I blushed and felt the need to mentally chastise myself. The man, good looking as he may have been, was my boss and I couldn't go about having the hots for my boss. It was unprofessional and impossible to boot. A wealthy boss falling for his young secretary? It was so clichéd, and I reminded myself to keep it together.

Even if shades of what Maddie experienced began to make me wonder if I'd ever have that with Mark.

Focus, Emma. This job is to make you money. That's it.

I repeated that a few times as he talked about something involving the building and the history of it.

"So, be here at nine every morning and be available until five. I'll probably send you home early some days if it's slow and there are no meetings to deal with. Should I need something extra that I think you can handle, I may come to you. I had you come in a little early today so that I could familiarize you with some of the things you'll be doing."

I looked around for his partner in the business but saw no one. "Mr. Tanchen, you mentioned a we? Will I be working for someone else as well?" I asked, hoping my sly way of trying to find out if he was referring to a wife or not wouldn't come off as too obvious.

He nodded, and as he wrote something down on a white board on the wall, said, "Sort of. I have a business partner who is more of the work away from the office type. Josh stops in here and there, but if someone needs to make an appointment with him, they'll go through you the same as they would for me. He's a good guy. You'll like him. If you ever see him, that is. The guy is usually in Hawaii working with some financiers there. I know that's code for hanging out with beautiful women, but the man sure can network, so I don't give a damn."

I smiled and nodded as he looked at a message that

came in on his phone and I looked around the place a little more. It was a genuinely masculine space, with no real art or color to speak of. The floors were hardwood, and everything else was either black or white. It wasn't the scheme I would have chosen as I thought about my apartment bursting with color, but it did suit the needs of an office space.

Mr. Tanchen looked up and must have caught me looking around as he said, "We just bought the place a few months ago and finished renovating it to be more like an office I can work at home from. I hate commuting into a huge building filled with people I don't know."

"It must be such a nice advantage to be able to wake up and just go straight to work, Mr. Tanchen."

"It's one of the nicer perks, yes," he said, gesturing for me to follow him into my little office area. "Come this way, and we'll go over some of the finer points of the job."

ark

I'D WOKEN UP WITH A SPLITTING HEADACHE THAT morning, but it had been tempered the moment I opened the door and found my new secretary waiting for me. DeVille had sent her paperwork over ahead of time and assured me Emma was the right person for the job. His exact words were that she'd be perfect and was sure I'd think so too, even though I'd specifically asked for someone older. I didn't have the patience or interest in taking the time to teach someone a job I didn't want to do myself, so seeing someone so young at my door made me question this whole thing with DeVille Staffing.

Then again, maybe I could afford a few days to try Emma out.

When I opened the door and saw the petite

brunette with the big blue eyes standing on my front porch before me, I was stunned by just how attractive she was. For a moment, I forgot that I'd made a point of requesting the secretary be in her forties.

But as we spoke, I reminded myself that I was running a business and I didn't intend to run it into the ground by getting preoccupied with the cute girl setting my appointments. Sure those stunning blue eyes and pouty lips were going to be a slight distraction, but I needed to keep my head in the game. I'd spent years focusing on getting my tech company off the ground, and I'd finally gotten to the point of success. I didn't have time for many women along the way, at least not anything more than one night with one, but that was something I could focus on when I reached my thirties.

Work was the name of the game, and I was winning that game.

I'd ordered a nice desk and chair for our new secretary, and as she took her seat, I stood next to her and logged onto the computer. "They haven't been delivered yet, but I do have some filing cabinets and more office furniture coming, so it won't be this sparse in here. Feel free to add your little touches as long as they're appropriate. Just no Red Sox stuff. We're diehard Yankees in this company," I said at an attempt at a joke.

She turned and made a face like she just sucked on a lemon before replying, "I wouldn't think of touching something Red Sox. I was born and raised a Yankees girl, even though we were from Minnesota. Anything else, even anything Twins related, would be the highest form of heresy."

I smiled but reminded myself to focus, no matter how cute she looked and how much I liked that we had something in common. I went over the programs she'd be using, none of which were too complicated, and she took to everything quickly. She appeared to have a knack for the work she'd have to do from the questions she asked, and she was personable too. I liked that. I'd thought Josh was a little crazy when he agreed with Louis DeVille about finding us a secretary that night at the bar, but she quickly proved me wrong.

"Did you go to school for computers?" I asked, noting that she had a natural aptitude for computers and the programs I showed her. I figured maybe she was involved in some kind of lower level computer science. That would have been an interesting person for DeVille to send.

Emma frowned. "Not yet. I want to, though, for psychology," she answered quietly as she typed the required personal information into the document I'd setup for her.

I was surprised. I hadn't taken her for someone who wanted to be a psychologist. When I was in college, all the psych majors had been as boring as hell. I hadn't spent much time talking to them, but every time they were around, they wanted to psychoanalyze everyone and acted far superior to those of us who worked with machines like computers. I didn't know why, but I hoped Emma wasn't like that.

Not wanting to make judgments too soon, I nodded. "I never took to the psych stuff myself. You want to be a therapist?"

"Sort of. My uncle joined the military right after September eleventh and came back with some severe PTSD. I want to help people like that. We send soldiers over to these places and then don't have people here to help them mentally when they come home. I consider it a bit of a calling really."

Her answer surprised me again. She didn't sound like those psychoanalytical pains in the asses from school. "Want to help the troops. That's noble of you. I respect that."

I didn't often understand the dumb career choices people made. Christ, every other student when I graduated seemed to be a business major. Emma's answer impressed me, though.

She looked up at me and smiled, but she didn't say anything else. She wasn't overly chatty, but she didn't seem cold either. So far, I liked everything about her.

After we finished going over some of the work requirements, I took a seat and said, "The man at the staffing agency didn't say how long you're looking to work for. The next semester of college is going to be starting soon. Are you taking night classes?"

Shaking her head, she frowned again. "No. College is just a goal right now. I'm here for as long as you'll have me. I don't have an end date as far as working goes."

Good. I liked hearing that. We didn't need a revolving door for secretaries that I'd have to break in, even though this whole idea was mostly Josh's and not mine. Mr. DeVille had made it clear that some people he sent to work for his clients were temporary, but he'd said nothing about Emma's situation.

"Okay. Well, as long as you're good at your job, you have one. I'm not a fan of training you and then having to hire someone else."

Emma nodded. "Then I'll be here, Mr. Tanchen."

There was something about the way she sounded when she called me Mr. Tanchen that made my cock begin to get hard. It was sexy but in that sweet and innocent kind of way. At twenty-one years old, it was unlikely she was either sweet or innocent, and I was finding myself more intrigued by the moment.

Shaking my head, I reminded myself that I couldn't be that guy going around fucking the workers some agency sent me. It was inappropriate, and great businesses had been killed and buried for far less.

As I chastised myself for my thoughts, the phone at her desk rang. I leaned over to answer it out of reflex, but she beat me to it.

"Thank you for calling Global Digital Solutions. My name is Emma. How may I help you?" she answered expertly.

I waited for her to tell me who called, but instead she said sweetly, "I'm sorry, but I believe you have the wrong number."

She smiled up at me as she hung up. "They were trying to order Chinese food. I don't think that's what you do here unless I'm very confused," she joked, making me chuckle.

"No, though now that you mention it I could go for some General Tso's chicken. What do you say to my ordering some for lunch for your first day? Great way to answer the phone by the way. You seem like you'll take to this quickly."

"I certainly hope so, Mr. Tanchen."

Jesus. There it was again, that sweet voice calling me Mr. Tanchen. I was starting to understand how better men than myself had fallen for the cute girl at work, especially when she worked under him. I'd been so focused on getting to the top of my field that any form of dating and romance had been put on the back burner. I was devoted and married, but only to my job.

I just needed to remember that now.

When I began to walk away, she asked, "Mr. Tanchen, is there a particular time I should be taking my lunch every day? I don't want to do anything that interferes with what you want from me."

What I wanted from her...*Mark, think with your brain and not your cock.*

"I'll leave that to your judgment. If you aren't busy, feel free to eat."

"Thank you." She hesitated for a moment before saying, "Oh, one more thing. Mr. DeVille said you'd let me know how much the salary is. I don't mean to..."

Before she could continue, I stopped her. "I'm sorry. I always hated when employers didn't say how much I'd be getting paid like I just did. It's twenty-five dollars an hour to start. After three months, we'll be willing to discuss benefits and pay increases. Does that work for you?"

Emma's eyes lit up. "Oh, yes. Thank you! That works perfectly."

"If you need me I'll be in my office. It's your first day, so don't feel like you can't bother me."

She smiled and returned to typing something into the document as I thought about how I'd never once even considered telling someone they could bother me while I was at work. I usually hated anyone interrupting me like that.

I nodded as she continued to type, unsure what was happening to me. I headed back to my office and tried to concentrate on work, even as I struggled against the urge to go talk to Emma. My mind drifted from thought to thought about her, making any focus on the things I had to do impossible. Each time the phone rang, I listened to her handle the call professionally, which was supposed to free me up to actually do my own work.

So much for that.

After a few hours, I walked out of my office toward hers across the hall. She spoke to someone on the phone and was all smiles. Instantly, from out of nowhere, I found myself jealously wondering if the call was personal instead of profession.

As my mind swirled with questions about who she might be talking to, she finished her call and smiled at me. "Mr. Tanchen, you have a few scheduled appointments for later in the week. I've logged them all into your calendar, along with notes about the client's reason for coming in and anything else you may need for your meeting."

My body relaxed with each word she spoke. What the hell was wrong with me? Even if she had made a personal phone call, I wouldn't usually care. I was running a business, not a prison.

"That's great, Emma. You're impressive jumping right in like that."

She stared up at me, her big blue eyes wide, and asked, "Is there anything I can do for you?"

There were plenty of things she could for and to me, and none of them had anything to do with making appointments. Christ, I wasn't going to be able to keep her around if my mind kept wandering to what she looked like bent over my desk with my cock inside her.

"I figured you'd probably be hungry soon. What would you like me to order for you from the Chinese restaurant?"

"Oh, Mr. Tanchen, you don't really have to do that," she said sweetly.

I shook my head. "No, I insist. It's your first day, after all."

"Okay. I guess General Tso's Chicken sounds good. Ever since you mentioned it before, I have to admit my mouth has been watering. I was thinking of grabbing some after I leave today, so thank you."

"It's my pleasure. I'll call the order in now. Just let me know when the food arrives."

The problem was after I ordered the food, I still couldn't concentrate on my work. I kept looking out across the hall toward where Emma sat, every moment filled with sexy thoughts about my new secretary.

Unable to fight the desire to be near her, I abandoned all hope of getting anything done before lunch and walked back across the hall. "Are you finding you have any questions about anything, Emma?"

She looked up at me with confusion in her eyes. No wonder. She didn't exactly have the most challenging job in the world, and she probably wondered why I kept hovering around her like some micromanaging asshole.

"I think I'm fine so far. I know it must be a big adjustment getting used to trusting a complete stranger with your business, but I promise that I won't do anything to disappoint you."

Great. Now I'd made her feel like I didn't trust her to make appointments for me. I actually was that micromanaging asshole I'd hated at every job I'd ever had.

Taking a step closer toward her desk, I shook my head. "It's not that at all. I guess I'm just not used to having another person around in the office. I'm so used to my partner being away all the time. I didn't mean to bother you," I said, adding pathetic to my list of traits I'd shown my new hire.

I turned to leave, but Emma said, "I'd be happy to hear any suggestions you might have for me. I'm here to serve your needs, so if you have any ideas on how I can do that better, I'm eager to hear them."

For a moment, I froze in place. Her words were

innocent enough, but the way my brain heard them made me think of all the delicious ways I would love for her to serve me. On her knees sucking my cock was the one my mind settled on, making me get hard just standing there.

I nodded and turned around as I hoped my hard on went away. Gesturing at the computer in front of her, I said, "I see you're alternating between programs a little slowly. It'll be easier for you if you do this." I showed her the keys to hit to alternate faster, and she tried it herself. "It'll make setting appointments while looking up any information you might need a lot faster. Trust me."

Emma turned to look up at me and smiled. "Interesting. I would have never known that. Thanks."

I liked being able to show her things, and before I knew it, I was showing her dozens of tips and tricks on the computer as I kneeled next to her. She would smile at me, and I couldn't help thinking she had the prettiest smile I had ever seen. It was small, not a big, toothy grin, and innocent just like she seemed. Just as I was allowing myself to delve deeper into thoughts I shouldn't have been having as I kneeled beside her, the doorbell rang.

"Oh, the food is here!" Emma said as she jumped up from her chair and ran to answer the door.

She set it down on the counter in the kitchen, where I waited for her. My partner and I never ate together at work, so I hadn't considered that I should have bought some furniture for Emma so she could enjoy lunch each workday. All we had were two barstools and a pub height table I'd grabbed from a friend when he was getting rid of his furniture after his wife left him.

"Sorry about the seating. I'll look into getting a table and chairs so you can have somewhere to relax and eat your lunch every day."

As she unloaded our two orders of General Tso's Chicken and fried rice onto the counter, she shrugged. "Oh, please don't feel like you have to on my account. I can eat standing up, if I have to."

She opened a drawer near her and then the one next to it before turning toward me. "I guess you don't have any silverware. It's okay. They gave us plastic forks in the bag, I think."

"Let me run upstairs to my apartment and get us some real forks," I said as I took a step toward the door.

Emma stopped me with her hand on my arm. "It's okay, Mr. Tanchen. I'm good with plastic forks."

For a moment, I didn't know what to say. Ordinarily, I would have just sat down, but something about her hand on my forearm made me wish she wouldn't move it. I knew she had to, though, and when she did, I took a deep breath and blew it out of my lungs slowly, hoping to stop myself from going full-blown fantasy on my new secretary.

"No problem. If you're good, I'm good too," I said as casually as possible and grabbed my container of food.

We ate in silence, which only made it more difficult not to daydream about her, so after a few minutes, I said, "I admire that you want to go to school so much. I hated every moment of it. I wanted to be out in the world doing things instead of wasting my time relearning what I already knew."

I grabbed two sodas from the refrigerator and handed her one as I gestured around the room, "The moment I got my degree I began putting all of this into motion. It took a lot of hard work. It didn't hurt that my family had some money and invested, of course."

"You're a lucky person, Mr. Tanchen. You've found something you love and you're succeeding at it."

Just then, the phone rang and she ran out of the kitchen to answer it. Alone, I rubbed my temples before pushing my hair out of my eyes. What had this DeVille guy gotten me into? Emma had been in my office for less than half a day, and I couldn't get my mind off what I wanted to do with her.

I cleaned up and walked back to my office. As I sat down, my cell phone went off. I looked down and saw it was my partner calling me. No doubt with a long and rambling story of his most recent conquest on the beach.

"The man himself. What's up, Josh?"

"Marky Mark!" he replied, using the nickname he'd bestowed on me our freshman year of college. I hated it then, and I'd hated it every time since.

Rolling my eyes, I sighed. "Dude, we're business partners now. You have to think of something different to call me."

"Not on the phone I don't," he joked.

Already tired of this conversation, I asked, "So, what's up?"

"Just checking in after the meeting with the Blithes. They're looking to invest, my man."

Now that kind of talk I liked to hear. "Excellent. Good job."

"As always. So, who is the pretty voice who answered my call the first time? I called the office thinking you'd just answer there. We have a secretary now?"

"Yeah. Remember that DeVille guy we were talking to in the pub the last time you were in town? He sent someone over."

I sounded distinctly defensive, and Josh heard it loud and clear. "Listen, man, if you want a pretty little thing running around the office, I have no problem with that at all."

Putting my feet up in a box next to my desk, I said, "You're going to get us a harassment suit if you don't cut the shit, Josh."

"You know I'm just kidding. You're so uptight, man. Maybe you should be the one to go to Hawaii next time. You need to relax. For example, last night I'm chatting these two coeds up at the bar, and one starts telling me how she's never been with a guy from the mainland. Can you believe that? It's like another world down here."

Leave it to my partner. The guy definitely knew how to mix business with pleasure.

"But seriously, is she good?" he asked with a chuckle.

"She's very nice and good at her job," I said, keeping my tone perfectly level and professional, even as I wished I could be like him.

"I'm sure. Well, listen, I'm flying out next week, so I'll be back then. Let's hang out and do lunch, and I can meet this new hire of ours."

Instantly, my chest tightened. I didn't love the idea of Josh meeting Emma so soon, but I couldn't quite figure out what about it put me on edge. I couldn't show that, though, or else Josh would never stop busting my balls, or worse, make his move on her.

"Sounds good. See you then."

We hung up, and I looked across the hall to see Emma working. I idly wondered what Josh had said to her. God, had he already tried to move in on her already?

"I hear you spoke to my partner. I hope he was polite with you. He's been known to be a bit of a wise ass sometimes."

She nodded, staring up at me with those big blue eyes and said, "Yes, Mr. Tanchen. Mr. Lanis was very polite. I explained who I was and he welcomed me aboard. He seems very nice."

"Good." I nodded and looked around the room, knowing I should just go back to my office.

"Slow day, Mr. Tanchen?"

"For once, yes. Usually, I'm up to my ears with things to do, but I cleared today to ensure I could train you. I guess I overestimated how much you'd need."

"I'm glad I could jump right in for you."

There was a long pause before I decided to say,

"It's three o'clock, and I don't anticipate so many people calling that I can't handle it. Why don't you take the rest of the day off?"

"Are you sure, Mr. Tanchen? I'm happy to stay."

As much as I wanted to her to stay, I knew it was better she leave. "It's fine. You did very well today, and you got here early anyway."

"Wow, thanks!" she said, grabbing her bag and logging off her computer. "I'll be here at nine tomorrow."

"Sounds good."

"Great! Have a good day, Mr. Tanchen. I'll see you tomorrow," she said cheerily as she waved and left through my front door.

As she walked away, I couldn't help staring at her again, wishing she was walking up the stairs to my bedroom instead. When the door closed behind her, I let out a long sigh.

"That girl is going to get me in trouble."

Something about her was just so enticing. I was drawn to her in a way I had never found myself attracted to a woman before. Sure, I'd dated and had my fun, but no one had left me with the feeling I had at that moment because of her.

Palming my hard cock, I mumbled to myself, "You better think with your head instead of your dick, Mark, or you're going to find yourself in a world of trouble."

And still I couldn't stop thinking about her and what I wished I could do with Emma.

CHAPTER 3

mma

BY THE END OF THE FIRST WEEK, I HAD ESTABLISHED a routine at my new job. I would get to work about ten minutes early so I could set myself up with a drink and get settled at my desk. Every day Mr. Tanchen would hear me unlock the front door and poke his head out to greet me with a smile.

That is, at least for the first week.

By the second week, he was meeting me just inside the door or in the kitchen where I always went first. We talked about the morning commute and how his was far preferable to mine. He told me about important things going on at work that day, but he also peppered in stories about other things, like his friends or family. I learned he had a crazy uncle who was in town and who he was trying to avoid due to his fondness for long rambling stories all related to drinking. His smile got bigger every time I walked in, and I couldn't help but think that my boss was flirting with me some of the time.

One day I walked in and skipped the kitchen stop, having too much on my mind to think of my daily routine and wanting just to sit down and busy myself with something that wasn't my personal life. I figured I was keeping it all together, so I was startled when I saw Mr. Tanchen walk around the corner with a concerned look on his face.

"Emma, are you okay?" he asked before taking a sip of his morning coffee.

I shook my head and said, "Yes, I'm fine. Is anything wrong?" looking around at my computer that hadn't even been turned on yet.

"No, I just...your face," he said, awkwardly.

I couldn't help it but something about how he said that made me laugh a little. Covering my mouth, I said, "Sorry, Mr. Tanchen. It's just that this is the first time I've laughed since Friday."

"Not a good weekend?"

"No, not really. Just a bunch of dumb drama that I won't get into since this is work and it doesn't belong here."

He nodded and smiled. "I understand. I'm glad that I could make you laugh then."

Then he set his hand down on top of mine for the briefest moment, and our eyes locked and something about the tingling sensation that ran through my entire body told me at least one of us didn't find the gesture to be wholly innocent. As if he realized it too, he quickly moved his hand back and he grunted to himself, moving to leave.

Despite my body still reeling from his touch, I quickly said, "Wait, I have your appointments for next week made up and the notes printed out for this week's appointments. I just forgot to give them to you before I left for the weekend. I'm sorry."

Smiling, he shook his head. "No apologies necessary."

He took a seat on the small, black couch near my desk, a remnant of what had once belonged there when it was a living room. His lean but muscular build was distracting, so I had to focus on the paper as I held it out to him, embarrassed that I'd let myself fantasize about my boss again for even a moment.

The truth was I'd been thinking about him all weekend when I wasn't dealing with my stupid ex-boyfriend and couldn't seem to get the thought of him off my mind, no matter how hard I tried. I went out with friends, and while I attempted to have a good time despite my ex showing up, I found myself retreating from the situation by fantasizing about what I wished we were doing in the kitchen or on my desk, and it certainly wasn't work. I got so lost in my thoughts that I didn't even hear the first half of Mr. Tanchen's sentence.

"Anyway, you've been doing great work for me, Emma. Why don't I buy us lunch again this afternoon?"

I nodded, thinking about the last and only lunch

we'd shared together. "That sounds great, Mr. Tanchen. I'll call and make an order, so just let me know what you want me to get. What are you in the mood for?" I asked, trying to drag myself back towards acting professionally.

He thought for a moment before answering, "Pizza."

"Great idea. Just tell me where you want me to call, and I'll be happy to order it."

"I've got it, Emma. I'll have it here for right around noon. Do you like anything on your pizza?" he asked in such a sweet way that I forgot myself and that he was my boss.

"Anything but anchovies or pineapple. Definitely not those."

Then I remembered that no matter what I'd thought about him for the past forty-eight hours, he was still my boss and not one of my girlfriends hanging out with me at my apartment. "Oh, I'm sorry, Mr. Tanchen. That sounded terribly ungrateful of me. You probably love both of those things on your pizza, right?" I asked, cringing at my mistake.

He smiled in a way that was nothing less than downright sexy and shook his head. "I'm a pizza purist, myself. Pineapple has its place, and it isn't on my pizza. I do like sausage. Are you okay with that?"

Nothing in his answer told me he disliked how opinionated I'd been about my pizza toppings, so I relaxed and breathed a sigh of relief. "I love sausage."

"Great. I'll order it and have a pizza with sausage here for our lunch."

He stood to leave my office and before I could stop them, words so inappropriate came tumbling out of my mouth. "It's a date then."

Instantly, I felt my cheeks begin to burn up like they were on fire. Surely, he had to know that I was attracted to him now and had been thinking the most impure thoughts I'd ever thought about a man in my life!

Mr. Tanchen didn't respond to my ridiculous statement, thankfully, so I quickly turned my focus to my work and prayed to God to make the phone ring so something could end this terrible moment I'd created by being too friendly.

As he turned to walk back to his office, I felt like I was going to be sick. It's a date, then. How could I have said that? Oh, God. I was such an ass.

And then as if God had heard my desperate silent plea, his phone began to ring. "Excuse me, Emma. I need to take this."

I looked up toward the ceiling and quietly said, "Thank you, God. Now if you could just help me not make an ass out of myself ever again while I work for this man, I'd really appreciate it."

Mr. Tanchen seemed to avoid me for the next few hours. I didn't blame him. I'd taken a friendly conversation and blown it to smithereens by saying something stupid and immature. I just hoped he didn't decide to fire me because of it.

At noon, I glanced at the clock on my computer and wondered if he'd decided against us having lunch together today. Again, I wouldn't have blamed him.

I leaned over my desk and looked across toward his office, but I didn't see him. Unsure what to do and certainly not wanting to make a fool out of myself again, I made my way to the kitchen to grab a bite of my sandwich I'd brought that morning. The mixture of ham with utter regret didn't make for a good lunch, and I tossed it back into the paper bag after two bites.

Disgusted with myself and my awful lunch, I slowly walked back to my desk. Mr. Tanchen seemed to have disappeared, which I thought was odd since he had told me every time he left the office since the first day. My ridiculous comment had changed everything for the worst, and I had no doubt he was avoiding me.

Lost in my misery, I heard a faint noise from upstairs. Craning my neck to listen to hear if it happened again, I distinctly heard a groan. Had Mr. Tanchen gone upstairs at some point and now something bad happened to him?

I quietly crept up the stairs to make sure he was okay, uncertain if I should even be anywhere near his apartment on the second floor. As I reached the top step, I heard the groaning noise again. Pushing the heavy wood door open, I poked my head into his living room and my eyes grew wide at the sight before me. Mr. Tanchen stood in just a towel that hung low on his hips, and my mouth dropped open in shock and delight that I'd been correct when I guessed he had a great body under those business clothes he always wore.

Lean, he was muscular in all the right places, from his shoulders to his abs to those incredibly sexy muscles near his waist that seemed to point like an arrow directly to his cock. Through the towel, I could see he was rock hard.

And big.

Before I got caught gawking at his beautiful body, I skirted back down the stairs to my desk and hoped the blush of my cheeks wouldn't give away what I'd seen. He had been so good looking, though. I bit my lower lip and had a feeling I knew exactly what I would be thinking of that night when I was home alone.

I waited, and soon he walked downstairs fully dressed in his usual work clothes of dress pants, dress shirt, and tie. He smiled as he passed my desk on his way to the front door, and as I watched him take the pizza box from the delivery man, I realized I'd been so lost in thought about how he looked that I hadn't even heard the doorbell!

God, I needed to get my head together. Why was I acting like a horny schoolgirl? I'd seen hot men before. I'd dated a few of them too, but never before had any of them had this kind of effect on me.

I took a deep breath and told myself to relax as I walked into the kitchen to find him setting out plates and silverware he'd gotten that first weekend after I started working for him. He heard me walk in and turned around.

With a smile, he said, "Lunch is ready. How many slices can I get you?"

Although I'd normally grab two, I didn't want to look like a pig in front of Mr. Tanchen, so I answered,

"Oh, just one. If I'm still hungry after that, I'll grab another."

That was possibly the biggest lie I'd told in a long time. Of course I'd be hungry after one measly slice of pizza. I wasn't a six year old girl with the appetite of a bird. If my friends heard me say what I'd said to him, they would have burst out laughing.

Well, that lie may have been the second biggest lie, but the first was one I told myself. All weekend I'd thought about my boss in a way that had nothing to do with work, and each time I swore I wouldn't do it again.

And then last night as I lay in bed, I did it again, complete with eyes rolling back in my head and an orgasm that made my toes curl. And that was before I saw him half naked in a towel that showed off the outline of a very impressive cock.

Oh, God. At the rate I was going, I'd be blurting out something stupid about how hot he looked before the end of my second week of work.

"How come you're not eating?" he asked, ripping me out of my daydream about having to go back to Mr. DeVille and beg for another position after I blew up this one with my stupidity and inability to remain professional.

"Sorry. Just a little distracted today. You know. Monday. I wonder if it's too late to start drinking coffee like the rest of the world," I said in a lame attempt to be clever.

It wasn't clever. It was more like rambling that I

thankfully stopped before something sexual popped out of my mouth.

"I don't think I've ever met anyone who didn't drink coffee. At least no anyone older than ten," he said with a chuckle.

With a smile, I said, "It's always been too bitter. I prefer sweeter tasting drinks first thing in the morning. The problem is I tend not to get the benefit of being bright-eyed and bushy-tailed from orange juice."

Mr. Tanchen took a bite of pizza and nodded. "Not good for your get up and go."

A tiny spot of oil slowly slid down from the corner of his mouth, so I pointed at it and as politely as possible said, "You have a little bit of oil on your face."

He quickly grabbed a white napkin from the stack of them in the center of the table and wiped around his mouth, but when he finished, a tiny bit of oil was still on his chin. I pointed at his face again, and he repeated dabbing around his mouth with another napkin, but still he missed that single spot.

Frustrated, I picked up my napkin and wiped it without even thinking that I shouldn't be touching his face. When I realized I'd once again overstepped the bounds of office propriety, I lowered my head and focused on my pizza.

But it was no use. My cheeks heated up until I was sure they were as red as the sauce on my lunch.

"I'm so sorry," I mumbled. "I swear I know how to behave in the workplace. I'm sorry."

He didn't say anything, so I ran out of the room

and rushed into the bathroom. It was stupid and juvenile, but I didn't know what else to do. That I couldn't stay in there for long made the whole action pretty useless, but at least for a few precious moments, I could hide out and cringe at my behavior in private.

This wasn't who I was. Why did he have such an effect on me? And why, dear God, did my usually sensible mind become lust-filled every time I was around Mr. Tanchen? I didn't even think of him by his first name. I actually came last night with the words Mr. Tanchen on my lips.

I leaned down over the sink and threw some cold water on my cheeks. Clearly, I would be fired today. He was a decent guy, but surely he couldn't keep me around now that I'd shown I didn't know how to act in the workplace. Maybe if I begged him to not tell Mr. DeVille I'd be able to get another position from the staffing agency.

If not, then I'd end up losing my apartment after all.

Looking up at my reflection in the mirror, I cringed and tears began to well in my eyes. God, how could I have behaved like this? It felt like I didn't have any control over my desires when this guy was around. Like something came over me and I couldn't stop myself.

That was no excuse, though. Maybe for a teenage girl, but not for a grown woman who wanted to keep her job.

After hiding for nearly ten minutes, I knew I had to go back out there and accept what was coming. Mr.

Tanchen likely waited in the kitchen to fire me, so I stuffed down my emotions and slowly made my way back there, but he wasn't there. My slice of pizza sat on my plate, but other than that and the napkins in the center of the table, there was no sign he'd even been in there to have lunch.

A thought settled into my brain. Maybe he was so disgusted with me that he just planned to contact Mr. DeVille and tell him he didn't want to work with me anymore. I couldn't fault him for that either. Why put himself through the hassle of having to fire me when the guy he was paying to hire people for him could do that job?

I made my way back to my desk for the last time as a knot formed in the pit of my stomach. I'd liked working for Mr. Tanchen. Too bad I hadn't been able to handle myself like a fucking adult.

Disgusted, I grabbed my bag and turned around to leave, nearly running into my boss. He stood staring at me like he couldn't figure out what was wrong with me. I got that. I didn't understand either, not that it made any difference.

"Mr. Tanchen, you don't have to say anything. I'll leave and I'm sure Mr. DeVille will be able to get the right person for the job here in no time. He's pretty good at figuring out who belongs with what job."

"He is. The problem is I don't want someone else, Emma. I want you," my boss said in a low voice.

Then before I could say anything to make up for my workplace mistakes, he took me by the hand and led me to a room off the kitchen that I hadn't seen before. He hadn't shown me this part of the house on the tour he gave that first day, so when he closed the door behind us and turned on the light because the blinds covering the windows were drawn, I was surprised to see it was a small lounge with a couch and TV.

Confused about what was happening, I waited for him to say something, but instead he leaned down and kissed me. For a moment, my eyes stayed wide open in shock and I stared at his long, dark lashes as they rested on his face. My mind couldn't process it all — his soft lips on mine kissing me better than any man had ever kissed me, the hardness of his cock pressing against my stomach when he inched closer to me, his hand tightening in my hair and sending ripples of pain across my scalp that turned into licks of need when the sensation rushed through my body. None of it seemed real, but there we were in that secret room with our tongues eagerly sliding into each other's mouths.

When he leaned back away from me, I whispered breathlessly, "I thought you were going to fire me, Mr. Tanchen."

He shook his head and slowly ran his tongue over his beautiful bottom lip. "No. What I want to do with you is the opposite of firing you."

I stared up into his dark eyes, lost in how wicked they looked now, as he slid his hand up under my skirt and teased the tender skin of my inner thighs. My eyelids threatened to close, an involuntary reaction to his touch, but I forced myself to keep my eyes open so I didn't miss a thing that happened between us.

The first brush of his fingertips against my panties made my breath hitch in my chest, and for a moment, I held the air in my lungs while I waited for him to slide his hand under the cotton. He looked up and suddenly stopped, making me say a silent prayer to God that he hadn't changed his mind about what was about to happen.

"Emma, I've thought about doing this since the first day you walked through my door," he said low and deep as his fingers drifted over my skin, leaving a trail of need in their wake.

I didn't respond, even though I could say the same thing. Instead, I let my actions tell my story and moved my hands to the front of his pants where his rock hard cock pressed against the dark fabric. I palmed him, eager to know if what I'd seen through the towel a short time before had been true or wishful thinking.

It only took one touch to tell me I'd underestimated how well hung he was. God, I wanted nothing more than to have my boss fill me up with that incredible cock.

He moaned as I slowly slid my hand down over him, my movement encouraging him to continue his exploration under my skirt. I didn't have to wait long for him to go exactly where I wanted him to, and the first touch of his fingertip to my pussy sent an electric shock through my body, making it come alive.

In a rush, he slid one finger and then two into me, their size easing into my body with the help of how wet I already was. His thumb pressed against my needy clit, and he began to finger fuck me. It felt incredible, but I wanted what he kept in his pants more.

Tugging his zipper open, I slid my hand in and found his cock ready for me. I pulled back his boxer briefs and finally saw up close what I'd fantasized about since last week. Long and thick, his cock stood ramrod straight and waiting for the attention it deserved.

He slid his fingers out of me, and in one smooth motion, lifted my skirt to my waist and me into the air. I hurried to move my panties off to the side, wishing I had forgotten to wear them that morning, and in one slow movement, he filled me completely.

"Pull your legs up to take all of me," he groaned.

I looked down in amazement and saw the last few inches of his cock outside me. Shocked, I did as he ordered and watched as the thick bottom of his shaft sunk inside my body. I didn't know how, but I didn't care because it felt so fucking good.

He held me in his arms, and I clung to his neck as he moved us backward toward the door. I felt the coolness of the wood against my skin, and then a second later, he began pumping into me. My boss, that polite and professional guy who I'd thought about in the most impure ways, fucked like an animal.

And I loved it.

With every thrust into my body, his cock touched parts of me that no man had ever reached before. Waves of the most delicious sensations washed over me each time his cock grazed those spots deep inside me. I'd never been with anyone who made my body come alive like this.

It wasn't romantic or sweet in the least. It was base and purely physical to the point that I didn't think I'd last long before I came. I wanted to put it off and enjoy this sensual moment for all it was worth, but his cock hitting one special spot made that impossible.

Pressing his head against the door, he grunted and that was it. My release raced through me, and my body surrendered completely to him. I pulled my legs up even further as something instinctive inside me knew to, and my orgasm exploded a second time just moments later.

He sagged against me a minute later after he came with one last hard thrust into me. Breathing hard, he kissed the shell of my ear, covering the side of my head in hot breath as he practically panted.

"That was fucking incredible," he said in a low voice.

I didn't know what to call what we'd just done. Incredible. Unbelievable. Fantastic. All those words ran through my head as I tried to get a grasp on what just happened.

Mr. Tanchen, my very attractive and well-built boss who I'd thought would fire me after my workplace faux pas, had just fucked me like no other man had ever done. I honestly didn't have a lot of experience in that area, having only a handful of boyfriends in my entire life and a singular one-night stand, but from everything I knew, everything I'd heard my friends say, and everything I'd read about sex, my boss was one phenomenal lover.

I wanted to tell him how much I enjoyed what we'd done, but I couldn't find the words. Needing to say something, I squeaked out, "Mr. Tanchen, I feel like I should tell you I don't do this. Ever."

Still holding me under my thighs, he leaned back and smiled. "I think you can call me Mark. We just had mind-blowing sex, so it feels like first names are appropriate. Since I'm still inside you, having you call me by the name people use for my father feels extra wrong."

My face felt like someone set it on fire from inside as a blush raced to my cheeks. I didn't know why anything he said made me feel bashful since he was right—his cock still filled my pussy even at that moment—but suddenly I felt shy.

I lowered my head and nodded. "Okay. Mark. The rest of what I said still stands. I don't go around doing this kind of thing."

"Fucking men who've been checking you out for over a week?" he said with a smile in his voice.

Looking up, I saw a silly look on his face. Why was he grinning like that?

"No, I don't usually do this with them either."

"Well, I'm glad you did. Not that I gave you much choice there. I guess I should have warned you that I'm a little wild when it comes to sex. Once I start into it, I'm like a man possessed. Then again, if I had told you that, you probably would have wondered why I was being so unprofessional."

His confession charmed me, and I smiled shyly. "I thought when I wiped the grease off your chin was so unprofessional that you were going to fire me."

As much as I didn't want him to, Mark slid out of me and set me on my feet as he tucked his cock back into his pants. Looking at me as he did it, he said, "To be honest, that's what made me think I should make a move. But I didn't plan on any of this. I swear I didn't plan this. This all just sort of happened."

Ordinarily, I might have been insulted by a man saying that about our first time together, but no truer words had been spoken between us. Now what would happen next was the question.

ark

AS I TRIED TO MAKE MYSELF LOOK PRESENTABLE and not like I had just had an early afternoon quickie with my secretary, I wondered if I'd made a mistake. Not that the sex hadn't been incredible. It had. More than incredible, in fact.

But any time sex got involved, it changed things. Was I ready to have my work life changed? I didn't know.

Emma stared down at the floor, looking as awkward as I felt. Damn. Maybe this had been a mistake.

"Mr. Tanchen..." she began and then stopped for a moment, pressing her lips together. "Mark, I can't afford to lose this job."

Fuck. That only made me feel like the biggest shit

in the world. She thought I might fire her even after what we'd just done together?

I slid my finger under her chin and lifted her head so she looked at me. "You didn't do anything for me to fire you. After that, I should give you a raise."

My attempt at being funny and lightening the mood failed miserably. Her eyes got wide, and all I saw in them was real fear.

"I was kidding. At least I was trying to. I'm not going to fire you, Emma."

Relief washed over her, and for the first time since we finished fucking, she smiled as her entire body relaxed. "Oh. Okay. So what happens now?"

"I don't know. I didn't plan on any of this happening, remember?"

"Maybe it might be better if I go back to Mr. DeVille and ask him for a different placement," she said quietly, her smile gone. "I feel like that might be the best idea."

"No, no. That isn't necessary. We'll figure this out," I said, hating the idea of not having Emma around in the office.

The two of us stood looking around the room as a strange and uncomfortable reality set in. In the heat of the moment, sex had been the best idea since sliced white bread. Now that we'd given in to our desires, we had to find a way to work together.

"Okay. Well, maybe I'll just go back to my desk."

And with that, she left me standing there not sure what the hell to do next.

· · ·

I STRAIGHTENED MY TIE AND SAT DOWN BEHIND MY desk to get ready for my two o'clock meeting. If I could get my head back into business and not stuck in that room behind the kitchen with Emma and her tight...

Okay, get your shit together, Mark. You're running a business. This isn't high school, and you aren't a teenage boy who just lost his virginity. You're a grown man who's had sex before, for fuck's sake. Get it together!

My pep talk to myself did little to clear my head of my desire to lock the front door and take my secretary by the hand up to my bedroom. I couldn't explain what had come over me. Ever since Emma walked into the building, I'd been able to think of nothing but being balls deep in her pussy. Now that I had actually lived out that fantasy, it's all I wanted to do.

Forget work. Forget how hard I'd struggled to make this business successful. Forget it all.

I couldn't let this go on. Maybe she was right. Maybe she sound have returned to that DeVille Staffing place and gotten another position.

The problem was even thinking that made me feel sick.

That meant I had to find a way to work with her and not want to bend her over the desk every time I thought about us together. How hard could that be? I'd spent nearly thirty years of my life, almost half of it sleeping with women, and never before had I been distracted by a woman so much that I couldn't get my work done. Why couldn't I do it now?

I could. I had to. Either that or the business I'd

worked my balls off to make a success would fall by the wayside. That couldn't happen.

At exactly two, Emma poked her head into my office and smiled like she always did when she interrupted my work. "Mr. Tanchen...Mark, your two o'clock appointment is here. Should I show him in?"

I nodded and hoped I'd eliminated the last vestiges of our time together an hour before. "Yes, please show him in. Thank you, Emma."

It all sounded perfectly normal that I thought for a moment that we could work together like this just fine. And then I saw how Steve Dumont looked at her like he wanted to devour her as he walked into my office and I knew I was in trouble. I'd never been jealous, but I had a feeling it didn't look good on me by the way Steve stared at me.

"What the hell is wrong with you?" he asked as he shot Emma one final leer before sitting down.

"Close the door, Emma."

I waited until I heard the click that told me Steve and I were alone and then plastered a smile on my face. "What are you talking about?"

He narrowed his eyes to slits and studied me for a long moment. "You looked like you wanted to kill me when I walked in here. I thought maybe I'd done something to piss you off, but since I haven't seen you in almost a year, I know that's not it. Did you have something that didn't agree with you for lunch?"

Nodding, I shrugged. "Yeah, something like that. So what can I do for you today, Steve?"

Happily, he seemed willing to let my odd

expression when he came in fade into history as he launched into an idea he had for his business. It was ludicrous, like most of the harebrained ideas he had every year when he came to see me. Our company handled all his websites for his restaurants, and his new plan to offer people the ability to instantly generate a review that could be posted on every popular site around simply wasn't doable.

And even if it was, it broke at least half a dozen rules each review site had about posting.

I spent the next hour explaining that to him and trying to dissuade him from attempting it himself like the last time he decided he could handle his sites on his own. Josh had to sweet talk our design team for nearly four hours to get them to fix that mess, and we'd had to pay six of them overtime just to get his sites back up.

Finally, he came around to understanding his idea wouldn't work and turned his attention to Emma. Glancing back toward where she sat in her office, Steve said, "So, you must be doing well, Mark. You know, needing a secretary and all. I never figured you for that, though. She's easy on the eyes, so that's nice. I just thought you tech guys liked to break the mold, but you've got a whole Mad Men thing going on here now."

I waved off his comments for the nonsense that they were. "I needed help around here since Josh is never around. It's nothing more than that."

"So what does she do? Schedule appointments?

Bring you coffee? Anything else?" he asked with a twinkle in his eye I hated from the moment I saw it.

The fact that I'd known Steve since college made it both easy and hard to deal with him. I had no problem telling him to fuck off since our business wasn't like I had with others, but at the same time, I didn't want to make him think anything was going on between Emma and me.

That left me with explaining to him the realities of the workplace and ignoring him. I chose the second option.

"So, your traffic is up from last year, which is good. We're still in good shape on the sites, so unless you have some massive surge of people visiting them, I think this yearly check-up is done. Any questions?"

"Is she single?" he asked, practically falling out of his chair as he looked back through the window in my office door toward her.

"Are you?" I asked, knowing full well that Steve's second wife would take his stupid ass to the cleaners if she found out he cheated on her. Bethany was a barracuda if there ever was one.

My question made his body sag like he was a tire and someone had deflated him. Turning back to face me, he twisted his face into a grimace. "You straight arrows are all alike. I was just looking. There's no harm in that, is there?"

"It's the touching that gets you in trouble, Steve. I would have thought you'd learned that with Ashley."

Just the mention of his first wife made him look sick. His grimace stretched out into a full blown frown, and he shook his head. "Fine. You made your point. No fun with the pretty girl in Mark's office. I better go anyway. There's no rest for the wicked, pal. If you ever got out of this office, you'd know that."

I forced a smile as the memory of just how wicked I'd been that day rushed through my brain. "You know me. Work, work, work. I leave the good times to people like you and Josh."

He stood up and shook his head. "You're going to regret it when you get old, man. I'm two wives ahead of you and I make millions a year. All work and no play makes Mark a very boring boy."

I rolled my eyes as I stood to shake his hand. "I'll keep that sage advice in mind. Thanks, Steve. Until next year."

"Until next year," he said as he walked out into the hallway, taking one last look at Emma as she sat in her office working.

After escorting him to the door, I watched him walk down the street and wondered if there was some truth to what he said. I didn't have any interest in being on my second wife and I made good money, but was I putting off happiness in favor of working too much?

I looked in at Emma as she typed something into the computer. Just seeing her there made me want to forget work, at least for a little while. I didn't want to fight that after hearing Steve warn me I'd regret it when I got old.

"You'll have my notes on my two o'clock later today, Emma."

She lifted her head and nodded, giving me a sweet smile like she always did when I spoke to her. "Okay. I'll make sure to get them logged in as soon as you get them to me."

We were both incredibly efficient, and it made me hate myself a little. Overcome by Steve's comment on regret, I walked into her office and held out my hand. "Let's go."

Emma stared up at me in utter confusion. "Go where?"

"Upstairs. Come with me."

She did as I ordered, putting her hand in mine, and we walked upstairs silently. I knew she probably wanted to know what I was doing, but I couldn't explain it, so I just stayed quiet.

Finally, we reached my apartment, and I closed the door behind us. Emma's eyes grew wide, and she said, "Neither of us locked the front door. Should I go down and do that?"

I shook my head. "No. I want you to stay here."

"Are you sure?"

"I'm always sure," I answered, lying but not caring at that moment.

I led her to the bedroom and sat her down on the edge of the bed. "But isn't this…wrong or something?" she asked hesitantly. "I mean, you didn't seem too happy after before."

Leaning down, I kissed her and smiled. "I'm the boss, Emma. I get to decide what's wrong and what isn't here. Unless you want me to tell you to get back to work."

A shy smile lit up her face. "No. That's not it at all."

"Then let's enjoy ourselves. We deserve it, don't you think?"

Nodding, she reached out to unzip my pants. My cock was hard and ready to go for round two. Emma slid her hand down the length of me and cupped my balls.

"I've never been with a man so big," she whispered, looking up at me with wide eyes as she licked her lips. "I wasn't sure you were going to fit before."

Before I could respond, she slid her mouth over the head of my cock and sucked, sending a jolt of need straight to my balls. I pushed her head down, guiding her as she took as much of me into her mouth as she could. When I nudged up against the back of her throat, I expected her to gag, but to my surprise, she opened her mouth wider and took another two inches in, nearly deep throating me.

"Oh… fuck…" I moaned as a woman took nearly all of my cock into her mouth for the first time ever.

But as good as that felt, that wasn't what I wanted for round two with Emma. Our first time had been fantastic, but I wanted to know what fucking her from behind felt like. It had always been my favorite position because I didn't have to hold back.

I slid out of her mouth and looked down to see her pouting up at me. Pulling her to her feet, I began undressing her while I explained, "Don't worry. I've got something even better than that, even though I have to admit sometime in the future I want you to go down on me again."

"Even better?" she asked as I slid her shirt off and tugged her skirt down her legs, leaving her in her bra and panties before me.

"Trust me. It's much better."

Emma slipped my tie from around my neck and then my shirt down my arms while I stepped out of my pants. "Better than before?"

I pushed my boxer briefs down my legs, setting my hard cock free, and kicked them off to the side. "Yeah, even better. Now take your bra off and get on your hands and knees on the bed."

As she obeyed me, I tugged her panties off her. She spun around and positioned herself perfectly for me, so I climbed onto the bed nudged my cock between her ass cheeks.

Emma looked back with fear in her eyes. "Mark, I don't think..."

Holding my cock by the base, I chuckled at what she thought I planned to do. "Don't worry. I accepted I couldn't be an ass guy a long time ago."

I slid the tip of my cock through her pussy and loved how wet she was for me already. I knew I should ease myself into her tight cunt, but after our first time, I could barely wait. I reared my hips back, and in one hard push, I filled her completely.

She grabbed the sheets in her hands and groaned, "Oh, God...fuck!"

Just as she wanted, I began fucking her in earnest. Like I expected, taking her from behind made sinking into her up to my balls much easier on both of us, and within mere seconds, I was thrusting into her tight cunt and she was pushing back to take every inch of my nearly ten inch cock.

God, she felt so fucking good! I pounded into her like I loved too—hard and fast, like a fucking animal rutting. She matched my rhythm with each thrust, moaning my name with each time I buried my entire cock into her.

Sliding my hand around her throat, I forced her to arch her back, making her body feel even better around me. I leaned forward and in her ear moaned, "Take it all. I want to fill your cunt up like before."

She whimpered and pushed her ass back toward me as I slammed into her. "God, yes! Fuck me! Fuck me hard!"

Her wish was my command, and as my balls tightened against my body in preparation of coming, I jackhammered into her and tightened my hand around her throat. "That's it, baby. Take it all."

Seconds later, her cunt began to milk my cock and she dropped to the bed, landing on her forearms. The angle made her coming feel even more incredible, and my body reacted, filling her with cum until it leaked out around me and down my shaft. While I watched the tremors from her orgasm rush through her, I realized I'd never come that hard in my life.

Emma collapsed to the bed, and I followed her, exhausted from fucking and my balls completely emptied. Turning my head, I looked over at her lying there with her eyes closed, and something about it looked so innocent.

I knew better, though. That sweet girl with the big

blue eyes who seemed practically virginal knew how to please a man like no woman I'd ever met.

"Mark, I don't think I can move. My legs feel boneless," she whispered hoarsely.

"If we keep it up, neither one of us is ever going to get any work done. Not that I'm unhappy about what else we'd be doing," I said, pulling her to me.

And then she opened her eyes and looked up at me in that way that made me want to protect her for the rest of time. "What are we going to do? At this rate, you'll be paying me to sleep with you. That's not right."

So that's why she looked so upset.

I quickly moved to reassure her that wasn't what was happening. Tilting her chin up so she had to look at me, I kissed her softly on the lips. "You're right, but that's not what I'm paying you for, Emma. You're an excellent secretary. That's what you get paid for."

She smiled and kissed me. "So would the other stuff we do together be considered benefits?"

Damnit, this woman could be so sweet.

"I hadn't thought about it that way, but now that you mention it, I guess so."

Emma snuggled against my chest and in a tiny voice said, "You know, Mark, I have to tell you I never imagined you'd be so incredible in bed when I first met you. I thought you were handsome, but you don't give off a vibe that you fuck like an animal. You look so...straight-laced and serious. Sort of nerdy, actually."

I held her to me and chuckled. That's what

everyone always told me. I liked that I could fool the rest of the world into thinking I was that man while at the same time rocking Emma's world. It would make keeping our relationship secret much easier.

"That's good to hear. I don't need the entire world knowing who I really am."

She looked up at me and smiled. "I like the idea that I get to see you in a way others don't."

Emma had no idea how special she was in that regard. Exes might tell people of my particular style of lovemaking, but no woman had gotten to see me in the way she had because no other woman in the world had ever made me want her as much as she had.

CHAPTER 5

*mma

SOMETHING ABOUT SLEEPING WITH MY BOSS FILLED me with a strange confidence and sexiness that I hadn't truly known I possessed. I'd become a new woman in the past month. It was like coming out of my shell in a way I would have never thought possible. I wasn't just some boring, average girl anymore. I was interesting and confident and knew I made him feel as good as he made me.

Making him feel right was only part of it, though. Something about the way he naturally desired me and wanted me made me feel special and alive in a way that no other man had. Sure, I'd been with other guys, but no one like Mark Tanchen. His power, his mystique, they were almost intoxicating.

When he came to my desk and kissed my neck,

193

running his hands down my body or up my shirt while I was on the phone, it was almost enough to drive me wild. I finished my work in record time most days knowing that the reward at the end of it was sleeping with a man who seriously knew what he was doing.

As I got ready that morning, I decided to wear something a bit more subdued than my usual skirt and blouse. I knew Mark preferred me in outfits like that, but his partner was going to be there today, and we needed to keep our relationship secret. Mark hadn't said much about Josh, who was three weeks overdue to showing up at the office, but I had the sense the man who rocked my world was more than a tad bit possessive. It wouldn't do any good to make his partner wonder what we'd been up to all these weeks.

I got to work, and I was startled when a man I'd never seen before met me at the door. He was good looking with sandy blond hair and a wickedly devilish way about him. His pale blue eyes lit up as he opened the door and gave me a pretty obvious once over.

"Good morning! You must be Emma. I'm Josh. It's a pleasure to meet you," he said with a sexy smile as he extended his tanned hand to shake mine.

His grip was strong and powerful, like that of a man who takes what he wants. At the moment by the way he was looking at me and smiling, I had a feeling what he wanted was me. "Hello, sir. The pleasure is all mine. Mr. Tanchen told me you'd be in the office today. It's nice to meet you."

I stepped inside, feeling like the office had taken on a different air from the night before. Instead of being pleasured by my boss that day, I would have to sit there and act as though we had no relationship whatsoever. I caught sight of him in the kitchen as I went to get my morning drink, and while he gave me a small smile and a curt nod, nothing else was said between us. It was almost painful, and I hated that a surge of sadness ran through me at not being able to reach out and touch him. It made me feel desperate and childish.

When I turned around with my orange juice Mark made sure to have in the refrigerator all the time, I saw his partner eyeing me from around the corner. Christ, this guy was a total horndog! I'd been careful to wear a long dress that hid that I even had a body. What else did it take with him?

"Was there something you needed, sir?"

He grinned and shook his head, clearly not ashamed at being caught looking at me. "Nope. I'm all good. You don't need to call me sir, though. Josh is fine. Sir makes me feel old as fuck."

"Dude, can we try to be professional? Emma is our secretary, and this isn't a bar," Mark said as he pushed past him on his way toward his office.

Josh looked embarrassed as he sheepishly said, "Pardon me, Emma. I'm used to far more relaxed working conditions. My partner runs a much tighter ship, though, so when in Rome. Please forgive my use of the word fuck."

Clearly, Josh was a bust ass. I wanted to laugh, but one glance at Mark and I saw he didn't find any of it funny. So I simply smiled and with a nod walked back to my desk. The two of them disappeared into Mark's office, and for hours after that, I didn't see either of them.

By the end of the day, I had to work not to let myself slip into pouting about how Mark and I wouldn't be able to be alone that night. I silently hoped Josh would be off on one of his adventures again soon. I didn't dislike him. I just wanted to get to spend time with the man I did like a lot.

As I completed my work and got ready to go home, Josh walked up to my desk, looking sheepish no longer as he confidently smiled down at me. There was no denying the fact that he was handsome, and I could see with those looks and his confidence how women would fall for him quickly. I preferred his partner and his proper businessman style, but I couldn't deny my other boss was hot too.

I finished typing and looked up from the computer with a smile for him. "Hi, Josh. Do you have some work you'd like me to do before I go?"

He smiled and leaned down toward me. "When I come into town, Mark and I always go out for wings. But see what I'm thinking is we turn it into an employee thing. What do you say? You up for wings tonight?"

I took a moment to think and felt a rush of panic go through me. If I turned his offer down, it could look suspicious or thought of as standoffish. I didn't want to offend him. As much as I knew Mark enjoyed being with me, I wasn't a fool. His business meant the world to him. If his partner started to give him trouble over me, who knew what would happen? Even worse, I didn't want to lose this job and all the benefits that came with it.

But if I said yes, that could mean trouble. The more time I spent around Mark and Josh, the more opportunities there were for a mistake that could get us found out.

As all these thoughts marched through my brain, I felt my phone vibrate in my purse. "Let me just look at my calendar."

"No problem. Take your time. I'm more than happy to just stand here and wait, beautiful."

I didn't like it when he referred to me in the same manner that Mark would have. It wasn't the same. When Mark said it, I felt beautiful, but when Josh said it felt like too much.

I suddenly wished that Josh could just go back to whatever vacation or business trip he'd been on and stay there. He wasn't the worst guy ever, and I did have to admit he could be funny. Still, something about him put me off.

Maybe it was the fact that I was having a secret love affair with his friend and business partner and trying to avoid his flirting with me.

I looked and saw a text from Mark on my phone. **You don't have to go if you don't want to, but he won't stop pushing if you say no.**

That didn't mean I couldn't try.

"It looks like I have some things to do at my place tonight. Thanks for offering, though. I'll try for the next time."

As if on cue, he said, "Stuff to do at your place? Nah! Come out with the two of us. Mark says you've been an amazing help to him here, and I want to hear more about the beautiful woman who he can't stop raving about."

I blushed and hoped it wasn't too obvious how much Mark's compliments meant to me. I sighed and out of the corner of my eye saw Mark watching from the door to his office.

Sensing I'd have to relent at some point anyway, I smiled and said, "Okay. I'll go."

Thrilled, he clapped his hands together and grinned. "Excellent! You hear that, Mark? She's coming for wings. Our first company retreat."

I couldn't help but chuckle at his eagerness. His personality was one of those that you couldn't help but be drawn in by, even if you didn't want to be. A glance over at Mark as he stood in his doorway, though, told me he wasn't at all happy with Josh being around. His body language screamed it to the whole room, but Josh didn't notice at all as he picked up his cell phone and went outside to make a call.

Mark smiled at me as I quietly said, "I can make an excuse and beg off, if you want."

He shook his head and tried not to frown. "It's fine. We just have to be careful. Besides, you'll have fun. Everyone loves it when Josh is around, and you clearly have another admirer."

I rolled my eyes and scrunched up my face to show him how much I didn't care about that, but Mark's expression never changed from the serious one he seemed to wear all the time when his business partner was around.

Josh came back into the office and clapped his hands together. "Okay, you busy bees! Enough of this working shit. I'm starving."

We filed out of the house, and as we hit the sidewalk, Josh took a deep breath and nudged Mark. "I've been all around the world, but there's no smell like New York City."

Without thinking, I said, "You must love the smell of garbage because that's all this city has with the sanitation strike."

Josh threw his head back and laughed as he elbowed Mark. "I like this one. She's a smart ass like me."

He winked as he looked over at me, and I felt myself blush once more. Maybe going out with my bosses had been a mistake. The look of disgust on Mark's face said he definitely thought it was.

We got to the restaurant, and for the most part, Josh and Mark just talked about business. It was a little tedious, but at least it seemed like he didn't suspect anything. The wing joint was a little hole in the wall place with brick walls and old wood floors. A sign on the wall claimed this was once where gangsters hid out, but I had no idea if that was true.

Halfway through our wings, Josh looked over at me and said, "Okay, I want to hear about this mystery woman who's come to save us from a mountain of paperwork and endless unanswered phone calls. You must be some kind of angel."

I had opted to sit next to him in the booth to stay as far away from Mark as possible, so for the first time, I felt like I was a captive audience who couldn't get away. "I don't know. It wouldn't be very angelic of me to say yes, now would it?"

"Not angelic at all," Josh replied with a devilish look in his eyes.

"Leave her alone, man. While you're off traveling the world, she helps me keep down the fort. Good secretaries are hard to find, so I don't want you chasing her off."

Josh pretended to be hurt by his partner's criticism. "Chasing her off? Why would you say that? I'm just trying to get to know her."

He turned his attention back to me and asked, "So what does a beautiful young woman like yourself want to be a secretary for a web firm like ours? You must have a million other career options available to you."

Shaking my head, I smiled. "Not quite a million, but I like working for your company."

He continued to try to get to know me, and I continued to give him coy answers. I thought doing that would make him less interested in learning about me, but it only seemed to encourage him. Every other guy in New York knew how to take a hint, but not Josh.

Flagging down the server, he said, "Can we get a round of drinks for our table?"

Mark raised his eyebrow, but Josh shooed him away, "It's one beer man. Loosen up. Anyway, Emma, tell me more about yourself."

I pushed my plate of wing bones into the center of the table and shrugged. "There isn't that much to tell. I'm like your friend here. Quiet. Down-to-earth. Just your average kind of girl."

Josh smiled and shook his head. "Oh, I don't think anyone is like Mark. This guy is as uptight as they come. You don't look uptight to me, Emma."

If I didn't get out of that booth, I had a feeling he'd be sliding his hand up my thigh in the next few minutes. I needed to leave right now.

"Okay, well it was really wonderful having dinner with you two. I'm lucky to have such cool bosses," I said, looking over at Mark. "But I better go. I do have things to do at home, so thanks, guys."

Literally, every word of that was the internationally accepted way to get away from people you didn't want to be around anymore. Unfortunately, Josh didn't seem to have ever learned that.

"You really have to go?" Josh asked, raising his glass. "We just got another around. Stay for this one, at least."

"I really can't. I'm sorry. But I'll see you at work tomorrow. Thank you again," I said as sweetly as I could without sounding fake.

"If you must, I'll walk you out. Mark, stay here and watch all this, will you? I want to have one more beer before we go, and we need to talk about the Boston meeting a little more."

As Josh chugged down the rest of his beer, I sat there stunned looking at Mark, who seemed like he was about to reach over the table and smack the hell out of his partner. There was nothing either of us could do. I knew it made Mark uncomfortable, but he just nodded and cringed.

"Good night, Emma. Be safe out there."

"Thank you, Mr. Tanchen."

Josh eased out of the booth as he said, "He has you calling him, Mr. Tanchen? Damn, dude. That's some funny shit right there."

Following him, I stood up and gave Mark a smile I hoped he knew wasn't genuine. I didn't want to leave with Josh. I wanted to go back to Mark's apartment and be with him since we hadn't been together in days.

Josh and I walked outside, and once we were on the sidewalk, I stepped away from him. "Thank you again for a lovely evening, sir."

"There you go again. Sir. Mr. Tanchen. They must have really taught you respect in that family of yours, huh?"

"Yes, I suppose they did. Anyway, thanks again."

"I'll see you at work tomorrow," he said as I shuffled my purse from one shoulder to the other, practically ignoring him.

Then he lowered his head and surprised me by kissing me softly on the lips. "It was great getting to know you, Emma. I look forward to finding out more about you while I'm in town."

I stood there on the sidewalk stunned by his kiss as people passed by on their way into the restaurant. My boss had kissed me, and he wasn't even the boss I liked.

When I finally got my bearings, I barely got three

steps away from the building before my phone vibrated. I pulled it out of my purse and saw a message from Mark.

Did he just kiss you?

I looked in through the window and saw him staring at me while Josh flirted with the waitress nearby. Mark's expression said he wanted to kill his partner.

Quickly, I typed a message back.

It's okay. It was nothing. I miss you.

He sent a message right back.

Go to my place.

I didn't need to be told twice. With Josh around recently, we hadn't been together for days. My body ached for Mark's touch.

But halfway to his house, I got another message that ruined my night.

He's planning on working tonight, so it's going to be late. I'll see you tomorrow. I miss you too.

Frustrated, I tossed my phone into my purse and headed for the subway. If Josh ever wanted me to think of him as anything other than a cock block, he needed to go out of town again. Immediately.

Over the next few days, Josh continued his flirting, which only served to frustrate Mark. Instead of working in his own office, he decided to plant himself right outside mine in the common area. It started out innocently enough, especially since I couldn't flat out ignore him. I tried steering the conversation towards professional talk, but he was having none of it.

The problem was I couldn't be rude to him because I didn't want to jeopardize my job or my relationship with Mark. At times I didn't even realize he was flirting until he'd touch my arm lightly as he spoke to me. He was charming in his way, and I couldn't help but laugh at his funny stories and blush when he complimented me.

Mark spent most of his time in his office and said nothing when we occasionally texted after work. It was like if he paid no attention to the matter that was frustrating him that it would go away completely.

Worst of all, I felt like we everything we'd become to one another was fading away with every day Josh stayed around. I wanted to talk to him, to tell him I missed him and couldn't wait until we were together again, but all I could do was text it. That wasn't the same, though.

One afternoon toward the end of the day when Josh was particularly busy trying to charm me, Mark sent a single text that stoked my fears. Just as I'd feared, he thought I wanted his partner and not him.

I've never seen him like this before. He must be really into you. You seem into him too.

I wanted to text back and tell him how wrong he was, but I couldn't because Josh was right there in my office talking me up again.

"Earth to Emma. You in there?" I heard from next to me as Josh tapped me on the shoulder.

"What? Yes, I'm sorry. I was just thinking about..."

"About hanging out with your hot boss tonight?" Josh asked confidently.

What? Did he mean what I thought he meant?

I was shaken by his response and replied, "Wh... what? No. I..."

"Emma, it's okay," he said with a smile.

But it wasn't okay. I'd tried so hard ever since he got there not to sneak looks at Mark or linger too long in his office when I had to talk to him about work. How could Josh have found out about us?

"No...I wasn't thinking about..." I said, unable to explain myself.

"It's fine to admit that you're into the boss, Emma. There's no real rule against it, and he's definitely into you."

"What? No, I mean..." I said, my mouth falling slightly open but the words got stuck in my throat.

Had we been found out? Had Mark said something to Josh and neglected to fill me in? A sense of panic raced through me, and I struggled to form words fast enough to try and cover our tracks.

Suddenly, Josh laughed. "Relax, relax. I was just teasing you, Emma. You really should consider it, though. I can take you to places you've never seen."

Oh. My. God. He'd been referring to himself the whole time. I silently thanked God that I hadn't started blabbing on about anything.

Relieved, I took a deep breath before shaking my head and with a smile said, "Oh, I'm sorry. No thank you. I'm with someone."

He leaned in close enough that I could smell the

faint hint of the soap he'd used that morning. I turned my head and realized he was right in front of my face.

"We could have a good time," he said before placing his lips on mine.

Startled, I didn't pull away as instantly as I should have. Maybe I was just a little starved for affection, having spent the better part of the week with only myself to be with. But after a moment, I pulled away and shook my head. "I'm sorry. No."

A moment later I heard a door open, and Mark said sharply, "Josh, you're needed in here. Now."

Josh rolled his eyes and give me a wink before walking over to his partner's office with a shit-eating grin on his face. Mark turned and gave me a sharp glare before shutting the door behind him.

Five o'clock came and went, and even though Josh stormed out the front door a few minutes after Mark demanded to talk to him in his office, Mark never came out. I waited, and at thirty minutes after my quit time, I started to pack up my stuff for the day. I slung my bag over my shoulder and glanced at Mark's door, but he never looked up from his computer like he always did.

Disappointed, I walked out and headed for the train. The whole time, I hoped to feel my phone vibrate with a message from Mark, but it never came. That night, as I went to bed, I looked one last time, but he hadn't sent me even a single word.

Had he seen the kiss and decided he didn't want me as his secretary or anything else anymore?

CHAPTER 6

ark

I STARED IN DREAD AT THE EMAIL ABOUT EMMA'S temp contract almost being up. I had no idea when, but Josh and that DeVille guy had decided she'd only be around for a month. Her time was almost up, and soon she'd be going to a new placement. I'd called the staffing agency, but nothing could be changed.

"Emma's talents are needed elsewhere, Mr. Tanchen," the woman answered flatly when I offered to extend her contract.

Talents were needed elsewhere? My pulse quickened as jealously raced through me.

"Fine. Then I'll hire her full-time myself," I said angrily, sick of that woman and my partner today.

"Mr. Tanchen, she signed a contract with us that

requires her to go wherever we send her or pay ten thousand dollars to break the contract."

My mouth dropped open in shock. Emma couldn't afford to pay them ten thousand dollars. She'd told me that she spent most of her money to keep her apartment, so I doubted she had a spare ten grand just hanging around.

I hung up on the woman at DeVille Staffing and went back to staring at the email that told me my time with Emma was nearly up. It didn't matter that I could see her after work and whenever she didn't have work. I hated the idea of her working for someone else.

Sitting in their office as they stared at her and wished the whole world would fade away so it was just the two of them.

What if her new boss felt like I did? What if she was sent to some extraordinarily wealthy client of DeVille's who could give her everything she ever wanted, including being someone who didn't have to work day and night to get their company to be a success?

What if she wanted that, which was more than I could give her?

Worrying about that on top of what the hell Josh was doing made me feel like my life was spiraling out of control. This wasn't who I was. My partner routinely spun out of control. Then he left town for a while and got his shit together.

That's how life worked for us. I didn't lose it. He did.

Yet now I felt like I was the one spinning out of control.

As I tried to logically think my way out of my problems, Josh appeared in my doorway. Our disagreement earlier about his behavior with Emma had ended in him storming out, very much in his usual style, but now he appeared contrite and seemed to want to talk.

But if he wanted a pass on his actions with Emma, he came to the wrong guy.

He knocked on the doorframe and smiled. "Can we chat?"

"Sure."

Josh sat down in front of my desk and nodded. "We haven't had a disagreement like that since a few months after we started this business. What's going on?"

I had to control myself or he'd figure out what Emma and I were up to. Taking a deep breath, I let it out slowly and then shrugged my shoulders. "Partners fight. It's not a big deal. I just don't think how you acted toward our secretary is a good idea."

"You know how I am with women," he said casually.

"Not that this makes a difference, but she's from that temp agency. What if she goes back to that DeVille guy and makes a complaint?" I asked, not missing the huge hypocrisy of every single word coming out of my mouth.

Josh chuckled and waved away my concern. "That guy? Trust me. He'll handle it. He's that kind of guy."

I had no idea what he meant, but I didn't care. At the moment, I wanted to know something else. "By the way, why did you and he decide that Emma would only work here for a month?"

"Oh, that? I thought it would be nice to have different people come in. Variety is the spice of life, you know."

"I like knowing the people I work with. You're not around, so I'll have to train every single new person who comes to work as our secretary."

Variety wasn't the spice of life. Variety was more work for me, and it also meant losing Emma from my everyday life.

"What does it matter?" Josh asked, clearly not understanding my irritation with that clause he and DeVille had agreed on. "Who knows? Maybe the next one will be even better than this one."

He didn't even bother to call Emma by her name. Clearly, I'd been jealous for nothing. That didn't change the fact that his decision pissed me off, though.

"I'm not interested in getting a new one, like a secretary of the month. You've just made more work for me."

"How can I make it up to you?" he asked, still not taking any of this seriously.

But I was.

"You can go to California early. I'm going to need peace and quiet to train the new person coming in next week, so go."

"Seriously? Are you kidding me? Come on. You're really upset about this, aren't you?"

I cracked my neck and tried to keep my cool, but all my emotions about Emma leaving my daily life threatened to come to the surface. "Not everyone is like you. You've never understood that. You blow into town and leave havoc in your wake every time. Normally, I can just slough it off, but this time you made more work for me, and to be honest, I'm pissed. So to keep everything between us good, you need to go. It's not like there's anything keeping you here, so just go."

"Damn, Mark. You're really mad. Okay, I'll head out for a while," he said. "We cool, though?" he added at the end, his eyes full of hope. Josh and I rarely fought, but he hated it when we did.

I nodded, tired of arguing with him. "Yeah, just go. I'll see you when you get back."

Josh walked upstairs to pack up his stuff, and an hour later, he was gone. It wasn't the first time we'd disagreed, but this time he'd gone too far. I knew the moral high ground wasn't mine to stand on considering I'd been sleeping with Emma, but he'd crossed a line.

He could go out to California and seduce all the secretaries he wanted out there. Emma was mine. I hadn't yet decided what to do about her, though. She had to know it was almost time for her to leave too. Maybe that's why she hadn't tried to talk to me much that day.

Or maybe she didn't feel for me what I felt for her.

· · ·

A RESTLESS NIGHT'S SLEEP MEANT I GOT TO MY office long before Emma showed up for work. When she walked past my door, I saw she wore a black skirt and pink silk T-shirt that looked incredible on her. I waited for her to say good morning, but after five minutes passed and she hadn't come out of the kitchen, I couldn't wait any longer to speak to her.

She stood with her back to me toasting a bagel, so I said, "Good morning. I got to work early today, so there are a fair number of projects I need you to update this morning."

She didn't turn around to face me and quietly said, "Okay. I'll get on them as soon as I get to my desk."

I waited for her to continue speaking, but she said nothing more, so I said, "Josh left. He's on his way to California."

Finally, Emma turned around and I got to see her beautiful face. She looked up at me with those big blue eyes of hers that never failed to make me want to kiss her and innocently asked, "Did you fire Josh?"

I shook my head and smiled. "No. I can't fire Josh. I just told him it was time to go. He'll find plenty of women to seduce out there."

That wasn't what I intended on saying since I hated that Emma had seen me jealous, but it came out of my mouth before I could stop it.

She lowered her gaze and said in a voice just above a whisper, "I'm really sorry. I think I caused a problem between you two."

I wondered again if she had enjoyed it. The

attention from Josh, his making moves on her, his kissing her.

"It's over," I said, wishing I didn't sense such distance between us at that moment. "He and I will be fine."

Emma nodded, but then she turned back to her bagel and didn't ask the question I thought she would. Did she think we were over?

Before I could say another word, the phone rang and she hurried out to her office to answer it. I stood perplexed at what to do. Part of me wanted to ask her to stay, but I knew she couldn't afford the ten grand she'd have to pay to break her contract.

I could pay it, though. It had occurred to me that would work.

She walked back into the kitchen and went directly back to the counter where her bagel sat getting cold. "That was the man from the company that's coming by on Wednesday to take care of the bats. They were just calling to remind you. I left the message on your desk."

I took a step toward her and stopped. "Emma, I'd like to talk to you about something."

"Okay," she said flatly, still with her back to me.

"Turn around, please."

She slowly turned her body until she faced me. "Yes, Mr. Tanchen?"

Mr. Tanchen? Why had we returned to that now?

"What's wrong? You haven't called me that in weeks," I said as hurt coursed through me.

Emma shrugged but looked away. "I just figured that was better."

"Why?"

"I just do. By the way, I got a call from the staffing agency last night. Tomorrow is my last day here with you. Time flies when you're having fun, I guess."

Stunned by her comment, I stood there and didn't stop her when she walked out with her bagel in hand. So that was it? Our relationship had fizzled to nothing in the space of a week, and now she'd be gone in twenty-four hours?

I couldn't let that happen.

I found her sitting at her desk but not eating that bagel she'd spent so much time bothering with. Clearly, she'd been avoiding me since she hadn't taken even a single bite out of it.

Leaning against the doorframe to her office, I said, "I know about the penalty if you break your contract with that staffing agency, Emma. I'm willing to pay it if you agree to stay."

Instead of being happy with my offer, she looked up at me and all I saw was anger in those beautiful blue eyes of hers. "So then I'd be your paid whore? Is that how this works?"

"No...no...wha..." I stuttered out, unable to get a full thought to move from my brain to my mouth successfully. How could she think that?

"Isn't that what the issue with your partner was, Mr. Tanchen? He rolls into town, and you get jealous because he clearly liked me. But you did nothing about that. Not a thing. You didn't make any effort to see me. You didn't even make any effort to text or call me. You just decided to ignore me while he was around because you were ignoring the fact that Josh wanted me. Men generally don't miss a woman twice if they have no interest in sleeping with them, you know. At least in the past week he bothered to pay attention to me, but then again, I'm just your employee. You just made that perfectly clear when you offered to employ me as your personal whore for hire."

Shaking my head in disbelief, I again tried to explain what I meant by my offer. "No, Emma. I didn't mean that at all. I just meant that I wanted you stay working with me."

But that answer didn't fix anything either. She stood from her chair, and as it shot back away from her toward the wall, she grabbed her purse and turned to face me with anger flashing in her eyes.

"You know what? I quit. And for your information, Mark, at least your partner is honest about what he wants. He doesn't couch his interest in a woman in a job that makes her feel like a bought-and-paid-for whore. Goodbye!"

And with that, she walked out of my business and my life, leaving me standing there not knowing what I'd do without her.

CHAPTER 7

mma

BY THE TIME I MADE IT BACK TO MY APARTMENT, I couldn't hold in my tears anymore. I'd been stupid to think Mark and I were something real. Oh, I was something to him. His in-house fuck toy.

God, I was so naïve! There I'd been going to work every day thinking I had what Maddie had with Eric, but the truth was I had nothing. When the time came for him to stand up for me and declare I was his, he did nothing.

Not a damn thing. And that's exactly what I meant to him.

I threw myself onto my bed and buried my head in my pillow as I sobbed uncontrollably. How could I have let myself be fooled like that? I knew as soon as Josh offered for the three of us to go out together that I meant nothing to Mark. A man who considered me his would have put his foot down, but he didn't.

Then when Josh kissed me outside the wing place, I knew Mark had seen it all through the window. And what did he do?

Again, nothing.

And I had a feeling I knew why. He was fine keeping me for his fuck toy inside his home, but I wasn't anyone he wanted to be seen with romantically in public.

Shame covered every inch of me. He didn't care at all about me. I was just another hole to fill.

I imagined there had been a long line of women before me who were merely that for him. A thing to get off on and nothing else. No wonder a man with a successful business who looked like he did was single.

He probably had two or three women just like me. I was his work whore, and then he likely had one to help with his business. Maybe someone at the bank who loved his big cock.

Ugh. I couldn't think about that anymore. I needed to feel better, not feel like a slut he used and discarded when it became inconvenient.

Fishing through my purse, I found my phone and called the only person I knew in the world who'd be understanding and not make me feel even more foolish. Her phone rang twice and then she answered in her usual shy voice.

"Hello? Em?" Tia said tentatively.

"Hi, Tia. Are you busy? Because I could really use

someone to talk to right now," I said, barely holding back the tears that threatened again.

"Yeah. What's going on? Did something happen? You sound like you're about to cry."

"I am. I just left my job, and I feel terrible."

"What happened?"

At that moment, I felt too ashamed to tell her the truth. Tia had always been the most understanding friend I'd ever had, but I didn't know how to explain that I'd let myself be fooled when all the while all I was to Mark was someone to fuck.

When I didn't respond, she said, "Did something happen with work? You were so happy at that job. What happened?"

Quietly, I answered in a way that didn't make me sound as stupid as I felt. "I was happy there, but I have to leave and things didn't end well."

"Why do you have to leave?" Tia asked. I hadn't told her about the clause in my contract, so I probably sounded like a crazy person leaving a job I liked after only a month.

"It's in my contract with the staffing agency. Long story. I didn't realize it until a few days ago. The important point is I thought I had something good there, but then it turned out to be nothing special."

Tia remained silent for a long moment and then said, "You slept with your boss, didn't you?"

As tears began to roll down my cheeks, I admitted the truth. "Yes, I did. God, am I the dumbest person in the world or what?"

"Oh, Em. You've been listening to Maddie too

much. What happened with her and Eric isn't going to happen all the time."

She was right. I'd let myself think that I would get to have the happy ending Maddie had with her boss, and what had it gotten me? Some great sex but little else. No declarations of love. No offer to stay with him forever.

Nothing.

I wiped my eyes and sniffled. "I thought he cared. I guess that sounds stupid."

"No, it doesn't sound stupid. I sounds sweet and trusting. You and I are like that. It's a good thing, Em, but it does mean we're apt to be taken advantage of far more often than women like Maddie and Cat. Don't beat yourself up over this. You can get another job."

"Yeah, I guess. Now that I think of it, the job wasn't much at all. Oh, God. He really was paying me to be his whore," I sobbed.

"No! Don't think that way, Em!" Tia cried out through the phone.

"I just don't know why people like us don't get that magical happily ever after. I thought maybe it was because we didn't go after it like Maddie, but I went after it this time and what did I end up with? A man who couldn't even be bothered to stand up for me when he had the chance."

"What do you mean?"

Wiping my tears away, I shook my head. "Forget it. That means nothing now. You're right. I can get another job. I don't know if I'll go through that same staffing agency, though. Mr. DeVille probably knows I walked out and wouldn't want to give me another chance at another position."

"Em, I know you well enough to know that if you walked out, you had a good reason. To hell with that DeVille guy anyway and his staffing company. Just because it worked for Maddie doesn't mean it's going to work for any of the rest of us. You'll find a great job. Don't worry. I know you will."

"Thanks, Tia. I needed to hear that. I'm going to crawl into bed and look forward to tomorrow being better. I'll call you then, okay?"

"Okay, Em. Don't give that man or that job another thought. You're better than both of them."

Her words made me smile, but I didn't feel better than anyone at that moment. I felt used and discarded by the only man I'd ever really wanted.

I curled up under my covers and tried not to cry, but it didn't work. No matter how I felt about Mark now, what hurt the most was that I thought we might have a future together.

God, I was so stupid.

THE NEXT MORNING, I AWOKE FEELING JUST THE tiniest bit better, but that counted for something. The first thing I needed to do was put Mark Tanchen out of my mind. That would be impossible, though, because I had to deal with Mr. DeVille to explain my leaving my position a day early.

As I sat on the edge of my bed getting ready for the day, I suddenly wondered if he would invoke that clause in my contract. I foolishly hadn't read it carefully, so when I found out that I'd have to leave after only a single month at Mark's office, my biggest concern had been not if I could break the contract but how often I'd get to see Mark after I stopped working for him.

That had been a misplaced worry, hadn't it?

Cringing at how wrong I'd been about Mark, I dug out the contract with DeVille Staffing and scanned it for that clause. As I read through the pages, I saw nothing about not being able to leave early from any assignment.

But then on the last page where the clause about only working for one month was I read the words that made things only worse. "Failure to fulfill any assignment will result in an end to the employee's ability to work for DeVille Staffing, barring extraordinary circumstances."

My body sagged as those words filled my brain. I had no extraordinary circumstances, unless being so humiliated and hurt that the man you thought cared about you other than for sex that you had to leave before you burst into tears counted.

I doubted that would work with Mr. DeVille. All the better. I needed a fresh start anyway.

And to do that, I grabbed my laptop and began searching for jobs. Whatever else I felt, I knew one thing for damn sure. I didn't want to lose my apartment over any man, whether he was a lame ex-boyfriend or a boss I should have never slept with.

After an hour, I'd found a few possibilities and

filled out a handful of applications online. Pleased with myself for doing something proactive, I headed out to my kitchen for lunch and heard a knock at my door.

I didn't expect anyone to come to see me today, so immediately my brain went to the idea that Mark was my visitor. I quickly chastised myself for thinking that.

He never even bothered to stand up and tell his partner to stop hitting on you, Em. He's not going to make the effort to come to see you now either.

Standing on my tiptoes, I looked through the peephole and saw not Mark but Mr. DeVille standing on the other side of the door. Why was he here?

Unsure what he wanted, I opened the door and saw the owner of the staffing agency smiling at me. Oddly enough, it made him look more sinister, not less. I had a feeling the light blue eyes contrasted next to his jet black hair created that effect.

"Miss Cooper, I hope I'm not interrupting anything."

I shook my head and smiled. "No, not interrupting. What can I do for you, Mr. DeVille?"

He stepped toward me as his smile faded. "I need to discuss a matter with you. May I come in?"

A tiny voice in the back of my mind warned that I shouldn't let strange men into my apartment. This was, after all, New York City. For a moment, I thought about telling him no, but I decided against it. He was technically my employer as much as Mark was, so whatever he had to discuss with me I had to deal with sooner or later.

So now seemed like as good a time as any to settle any issues with him and move on with my life.

I stepped back out of the way and extended my arm. "Please, come in. Take a seat at the table."

He did as I suggested, and I watched him place his black leather briefcase in front of him to pull out a file folder I assumed was about me. My stomach promptly knotted up when he laid it on the table, slowly opened it, and I saw a red arrow sticky note on the top sheet of paper.

Waiting for him to say something made me nervous, and I suddenly blurted out, "I just want to say that I think Mr. Tanchen and his partner were quite pleased with my work, Mr. DeVille."

For a moment, he simply nodded his head before looking up at me. "I see that."

"I'm sorry that I had to leave a day early, but I had extenuating circumstances. Really."

Mr. DeVille smiled and nodded again. "Mr. Tanchen said the same thing. I understand you had to deal with an uncomfortable situation with his partner. Can you tell me a little about that?"

An uncomfortable situation with Josh? Was he referring to the kissing?

I sheepishly looked at him and then turned away. "It wasn't that big a deal. I'm a big girl. I can handle myself, Mr. DeVille."

Lots of bigs in that answer.

"Well, I'm sorry if you found anything made your time there difficult, Miss Cooper. Mr. Tanchen has assured me you were a wonderful secretary and what you had to deal with was extraordinary, so there will be no penalty imposed on you for leaving early from that position."

"Oh. Okay," I said, shocked Mark had gone out of his way to help me.

"I'm assigning someone new to that position, so I'd appreciate any comments that will help me find the perfect person for it," he said as he pushed a sheet of paper toward me.

My chest hurt at the idea of another woman working for Mark, and as I scanned the questions in front of me, the only answer I had was me. I should have been still working for Mark.

I looked up and sighed. "Mr. DeVille, would it be possible for me to go back to working there? I really liked it, and even though I left a day early, I don't think there would be any problems since Mr. Tanchen's partner is usually out of town."

He shook his head. "No, I'm sorry, Miss Cooper. While Mr. Tanchen also made that same request, I'm afraid I can't go against the contract."

Disappointed, I filled out his questionnaire and pushed the paper back toward him. "Here you go. Thanks again."

As he filed the form away in my folder and stuffed it into his briefcase, he said, "You can come in first thing in the morning and we'll get you another position that pays even better than the one with Mr. Tanchen and his partner."

"A position that pays even better?" I asked, suddenly feeling hopeful.

Mr. DeVille smiled in a way that was nothing less than wicked. "Oh, yes. You've shown yourself to be a real go-getter, Emma. We at DeVille Staffing believe that should be rewarded. So I'll see you tomorrow morning? Let's make it ten o'clock."

He stood to leave and I followed him to the door. "Okay, ten it is. Thank you so much."

Turning his head, he looked back at me as he began walking down the hallway. "My pleasure, Emma."

I closed the door and couldn't help but smile. Things had gone horribly off the rails with Mark and my position at his company, but now I'd be getting a better paying job somewhere else. If there was something else that would make me feel better about everything that had happened, I didn't know what it could be.

But then that ache in my chest reminded me that only my money situation had been improved. I still wished Mark and I hadn't crashed and burned. He had done me that favor with the contract, and he had said wonderful things in his reference for me to Mr. DeVille.

Was there a chance at all he cared for me other than as an employee?

$\mathcal{M}$ark

HALFWAY THROUGH MY DAY, I LOOKED OUT ACROSS the hall for at least the tenth time and felt like shit every time I didn't see Emma. It was like my brain has some malfunction and kept thinking that if I thought about her enough she'd be there.

My shoulders sagged from the disappointment of not having her in the office anymore. The guy from the staffing agency was scheduled to come in to talk to me right before lunch, so that made me think of her even more.

Not that she hadn't been on my mind every minute since she walked out. I thought about how she smiled at me whenever I told her a stupid story or how her big blue eyes looked when she walked out of my life.

They'd lost their innocence and instead were filled with anger at me.

Not Josh. Not anyone but me.

Fuck. I'd never felt this about any woman. I didn't know when it happened, but Emma changed from someone I couldn't fuck enough to someone I couldn't live without. I'd never been this miserable after breaking up with anyone. That wasn't my style. I fucked and moved on. I didn't have time for a relationship because my work life came first until the business became as successful as I'd always dreamed it could be.

That hadn't happened yet, at least not like I'd planned, so why the hell was I pining over Emma?

I knew the answer. Because she wasn't just another lay. She made me want to tell her about my idiot uncle who always showed up drunk to every family affair and all my plans for the future of the business. And with each story and goal I told her about, she listened like it meant something to her.

She made me realize that what Steve said was true. All work and no play did make me fucking boring.

With Emma I had it all. She helped me with work, and she filled the hours I usually spent alone in ways I'd never dreamed I'd want.

And now she was gone because Josh had that DeVille guy put in a clause in her contract that she couldn't work for me for more than a month. What kind of bullshit was that?

While my brain conjured up half a dozen ways a

decent lawyer could find loopholes in that asinine clause, it began to dawn on me that the contract wasn't the only reason she was gone.

Emma was right. I didn't do what I had to do to keep her in my life. My pride had kept me silent when I should have punched Josh in the head for kissing her. My fear of getting too attached to anyone had kept me from explaining to her that even though I loved when I was inside her, sex wasn't all I gave a damn about when it came to her.

All she'd wanted to know was that I didn't consider her bought and paid for, and yet, I couldn't say the words I had to so she'd stay. Whether it was pride or fear, I fucked up. So she left.

I needed to find a way to show her I wanted her in my life—all of it, not just the part that included her naked under me. I stood from my desk and grabbed my phone, saying into it, "What's Emma's home address?"

As my phone rattled off where she lived, I hurried toward the front door but found Mr. DeVille standing there for our appointment. Fuck. The last thing I wanted to discuss was Emma's replacement. No one could replace her. I knew that now.

I opened the door and quickly said, "I have to reschedule our meeting, Mr. DeVille. How does tomorrow sound? Any time you want."

His expression darkened, and he shook his head. "No, I'm sorry, Mr. Tanchen. That won't do. I really must speak to you now. I can't reschedule, unfortunately."

Something about this guy made me think he was a lot like Josh. Neither one of them understood the word no, and I'd be wasting my time trying to convince him to come back tomorrow.

"Fine. Now's great. Let's go into my office," I said, relenting only because I felt sure I could get this done and out of the way quicker than trying to put him off.

I rushed back in and sat down behind my desk as Mr. DeVille casually strolled to my door. Looking across the hall, he said, "Miss Cooper's former office, I presume?"

"Yes. That was her office."

"Very close to yours. Did you like that set-up or did you find she was too close?" he asked, still not in my office yet.

His question sounded inane. I'd chosen that location for her office, so why would I not have liked it?

"Where her office was didn't bother me," I answered, losing patience with this guy just one question in.

"Miss Cooper has a wonderful way of lighting up a room, doesn't she? I can't decide if it's her smile or those beautiful blue eyes of hers," DeVille said. Smiling, he added, "Then again, I might not be an impartial judge since I do favor blue eyes."

"Yes, she does. I think it's her personality, to be honest, and nothing physical she possesses," I answered, suddenly very defensive about the way he talked about Emma.

"Her personality?" he asked, arching a single black

eyebrow. "I haven't found her to be particularly bubbly, and she's certainly not giggly, especially considering her young age."

"No, she isn't any of those things, thankfully. She is, however, bright and intelligent, which makes talking to her much easier than if she was a bubbly or giggly young girl."

Finally, he stepped into my office. "Bright and intelligent I can definitely agree with."

Our conversation had already frustrated me since the man seemed to have nothing better to do than waste my time. Clearly, he ran his business differently than I ran mine.

"So what can I do for you today, Mr. DeVille? You said you wanted to discuss what I was looking for in a replacement secretary. To be honest, I don't want one, but since you and my partner decided I'd only get a month with each new one you sent, all I can say is I'd like her to be exactly like Emma."

He studied me for more than a few moments and then tilted his head. "The job you have the prospective employee perform isn't terribly difficult, Mr. Tanchen. There are a very limited number of tasks she would have to do, and the hours aren't oppressive, so I'm thinking just about any of my people could handle it. Was there something about Ms. Cooper that made her superior in any way to another secretary?"

His question made me sit back in my chair. I couldn't tell him how I felt about Emma. That would be unprofessional, and even though I didn't care if he ever sent another secretary to me, I prided myself on being a professional.

So what was an answer I could give him?

He focused his attention on me, his pale blue eyes staring into mine as I tried to find a way to convey what about Emma made her superior to everyone else. Finally, after nearly a minute of thinking of an appropriate answer, I said, "Sometimes in business, it isn't about the abilities of the employee so much as the way they click with an organization. Emma clicked immediately. I can't explain why. She just did."

A slow smile spread across his lips. "Isn't it wonderful when that happens? Almost as if fate stepped in and helped bring the exactly right person into your life. I love when that happens. It makes what I do so fulfilling and rewarding."

"Does that happen often in your line of work?" I asked, suddenly curious about this man sitting in front of me.

He nodded slowly as his smile grew broader. "Oh, every time."

"Really? Every time? You must be quite good at your job, Mr. DeVille."

"Oh, I am. I have a knack for these things. I know exactly what people need. In your case, the right person to help you."

Interested to know if he understood his employees as well as the businesses he worked with, I asked, "And the people who come to you looking for positions? Do you have a knack with them too?"

"Oh, yes. You see, it must be perfect on both sides.

You needed the right person to help you. For Miss Cooper, she needed a position that would allow her to use her organizational talents while giving her the confidence she needs in other areas."

His final words hit me like a sledgehammer to the side of my head. Other areas? What other areas did he mean?

I opened my mouth to ask him, but he was already out of his chair and heading toward the door. Confused, I rushed after him and caught him just as he was about to walk out the front door. "Mr. DeVille, what did you mean other areas?"

Turning to look at me, he smiled. "Ms. Cooper has organization down to a science. It's what makes her such a wonderful assistant to men like you. But she's lacking confidence in what I'd call social areas. I think that might have been the reason the issue with your partner and her occurred."

I didn't know what he was referring to, but I had a feeling Josh had been filling his head with bullshit in his defense of what he'd done. I shook my head and blocked DeVille's way out, intent on telling him how wrong he was about Emma.

"What happened with her and Josh had nothing to do with any problem Emma has in social areas. In fact, I'd say she isn't lacking at all in anything I'd consider social areas. Regardless, she had a problem with him making advances toward her because she's seeing someone else. I heard her tell him that myself. So whatever you've been told by my partner, I'm telling you it didn't happen that way. Emma is not to blame for anything."

Again, DeVille smiled and nodded. "I always enjoy hearing employers defend their employees, even former employees. Your comments will help me place her with someone else, and I can assure you that they will help her move into an even better pay scale."

I hated hearing that Emma would be working with anyone else, but now he'd sweetened the deal for her and she'd be getting paid more. Maybe if I offered more he'd let her stay here with me.

"I'd be happy to offer to pay her more. Just tell me how much and I can match it."

Mr. DeVille patted me on the shoulder and shook his head. "I want you to know it's all because of you that her work will be worth more money from now on. First, you told me about the extenuating circumstances that required her to leave a day early, and now you've shown me that you think she's worth far more than before. You certainly do value her work, don't you? I'll be sure to tell the next employer about that."

"Why won't you just let her come back here to work for more money? It's got to be more paperwork for you to place her with another company. Let me save you the time and effort. I'll increase her salary. Just tell me how much and I'm fine with it."

Again, he shook his head. "I can't do that. To do so would break the contract I have with you. Just as your side of our deal must pay ten thousand if you break it, so I must do the same if I break it, and I am not a man who gives out thousands of dollars lightly."

"I thought that was only the penalty for Emma. You told me she'd have to pay that if she broke the contract," I said, hopeful I'd tripped him up on his details.

But no. I hadn't.

"You're correct in saying that she must pay if she refuses to go to where she's assigned tomorrow. However, if you'll check your contract with my company, the same penalty holds if either one of us breaks our deal. These clauses are inserted to ensure everyone remains professional and committed to the contract."

My heart pounded as my mind raced to find a solution to this. Emma felt like my paying for her to get out of her contract would be tantamount to paying her to be my whore. That wasn't what I wanted for her at all, but what other way was there to ensure she could work here with me?

I couldn't bear the idea that she'd go to work for some other man. Emma was mine, and it was about time I stood up for her.

"Fine. Then I'll pay the ten grand to break my contract with you. That will solve this problem. Then I can hire Emma full time and pay her on my own, without you as the middle man. She deserves that, don't you think?"

A strange look of surprise came over his face. "You'd do that for her? For your secretary? She must be very valuable to you, Mr. Tanchen. She will have the choice once she's not under contract with me to decline your offer of employment without my having any ability to help you. That's a risk I fear you may not have taken into consideration. Are you sure you want to pay that amount for someone who isn't even your employee at the moment?"

I didn't have to think twice about my answer. "I'm not paying for Emma. I'm paying a penalty so she doesn't have to. That's it. But I'd like to make one request."

"Insisting she return to her job here isn't possible. As long as you understand I can't do that."

"I understand."

"Then what's your request?"

"Don't tell her until tomorrow morning. That's all I ask."

He thought about my demand for a moment and then nodded. "That I can do. I will inform her of her ability to choose wherever she'd like to work without being penalized tomorrow at ten a.m. Remember, though, that I cannot help you if she chooses to stay with my company and go to work somewhere other than here for you. It's a sizable risk, don't you think?"

I stepped back out of his way so he could leave. "No. I'll have the money sent to you. Expect it by end of business today."

"You know, I initially thought your partner was the stronger member of this company, but I think I was wrong, Mr. Tanchen. I hope things turn out the way you want them to, but regardless, I've been impressed by the lengths you've been willing to go for Miss Cooper. Good luck."

As he left, I hurried back to my office to grab my phone and keys. I needed more than luck to get Emma back. I needed to be the man who could stand up for her when it counted.

And I needed her to know I did it because I was crazy about her.

CHAPTER 9

mma

I HANDED TIA A GLASS OF WINE AND TOOK A SIP OUT of my own. Normally, I wouldn't have been a fan of day drinking at two in the afternoon, but after the week I'd had, I didn't care what society dictated. I'd pretty much jumped the shark on following the rules when I began sleeping with my boss—now ex-boss, but no matter—so what was a little wine in the middle of the day?

"To new beginnings!" she said with a forced cheer I knew was intended to help me get out of my funk.

"New beginnings," I repeated with a smile.

That I didn't want to start anew with another boss or another man wasn't something I told her since I knew it sounded pathetic. Mark wasn't the right man for me, and being his secretary wasn't the job for me. End of story.

"So you were telling me about that staffing company guy, Mr. DeVille?" Tia said as she leaned forward to set her wine glass on the coffee table. "What did he want?"

I shrugged. "I'm not sure, but I think he came over to console me in his strange way. He did tell me that my next assignment with him will come with a higher rate of pay. That was good. I just don't know if I want to stay with his company."

Tia made a face like she just sucked on a lemon. "Because the first assignment with him went so well? I think the guy is weird. I don't care what Maddie says about him."

I took a sip of wine and let it slowly run down my throat. "She only likes him because she credits him with her and Eric getting together. You don't like him because you blame him for my current misery. I'm guessing somewhere in between those two extremes is the truth about the very interesting Mr. Louis DeVille."

"I'm not disagreeing with you on that. I hate seeing you sad, Em. And yes, I think he had something to do with it. Does he do any research on the companies he sends his temps to? I mean, from what you've told me your position was a good one, except for the people you had to work with."

I'd probably made my situation with Mark sound far worse than it was because I tended to be overly romantic. That was what got me into this situation in the first place. Mark had wanted a woman to fuck, and I'd misconstrued that desire to mean he cared for me.

Now I knew better.

"Let's not talk about any of my employment or romantic woes. What about you? Have you found anything in the past month?" I asked, eager to move the attention away from my pathetic life to Tia's.

She sighed. "Well, I did get a few bites on my posts online. None of the positions are full-time, but I've made some money. Enough to tide me over for another few weeks. I just need something a bit more permanent."

"Don't give up. I have no doubt that you're going to find something. What about Cat? Have you heard anything from her?"

"I think she's doing something with driving. I still don't see that as a permanent job, but whatever. Why isn't she here today? Is she working?"

The truth about why I didn't invite Cat centered more on how gung-ho she could be and not how busy she was. I just didn't feel like hearing her claim I'd conquer this, or whatever else uplifting shit she'd say. I loved Cat, but at the moment, I needed something far less up and far more subdued, like what Tia offered.

"I didn't call her," I admitted and then quickly changed the topic. "So did you ever finish binge watching that series you were eating, drinking, and sleeping last week?"

Tia laughed at my description of what had recently been her obsession. "Believe it or not, no. It got boring in the third season, so I dropped it and started a new one. This is a series about stalkers. If you have Netflix, we can watch some of it this afternoon. There's nothing like getting drunk and watching some bingeworthy TV."

"Aren't all the shows you watch about stalkers? I swear you have a thing for them," I teased.

She began searching for the remote and mumbling something about us not having anything better to do, which I hated to admit was the truth, when I heard a knock on my door. For the second time in the same day, I wondered who could be visiting me since the only person I'd invited over was at the moment digging in my couch cushions.

Tia looked up and smiled. "Found it! And was that a knock I heard?"

I stood up and nodded. "Yeah. If it's Mr. DeVille, promise you'll be nice."

My friend pouted in response to my warning. "Why would you say it like that? I'm always nice."

As I walked toward my front door, I smiled. "Yes, but when you're feeling protective of your friends, you can get a little mean. We all love you for it, but you have a whole Mama Bear thing that comes out every so often."

She rolled her eyes and pointed the remote at my TV on the wall across the room while she mumbled, "I don't know what you're talking about. I just care when people dick over my friends. That's all. But I wouldn't call it a Mama Bear thing. That would require you to be my kids, for God's sake."

Her comment made me laugh, and I didn't bother

to look through the peephole before I opened the door. I stared out into the hallway and nearly fell to the floor when I saw it wasn't Mr. DeVille at all.

"Hi, Emma. I was hoping we could talk."

I pressed my lips together so my mouth didn't hang open, but that didn't make the shock of seeing Mark Tanchen standing at my door any less stunning. In the month he and I had known each other, he'd never come to my apartment. He'd never even asked me about where I lived.

"You're here. I'm surprised," I heard myself say as I gaped at him in amazement.

He looked as incredible as always, but something in his dark brown eyes told me he didn't feel as comfortable outside the office as he had when we talked at his place. I didn't know why being on my turf should make a difference, but it seemed to, for some reason.

"Can we talk?" he asked in a way that told me he had something important to say.

"Okay. Come in," I said as I stood back to let him into my apartment for the first time.

He walked past me and stopped dead when he saw Tia. I looked over at her and saw her eyes were as big as saucers. For a minute, I forgot they'd never met before, so I said nothing and simply stood there, still in shock that he'd bothered to come to talk to me.

When I finally came to my senses, I quickly said, "I'm sorry. Mark, this is my friend, Tia. Tia, this is my former boss, Mark Tanchen."

They both nodded and said their hellos, but I could

practically feel the tension grow among us. Tia looked over at me for a sign for what to do, so I gave her my best look that said, "I promise to tell you everything, but I need you to leave now, okay?"

A second later, she jumped up off the couch like a jack-in-the-box and hit her leg off the coffee table, nearly knocking her glass of wine over. She caught it before it spilled everywhere and let out a nervous laugh.

"I'm like a bull in a china shop. That's a thing, right? Sure, it's a thing. Oh, well. I better go. Nice to meet you, Mark. Em, I'm going to go now. I'll talk to you later, okay? Okay."

By the time she finished rambling, she was heading out the door. Tia hugged me on her way out and whispered in my ear, "I want to know every detail. Oh, my God, is he delicious! Okay, I'm going. Call me."

She slammed the door behind her, leaving Mark and me awkwardly looking at one another. I had a feeling he'd heard every word she said, but I didn't care. Whatever he came to talk to me about had nothing to do with the girl code Tia and I kept to in situations like this.

"Your friend seems nice," he said quietly. "I didn't mean to intrude on anything."

"You weren't. The two of us are unemployed at the moment, so we decided to do some day drinking and watch some shows on stalkers."

Mark gave me a strange look that said he didn't share our interest in either of those activities. "About that. I was hoping we could talk."

I walked past him and grabbed my glass of wine off the coffee table. Taking a drink, I gulped down a mouthful of Cabernet and then asked, "Which did you want to talk about, stalkers or day drinking?"

Whether it was the fact that I was no longer his employee, we weren't at his home, or that I'd had nearly a glass of wine in a matter of minutes, I felt bolder than usual around him at that moment. I liked it too.

He smiled at my teasing him and shook his head. "Neither, to be honest. I don't know much about either topic. I wanted to talk to you about working for me."

I walked back to the coffee table and grabbed Tia's glass of wine as a rush of nervousness ran through me. Had Mark actually decided to stand up and fight for me?

"I can't, remember? I signed that contract with Louis DeVille. I guess I have you to thank for making him bump me up to the next salary level on my next assignment, so thanks."

Mark didn't say anything for a few moments, which only served to make me more nervous, so I took a drink of Tia's wine. When he finally spoke again, I nearly spit it all over.

"About that. I paid him the ten grand. I just need you to please listen to me before you get all upset like you did the other day," he said as he walked toward me, his eyes pleading for me to give him a chance to explain.

I didn't know if it was the wine's effect on me or that I was just so happy that he had understood he needed to do something if he didn't want to lose me, but I didn't want to tell him to fuck off this time. Now, I felt like I could listen.

It must have been my midday wine buzz.

"I'm listening."

Mark's entire body relaxed as he realized I wasn't going to order him out of my apartment. With the chance to tell me what he came to say, he took a deep breath and began.

"I paid him the money because I don't want to lose you from my life. All of it. I miss having you there with me in the office, and I don't want another secretary, and not just because training someone new every month is stupid and typical Josh bullshit that he thought would be great but in reality only causes more work for me. I miss seeing you there across the hall. I miss your smile and the way you look at me when I talk to you. I don't talk to anyone, but when you're around, I want to tell you things."

He stopped speaking for a moment, so I asked the biggest question I needed the answer to. "So it isn't just about sex? Because if that's the case, I can't help you. I mean, I loved sleeping with you, but I won't be someone's whore. No thanks."

Mark shook his head as I spoke, and when I finished, he said, "No. I'm not going to lie. It definitely started out being about sex with you. I didn't know you, but I couldn't stop thinking about you from the moment you started working for me. I guess maybe in retrospect how things happened wasn't the best way to start off between us, but I can't change that now. All I can say is I didn't pay that DeVille guy to get you out of your contract so you can be my in-house whore or anything like that. I broke my contract with him and paid the ten grand I had to so you can come back to work. I'm crazy about you, Emma. Since you've been gone from the office, the place feels empty and lifeless. Pretty much like it did when I was the only person there before you came along."

As he spoke, he began to sound lost, like he didn't think what he was saying was convincing me that he was the kind of man I'd want to work for and be with. But he was wrong. Every word made me realize how crazy I was about him too.

"So what are you saying, Mark? You want me to come back to work for you to liven up the office?"

"No. I mean, yes, but that's not the only reason I came here today. I've been so focused on making my company a success that I never cared about anything having to do with what happened after work. Relationships were for other men. Since you came into my life, though, I want more. I want more with you."

His expression twisted in a look of anguish. I didn't want to see Mark like this, so I gently took his hand in mine and lifted to my mouth to kiss it.

"I know what you're trying to say, I think. You want me to come back to work as your secretary. I can do that. But if we're going to be anything other than employer and employee, I need to know that isn't what I'm being paid for. I need to know that even if I didn't come back to work for you that you'd still want to be with me. Can you say that honestly, Mark?"

He frowned and let out a sigh. "If that's what you want, then I can do that. But I would still miss working with you, Emma. You might not realize it, but you were the reason I wanted to be in the office most days."

"Mark, you're a workaholic. You like being in the office because of that, not me."

"I thought that too, but since you've been gone, I don't want to work or be in the office," he said quietly. "Will you come back to me in every way?"

He looked so sweet staring down at me with hope filling his deep brown eyes that I couldn't deny him anything. Standing on my tiptoes, I kissed him softly on the lips.

"Yes. I'll come back to you in every way."

Sliding his hands down my back, he cupped my ass and pulled me to him. "I've missed you so much, Emma. I don't want to think about anything but you."

Then he kissed me long and deep to prove it, and all I could think of was how much I wanted exactly what he wanted.

My fingers fumbled with his belt and zipper as Mark kissed my neck and slid my shirt over my shoulders. It took just a few seconds for us to strip one another's clothes off and toss them to the side, leaving us naked and standing in my living room in front of the huge window that I'd never been able to find the right size curtains for.

"We're pretty much putting on a show for my neighbors," I said with a giggle, pointing at the window.

"Just wait until they see what happens next," he said with a devilish grin before he lifted me to the perfect height where he could slide into me.

I wrapped my arms around his neck as I waited for him to fill me up and whispered against his lips, "I thought you didn't like this position much."

His hands squeezed my ass while he lined up his cock with my already wet pussy. "I didn't want to wait any more. I need to be inside you now."

And with that, he pushed his hips forward and eased into me. I knew to lift my legs so every beautiful inch of him could fit, and he groaned as he filled me until his entire cock was nested inside me.

Mark kissed me hard, pumping into my body like a man on a mission to make me come. I sucked on his tongue, and snaked mine into his mouth while I moaned at how unbelievably good it felt to have him fucking me again.

Everything around us fell away, and we stood there in my living room racing toward that sweet release we could give one another. I felt his cock swell inside me until I was sure he was too big for me to take, but my body wanted to be claimed and took every inch of him every time he pumped into me.

As we rushed toward the moment we craved, he turned into that dirty talking man I adored. In my ear, he moaned, "You feel so fucking good. I missed that tight cunt of yours, Emma."

I loved that the serious man who seemed to be all business could be so erotic when he fucked me, and I knew he loved when I talked like that to him too, so I scratched my nails across his shoulders and whispered, "Give me that big cock, baby. I want you to fill me up until there's nothing left inside you."

I'd never spoken like that to any man, but the way he became so sensual when we were together made that part of me come out without fear that I'd shock him or turn him off. Just my words made him fuck harder, and seconds later, I came with a rush that nearly took my breath away.

"That's it. I love when your cunt milks my cock. Milk all that cum out, baby."

I clung to him as my orgasm roared through me, and just when I thought the aftershocks had subsided, he thrust into me one last time. I felt his cock twitch with each time he shot into me, and in my ear he moaned my name low and deep.

When he finished, he took a deep breath and sighed. His dark hair glistened with sweat, and when I kissed his neck, I tasted the saltiness on his skin.

"God, I missed you," he said as he pushed my damp hair off my face to kiss me sweetly.

"I missed you too."

I didn't know how long we stood there exhausted from our lovemaking but not wanting to separate. My neighbors probably saw the entire thing, but I didn't care. All I cared about was being back with the man I adored.

CHAPTER 10

ark

FOR THREE MONTHS, EMMA HAD WORKED FOR ME. Three incredible months. In that time, I'd fallen madly and completely in love with her. I'd never said those three words, though. Neither of us had. I knew she felt it like I did, but I'd learned that the woman who rocked my world each night was more than a little old fashioned. She wanted me to say I love you first.

Not that I didn't find that charming. It just came as a surprise after the way we started together.

The last vestiges of that man who kept everyone at arm's length still clung to me during those three months, but finally one day as I watched her from across the hall as she worked to help me make my business better than it had ever been, I knew the time had come.

But it had to be special. I had to show her how much I couldn't do without her.

Emma pushed her chair back away from her desk and looked over at me. I'd been watching her for the past few minutes, eager to begin our night together, and smiled at her.

"You look like a little boy who has a secret he can't wait to share," she said as she walked across the hall into my office. "What's going on?"

"I want you to go upstairs and wait for me. I'll be up in a few minutes."

"We aren't going out to dinner?" she asked, confused since I'd made a point to tell her all week how much I wanted to take her out tonight.

"No, but I promise you won't be disappointed."

For a few seconds, she gave me that adorable pout that never failed to charm me, but then a tiny smile lifted the corners of her mouth. She walked around my desk and sat across my lap, threatening my entire plan because I might take her right there and ruin everything.

"I'm never disappointed, Mark. I don't want you to ever think that."

I pulled her to me and kissed her long and deep, my cock getting harder by the second and making me want to abandon my entire plans for the night. "If you don't go upstairs right now, I'm going to fuck you right here, which sounds great but I have other ideas for us tonight. Please don't tempt me."

"Okay. Should I just wait for you in bed?" she asked sweetly.

Shaking my head, I lifted her off me, instantly missing the feel of her body against mine. "No. Wait for me in the kitchen."

She expected me to tell her more about what would happen, but I merely smiled and pointed toward the door. "Upstairs right now. I'll be there in a few minutes."

Emma leaned down and kissed me. "Okay, but I'm going to be hungry after, so you're going to have to feed me real food."

"I promise. Now go."

As she trotted off to follow my orders, I closed my laptop and waited for the delivery person from Emma's favorite Italian restaurant. We'd worked hard that week, and in addition to my usual treating her to dinner, I intended to make this night one she'd never forget.

Right on time at exactly five, he followed my directions to the letter, knocking once and leaving the food I'd ordered outside the front door. As soon as I picked up the box, I smelled the buttery lobster and risotto that Emma loved. With a smile, I inhaled a deep breath and closed the door behind me.

I slowly climbed the stairs as a hint of lemon wafted up toward my nose, and suddenly I became nervous about what I planned. Was it enough? I'd never said those three magic words to any woman. Emma was the first woman I'd dated for more than a few nights. She meant the world to me, and I wanted this night to be perfect.

I pushed those worries down inside me and opened

the door to my apartment. The scent of our meal reached the kitchen before I did, and I found Emma on her feet waiting for me when I walked in.

"Oh, Mark! I'd know that smell anywhere. You got us that lobster risotto I love from Caravaggio's, didn't you?" she squealed.

Placing the boxes on the counter, I nodded. "I know it's your favorite, and you did say you're hungry."

Emma got dishes and silverware, and I plated the food. The mouthwatering combination of butter, lemon, garlic, and wine filled the air around us. Thrilled by the first part of my surprise, she leaned over the table to kiss me before bringing the first forkful of lobster risotto to her mouth.

Closing her eyes, she moaned sweetly, "Oh, this is better than sex."

I smiled, happy to see she was pleased, and she opened her eyes and gave me a cute grin. "Well, not better than sex with you, but better than sex with every other man on the planet."

"Eat. I have two other surprises after this."

Her blue eyes grew wide in anticipation. "Ooooh, two more surprises. For me? What's the occasion?"

I almost let those three words spill out of my mouth at that moment, but I wanted to save that for a little later. Shrugging, I answered, "Just a Friday we get to spend together."

Emma gave me a skeptical look that told me she didn't believe that, but she wouldn't have to wait much longer. "The second surprise is dessert, but that can't happen until you finish this."

With a cute pout, she nodded. "Okay. You're twisting my arm to eat my favorite meal ever, but I can't wait for surprise number two and three."

She quickly finished her meal and leaned over to kiss me again. "Thank you for that. No matter what else comes next, that was delicious. It was so sweet of you to get me the lobster risotto, Mark."

I brought over a second box from the restaurant and placed it in front of her on the table. Before I opened it, I whispered in her ear, "I had them make this especially for you, Emma."

Turning to look up at me, she had tears in her eyes. "Why? What's this about?"

Without answering her questions, I lifted the top of the brown box to reveal a heart shaped panna cotta dessert in the shape of a heart. Drizzled over the top were ripe red cherries and the largest, most succulent looking blackberries I'd ever seen. I'd told the man at Caravaggio's that I wanted something they could make into a heart, and they hadn't let me down.

"Oh, my God!" she said, her eyes wide as she looked at the dessert and then at me. "It's beautiful. I'm afraid to eat it. Did you get one for yourself?"

I shook my head. "No, this is only for you. Let me get a fork."

Grabbing one from the drawer, I returned to the table and sat down in my chair. I cut a piece of the dessert off and lifted it to her mouth as she watched me in rapt attention.

"I bet it tastes as good as it looks," I said as I let the panna cotta drop off the fork onto her tongue.

Emma closed her eyes and sighed as a smile spread across her lips. "It takes perfect. I love it."

And that was my cue.

"I love you, Emma."

Her eyes slowly fluttered open, and she stared at me for a moment before she said, "You love me?"

"I love you. I've been in love with you for so long but I didn't know if I could say it. So I arranged to have all of this to show you just in case it didn't come out right when I finally said it for the first time."

She took the fork from my hand and cut off a piece of the dessert before lifting it to my lips. I savored the lightness of the cream and sweetness of the berries as they hit my tongue. The taste was pure perfection, and I closed my eyes just as she had.

"I love you, too, Mark," she said softly.

I opened my eyes and smiled. "That was my third surprise, by the way."

Emma licked her lips and stood from her seat. "Now I have one for you."

Taking me by the hand, she led me to the bedroom. Stripping out of her clothes, she draped herself across the bed so her head hung off the front.

"Move closer," she said, and added, "and take your cock out."

I didn't know exactly what she planned to do, but anything that involved my being told to take my cock out and Emma naked in front of me couldn't be bad in the least. She looked up at me, her blue eyes seeming more innocent than usual and wide in anticipation, and I unbuttoned and then unzipped my pants. My cock sprung out as soon as I yanked my boxer briefs down past my balls.

With a sexy smile, she said, "Maybe you should just take everything off. No need to make this harder than it is."

I stroked my cock and chuckled. "I don't think I could get harder, to be honest."

A few seconds later, I stood over her naked and ready for whatever she wanted to do to me. I slid my gaze down over her breasts with nipples taut and needy for my mouth to the smooth space between her legs. It took everything in me not to lean over and bury my face in her pussy I knew was wet and waiting for me.

Reaching back, she cupped my balls and gently squeezed, sending ripples of need through me. My breath caught in my chest when I saw her tilt her head back as far as it could go.

And then a second later, she whispered, "Feed me your cock."

She opened her pretty little mouth, and I gripped the base before angling the long shaft so thick it filled her cunt completely toward her pouty lips. The first touch of her tongue nearly blew off the top of my head it felt so good. I bent my knees and slowly slid into her, loving how she looked sucking my cock for the first time.

I slid my hand over the front of her neck and felt her muscles contract around my shaft. Enthralled at how good it felt, I slowly pushed my hips forward to sink further into her and felt the head of my cock bump up against the back of her throat.

She didn't gag or make a noise, so I pushed a little further and was rewarded by a moan that resonated against my cock. Fuck that felt good!

Emma squeezed my balls gently in her hands and then slid her palms over my hips. She sank her fingertips into my skin and urged me on to fuck her mouth. I didn't want to hurt her, so I retreated until only the head stayed in her mouth and then made slow and shallow jabs into her. She flicked her tongue along my shaft, sending jolts of need straight through to my balls, and I had to fight the urge to fuck her as hard as I usually did when I was buried in her cunt.

I slid out of her so my cock just teased her lips, and she smiled. "You can go a little faster if you want. I'll let you know if I can't handle it."

That's all I needed to hear. Bending my knees even more, I stuffed my hands into her hair and tugged hard as I began pumping my cock into her mouth, barely able to walk that fine line between control and my animalistic tendencies. Emma dug her fingernails into my hips and moaned with each thrust into her mouth as she flattened her tongue to slide it up the underside of my shaft. The feeling was like nothing I'd ever experienced in my life. Having a big dick had a lot of advantages, but one of the disadvantages was rarely, if ever, having a woman suck me off. I didn't know where Emma had learned to do this and couldn't think about it as she inched me toward coming straight down her beautiful throat.

She sucked hard while I pumped in short stabs into her mouth. I knew I wouldn't last long and tightened my hold on her hair. My need to fuck her hard began to take over, making me think I should stop before I hurt her, but with one teasing flick of her tongue near my balls, I slipped over that edge to a place where I lost control.

With her throat completely exposed, I watched as my thick cock disappeared past her lips and then pressed against her throat so the outline of it made her neck muscles bulge. I pumped into her with abandon, and seconds later, I felt the first twitch of my cock as I came.

Quickly, she moved her hands from my hips to my cock, stroking me as I shot down her throat. She looked so perfect there taking everything I had into her and doing it to please me. I heard myself groan as the last drop of cum shot out of me, and then it took all my strength to even stand.

I eased out of her mouth, loving how sexy she looked at each glistening inch passed over her lips. Taking a few steps back, I steadied myself with my hand on the dresser while she lay there looking back at me.

"Holy fuck! That was the most incredible thing I've ever experienced," I said with a smile as I struggled to recover my strength. "I thought I was going to black out for a second there."

"I'm glad you didn't. I'd hate to have to explain to

the paramedics when they finally found us that I was giving my boyfriend a blowjob for the first time and he landed on me. That's if they found us at all, I guess."

I laughed at how cute she could be after sucking my cock so well that I nearly passed out. "That might have been awkward."

Fully recovered, I walked around the bed and pulled her up so her head wasn't hanging off the edge. "I think someone deserves to have their pussy eaten, and thankfully, I'm happy to do that for you."

She looked down her body to see me positioning myself between her legs. With a sweet smile, she asked, "Are you sure you're up to it? Want to rest for a few more minutes."

I shook my head. "Nope. After that, I have to make you come at least as hard."

"Is this a competition?" she asked as I slid my tongue up her slit.

"No. Just giving the woman I love what she deserves."

Pressing my mouth to her beautiful pussy, I heard her moan above me. I pushed her legs open wide and slid two fingers into her cunt while I flicked my tongue over her clit. She tasted so fucking good that I could have spent the rest of my night eating her out.

"Oh...God...I don't think I'm going to last very long, Mark. I almost came while I was sucking your cock, so don't be surprised when I come any time now."

I rammed my two fingers into her like I knew she

liked and sucked her clit into my mouth as I said, "Mmmm...let me feel you come apart, baby."

A few seconds later, I felt her cunt squeeze my fingers as the first hint of her orgasm ripped through her. She pulled my mouth into her pussy, grinding it against my face as she came harder than ever before with me.

"Oh, God! Don't stop. Lick me...fuck me harder...oh, God..."

When she finally finished coming, she let out a heavy sigh. I pulled my fingers out of her cunt and pressed a soft kiss on her clit.

"That feel good?" I asked, knowing the answer before she gave it.

Emma nodded. "So fucking good. God, you have totally ruined me for sex, you know that? I'm spoiled now because of you."

I slid my body over hers until I hovered over her and kissed her softly on the lips. "Then I guess you're going to have to only fuck me for the rest of time so you're never disappointed."

She looked up at me and smiled. "I can do that."

And that's how a man who never thought much about love made plans to spend the rest of his life with his beautiful secretary. Everything had worked out. She was mine, and I was hers, and that's the way it would stay.

MARK TANCHEN THOUGHT HE NEEDED SOMEONE TO HELP schedule his appointments and do his filing. I knew the first time I met him that's not what he needed. Or wanted, deep down. So I sent him a woman who would help him see that business wasn't the most important thing in life.

With her talent at organization, Emma was the perfect secretary, but even more, she was the perfect distraction for a man desperately in need of one. Sweet and giving, she deserved a man who could satisfy her. She also wanted a man who would fight for her. I had my doubts for a few moments there, but in the end, Mark found his way to the one woman who could give him what he needed at work and what he wanted after work.

As I told him, I have a knack for these kinds of things. It's a gift I willingly share because I like to see people happy. As you can see, I'm very good at what I do.

PLAY DATE

K.M. SCOTT

CHAPTER 1

ia

THE RAIN POURED DOWN IN SHEETS, DRENCHING ALL of New York City in water that had lasted for days. I clutched my umbrella tightly as the deluge battered against it, desperate to keep myself dry for this appointment. I could practically feel the humidity flattening my hair to a pancake against my head.

So much for all that effort I took to make myself look good before I left my house.

My insecurities began to get the better of me, so I took a deep breath and stopped under an awning to let it out slowly. "Okay, Tia. You've got this. So what if you don't have a four year degree? You have skills, and the people at this place are going to see that."

After my quick pep talk, made even quicker by the downpour that now ran in rivers off the end of my umbrella as I hurried to my destination, I rushed into the DeVille Staffing office. The office was warm and welcoming, and as I approached the reception desk, I heard the faintest sound of classical music playing in the background. The receptionist was tanner than anyone usually looked in October, but it somehow suited her, making her blond hair look even lighter next to her skin.

She looked up and gave me a genuine smile as she said, "Good morning. It's a nightmare out there, isn't it?"

I nodded in agreement while I wrapped my umbrella up in a bag and stowed it near my purse on the floor. "It really is. This is crazy. I guess it could be worse. It could be snow."

A look of horror filled her expression. "Don't even mention snow. I swear every winter I'm going to move to an island or something, but here I am getting ready to spend another season right here in the city."

Her Brooklyn accent, one I recognized immediately, became stronger as she talked about the cold weather coming, and I suspected she usually hid it but couldn't when she got excited about something. As she complained about what we'd all be seeing in just a month or so, I nodded and smiled, refraining from joining in with how much I hated the cold weather.

"Well, welcome to DeVille Staffing. I'm Tina. Did you have an appointment?"

I smiled as I replied, "I'm Tia Morton. Nice to

meet you. I have an appointment with Mr. DeVille at ten."

"Tia! Just dropped the n, huh?" she teased before smiling and nodding again as she typed into her computer. "I see you right here, Tia. Mr. DeVille will be ready in just a few minutes. Would you like something to drink while you wait? Something to take the chill out of your bones from that rain?"

Holding the paperwork I'd filled out from online, I shook my head and smiled again as I handed the papers to her. "No, I'm fine, thank you."

"Okay, well, have a seat and he'll be out in just a few."

"Thanks."

The lounge area was well put together and chic with modern furniture, like the rest of the office, which made me feel better. I would have felt absolutely terrible if DeVille Staffing resided in one of those cramped and dirty offices that a lot of temp agencies seemed to specialize in. Upscale and recent magazines sat on the oak coffee table in front of me, and I found myself feeling very relaxed in one of the plush black chairs around it.

After only waiting for the few promised minutes, I saw a door open at the far end of the office and a man in a dark suit walk out. Tall with black hair, he had an air about him that commanded attention. He said something to Tina before smiling a wickedly charming grin and gestured for me to come over.

Quickly, I grabbed my soggy belongings and hurried over to him at the reception desk. As I drew closer, I saw he had the bluest eyes I'd ever encountered. Their color was nothing less than piercing.

"Tia, is it? I'll have to be careful not to call you Tina. How do you do, Tia Morton?" he said in a smooth voice as he held out his hand to shake mine.

"I get that a lot actually," I joked back. "It's very nice to meet you, Mr. DeVille."

"So, Tia, you're the one who likes kids, right?" he asked as he escorted me into his office.

"Yes, sir. I have a two year degree in early childhood education. I know it's not a full degree like many places want, but I love children and they love me."

"I understand completely. Well, let's chat and by the time you leave, I'll see to it you have a temporary position somewhere."

I beamed my happiness at how positive he sounded about my finally getting a job. He sat down behind an enormous old desk that reminded me of my grandfather's mahogany desk he loved so much, and I took a seat in front of him in a black leather chair as I looked around at his office.

Beige walls and deep brown carpeting gave the impression that this was just another nondescript room in a business, but as I glanced over at the dark wood bookcases that filled the wall behind him, I saw a variety of interesting books from what looked like first edition classics with fine covers to paperbacks of romance novels. Expensive picture frames held images of beautiful women and Mr. DeVille, all different in each of the five of them.

What an interesting man he must be, I thought to myself.

"Now, I can't guarantee that you'll be hired on full time. I don't make that call, but we're here to place you somewhere else in the event that you don't get hired on permanently somewhere."

Nervously I asked, "Do many people not get hired on permanently?"

He shook his head and smiled. "Oh, most of them do, but I'm not allowed to guarantee anything. You understand, I'm sure."

"Yes, sir."

He slowly stroked down from his lower lip to his chin with his forefinger and middle finger and nodded. "If I do say so myself, I'm very good at matching people to the perfect place they should be, so it's quite rare that I don't succeed. It happens from time to time, though."

I smiled, liking how confident he sounded. Two of my friends had found great jobs and so much more through Mr. DeVille, so I had high hopes I'd at least get a position that would help me pay my bills.

Anything more would be like a cherry on top of the cake.

Lowering his head, he looked over my information I'd filled out online, nodding and humming as he read it. Finally, he lifted his gaze and flashed me another of his charming smiles.

"Tia, this all looks excellent. While you don't have

much work experience, you're young so that's to be expected. I'm impressed with how much you love children. I see from all your previous positions that everyone says they love you too."

"Oh, very much so. What work experience I do have almost all consists of working with children. I enjoy being around them so much. I've never met a child I didn't like."

Mr. DeVille sat back in his chair and nodded slowly as I gushed about loving kids. "To have found your specialty and calling at such a young age, I'm envious. So many of us have to try things that aren't right before we find what's good for us."

I wanted to tell him that I've had a lot of side jobs that were awful and definitely not right for me, but I pressed my lips together and simply smiled. He didn't need to know about those.

"Okay, I have something that I think will be perfect for you."

He handed me a sheet of paper, but before I could begin to read the information about my new employer, Mr. DeVille said, "His name is Mr. Nico Allen. He's a great guy. He used to go through me for temp workers for his real estate business, but he's grown so big that he needed more than my modest staffing agency could offer. However, he's got a very different issue now. He's taking care of his five year old niece, and I don't think he'd be offended by my telling you he's completely lost. Think you're up to the task of helping him?"

"Yes, absolutely!" I said happily.

Taking care of a five year old sounded like the perfect job. I'd babysat ever since I was young and my degree was in early childhood education. It was perfect. And five was such a great age.

I looked down at the address for Mr. Allen's home and saw it listed as Scarsdale. Looking up, I asked, "Mr. DeVille, is this a live-in position?"

My beat up car likely wouldn't make the trip from Brooklyn to Scarsdale too many times before it gave out.

"It is. Do you need transportation to Mr. Allen's home?"

I thought about my old car looking completely out of place in one of the wealthiest suburbs of the city and cringed. I definitely did not want to take that piece of junk out there and make a bad first impression.

"Yes," I lied. "That would be great. Thank you."

"Excellent. I'll have my driver pick you up at your apartment at eight sharp Wednesday morning. That will give him a couple days to prepare. I'm sure he'd love if you would come tomorrow. He's definitely struggling with his niece."

"Does he have any experience with children?" I asked, imagining a grown man not knowing the first thing to do with a five year old girl if he didn't have any of his own.

"Other than some of his whinier clients, no," Mr. DeVille joked. "Now if you have any questions, please feel free to call or email me."

He stood up from behind his desk, a clear sign he

believed our meeting had ended, and began walking toward the door. Just as he reached it, he turned around to face me, and for the first time, I saw something different in his expression.

Something far more serious.

"Tia, I want to warn you that your new employer can be a bit brusque. He doesn't mean to be, but it's his way. Don't be discouraged if he doesn't warm up to you for a while. Anyway, no matter how he acts, I know he's going to be thrilled to have your help with his niece."

I nodded, taking all he said in before asking, "Do you know the child's name, Mr. DeVille?"

"Grace. Oh, also, don't ask about her parents. It's nothing terribly tragic, but just know that they aren't around right now, so Mr. Allen is in charge of her welfare. Now enjoy your new position, and remember, if you need anything, we here at DeVille Staffing are always available to help."

"Thank you so much. I'm sure it's going to be a wonderful experience."

As Mr. DeVille escorted me to the front door, I noticed the rain had finally stopped and the sun appeared to be poking out from the clouds. That seemed like a good sign.

So what if my job involved a cranky uncle? It also came with a five year old girl I was sure would be wonderful to be around. The best thing was I had a job and could finally pay my bills and not be forced to ask my friends for money anymore.

Wednesday couldn't come fast enough.

. . .

TWO DAYS LATER AFTER A LITTLE SHOPPING FOR some more appropriate work clothes than the yoga pants I'd spent the last few months wearing, I sat in the back seat of Mr. DeVille's black Town Car as his driver shuttled me up to Scarsdale and I thought about the place I was going. People from there were like some kind of dream to me. They lived perfect little lives in perfectly huge houses and drove gorgeous luxury cars. Everything my life hadn't been.

I just hoped I'd fit in.

The last remnants of the fall leaves clung to the all but bare branches, dotting the sides of the road with the final hint of color of the season. I looked out the window for a little while and then down at my lap where my manila folder of information about my position sat. I'd done a little research on my new boss the day before and hadn't found anything particularly interesting. He looked like any other businessman in the photos, but most of the things I found were just articles about how he rose so quickly to a place of prominence in the New York City real estate elite. I imagined he must have been quite the man to do something so monumental before the young age of thirty-five.

Finally, the driver said, "We're here, miss. I'll let you out in front of the house and then I'll get your things for the staff to take in."

Staff? Mr. DeVille hadn't mentioned anything about Nico Allen having staff. But one look out the window at the home in front of me said he needed staff, even if it was only himself and his five year old niece living there. The house had to be over five thousand square feet, and just the front porch alone looked spacious enough to house half a dozen people comfortably.

I stared in amazement at how gorgeous Mr. Allen's home was. Light gray stone covered the façade, making it look like a castle, and the home's three floors climbed high into the bright blue sky. The yard was huge and sweeping, perfectly manicured by expert landscapers, no doubt. I felt like I could look at this place for the rest of my life and still not take in all its grandeur.

"Mr. DeVille said to have you go to the front door, although the staff uses the side entrance," the driver said, breaking into my thoughts about how incredible my new location was. "I'll take your bags to the side, though. Good luck, Miss Morton."

"Thank you, and thank you for handling my bags," I said, barely able to get words out as my mind reeled from what lay in front of me.

I walked to the front porch and rang the doorbell. After just a moment, the large wooden door opened to reveal a woman dressed in all black. Her hair pulled back, she had a serious look about her, but she cracked a tiny smile as she opened the door to welcome me inside.

"You must be the nanny. I've been waiting for you. I trust the driver deposited your bags at the side entrance?" she asked as she guided me into an enormous foyer with a crystal chandelier hanging in the center of the room.

As I looked up to admire it, I answered, "Yes, he's doing that right now."

"Your name is Tia, correct?" she asked in a clipped tone.

Sensing she didn't like how distracted all the beauty around me had made me, I snapped my head in her direction and pasted a smile on my face. "Yes. I'm Tia Morton. It's nice to meet you."

"I'm Agatha. It's nice to meet you too, Tia. Now follow me and I'll give you a tour of the house before you go to meet Mr. Allen."

Clutching my purse and manila envelope in my hands, I nodded and followed her down the hallway as she gave me a rundown of how many bedrooms and bathrooms the home had, where the laundry was since Mr. Allen's niece needed her clothes washed constantly as she got into everything under the sun, and where the kitchen was since I was in charge of feeding the child. With each room, we poked our heads in and I looked around quickly before she whisked me off to the next location.

At the end of the whirlwind tour, Agatha turned to face me and nodded quickly. "That's the house. I'm the head of the housekeeping staff. Michael is the head of the kitchen staff and the cook, and Anthony is Mr. Allen's driver. There are also groundskeepers and landscapers, but you don't need to know about them. Now let me take you to meet Mr. Allen. This way."

She pushed against my elbow to turn me to the left

before we hurried down a long hallway that comprised an entire wing of the home. Each door on our way was closed, so I couldn't see what type of rooms were on this side of the house, but at the end of the hallway I saw an open door as Agatha and I stopped.

"This is his office. He's instructed me to bring you here upon your arrival. Go in and sit down and he'll come out when he gets done with his work."

"Oh, okay. Thank you," I said quietly as she hurriedly pushed me into the room.

A dark wood floor met deep blue walls covered nearly entirely with wood bookcases a shade or two lighter than the floor, and as I walked toward a white loveseat, I immediately wondered how a five year old child would handle being in a room like this. Everything felt very off limits.

I barely had time to sit down and get my bearings before the door on the far wall opened and a man wearing a three piece suit strolled out. Immediately, I couldn't help but be struck by how handsome Nico Allen was. The pictures I'd seen online had really done him no justice at all. He was tall and muscular with dark eyes that seemed to swallow me up as he looked down at me. Near his temples, he had a hint of gray, and his dark brown hair hit just at his collar and hinted at a more casual man than the businessman the world saw.

"Are you the nanny from DeVille's place?" he asked curtly, almost as if he didn't care to know the answer even thought he'd asked the question.

I quickly stood and nodded. "Yes, I'm Tia. Tia

Morton, Mr. Allen. Your house is beautiful. Agatha took me on a brief tour on our way here, and it's breathtaking."

Grimacing, he answered, "It should be for the price. Follow me and I'll introduce you to my niece Grace. She's five and I swear to God she hasn't stopped crying since she got here last week. I hope you can do something about that because getting work done with that kind of insanity in the house is next to impossible."

Before I could say anything in response, he took off out the door and down the hallway. I hurried to catch up to him, remembering Mr. DeVille's warning about him being brusque. He wasn't kidding. Brusque was the nicest thing I could say about him right now, other than thinking he might be the sexiest man in his thirties I'd ever laid eyes on.

We walked through the central area of the home that I would have sworn was as big as my apartment and then to the far end of the other wing before stopping. I didn't need to ask where the child was since the sound of her screaming and crying could be heard nearly from the moment we left his office.

With a huff of disgust, he rolled his eyes and threw open the door to reveal a little blond girl sitting on the floor of an enormous bedroom, tears rolling down her face. She instantly stopped crying and looked at the two of us, clearly hoping someone would pay attention to her.

"This is Grace. She cries. A lot. Your job is to make sure that doesn't continue using any means necessary. I don't care what that entails. I'm a very wealthy man, Miss Morton, and I can make most problems disappear just by throwing money at them, so do whatever you have to so I get peace and quiet again."

Before he could say another unkind word, I stepped into the room with the white carpeting and pink walls and smiled at Grace. "Well, children don't really respond to that kind of thing."

Mr. Allen leveled his steely gaze on me and said, "What I meant was don't worry about whatever you have to do to calm this child down. If it ends up having to involve the authorities, I can simply make the problem go away with money. Good luck. Don't fail as this is literally the only thing you have to do here."

And with that, he slammed the door, startling Grace into tears again and leaving me with nothing but a bad taste in my mouth for Mr. Nico Allen.

CHAPTER 2

ico

BY THE TIME I GOT BACK TO MY OFFICE, THE SOUND of that infernal crying had ceased to be the soundtrack of my day, instantly cheering me up. As I settled into my chair and closed my eyes to enjoy the beautiful sound of nothing in my home, I silently swore to let my sister know how much I hated her for saddling me with her kid while she gets to spend eighteen months in some white collar prison-like setting where she probably has more freedom than I do at this moment.

Leave it to Fiona to get caught up with insider trading. Who the hell does she think she is? Martha Stewart? All that intelligence and she pissed it away by getting sentenced to eighteen months in jail.

Talk about nearly knocking me over with a feather when that woman from social services came here that

276

day with Grace in tow. First, Fiona has a child with some gigolo from God only knows where and then she's stupid enough to get sent to prison.

If our father was alive today, he'd kill her. I thought about finding some way to sneak into her cell and strangle her, but I decided against it. I have too much to lose, and unlike her, I understand how to act like a goddamned responsible adult.

I smiled to myself as the wonderful silence surrounded me. I intentionally never had children, which is why my home used to be my sanctuary. Since that little girl showed up, it's been nothing but chaos, a horror show full of wailing and dirty hands messing up the walls and furniture. I finally had to close her in that bedroom I keep for guests because all she did was cry.

She's at the wrong house to do that. There's no crying in my world. Not in my personal life, and certainly not in my professional life as a real estate magnate. I made others cry by buying and selling buildings. I didn't cry, and I certainly didn't need to hear some kid's sobbing day and night.

I knew DeVille would have just the right person for the job. He's always on top of things, like I preferred the people I pay to be. He tried to talk me into some other nonsense like he did with my friend Eric, but I wasn't hearing any of it. Eric may have been gullible enough to let him send out a baker when he needed a housekeeper, but I put my foot down and demanded a nanny who could handle Fiona's kid.

Now that Tia had arrived, I could finally get back to living my life the way I wanted to.

My phone tore me from my reverie of how happy things would be from now on, and I saw it was Charles calling. The last two bachelors left in our circle, he nearly had a heart attack when he found out I had a child staying with me. He probably ran out that night and bought a gross of condoms just to ensure that never happened to him.

"Charles, I'm talking to you from the silence of my office, and I can tell you, it's perfect living in this house again," I said into the phone, punctuating my statement with a chuckle.

"I was wondering if you fixed that problem. You're not a man who should be around kids. Not that I am either, but Christ, whoever thought you were a good guardian must be out of their mind."

I shook my head even as I agreed with that more than he could ever understand. "My sister, the felon who's currently serving eighteen months upstate for insider trading. Clearly, good parenting skills do not run in my family."

That got me a full-throated laugh. "You Allens sure do like to keep things interesting. So you finally got someone to take the kid off your hands? Good for you! That means we can get back to our Friday night poker games. I'm dying to get cards back in my hands after nearly two weeks."

"You better believe it," I said, practically salivating at the chance to take him for all he's worth. "But the kid is still here. I just brought in a nanny to take care of her. From the sound of no crying, I'd say she's working out fine."

"A nanny? What are we talking here? Barely out of high school and totally fuckable, or warden from a German women's prison?"

I shuddered at the thought of the latter and tried to find the right way to describe Tia Morton. "I didn't really pay that much attention to her, but she smells nice. Like flowers."

Charles let out a sigh of exasperation. "Man, is she old or young?"

"Young," I said, trying to gauge her age in my mind. "Maybe early twenties."

"Okay, now we're getting somewhere. Pretty? You would have noticed if she was hideous, right? I mean, you're all business all the time, but you do notice good looking women occasionally, right, Nico?"

I preferred when we were discussing poker and enjoying the idea of him losing his shirt to me. "I don't know. She wasn't hideous, no. I guess she might be pretty. I want to say she has reddish blond hair."

"A strawberry blond?" Charles asked in a tone full of amazement.

"Yeah. That might be what color it is. Why do you say that like I have some rare gem in my possession here? Fuck, I don't care what she looks like as long as she gets that kid to stop her goddamned crying."

I really didn't. She could have looked like that warden from a German women's prison he mentioned for all I cared. Her looks had nothing to do with what I was paying her for.

"You know, Nico, my father used to say strawberry blonds were the sexiest women on earth," Charles said in a dreamy voice. "We might have to set up the poker game at your house this week so I can catch a glimpse of this nanny of yours."

"Your father was married six times, Charles. He thought every women he ever met was the sexiest thing in the world. Then he married them and they got unsexy really quick."

My assessment of his father's outlook on women made Charles laugh. "The old man sure did love being married. I swear he would have gone for a seventh time if he didn't drop dead. Thankfully, he only had one child with each wife, so I only have five siblings. Can you imagine if he had a handful with each? Jesus, we could fill our own bus just with our family."

The mere thought of that many children made me cringe. I'd had one in my house for less than a full week, and I was fairly certain a few more days of her racket and I would have gone straight out of my mind.

"What happened with you then?" I teased him.

Charles had no children and didn't seem on the path to ever having any. A sports agent, he was completely immersed in his work and his clients' success.

"I've got better things to do than run around after rugrats. There's a world to conquer, and that won't wait for me to change diapers. Plus, can you really imagine me having a kid with any of the women I sleep with? Christ, I don't think a single one of them would know what to do with the business end of a baby."

Spoken like a true bachelor.

His way of describing what I assumed was the part that needed a diaper made me laugh, and I lifted my feet up onto my desk to relax as I tried to imagine him with a baby. Nope. There was a picture my mind simply couldn't conjure up.

"Tell the guys that we can do the poker game here this Friday, but you better come ready to go home poor," I said with as much cockiness as I had inside me.

"Big talk from the one guy who couldn't find an ace to save his life last time," he teased.

With a shrug, I said, "That was then. This is now. I'm a new man today. Plus, you don't need an ace in every hand to win."

"Fine. I'll give you that. What time Friday? So I can tell everyone else. Regular time? Eight?" he asked just as something flew by my office window.

I stood up to see what it was and answered, "Eight works. Come hungry. I'm in the mood for wings like my cook makes them. You know the ones with that tangy sauce he swears doesn't have red pepper in them but my tongue says it definitely does? I'm going to have him make a ton of them, so you guys need to bring your appetites."

Outside in the backyard, Tia and Grace played ball, tossing it back and forth. The little girl missed it every time, and when she threw it back to her nanny, she didn't come anywhere close. Tia had to run to get it every time before the wind took it away, but for the first time, I noticed Grace smiling like she was genuinely happy.

"Hmmm, maybe she isn't the worst kid in the world," I mumbled, forgetting I was still talking to my friend.

"What?"

"Nothing," I said as I continued to watch the two of them playing outside in the grass. "Just that the nanny has my niece outside and the kid is actually smiling and laughing. I wasn't sure she had the ability to do either of those things after watching her for the past few days."

Completely disinterested in the child, Charles asked, "So what's your assessment of the nanny? Hot or not?"

I stared out at Tia and took a good, long look at her. She had a nice body, but she was petite. She seemed athletic, or at least it appeared so by the way she ran after that ball Grace kept chucking all over the yard. She was laughing too, and I had to admit she looked beautiful at that moment.

"She's not bad. Young, but she has a nice smile."

"Man, I'm not interested in her teeth. What the fuck do you think I am? A goddamned horse doctor? What about her body? Does she have a nice rack? Hot ass? Give me some details, Nico. I'm dying here."

For a guy who didn't want kids and had no interest in getting married, Charles was a horndog.

I let my gaze travel down Tia's body and sighed. "Okay rack. They look a little small for your taste since you prefer bigger tits, but not bad. Her ass is sort of small, again not really your style. Come to think of it, Tia might be the polar opposite of your taste."

A heavy sigh of disappointment filled my ear before he said, "Oh, well. They can't all be movie stars. I'll have to check her out this Friday when I come to take you to the cleaners. See you then!"

"Right! Eight sharp," I said before ending the call and stuffing my phone into my pants pocket.

I should have gone back to work, but something about the way Tia and Grace looked playing outside kept me standing at that window. Who would have thought that not even an hour after arriving at this house the nanny would have made my niece change so much already?

Thanks to Mr. DeVille, my life was my own again and the kid was happy. I knew calling him would be a good idea.

CHAPTER 3

ia

GRACE AND I SAT AT THE TABLE IN HER UNCLE'S cavernous kitchen eating breakfast, but I noticed she kept glancing over toward the empty chair where I assumed Mr. Allen sat for meals. She seemed almost sullen this morning, but then again, maybe she wasn't a morning person. I'd only known her for slightly more than a week, so we hadn't exactly learned all there was to know about each other yet.

"How is that French toast, Grace? I think Michael tried to make it extra special for you this morning," I said sweetly.

Without looking at me, she answered, "Okay," in her tiny voice but didn't take another bite of her breakfast.

Something was definitely wrong.

"French toast is your favorite, right?"

She nodded once. "Yeah."

"Is something wrong? Do you want to talk about it?"

For a moment, she simply stared down at her plate, but then she finally turned to look at me. In her eyes, I saw real sadness. I didn't know the full story behind where her parents were that meant she had to stay here with her uncle, but I silently wondered if maybe that was the issue this morning. This was an entirely new experience for her, and from the way Mr. Allen acted toward her on that first day when I arrived at this house, it had to have been a traumatic one.

Thankfully, he'd been absent from all the areas of the property where Grace and I spent time since that first day. All that anger and negativity wasn't good for a child.

It wasn't good for anyone.

"Why doesn't Uncle Nico like me?" she asked quietly.

In her big blue eyes, now I saw something more than sadness. In them, I saw hurt. What a son of a bitch he was! The child had to be without her mother and father. Wasn't that bad enough? Did he have to make things worse for Grace by acting like an ogre?

It was up to me to make sure she knew whatever he felt had nothing to do with her. All she needed to worry about was if it would rain today and cancel our plans to go outside and if Michael would make her grilled cheese for the fourth day in a row. She didn't need to worry herself about the utter rudeness and unkindness of her uncle.

Reaching over, I gently touched her forearm and smiled as I shook my head. "Your uncle likes you, Grace. I'm sure he loves you. You're his family. He's just a bit tense because of work. That's all. I'm sure if he could take a vacation, you'd see he'd be so much fun."

Every word of that was a lie. I didn't think Mr. Allen liked her. In fact, I was relatively sure he didn't like anyone in this house, including himself. As for her being family, I didn't think he gave a damn about that either. I hated making excuses for his bad behavior. No matter what hassles his work threw at him, he shouldn't have ever been so callous with her.

Not that I actually thought he was a miserable bastard because of his work. I suspected that was just his personality. He didn't think about other people's feelings before he opened his mouth. In truth, I thought he was merely a selfish son of a bitch who chose not to be nice, even to a five year old little girl.

"He never smiles at me like you do. He just frowns and stomps his feet when he walks away," she said sadly.

"I have a lot to smile about. Maybe he doesn't. I mean, having a big house might not make him happy. Some people are like that. Me? I'm happy because I get to spend time with you."

That brought a smile that lit up her round face. "I wish he was like you."

Me too, honey. Me too.

"Do you think if I made him something he'd be happy? At school, we made macaroni pictures, and it was fun. Can I make him one?" she asked with such hopefulness that I couldn't say no.

Even though I worried he'd throw the thing back in her face the second she handed it to him. I wasn't sure I'd be able to hold my tongue if he did that.

"Sure! Finish your breakfast, and then we'll have your uncle's driver take us to the store in town. Let's see, we'll need those little elbow macaroni, right? And glue. Are we thinking glitter, or are we going low key?"

As she rushed to stuff the remaining piece of French toast into her mouth, she said, "Defritly glibber. Purple wif silfer amd gof sparfles."

Laughing, I tried to figure out what she meant. "What? Swallow first and then tell me."

Grace gulped the rest of her breakfast down and smiled. "Purple glitter with silver and gold sparkles."

"Okay. Purple, silver, and gold it is. When you're done, we'll get busy."

"Can we make it outside?" Grace asked with big eyes full of hope.

Turning to look out the window, I saw an autumn breeze blowing the leaves around in the yard. I hated to disappoint her, but as much as I loved going outside, I was pretty sure this morning's project wouldn't survive the gusts.

"I think inside might be a better idea. We don't

want all that glitter flying off the macaroni. That would ruin the whole look, don't you think?"

A bright child, she understood completely and nodded while she lifted her glass of milk to her lips. "Yeah. I want the glitter to stick to the macaroni elbows."

The way she said that made me giggle. The thought of a doctor telling a patient they were afflicted with macaroni elbow settled into my brain, and I shook my head at the silliness.

With pride, Grace pointed down at the empty plate in front of her and beamed a smile. "All done. Time for macaroni art. My teacher said that every mommy and daddy loves macaroni pictures. Do you think uncles do too?"

I stood up and moved her plate full of syrup away from her so her long blond hair didn't dip into it when she got up from the table. "I'm sure uncles and aunts love them too. All adults do. I mean, who doesn't love food stuck to paper with glue and covered in glitter? You'd have to be crazy not to love that."

As she slid off her chair and bounded across the room, I yelled after her, "We need to brush your teeth before we go anywhere, so head to your bathroom. If you didn't get any French toast or syrup on your clothes, you can wear the ones you have on, but we need to brush away all that sugar before it settles into your teeth and gives you cavities."

She skipped into the hallway toward her room on the other side of the house singing, "First I brush, and then it's art time!"

How Mr. Allen could ever be cruel to her I had no idea.

GRACE SQUEEZED OUT ANOTHER GLOB OF GLUE IN the top corner of the piece of blue construction paper and then dumped the last of the purple glitter onto the white liquid, covering it completely. We couldn't get purple with silver and gold specks, but she'd been happy to find the last tube of bright purple glitter on the very back of the shelf at that store in town. I worried it had been sitting there for a decade or more, so I cautioned her that sometimes glitter didn't act like it should, but as soon as she got the top off and started shaking it over the glued macaroni, it came out perfectly.

Well, too perfectly, I suspected by the way Agatha gave us a disgusted side eyed look as she passed through the kitchen where we set up our art project. I made sure to tell her that I'd clean everything up, including any stray glitter that made its way off the table. When she pursed her lips and groaned, I got the sense she didn't believe me, but I'd take care of it.

You'd think no one in this house had ever been a child at some point. Were they all born old and miserable?

Her hands covered in glue and glitter, Grace sat back in her chair and pointed at her creation. "I hope Uncle Nico likes it. I've never made any macaroni art as good as this one."

She moved to touch her face, so I quickly lifted her

up in my arms and carried her over to the farmhouse sink at the other side of the kitchen. "Let's get you washed up and brush off any glitter you got on your shirt before you take your present to your uncle. We have to let it dry for a few minutes, so let me have those hands."

Grace lifted them in front of my face and giggled. "I'm like a purple monster, Tia! Grrr!"

I turned on the water and grabbed her wrists before she made me a purple monster too. "Under the water you go. Here's the soap. I want you to get under your fingernails too. I think we might have to trim them today. Suds up!"

She did exactly as I told her to, and after I brushed off all the remaining glitter clinging to her pink and white polka dot shirt, I stood her on her feet next to me. "I just have to clean out the sink and the table and the floor so nobody gets glitter all over them when they come in to eat. Then I think we can take your picture to your uncle. How does that sound?"

"Yes! Do you think he's going to love it? I love it. Don't you?" she asked excitedly.

As I rinsed away the last of the glitter down the drain, I nodded. "I do. Lots of blue and purple is perfect for an uncle. Very masculine."

"I used only a little silver glitter for his name. I thought that would make it look good," she said confidently, sure her art was the best ever.

Taking her hands in mine, I led her over to the towel sitting on the counter. "Let's dry those hands.

We don't want to ruin the picture with wet hands, do we?"

A look of terror settled into her beautiful face, and she shook her head. "No. Not after all I did to make it perfect."

"Then let's make sure there's not a drop of water on your skin. Dry really good, okay?"

As obedient as always with me, she did exactly as I told her to and then lifted her hands to show me they were dry. With a smile, she said, "All dry. Can we take the picture to him now?"

I loved how sweet and caring she was, so even though I worried he wouldn't accept her gift with the same kindness of spirit, I nodded and forced myself to smile. "Now seems as good a time as any. Just let me wipe down the table so Agatha doesn't get any stray glitter on her."

"Why?" Grace asked as we walked back to where she'd created her masterpiece. "Doesn't she like glitter?"

I shrugged, thinking to myself that Agatha didn't seem to like much of anything. Maybe prunes. I could see her liking those. Not glitter, though. That was too happy, too lighthearted for her.

With the kitchen cleaned of all hints of our time in there, I walked with Grace as she clutched her gift for her uncle in her hands. She beamed such happiness with every step that I told myself he had to melt at least a little bit today.

When we got to his office, I stopped her just

outside the door. "Let me knock first just in case he's in a meeting."

Wide-eyed and excited, she nodded, bouncing on her toes as the moment had nearly arrived to unveil her art for him. I knocked on his office door and heard him grumble something about coming in if I had to. Not exactly the welcome I had hoped for, but I still wanted to think this would turn out well for Grace.

Taking her by the hand, I walked her into his office and said, "Mr. Allen, Grace made you a little present and wanted to give it to you as soon as she could."

She held out the piece of construction paper, now rigid from all the glue and macaroni plastered to it, and smiled up at him as he sat at his desk. "This is for you, Uncle Nico. I made it with macaroni and glue and two kinds of glitter. It's a picture of birds flying over the house like I saw yesterday when Tia and I were outside. Do you like it?"

A look of pure disgust twisted his expression into something one might expect at seeing a dead body or a car wreck. Reluctantly, he took the paper by the very edge and dropped it onto the corner of his desk without a word.

I waited for him to say something—anything to let Grace know her gift was appreciated—but he merely sat there staring in horror at what she'd made him. The feel of the room grew tenser by the moment, and when I looked down at her, I saw she understood just how little he valued her thoughtful gift.

"Isn't it nice, Mr. Allen? Grace made it all by

herself," I said, hoping to shake loose something kind inside him.

But all he did was look up at me with that same expression of disgust he'd worn since she handed him her artwork made especially for him. "It looks like it. Isn't the glitter supposed to stick to the glue? It's getting all over the place. I can't have that in my office here. This is a place of business, for God's sake."

Out of the corner of my eye, I watched as Grace's entire body sagged, her spirit deflated from his ungrateful attitude and his unwillingness to utter even a single caring word after she gave him a present. She ran out of the room crying, leaving me standing there alone with him, and something inside me snapped.

I'd had enough of this man, and now he was going to get a dose of his own medicine.

"You couldn't even say thank you? What kind of person gets handed a homemade gift from a child like that and can't say thank you?"

Rolling his eyes, he sat back in his chair and shook his head. "I don't thank people for bringing me garbage. Are you going to clean up this mess? No. I'm going to have to get someone in here, and that's going to take more time out of my busy day."

"You are the worst person I've ever met in my life. How on earth did anyone in your family think you were the best choice to take care of this little girl?" I barked.

"My sister, in her infinite wisdom, got herself thrown in prison for insider trading, and since she reproduced with some nutjob who spends his time worrying about his aura or other bullshit real adults don't give a damn about, I got stuck with this job since I'm her only sibling. That's how this happened."

I shook my head, utterly disgusted by the man sitting in front of me. "She asked me this morning why you don't like her, and then she made that picture just for you because she so desperately wants you to like her. We had to go shopping for the construction paper, the glue, and the glitter, which by the way, she agonized over what colors to use to make it manly enough for you, her dear uncle. She shouldn't have bothered. You're no kind of man. A real man would be kind to a child no matter what when she handed him a gift."

As I turned on my heel to leave, he tried to stop me. "Now see here, Miss Morton. I won't let you insult me like that. You work for me."

I glanced back and him and shrugged. "I work for Mr. DeVille, who warned me you could be brusque. He didn't warn me you were a petty asshole who got his kicks being cruel to little girls. Feel free to fire me, Mr. Allen, but I'll tell you this. I won't let you be nasty to Grace anymore, and if I go, then I'm going to make sure I contact the authorities to tell them how you treat that child. Good day!"

My entire body shook as I marched down the hallway from his office. I'd never spoken to anyone like that in my life. I was usually mild mannered Tia, the woman who barely made a peep when people did things to upset me. But something about the way he made her feel so terrible and the look on her face as she ran out of his office made it impossible for me to hold back my anger.

Unfortunately, I probably just got myself terminated. I hurried toward Grace's room to comfort her, pushing that reality out of my mind for the moment. I found her on her bed crying, so I climbed in next to her and wrapped my arms around her as her tiny body shuddered from her sobs.

"I'm sorry, honey. Some people just don't know how to accept gifts."

"He hated it. I tried to make it pretty, but he hated it. Why did he hate it, Tia?"

Because he's a selfish jackass.

I couldn't tell her the truth, so I gave her a tiny squeeze and said quietly, "Some people just don't know what to do with kindness. You're going to find that in the world, but don't let that change you, Grace. You keep being exactly how you are, okay?"

She took a deep breath and sighed. "Okay."

Desperate to make her happy again, I whispered into her ear, "What do you say we go outside this afternoon and eat s'mores at the picnic table in the backyard? Michael told me he has all the things we need."

Grace eagerly rolled over to face me and smiled. "Can we do it now?"

I nodded, unsure if I'd still be here as her nanny this afternoon. Better to let her last memories of me be happy ones full of chocolate, marshmallows, and leaves swirling around us as we gorge ourselves on too many sweets.

"Sure! Let's go!"

A half hour later, the two of us sat at that picnic table with the autumn wind making our cheeks red and stuffed from too many s'mores but happy. And that's all that counted. Kids needed to know nothing, not even the hurt a family member could deliver, lasted longer than a good time and chocolate.

While she chased leaves around the yard, her energy level amped up from way too much sugar that morning, I saw Mr. Allen standing in his office window watching us. How a man could be so cruel to a child who simply wanted to show him she cared left me wondering what in the world could have happened to make him so empty and cold.

Not that it mattered much. He was who he was. Nothing was going to change that. I likely wouldn't have much of a chance to do anything at this house since he probably had called Mr. DeVille and fired me already.

I regretted nothing, though. If defending a child's happiness got me canned, so be it. There were far more egregious things done in this world, and if that was my biggest crime, I'd wear it as a badge of honor.

When I glanced over at his office window again, I saw him standing there with a woman who looked like some supermodel. Nearly his height and definitely around six foot tall, she wore a long black sweater dress that looked like someone had spray painted it on. Like him, she didn't seem to be impressed by Grace's joyful racing around the yard chasing leaves either.

The two of them made a perfect pair. Both

attractive people who couldn't find a reason to smile to save their lives. I just hoped she wasn't going to be a fixture around this house because after I left, I didn't know who would make sure Grace was protected from Mr. Allen's cruelty.

It certainly wouldn't be his model friend there, that's for sure.

ico

AMANDA HUFFED HER DISGUST AT THE SCENE unfolding outside in my yard and then marched over to sit on the couch near my desk. I stood at the window for a few seconds more, staring out at the mouthy nanny who had basically told me to go fuck myself not an hour before. She saw me looking at her and glared at me, practically boring holes through my head and never turning away.

She certainly did have courage. Not that I necessarily liked courage in people who told me off and made me feel like I was second only to Attila the Hun when it came to hurting children.

As I turned to deal with Amanda, I could have sworn Tia threw me the finger. So much for her being a typical nanny. Mary Poppins she wasn't, for sure.

"Do you have another family member shacking up here at your house?" Amanda asked as she leaned back against the couch to show off her long legs peeking out from under her black dress.

"No. That's the nanny. Tia. She's very good with my niece, thank God," I explained as I sat down next to her on the couch.

"She looks like some kind of reject from the Good Ship Lollypop," Amanda said before smoothing her long brown hair along the side of her face. "I didn't realize women actually looked like that anymore since the internet. Has she never seen the way real women do their makeup and hair?"

Typical Amanda. Christ, was she ever not a bitch?

"I don't care what she looks like. She could look like the wicked witch of the west for all I care. As long as she handles my niece, I'm happy."

"What does she do with her exactly? I mean, how old is the child?" Amanda asked like just saying the words made her feel queasy.

I thought about that question and realized I didn't know what Tia and Grace did all day. All I knew was the past nearly two weeks had been far quieter than that first week and the little girl hadn't cried since Tia's arrival, so my workdays weren't interrupted.

Well, not until this morning.

"She does arts and crafts with her. That I know. She sits with her for meals, I think. Not that I've eaten any with them, but I think she does that since Agatha was happy to tell me she doesn't have to perform that job now that Tia is here."

Amanda turned her body toward me and ran her fingernail across my sleeve just above my wrist. "So she's a live-in?"

"Yes. I didn't want to take the chance that my niece would need someone at night and there would be no one around to take care of her, so Tia stays in the room next to Grace. So far, it's worked like a dream."

With a sexy grin, she let her gaze run over my body. "So you aren't alone at nights? Pity. I was thinking I should stop over sometime and we could get together."

She never failed to hit on me when she came for an appointment, even though we'd been broken up for over a year already. Neither one of us really wanted to get together, even to sleep with one another, but it was so ingrained in Amanda's DNA to flirt with men anytime they were close that she couldn't help herself.

It's one of the reasons why we weren't a couple anymore. That and her cheating on me with some stockbroker she met at a party a few weeks before we broke up.

I stopped her hand as she made her way up my thigh. "So you want to buy a building for some business you want to start? Is that what I understood from our phone call?"

Her expression fell, like she was having fun and I ruined it for her. "Yes, but I don't know why you can't let me enjoy myself for a few minutes before we get all involved in talking business. You really need to learn to lighten up, Nico. Smile for a change. Let a woman admire you. You have a great body. I should know. Relax and enjoy a good time when it's offered to you."

She sounded vaguely like Tia had when she was reprimanding me a little while ago. Of course, Amanda's admonitions were couched in her own pleasure while Tia's were centered in my not being a complete and total dick to my five year old niece, but at their foundations, both women were saying essentially the same thing.

"I prefer sticking to business," I said as I stood up to walk over to my desk. "It's far less messy than anything you're suggesting."

Amanda followed me, and as she leaned over to show off the two best body parts she possessed, she knocked over Grace's pasta art onto the floor. Looking down at it as it sailed to its landing place near her feet, she kicked the paper away in disgust.

"Ugh! What is that? Did that just get glitter all over my brand new suede boots, Nico? Why is that in here?"

I leaned down to pick up my gift and set it down on the other side of my desk. "It's from my niece. She made it this morning. I'm sure if any glitter got on your boots that you can just brush it off," I said calmly, pretty much dismissing her near hysterics about a little shiny stuff getting on her.

She frantically rubbed her black boots like paint had been dumped on them. "Why are children always so messy? Oh my God! How are you living like this, Nico? When we were together, you couldn't handle a single piece of lint on you, and now you're dealing with glitter, of all things, all over the place?"

Clearly, we had moved into hysteria mode already. I didn't exactly like children or having them around, but at least I didn't act like this over a tiny hint of glitter in the air.

Well, not really. I had good reason to be surly before. Tia and Grace interrupted me at work. My work was the most important thing in my life. Everyone on staff here knew, so why didn't she think about that before bringing that child to my office in the middle of the day?

"It's my cross to bear, for sure, but I'll handle it."

"It seems like my brand new Louboutins are handling it. These boots cost more than that child is worth. Doesn't she know not to get glitter all over the place? God, what is that nanny of hers doing all day? I'd fire her, Nico. It's not like nannies aren't a dime a dozen."

Ignoring her, I focused on the reason for her being here today. "Now about that building you want to buy. I say we map out a strategy today and then I'll see what I can do to get the price down to somewhere in the ballpark of what you'll want to pay."

Again, Amanda leaned over my desk to show off her assets courtesy of the best plastic surgeon in New York and turned her attention to her favorite subject. Her. "See, that's my Nico. That's the man I came to see. Let's get me that building."

As I typed into my laptop to bring the listing up on

my screen, I asked, "What is this business you want to start again?"

She began talking about some idea of hers to make dog biscuits with peanut butter in them like her two Chihuahuas loved, but I stopped listening a few sentences in. I always hated those dogs when we were together. She'd bring them on our dates, and it never failed whenever she had her head turned, one of the damn things would come up out of her oversized purse and bite me.

Thank God she knew better than to bring them here to my home. That's all I needed. I already had enough hassle with a kid. I didn't need two yapping dogs around too.

An hour later, she breezed out of my office, happier than when she walked in and just how I prefer my clients to be when they leave an appointment with me. I made a few notes about the property in Amanda's file and then walked over to the window to see if Tia and Grace were still outside.

Oddly enough, I felt disappointed when I didn't see them. I didn't know why. It's not like any of us were close. In fact, I wasn't close to anyone.

I pushed that ridiculous thought out of my mind and made my way to the kitchen to get lunch. I walked in and saw Tia sitting at the table reading a book, and for some reason, I couldn't stop myself from mentioning part of what Amanda had said about her.

"My client thought you were another niece of mine. You must have looked very young to her," I said with a chuckle.

As I walked to the refrigerator, I heard her say, "Well, I guess a man your age could have a niece my age, so maybe she was only stating the obvious."

Slamming the door, I spun around to face her. "I don't know how old you think I am, but I'm not even forty. I'm barely thirty-five, so the idea that I could have a niece your age is ridiculous."

Tia carefully set her book on the kitchen table and nodded. "Your sister could be much older than you. Maybe you were a late-in-life baby for your parents."

"Well, she isn't and I wasn't," I said, correcting her even as my temper began to rise.

Standing up, she picked up her book and shrugged. "You act much older than your age, so you can't blame me for thinking you were in your mid-forties."

"You know, you might want to try to show some respect. I am your boss," I said, furious by this time.

"I'll tell you what, Mr. Allen. Since it seems like you don't plan to fire me, I'll take that criticism if you'll take mine. Respect isn't just for bosses. It's for little girls who cared enough to make you and purple and silver macaroni picture too."

I watched her walk out into the hallway, leaving me stunned and feeling like I'd just been slapped across the face. Not only didn't she like or respect me, but she thought I was old.

Mid-fucking-forties old.

CHAPTER 5

ia

AFTER AN EARLY MORNING DRIZZLE THAT evaporated as soon as the warmth of the day settled in, Grace and I decided to take a walk through the neighborhood to get to know it better. Hand in hand, we strolled down the streets around Mr. Allen's house. Each home in the area had all the hallmarks of opulence like his home, and as she and I took in all the sights and sounds, I told her about my childhood growing up in Brooklyn, a very different place compared to this one.

"Was it noisy?" Grace asked after the lone car on our journey whizzed by us.

I thought about that for a few seconds and nodded. "Sort of. I think it was just that there were so many more people around than here. Like you see how there's all this space between houses around here? Like everyone has big yards and huge walls and fences around their homes? That isn't how it is where I come from. We lived in a little house compared to your uncle's. It was my mother, my father, my sister, and me. We didn't really have much of a yard, but we had a little one where we would sit and play for hours."

"What's your sister's name?" she asked with a look of utter curiosity in her eyes.

"Sara. My mother has a thing for the letter A," I said with a laugh.

Grace didn't understand what I thought was funny, of course, since she was only five, but I had a feeling she understood quite clearly that she wished she had someone close to her age like a sister to play with. I'd never met an only child who didn't wonder if life would have been better if they had a sister or brother to play with instead of always being alone.

After a minute or so, she said quietly, "I wish my mommy had a sister for me. Then I'd have someone to play with."

I squeezed her hand and swung our joined arms out in front of us. "Well, you have me. What do you want to do? You tell me, and I'll make it happen."

Grace pointed her little forefinger toward the woods in front of us at the end of Revere Road. "Can we go for a walk in there? I can pick up leaves and acorns. There aren't any left in the yard."

Swiveling my head left and right to check the area for anyone who might look like they would take advantage of a young woman and a little girl, I saw no one. I didn't want to tell her no since I said I'd make whatever she wanted to do happen, but taking her into the woods hadn't been in my mind when I made that promise.

Nevertheless, I nodded and smiled down at her. "Sure!"

When we reached the edge of the trees, she eagerly began pulling on my arm to get me to move faster, but we had some prep to do before we walked in there. "Not so fast, Grace. We need to tuck your pants into your socks first."

I crouched down and began getting her ready for whatever nature may have had waiting for us. Above me, she asked, "Why do I have to have my pants like that? I don't when we play in the yard."

Every warning about Lyme Disease my parents repeated every summer when my sister and I would go off to summer camp repeated in my mind as I moved to her other pant leg. When I finished, I looked up at her and explained, "We want whatever is living in the woods to stay there, and if it decides to come back home with us, then it needs to travel on the outside of your clothes. No hanging out on your legs. Those are for you only."

I punctuated my words with a smile and patted her ankles, now protected against ticks. "All set! Ready to do some exploring?"

"Yes!" she squealed before running down the well-worn path into the woods.

"Wait for me! And don't touch anything! The last

thing we need to do is bring back poison ivy to your uncle's house. His head will explode."

Not that I wouldn't secretly enjoy that after how nasty he'd been.

OUR TIME IN THE WOODS NETTED GRACE ENOUGH leaves for her to create an autumn picture she had planned, ten acorns that would adorn the outside of the paper as a border to frame her masterpiece, and zero ticks, thankfully. I still made her undress completely and put on all new clothes while I shook her old ones out in the yard, just in case.

By the time she finished, she looked so exhausted I wasn't sure she'd make it another hour to lunch, so nap time took precedence. She barely got her head down on her pillow before her eyelids fluttered closed and she was out like a light.

As my mother always told me, fresh air can do wonders for a body. Maybe if Mr. Allen spent more time outside, he wouldn't have been such a bastard.

Happy to let Grace sleep until lunch, I made my way down to the kitchen to find a snack and to read a little more of my book. Oddly enough, in my time at this house, I'd found that the quietest place always seemed to be the kitchen. In most homes, the kitchen was the hub of the family, but since there was essentially no family here and merely a collection of people who worked for Mr. Allen, I guessed it wasn't a big a surprise that no one gathered in that room.

After grabbing some graham crackers and a cup of

hot chocolate, I settled into my favorite chair at the kitchen table right next to the window that overlooked the backyard and began reading at Chapter Thirteen. Someone was about to die, and the FBI agent on the killer's heels wouldn't get to the abandoned house in time.

Lost in the story, I didn't hear anyone join me until someone cleared their throat. I looked up from the page and saw Mr. Allen staring down at me like I was doing something that wasn't allowed in his home. Didn't he let anyone read in this place?

"Yes?" I said with so much sass that my dislike for him was obvious.

"What are you reading?" he asked in a far kinder tone.

I held up my paperback for him to see the cover. "Just a thriller I picked up one day at a used book store."

"Is it an interesting story?"

Nodding, I answered his question. "It is. On a chilly fall day, there's nothing better than a cup of hot cocoa, some cookies, and a good book. Grace is in her room taking a nap after our field trip this morning."

I honestly had no idea why I bothered telling him all of that. He never cared enough to ask me a thing about what she and I did together each day. As long as I kept her out of his sight, that's all that mattered. At any moment, I expected him to grumble about how he doesn't give a damn what we do as long as she stays away from him.

But he didn't seem to be in the mood to snap at me

like that this morning and walked over to the refrigerator as he said, "I haven't read a book in years. Not fiction, at least. You're right about there being nothing better than curling up with a good book. Some of us forget that sometimes."

For a few seconds, I didn't know what to say. He sounded downright pleasant now, and I definitely didn't want to do anything to put a stop to that. The problem was I had no idea how to respond to Mr. Allen acting like a decent human being.

So I said nothing. Instead, I simply waited for him to walk out and leave me to the impending death of that secondary character I was sure would occur on the next page.

He didn't leave, though.

As he pulled out the chair across the table from me, he asked, "Do you mind if I join you?"

Part of me instantly wanted to say, "Yes, if you're going to be that jackass you've been to me since I arrived here." However, he appeared to be making some kind of effort at kindness, so I gave him a tiny smile and said, "No, please do."

It was his house, after all.

He set his coffee cup down on the table and sat down, and all I could think of was how proper he sounded. Then again, wearing a three piece suit did tend to bring out the formal in anyone, I guessed. I wondered why he dressed like he had to go into the city when he worked out of his home.

"So my niece...Grace, is taking a nap? Where did you take her on your field trip?"

"Into the woods at the end of Revere Road a few blocks from here. Do you know if she's ever spent any real time in nature like that? Because she had a great time but I got a sense it was something brand new to her."

For the first time since I'd come to his home, Mr. Allen relaxed and sighed, blowing the air out of his lungs like I'd brought up a subject so weighty he didn't know how to answer. I opened my mouth to apologize, thinking I must have said something wrong, but then he began to speak, and I realized exactly how lost he was when it came to his niece.

"I doubt Grace has seen much of anything in the outdoors. My sister isn't much of a nature girl. Not that I am either, but I think I'm better than she is. Then again, that might change now that she's getting to enjoy the fine accommodations of prison courtesy of the State of New York for the next year and a half. As for Grace, I'm happy you take her out as much as you do. Children need that. I tend to forget those things."

"I'm sorry. I didn't mean to bring up a sore subject, Mr. Allen."

He shook his head and smiled. "You can call me Nico, Tia. I know you think I'm as old as Methuselah, but I don't require you to call me Mr. Allen. Really."

As he joked about how old I thought he was, referring to my snappy comments from yesterday, he winced. I shouldn't have been so mean. No matter what he did or said, I didn't need to be that way too.

Looking down toward my book, I closed it and

pushed it off to the side. "I'm sorry about what I said. I didn't mean to be so hurtful."

"You had every right to be. I acted like a goddamned monster when Grace gave me that pasta art she made me. I deserved everything you said and about a hundred things you didn't say but were probably thinking."

I looked up, surprised to hear him say that, and saw an expression of contrition on his face. He genuinely seemed to be sorry for acting so terribly toward Grace.

With a smile, I tried to make him feel a little better since that was my nature. "You know, I think if you showed her this side of you, she'd love to see it. She really only wants you to like her. She said that to me just the other day."

He nodded and sighed again. "I'm not really good with kids. I never have been. Maybe when I was a kid, but since then, nope. When I heard Fiona had given birth, all I could think of was why. She's no better with kids than I am, and even worse, she doesn't work at home where she can see the child whenever she wants. I mean, she didn't."

Nico stopped talking for a moment and ran his hand through his dark hair as a look of anguish settled into his chiseled features. "What a mess. Then they come to me and say I'm her only family since her father is God only knows where. Probably catching some wave on the coast of wherever. I don't think he was more than a fling to begin with, so I wouldn't be surprised if nobody even tried to locate him before they brought her here to me. As you have seen more than clearly, I'm not good for her either. Thank God DeVille Staffing found you."

"Anyone can be good for a child. You just have to open up a little."

I didn't know if I was overstepping my bounds, but I wanted to do whatever I could so Grace would know her uncle didn't hate her. He just had trouble understanding what children needed.

For a long moment, I held my breath and every muscle in my body tensed as I waited for him to lash out or bark at me, but nothing like that ever came. He simply sighed again, blowing the air out of his lungs even harder that time, and nodded.

"She seems like a nice kid."

"Oh, she is! She's incredible. You can have entire conversations with her, and don't think you need to do any of that baby talk with her because Grace is very bright. Your sister must be an exceptionally intelligent person because her daughter is so smart. I think you'd really enjoy talking to her if you took the time to have a conversation. And she's fun. She likes to laugh and tell stories and run around after leaves when they blow in the wind. She really is just the sweetest little girl."

I knew I was gushing about Grace, but not a word I said wasn't the absolute truth. In only a couple weeks, she'd become one of my favorite people in the entire world.

"I'm happy she has you around, Tia. Everyone deserves to have a fan like you are of Grace," he said, and underneath his words I sensed a hint of sadness.

Was it that he didn't have anyone to be a fan of him? Was that why he didn't know how to relate to his own niece? Was that why he seemed so cold and distant all the time?

Well, until now.

Something about the sound of his voice made me want to be nice to him, so I smiled and said, "You and your client yesterday seemed very much fans of one another. It's a lot like that for me and Grace."

My suggestion made him laugh, and he shook his head. "Not at all the same. You genuinely like her and she obviously feels the same way about you. Amanda is my ex-girlfriend, and while it looks like she actually likes me, that's not how it is at all. As for what I feel for her, let's just say that I don't need to touch a hot stove twice to know I'll get burned if I do it again."

I watched as he forced himself to smile and quickly stood up from the table. "Well, enough time off for me. My boss is a slave driver, so off to work I go."

"You should tell him you deserve time off," I said with a smile.

That made him laugh again. "I'm my boss, Tia. That was my attempt at a joke. Not very good, I guess."

Instantly, my cheeks felt like they were burning up. How embarrassing. I must have sounded like the dumbest person in the world. Of course, he's his own boss. What a dolt I could be sometimes.

"Oh, yeah. Duh. Sorry. Your joke was fine. I was just off in another world, I guess."

Grabbing his coffee cup, he looked over at me and

in his dark eyes I saw he didn't seem unhappy anymore. "Thanks for the talk. Maybe we could do it again sometime."

"I would like that. And as for Grace, just give yourself a chance with her. You'll see. It will pay off."

Nico smiled, and for the first time, he looked like a different man. A kinder man. A nicer man.

A sexier man.

"I'll do that. Thanks."

I watched him walk out of the kitchen and a thought hit me like a bolt of lightning. This Nico was downright hot. Who would have dreamed that would ever pop into my head?

On top of that, I had to admit something, even if only to myself. I think I wanted my boss. But that couldn't be possible for a dozen reasons. He was my boss, first of all. And doing anything with him could jeopardize my position as Grace's nanny, and that's the last thing I wanted to do.

Even more, I'd seen the type of woman he liked. His ex looked like a model, and I certainly didn't come anywhere close to that. He likely would never even give me a second glance.

But the most important reason even thinking about wanting Nico was impossible was that I hated him until about fifteen minutes ago.

ico

ALL DAY, I TRIED TO FOCUS ON MY WORK, BUT MY mind refused to obey and instead wandered off to focus on Tia. What was she doing? Where in the house was she at that moment? Were she and Grace outside playing in the side yard?

I lost count how many times I got up from my desk and walked over to glance out the window, my heart sinking every time I didn't see her. If I didn't know me, I'd have grabbed me by the shoulders and shook some sense into me.

Why was I getting all moony-eyed over the nanny? How fucking clichéd. The nanny. I didn't want to think of her like that. If I did, I worried my life was devolving into some sad Lifetime movie.

Christ, where did the Nico who could have any

woman he desired go? Maybe this was an aftereffect of having a child in the house. I'd heard that changes a guy.

No, that's fatherhood that changes a guy. Just having a kid around you didn't change anything, other than how much work you completed. First, it was Grace with all that screaming and crying, and now I sat in my office distracted as all hell hoping to catch a glimpse of Tia.

My life worked so much better before all these females started inhabiting my home. Before, my days ran like clockwork. Now, my days hobbled along like a pig on stilts.

As I silently wondered if I'd ever go back to the man I remembered being, I heard footsteps outside in the hallway. My heart skipped a beat, and I jumped up to rush over to the door.

"Who's there?" I asked in an eager voice I didn't recognize.

Agatha looked at me like she didn't know how to answer and stared for a few moments before answering, "It's just me, Mr. Allen. Is there something I can do for you?"

I shook my head, more in disbelief that I was acting like some lovesick schoolboy than answering her question, and gruffly said, "No. I'm fine. I don't like noise outside my office when I'm working. You know that."

"Yes, sir, but I didn't want the mess I saw in your hallway to turn into something bigger."

Looking up and down the spotless hallway, I

couldn't imagine what the hell this woman was talking about. Maybe it was something affecting the entire household because she was acting as out of character as I was.

"I don't see a thing, Agatha. What are you talking about?"

She opened up her hand to show me two tiny elbow macaroni pieces with glue and purple glitter stuck to them sitting in her palm. "Food on the floor, sir. That's the surest way to get ants, to say nothing of other creatures. I told that nanny not to make a mess, but here is the proof she didn't listen. If you ask me, she's too permissive with that child, and we're all going to pay for it."

As I listened to her attack Tia, the only thought in my head was to defend her. Since this was my housekeeper I was talking to, I didn't have to do that, but I intended on setting her straight.

"I didn't ask you, so keep your opinions about Tia to yourself. I haven't heard a single sob or seen a single negative thing with her or my niece in the entire time she's been at this house. Whatever she is, she's good for Grace, and that's all I care about."

The shocked look on Agatha's face told me I'd made my point. I turned on my heel and strode back into my office, slamming the door behind me. I didn't need my housekeeper telling me how to deal with my employees.

Not that I'd thought of Tia as anything close to an employee for the past five hours. My fantasies involved her being naked on my bed, not cleaning my niece's face after a fight with a peanut butter and jelly sandwich her lunch had won.

I needed to stop myself from thinking those things about Tia. I wasn't some newbie kid in business who didn't understand what kind of havoc sexually harassing some young woman would bring to my professional world. Christ, I'd laughed at men who couldn't be smart enough to keep it in their pants when it came to a co-worker.

So why was I sitting here at my desk rock hard and unable to think of anything but bending Tia over it?

Damnit, Nico. Get it together, man. If you need sex, Amanda is a phone call away.

But I didn't want to get back together with my ex. She didn't make me smile or make me want to be a better man. Only Tia did that.

Jesus. I was lost. How the hell had that happened?

I HID OUT IN MY OFFICE UNTIL I KNEW GRACE would be asleep in bed, and by ten o'clock I couldn't look at the four walls of that room any longer. Unsure what I'd say if I ran into her, I crept into the kitchen and grabbed some of the cook's leftover lamb stew before hurrying to my room.

That was what I had been reduced to by a beautiful young woman with big brown eyes. Hiding out in my office all day and then skulking around to go hide out in my room all night.

The lamb stew tasted incredible, as all of Michael's

food always did, and by the time I had gotten something in my stomach, I knew I'd been acting stupid all day. I wasn't some mindless thing who couldn't control his urges. So I wanted Tia. That wasn't a reason to lose my mind. I simply had to accept we couldn't be together.

There were millions of women in the world. I could be with any one of them. Problem solved.

Happy I'd gotten my focus back, I took my dinner dishes to the kitchen and headed back to my room. A good night's sleep would do wonders for me, and tomorrow I'd be back to my normal self again.

"Mr. Allen? I mean, Nico?"

Just the sound of her voice made my cock harden, and I looked behind me to see Tia standing in the main hallway. Her hair up in a ponytail and wearing pink yoga pants with a white T-shirt, she looked completely fuckable, like some perfect wet dream standing just feet away from me.

"Hi, Tia. Everything okay?"

With a smile, she said, "Oh, yeah. I was just bored and thought I'd stretch my legs. I hope I didn't wake you up."

"No, not at all. I was thinking the same thing. Long day at the office. Sitting all day. You know."

Christ, I used to be able to charm women merely with a smile and a few words. Now I sounded like a pimply-faced teenager who had never had sex. What power did this woman possess over me?

"I guess running your own business is pretty stressful. I don't think I'd be able to do it."

And now we'd transitioned to talking about work. The next topic would be the weather and then I'd be listed in the hall of fame of losers when it came to women. People would walk by my exhibit in that sad and pathetic museum and shake their heads at how pitiful a grown man could be in the presence of a beautiful woman.

"I'm sure you would. It just takes discipline."

I'd never been this close to woman I wanted to sleep with and said such mundane things. She probably regretted her decision to take a walk tonight.

Tia took a few steps toward me and stopped before taking a deep breath. "I'm not going to sleep anytime soon. If you wanted to have that talk you mentioned earlier, that could be nice."

I knew I shouldn't take her up on her offer. I'd told myself I wasn't going to do anything stupid. Yet having her this close and being able to smell the vanilla scent of her shampoo as it wafted up to my nose made saying no impossible.

"That would be nice. Do you want to go to the kitchen? There's some lamb stew left, if you're hungry."

Tia took another step and stopped right in front of me. Looking up at me with those big brown eyes, she said, "If you want. Or if there's somewhere else you'd be comfortable, we could go there too."

I didn't say a word before I took her hand and led her to my room. Red flags were flying up in my head all over the place, but I didn't care. I wanted to feel

K.M. SCOTT

this beautiful woman beneath me screaming my name in the heat of passion.

Closing the door to my room, I thought about talking but the truth was I didn't want to talk. I wanted to fuck this woman. Tia had been on my mind all day, and now that she'd given me the signal she wanted me too, I didn't want to hesitate.

She smiled up at me, her eyes wide and looking so innocent that for a split second, I wondered if this was right. Tia was my niece's nanny, and that technically made her my employee. I'd sat through enough seminars on proper workplace behavior to know I shouldn't act on my desires.

That thought flew out of my mind when she pressed her palms to my chest and need rushed through me. Right or wrong, I was having the nanny tonight.

I took her beautiful face in my hands and kissed her perfect mouth. My cock stiffened so it pressed against my stomach, making an ache form in my balls. It had been too long since I enjoyed a night with a woman. All work and no play made for a very horny Nico.

When I pulled away, she asked, "So I guess you don't want to talk?"

Her sexy smile told me that was meant to be playful, so I shook my head and answered, "Not tonight."

She trailed her fingertips over my ribs and down to my waist. Staring up into my eyes, she slowly unfastened my belt and opened my pants.

The nanny wasn't so innocent after all.

"Can I confess something?" she asked as she slid her hand under my boxer briefs.

With the first touch of her fingers on my cock, I had a hard time forming an answer to her question, so I nodded and closed my eyes to revel in the feel of her stroking me.

"At first I didn't like you at all, but once the mean guy turned into the nice guy I was talking to in the kitchen today, this was all I could think about."

She stopped jerking me off, and I opened my eyes to see her on her knees in front of me. Tia looked like a fucking goddess with a mouth that needed to be fucked.

And I was the man to do it.

"So you like nice guys?" I asked, sure what I planned to do next disqualified me from that description.

Tia smiled and shook her head. "Not so much."

I stuffed my hands into her hair and pulled her mouth toward my cock, but she took it from there and a second later, her lips wrapped around the head and nearly sent me into outer space with how good it felt. Inch by inch, she swallowed all of me, her tongue flicking the underside of my cock as she moved down to the base, all the while looking up at me with those innocent doe eyes that only made me want to fuck her even more.

Jesus, this felt like heaven. My fantasies about Tia all day had been nothing compared to the real thing. I clearly had suffered from a lack of imagination when it came to how good it would feel to have her suck my cock.

I tightened my hands in her hair and felt the silky strands pull against my fingers when I began thrusting my hips. Her eyes grew wider for only a second, but then it was as if she knew exactly what to do. Grasping my thighs, she took everything I gave her without gagging or wanting to stop.

Every time I hit the back of her throat, I moaned, each one growing louder and louder until the room filled with the sound of her giving me the best blowjob of my life. I hadn't been with anyone after Amanda, so it didn't take long before every cell in my body wanted the one thing it hadn't had in far too many months.

The pure pleasure of coming with a woman.

Tia sensed it too, and she closed her eyes while she sucked all of me into her mouth. That's all I needed, and a second later, I came harder than I ever had. She took it all too, and when I finished, I stumbled back against the door, my legs barely able to hold my weight.

With a smile, she stood up and said, "That was fun. Reciprocating is fun too."

I knew what she meant, but that would have to wait for another time. Now, I wanted to know how great it felt to be buried inside her.

Pulling her to me, I kissed that mouth that had just given me such incredible pleasure and made quick work of her clothes, tossing them off to the side so I could see her body for the first time. When she was naked in front of me, I stopped to appreciate how beautiful she truly was.

Full breasts led to a tiny waist and shapely hips that gave her an hourglass figure. I'd spent so much time with women shaped like Amanda that I'd forgotten how much I enjoyed curves on women.

I ran my hands along her sides and moaned. "You are more beautiful than I even imagined."

Tia's cheeks turned light pink, and she bit her lower lip as she gave me a shy smile. "Thank you. I was worried you might be disappointed since I'm not tall and thin."

I shook my head and leaned down to kiss her again. "Not at all."

Something changed in her at that moment, and suddenly, she didn't seem sweet like she had before. We fell back onto the bed, lost in the ecstasy of how our bodies felt together, and by the time she tugged my pants down my legs, I was ready for round two.

Tia wrapped her ankles around my waist and pulled me into her. She was warm and wet, and I sunk into her cunt like it was pure paradise. It only took a few moments before we found our rhythm, my thrusting and her rolling her hips to take all of me.

Her moans made me want to give her what she'd given me, so I pumped into her as my mouth devoured hers. We were like need and desire mixed so completely that someone watching us wouldn't have been able to tell where one of us ended and the other began.

I'd never felt anything like this with a woman

before. For me, sex had always been to make me happy. But now I wanted Tia to feel good.

I slid my lips over to her ear and whispered, "Tell me what you want."

Whatever it was, I'd give it to her. She merely had to give voice to her desires.

With a moan, she answered, "I want you. This. Don't stop. God, don't stop."

So I gave her what she wanted, and every moment of our fucking felt better than the last. When I felt the first squeeze of her cunt around my cock, I knew I'd given her all I could.

Her fingernails tore across the back of my shoulders, making me rear back, and a second later, I came for the second time. It felt like nothing had ever felt like before.

"Wow, I didn't expect you to be so incredible," she said in a soft voice beneath me.

I laughed, another first for me during sex with a woman. "What were you expecting?"

Tia shrugged, and with a sheepish look said, "I don't know. Maybe something more businesslike?"

"I leave business for the office. When it comes to fucking, I take a more intense approach."

She ran her fingernails down over my biceps and nodded as her eyelids slowly closed. "I'd definitely say that was intense."

It was, but even more than that, it was the first time I'd actually cared more for the woman I was with and her happiness than for my own.

CHAPTER 7

ia

My eyes flew open, and I saw nothing but darkness all around me, except for a tiny stream of light coming in where Nico's blackout curtains joined. Oh my God! What time was it?

I tried to roll over to get out of bed, but his arm kept me pinned to him. Nudging his muscular bicep, I said, "I have to go. Can you move your arm? I can't get up if you don't."

Nico mumbled something and pulled me tighter to his warm body. "Not yet. The alarm didn't go off."

"Grace doesn't wake up to an alarm. If she goes to my room and doesn't see me there, she might get scared. I need to get up right now, Nico."

For a few seconds, he did nothing, and I was sure I'd need to find a way to slither out of his hold, but

327

then he lifted his arm and rolled over to turn on the lamp on his nightstand. I jumped out of bed and frantically searched for my clothes. Where did we throw them last night? I vaguely remembered him tossing my underwear onto the floor. Or at least I thought I did, but now that I looked for them, along with every other piece of clothing I'd been wearing when I came to this room, I couldn't find anything.

"Oh God! Help me find my clothes. Please!"

One glance at him sitting up against his headboard looking all too pleased told me he wouldn't be jumping up out of bed anytime soon. Nico laughed at my panic attack, shaking his head.

"It's not even six in the morning, Tia. Relax. She doesn't get up for an hour."

Finally, I located my bra and quickly slid into it. "But what if she does and I'm not there? I don't want her to feel frightened I'm not around. I'm sure she's got feelings of abandonment from having her mother taken away. She doesn't need to have those compounded by thinking the only person she's spent time with in the past few weeks suddenly disappeared. So would you please help me find the rest of my clothes?"

He smiled and pointed at the mauve upholstered chair in the corner of the room. "I think those are your underwear. They're definitely not mine, for sure."

As I made my way over to another piece of my clothing, I rolled my eyes. "Shamrock green panties would look so great on you. I can't imagine why you wouldn't wear them."

"Bright green isn't my color."

As I shimmied into my panties, I swiveled my head back and forth looking for my shirt and pants. At the rate I was going, Grace would graduate from kindergarten before I got dressed and ran to her room.

Spinning around to face him, I saw he wasn't taking this seriously at all. "Please, Nico! This is important."

"Okay, okay. Your pants are over there on the end of my dresser, and if I'm not mistaken, your shirt is down near my feet. Come over here and I'll see what I can do to help you into it like I got you out of it."

Ugh! This man was nothing short of infuriating!

I grabbed my pants and got them on before I headed over to where he sat still naked, the covers barely concealing his hard on. "Where are they? Can you grab my shirt and hand it to me?"

He lifted the sheet and grinned wickedly up at me. "I think you should climb under here and fish it out."

Utterly exhausted not ten minutes after waking, I sighed, my shoulders sagging under the weight of worry that at any second Grace would go to my room and find me missing. "Please take this seriously. Give me my shirt, please."

"Are you always this stressed out when you wake up? You must be growing a hell of an ulcer."

He pulled me down to kiss me hard on the lips, but as much as I wanted to straddle him and go for another round of phenomenal sex, I kept my focus on my job. I snaked my hand under the sheet and found my shirt, thankfully, before Nico had the chance to pull me into his arms.

"Thanks for all the help," I said.

With a pout, he said, "You don't know how to have fun."

"I have to go." I stopped and suddenly felt uncomfortable now that our time together had ended. "Thanks for last night."

That sounded distinctly cheap, and I couldn't stop myself from blushing. I didn't have one-night stands. How I ever had the nerve to let him know I wanted him I'll never know, but I never thought that far ahead to make it just a one-time thing for me.

"It doesn't have to end," Nico said with a sexy grin.

I hung my head, tired of fighting against him for the past ten minutes. "I can't. I swear you aren't listening to me. Grace is going to be up at any minute. I need to go."

He took my hand in his and nodded like he actually understood, finally. "I know. I mean, we should do something later today. Would you like to go out with me for dinner?"

"Oh. Yeah, that would be great. I thought you meant —"

With a chuckle, he finished my sentence. "You thought I meant that I wanted to fuck you again right now. I do, more than you can imagine, but I'm a patient man. I can wait until tonight."

Now my cheeks felt like they were on fire. Just the

mention of us together again made my stomach flip, and an ache settled in between my thighs.

"I have to go. I should warn you that I don't have anything really great to wear for any decent restaurant. I just thought you should know."

He pulled me down on top of him and kissed me. "I'll keep that in mind."

I felt his hands at the back of my shirt and knew exactly what he was trying to do. Pulling away, I shook my head at his one track mind.

"Typical man."

Nico shrugged and gave me another wicked smile. "Guilty. Tonight then."

Nodding, I turned and ran out his bedroom as I silently prayed to God Grace wasn't awake yet. By the time I reached my room, I had to catch my breath since I'd sprinted all the way across the house.

But it was all worth it because a few minutes later when Grace knocked softly on my door, I was there for her. With a drowsy expression, she rubbed her eyes and asked, "Can we go back to the woods today?"

I nodded and smiled at how cute she looked in her pink and white nightgown, her bare feet sinking into the white carpeting in my bedroom. "Absolutely, as long as it isn't raining. I don't want you to catch a cold. You look pretty sleepy, though. Do you want to go back to bed for a while?"

Grace nodded but didn't turn to leave. After a few seconds, she asked in a tiny voice, "Can I come in your bed?"

How anyone could turn down such a sweet little

girl I had no idea. I lifted up the bedspread and sheet and waved her over.

"Sure. Come on in!"

She ran over to my bed and climbed up under the covers. Smiling, she turned to look over at me. "Thank you, Tia. I used to like sleeping in my mommy's bed."

Suddenly, I wondered if she and her mother had always shared the same bed. If so, then she was probably feeling even more abandoned than I already believed.

"I'm sure your mom liked that too."

Nodding, she smiled, but it was half-hearted. "Only on Sundays when she didn't have to go into work. That was the only time I could get into her bed."

"Oh. Well, I can understand that. It's next to impossible to get out of bed to go to work when you want to stay right where you are."

Grace said nothing, but after a few minutes, inched herself over closer to me. "Do you think my mommy misses me?"

Her tone of uncertainty broke my heart, so I wrapped my arms around her to give her a hug. "Of course, she does. Your mommy loves you, honey, and being away from people you love is hard."

"It is. She doesn't have a Tia either," Grace said sweetly. "Can I make her something to send to her after we get back from the woods?"

I pressed my cheek against the top of her head and smiled. "Absolutely. I'm sure she'll love it."

Against me, Grace's body got small all of a sudden. "Not like Uncle Nico."

Since I couldn't share with her what I knew about her uncle as of just a few hours ago, at least I could let her know he may not have been the man we both saw these past few weeks. "Well, I suspect he was just getting used to having a girl in his house. I bet now he's going to be better. In fact, I'm sure of it."

But that didn't convince her. Nico was going to have to prove to his niece that he wasn't the son of a bitch monster she had seen time and again in the weeks she'd lived here.

I hoped he was up to the challenge.

WITH A GALLON SIZE PLASTIC BAGGIE FULL OF leaves, Grace marched down the path back toward the house. "I want to make my mommy's card pretty. The big red leaf will be perfect, don't you think?"

"I do. I think it will look like the most beautiful card she's ever received."

As we walked, I looked up and saw someone coming toward us. For a few seconds, I couldn't tell anything except it was a man, but then I realized it was Nico! What could he be doing here in the woods?

"Tia, Uncle Nico is here," Grace said in utter surprise.

Nearly stunned into silence, I mumbled, "He is. I wonder why he's come here."

"Do you think he's mad we went to collect leaves?" she asked in a worried voice.

She searched out my hand and squeezed it tightly, her tiny fingers grasping mine. Clearly, she was frightened. I wanted to tell her he wouldn't act like he used to, but I didn't know how to say what I hoped would be true in a few seconds.

Praying I was right, I waved as we continued to walk toward him. When he didn't wave back, my heart sank. What happened to the man I spent all those hours with last night? Why did he have to be so mean when it came to Grace?

She stopped walking, and when I looked back at her, she shook her head. "He's going to yell at us. He's mad."

"No, he isn't, and I won't let him yell at us. We did nothing wrong by coming out here, so don't worry. I'm sure he's just not used to nature. He spends all his time in that office of his. He's probably afraid of bugs or something," I said with a smile.

That made her happy, and she nodded. "Bugs are scary. Spiders are really scary. Maybe he saw a spider."

"Maybe. But everything's better when there's someone else around, so he'll be happier when he joins us since we know our way around the woods, don't we?"

With a confident nod, Grace began walking again. "Yes. We're not afraid of the woods. Maybe we can show him how nice it is here."

She loosened her hold on my hand just a little, and I held my breath, hoping he wouldn't be that miserable man he'd been to her before. As he got closer to us, I saw not anger but almost what looked like confusion on Nico's face.

But what could he be confused about?

Finally, I called out, "Hi! Did you decide your office needed a break and you wanted to join us in the woods?"

He simply kept walking toward us, and now I felt like I wanted to hold Grace's hand more tightly. I had no idea what could have brought him out to this place, but nothing about his silence felt good.

Finally, when we got close enough that I could see his face clearly, I saw a tiny smile. Maybe this would be okay, after all.

"So this is where you two come when you leave the house?" he asked and then looked down at Grace. "Your grandmother used to love to spend time in the woods too when she was a little girl. She used to tell me and your mother stories about it. Did you know that?"

I turned to see Grace shaking her head. "Mommy never takes me to woods like this."

"That's probably because she's too busy," I quickly said. "Mommies can get very busy with work, you know."

She nodded her head and then tugged on my hand to bring me down to her. In my ear, she whispered, "Can I show him my bag of leaves?"

With a smile, I answered, "I think that would be nice."

Her face lit up with happiness, Grace held out her large plastic baggie full of leaves to show her uncle. "I got these to make a card for my mommy. Tia said I could send her one. I want to give her the big red one in the middle."

Nico hesitated for a long moment, and concern raced through me. He didn't know how to act with her. Would he revert to his former nastiness?

But finally, he crouched down in front of her, and dressed in his dark grey business suit, white dress shirt, and grey striped tie, he pointed at the red leaf in the middle of the baggie and smiled. "That one? I bet she'll like it. She'll like anything if it's from you."

I let out a sigh of relief, my shoulders sagging as the weight of utter fear that he'd crush her hopes again evaporated into thin air. So he could be sweet in addition to being sexy. Good to know.

"Let's go home now so I can make her card. I can't wait to send it to her!"

Grace yanked her hand from my hold and began running down the path. I hurried behind her, calling out, "Don't run out onto the street. When you get to the end of the path, stop!"

Beside me, Nico took my hand in his. "Any chance you're going to have to run after her?"

"No. She's a good kid. She listens when I tell her not to do something. So what are you doing here?" I asked, turning to look at him.

He smiled and shrugged. "I don't know what kind of magic you hold, but I couldn't stop thinking about you all morning. I think you've put a spell on me."

My spirits soared as he said those words. I hadn't done anything of the sort, but to know he was thinking about me after our time together last night thrilled me.

"No spell. I'm just little old me, Tia."

Nico slid his arm around my waist and nuzzled my neck. "Well, little old you has possessed my mind."

As much as I loved the feel of his body next to mine, I pulled away, unsure Grace should see us together like that. Instantly, his expression darkened from disappointment.

"I don't want to confuse her, Nico. She already had to leave her home to come here to yours where she didn't know anyone. I think it's incredible how kind you were to her about her bag of leaves, but to see us together like a couple might not be something she understands."

He didn't like what I was saying, but he nodded anyway. "Fine. While we're around her, no touching. But tonight, you should expect me to be all about the touching and more."

After glancing at Grace and seeing she was getting close to the road, I gave him a quick peck on the cheek. "That's a down payment for tonight, okay? Right now, I have to run after a five year old who wants to make a card."

Nico smiled as I ran away and called after me, "Eight o'clock. I'll pick you up in the kitchen."

I beamed a grin of anticipation for what would happen in just a few hours from now, but I hoped Grace didn't hear him say that. I didn't know how I'd explain it to her.

CHAPTER 8

ia

AFTER HOURS OF CARD-MAKING WITH GRACE AND then dinner with her, I put my favorite little girl to bed with a bedtime story about a princess who loved nature and her kingdom full of leaves of every color in the rainbow before walking to my room next door. I didn't have anything to wear to this date, but even more, now I realized if we were going out to a restaurant, who would be here with Grace?

I didn't feel right leaving her with Agatha. That woman could ruin all the progress I'd made with the little girl in one night. A single horrible grimace from her and who knew what would happen with Grace.

No, Nico would just have to understand that if we were getting together tonight, it had to be here at the house or I couldn't go.

On my bed, I found an envelope with my name written on it. I opened it up and saw he'd left me instructions for our date. Happily, I wouldn't have to cancel after all.

DEAR TIA,

Since I didn't think you'd be willing to leave Grace with a sitter yet while I took you to a restaurant, I brought the restaurant to us. Feel free to wear something comfortable. Easy to get off would be best because I don't plan to let you stay dressed for long. Meet me on the lower level of the house.

Nico

FOR A FEW MOMENTS, I MARVELED AT THE CHANGE in the man. He'd gone from being an insufferable bastard to someone who took into consideration my need to be there for Grace. I wondered what had brought about this sudden change, but I didn't want to jinx it.

Better to be thankful it happened at all and not question it too much.

So he wanted me to be comfortable? That I could do perfectly well.

I chose my favorite black yoga pants and my nicest purple T-shirt with the black butterfly outline design to go over my best black bra and panties set. I only wore it on special occasions, and I almost didn't pack it when I was getting ready to come live here.

As I spun around to check myself out in the bathroom mirror, I smiled at my inability to pack light for anything. Thank God for that, though, or I'd be wearing my boring old white bra tonight.

After slipping into my most comfortable clothes, I took one last look in the mirror and tried to calm my nerves. Last night when I approached him, that had been a spur of the moment thing. I didn't think about it at all. I just went for it.

Tonight was different, though. Now I couldn't stop myself from shaking and overthinking everything. Doubts filled my head, and I felt like I might throw up at any moment.

I swallowed hard and took a deep breath as I walked away from the mirror. He liked me well enough last night, and I looked pretty much the same as tonight. Everything would be fine.

As long as I didn't get sick all over the table.

I'd never been to the lower level, so as I walked down the stairs, I wondered what it looked like. Our house back home had brown wood paneling on the walls from the seventies in the basement and a dart board my father claimed was in some famous Prohibition era speakeasy at one time. Nobody believed that story, but the dart board fit in with the lame décor perfectly.

The heavenly scent of fresh baked bread filled my nose and pushed out any thoughts of my ugly childhood home's basement. It smelled buttery, like the kind of rolls my mother always made for holiday dinners.

If I saw a turkey sitting in the middle of the table, I might fall in love with Nico right then and there.

As I stepped down off the final stair, I looked around at what he called the lower level. No wonder he didn't call it a basement. Those looked like my parents' back in Brooklyn with the hideous old-fashioned paneling. This looked like some high-end man cave.

"Welcome to my secret hideout. Let me show you around."

Nico, dressed in his dark grey suit pants and white dress shirt from earlier in the day, took me by the hand and began walking through the room. Pointing at the tan wall across from us with a picture of him on some mountain, he said, "That was the time my friends and I decided to climb the highest peak in Vermont. Have you ever been up there?"

I nodded as I remembered my family's summer vacation to Canada when I was twelve. "Only passing through. The mountains are very pointy compared to the ones we have here."

He stopped and studied my expression for a long moment before smiling. "Now that I think of it, they are, aren't they? We weren't prepared to tackle any mountain, much less the highest summit in the state, so we didn't pay much attention to how they looked. We were more focused on just getting down alive. That picture was taken on the way up. If they took a picture on the way back, it would have looked very different, that's for sure."

I studied him standing there in the outdoors

looking so strong and confident and liked that version of him. Perhaps he hadn't always been some mean guy who preferred his office to the outside world.

As he walked me over to the mahogany wood bar, I marveled at how impressive it looked. "I think this is nicer than most places my friends and I go to hang out. No wood paneling here, I guess."

Nico shook his head and walked behind the bar to pour us both a glass of red wine. "I had this part of the house completely demolished and redone when I moved in. It wasn't paneling down here, but wall to wall carpeting that reminded me of tall grass. It was an ugly green and I swear it covered your feet. Nasty stuff."

Handing me my glass, he made a toast. "To you and me in my secret hideout."

"It's beautiful down here, Nico. I've never seen a man cave this nice," I said before taking a sip of wine.

With a smile, he shook his head. "Man cave sounds so typical. Like I have some kind of recliner and I watch sports on a big screen TV. This is a hideout. Any time I don't want to deal with the world, I come here and become invisible to the rest of the planet."

"Why do you want to turn your back on the world?"

The sexy man in front of me changed into that miserable soul I'd known for most of my time in this place for just a moment before he forced a smile. "The world wants me to be one way, so that's the way I have to be. In this place, though, I get to be just Nico. No pressure. No expectations. Just me."

I wanted to ask why he thought he couldn't be this wonderful man so the rest of the world could see what I saw, but instead I simply smiled and took another sip of wine. "So are we hiding out tonight? I thought I smelled fresh baked bread when I was walking down the stairs. Did my nose lie to me?"

"No, it didn't. Let me show you the other side of my hideout where we'll have dinner from the finest restaurant in town. I had them make their specialty, so I hope you like duck."

He took me by the hand and began walking to the other side of the lower level as I quietly admitted the truth about dinner. "I've never had duck."

I turned my head as I waited for him to express shock that I'd never eaten what seemed commonplace to him, but then I heard him say, "Great! I always like when I get to introduce people to this meal. I promise you it's the best you'll ever have."

When we stopped in front of an intimate table set for two and covered with dishes filled with our dinner, I asked, "Why aren't you always like this? I have to know. Because for ninety percent of the time I've been in this house, you've been doing your best ogre impression. Now you're like a completely different man. Why?"

He dipped his head to kiss me softly on the lips and whispered, "Maybe this is who I really am and the ogre is just an act. Or maybe this is your effect on me and I'm a changed man."

Instead of telling me which was the truth, he escorted me to my seat on the other side of the table and then took his seat. When one of his staff appeared from a room behind me, I knew I wouldn't be getting my answer anytime soon.

DINNER TASTED AS INCREDIBLE AS HE PROMISED, but I sensed something different about Nico as we made small talk about the weather and how wonderfully the card for Grace's mother turned out.

True, I didn't know him well yet, but with every word, I felt like a wall was going up between us.

But why?

"The duck was delicious, Nico. I guess I should have tried it before this since I loved it."

"I'm happy you waited until tonight. I loved seeing you take that first bite. You looked like you weren't sure you wanted to keep eating or spit it out," he said with a laugh.

My cheeks instantly heated up from a blush of embarrassment. "No, not at all. God, I hope it didn't look like that. Now I feel silly."

He stood up from the table to come around behind my chair. Leaning over, he whispered in my ear, "Enough talk about duck. Let's move on to the rest of our night."

Taking my hand, he led me to yet another room in his hideout. This one had furniture that made it look like a living room, but unlike the one upstairs in the main level of the house, Nico's hidden one felt less stuffy.

That worked for me since I looked like I was

dressed to hang out on a Thursday night at home, but he still looked like the businessman he always seemed to be. Well, except for last night.

"I thought when you said dress casually that you would dress that way too," I said as he guided me to the navy blue upholstered sofa.

He shook his head and smiled. "I either wear this or I wear nothing. Sitting naked at dinner seemed like a bit much, so regular clothes it is."

I waited for him to sit next to me, but instead he crouched down on the floor in front of me. Confused, I asked, "Why are you down there?"

With a wink, he smiled and slid his hands up over my thighs. "Because as much as I love this piece of furniture, it isn't right for what I want to do at this moment."

A second later, he tugged my yoga pants down my legs and I understood what he meant. After he slipped them over my ankles, I watched him take such care with a pair of pants that cost less than the corkscrew he used to open the bottle of wine at dinner.

"You can just ball them up, if you want. My clothes aren't as nice as yours," I said sheepishly, suddenly all too aware of how different our levels in life were.

He didn't say anything but continued to carefully fold my yoga pants and set them on the table nearby. When he turned his focus back to me, I saw a look of appreciation in his eyes for my black panties.

Nervous, although I didn't know why, I mumbled, "They go with the matching bra I'm wearing."

"Good. I want to see that, so let me take off your shirt."

No one had ever undressed me like this. It had a methodical way about it while at the same time having him so close felt incredibly sexy. He smelled like the cologne he always wore, something woodsy and warm that made me think he really did like the outdoors more than I had imagined.

When he finished and placed my shirt carefully on top of my yoga pants behind him, he turned around and smiled, humming as if he liked my black bra and panties. "Now your job tonight is to sit back and enjoy everything I do to you."

I liked the sound of that, even as I watched him take his place on the floor between my legs and look at up me with a wickedly sexy expression. "Okay. I can definitely do that job."

Nico sat back on his heels and lifted my right foot to place it on his shoulder. I watched in rapt attention as he pressed his lips to the inside of my ankle and lightly kissed my skin. No one had ever kissed that part of my body before. If they had, I may have been theirs forever. With every second his mouth stayed on my ankle, I felt like waves of electricity were sweeping up my legs directly to my pussy.

A soft moan escaped from between my lips, and Nico lifted his gaze to look up at me. "You're doing your job well, Miss Morton. Keep up the good work."

"Mmmm...you too, Mr. Allen. You're quite the inside of the ankle kisser. I can't wait to see what you do with those lips on other parts of my body."

My cuteness made him smile. "Patience. We have all night."

As he moved up from my ankle to drag his tongue along my calf, I wondered if I'd make it all night. My job had sounded easy when he told me all I had to do was enjoy myself, but with every inch of me he kissed, I felt like I was losing control.

"Are you going to kiss all of me?" I asked as he flicked his tongue over my right knee.

He lifted his head and nodded. "Patience. I had no idea you were so tense. I should have started with a massage."

Oh, God. If he had started the night with that, I don't think we would have made it through dinner.

By the time he made it to the middle of my thigh, my leg was quivering in anticipation of where his mouth was headed. I wanted to feel his tongue on me so badly I would have begged him if he stopped at that moment.

Against my skin, he asked, "Are you cold? I can get a blanket if you want."

Just then, he skidded his lips up the inside of my thigh and stopped to nip at my skin. I opened my mouth to say don't stop, but all that came out was another moan, this one needier than the last. He was so close. All it would take was just another few seconds and then he'd be there.

And a moment later, he lifted his head, smiled a wicked grin, and sat back on his heels to begin all over again on my other leg. I wanted to scream as utter frustration filled me.

"No...please. You were right there. Why did you stop?"

"I didn't do the other leg. You have to do both legs."

Never before in my life had the need to be complete left me so unhappy.

"Yes, but in this case, you really don't have to. You could just do one leg. Like pretend I'm a peg leg pirate."

Slowly, a smile brightened his face, and at that moment, he reminded me of a little boy. "Sex with a peg leg pirate. That's not something you hear happening every day."

"I say we make it our thing. Only one leg and then onto the main event."

Nico lowered my leg off his shoulder and leaned forward to kiss me. "Trust me. That's not going to be the main event. That's going to be a delicious appetizer, a nice start, but definitely not the main event."

"Can we have the appetizer now then? I'm sort of starving here," I said with a pleading smile.

Shaking his head, he chuckled. "After that incredible dinner, you're starving? That doesn't make sense."

I leaned down and kissed him full on the lips, hoping he'd see all this foreplay was driving me mad. "Stop teasing. You know what I mean."

"That I do, and I like seeing you like this. I'm thinking by the time I give that pussy of yours a first lick, you're going to be more than ready."

I squeezed my thighs together to ease the ache inside me. "I'm ready now, Nico. Trust me. More than ready."

He eased me back against the sofa and pushed my legs open. "I guess to know for sure, I'm going to have to take these black panties off."

As he said that, I hooked my thumbs along the tops of them and tugged my panties halfway down my thighs. "Let me help. I like to do something other than watch a man seduce me."

Nico picked up where I left off and pulled the black underwear down to my ankles before he eased them over my feet. "An active participant. I like that. I had a feeling from last night that you weren't the type to just sit back and lie there."

All his talking made me even crazier, so I slid my feet around his back and pulled him toward me. "Definitely active."

"And eager," he said with a big smile as he settled in between my legs.

I opened my mouth to agree with him, but just then he flicked his tongue against my clit and nearly sent me through the roof. Definitely more than ready. In fact, I doubted I'd last long at all.

Against my tender skin, he moaned in a low voice, "You taste like heaven."

This felt like heaven. With every swipe of his tongue over my pussy, waves of pleasure washed over me. I spread my legs as wide as they could go because I didn't want an inch of me to not get to enjoy this man's talented mouth.

"Oh, God..." I moaned after he gently sucked my clit between his lips.

It wouldn't be long before my orgasm rolled over me, but I thought I had a little more time before that delicious moment. When he slid a finger inside me and stroked just the right spot men so rarely ever found, that was it.

My hand shot out and clamped down on the back of his head to hold him exactly where I wanted him to stay. I rode his mouth, bucking and rolling up and down to feel as much of this ecstasy as I could.

I didn't think he could be better than last night, but oh how wrong I was.

When the last tremor from my orgasm subsided, Nico sat back and smiled up at me. His lips glistened with my juices, and when he licked them, he looked like he couldn't be happier.

"I do love when a woman lets me know how much she likes what I'm doing. It's like cheering from the crowd."

Pushing my hair off my face, I admitted the truth of how much I'd held back. "If I knew that, I would have let myself go."

Nico slid his palms up over my thighs and sat up to kiss me. "Definitely let yourself go. I want to see that."

His wish was my command.

CHAPTER 9

ico

"So now that I've reciprocated, tell me what your fantasy is so I can make it come true."

Tia bit her lower lip in that way that made her look so perfectly sexy. "This is my fantasy. Having a gorgeous man want me and no one else."

I kissed her lips softly and smiled. "Then that's what you'll get."

Easing her back against the sofa pillows, I quickly removed my clothes. I wanted no one but her. Now and forever.

She smiled while I unhooked her bra and said, "Actually, I do have something else I like. It's not really a fantasy since I've done it before, but it's a favorite position."

"I'm all ears."

"Over on your back then."

I did as she wanted and watched as she straddled my hips. She sighed and slowly eased herself down onto my cock, taking all of me into her. It was something so commonplace but now felt incredible, like I'd never had a woman ride me before.

"This feels so good," she said, leaning down to kiss me a moment later.

I wanted this to be the best time she'd ever had in this sexual position. No, it wasn't a fantasy, but it made her happy, so I wanted her to have this and anything else I could give her.

While she rolled her hips and moaned with every time my cock filled her, I cupped her breasts and adored their full size. I'd forgotten how much of a boob man I was. When I pinched those deep pink nipples to hardened peaks, she kissed me, sighing against my lips.

"I love it when a man plays with my nipples," she said in a needy voice. "It's like it's a straight line between them and my pussy."

So I pinched them harder and her cunt contracted around my cock. Maybe she was onto something there.

"Do you like anything in particular?" she asked as she lifted herself off me only to slide down my shaft again.

I lowered my head and sucked one of those pretty tits between my lips as I held her ass to keep my cock inside her. "This."

All of it.

But I didn't say that. Getting burned by a woman taught a man not to let anyone know what he really felt. Tia made me want to, though.

Just not yet.

My teeth gently bit into her tender skin, and that was all it took to kick her into overdrive. She rode me like a wild woman, like a woman on a mission to come. She moaned against my neck, and then a minute later, she came hard on my cock, her hands grasping at my shoulders so she could keep her balance.

When I came a few seconds later, it was like I'd finally found the person I was meant to be with. After a while, she stilled against my chest, and I wrapped my arms around her to keep her next to me.

I wanted her to stay with me forever. I knew my niece wouldn't need a nanny next year, but by then, I wanted Tia to be more than an employee.

But I didn't know how I'd tell her that.

STILL IN THE HAZE OF MY TIME WITH TIA hours earlier, I made my way to my office and realized I didn't want to work today. I wanted to find the woman who had turned my life upside down and keep her in bed with me for another day.

She'd protest, of course, since there would be no one to take care of Grace, but even that didn't bother me. Tia truly cared about my niece, and for that, I couldn't get angry with her. After all the little girl had been through, including dealing with me when she first arrived here, she deserved to believe she had someone like Tia in her corner.

The sound of my cell broke into my happy daydream, and I answered it still smiling. "Hello?"

"Mr. Allen, this is Sadie Sanderson, the woman from child services. How are you today?" a squeaky voice asked.

My mind quickly flashed an image of Miss Sanderson. Short with spikey white hair and big dangly earrings that looked like at any moment they might tear through the holes in her ears, she made quite an impression on me that day she brought Grace out to the house for the first time.

"What can I do for you today?" I asked.

She hesitated for a moment and then in an uncomfortable voice said, "Well, there have been some developments in your niece's case that have changed the situation somewhat."

I'd heard people use a lot of words to say next to nothing before in my life, and never had it been a sign of anything good. What could have changed in Grace's case? My sister hadn't been released from prison, so did we have some long-forgotten sibling neither one of us knew about who suddenly had an interest in being his or her niece's guardian?

Then a thought hit me. Had someone called the authorities and reported me for how I'd treated Grace? Tia had threatened to do it, but she wouldn't have. She'd seen the way I changed since she arrived here.

But if not her, then who? None of my staff would do that.

"What exactly has changed, Mrs. Sanderson?"

"Mr. Allen, Grace's father has applied to take his daughter with him."

Her father? I didn't realize my sister even knew for sure who the guy was who impregnated her. And now we were calling him Grace's father? Where had he been for the past five years?

"And who is this person purporting to be her father? Is child services in the habit of just letting any man walk in off the street and say he wants to take a child? My niece has never met her father. How in the world do you think it would be a good idea for her to be uprooted again in the span of a month and sent to live with a total stranger?"

"Well, you were a total stranger to her, Mr. Allen, but she went with you."

I wanted to snap at her for that smartass remark, but I held my tongue. "Exactly. Once was bad enough. At least I had seen the child, although it had been when she was small. This supposed father of hers has never even met her. And even more, Grace is happy here. I don't think she should be taken away from my home."

"Really? You didn't seem thrilled to have this responsibility thrust upon you earlier this month."

This woman was testing my patience and ruining what had been a fantastic morning.

"I wasn't thrilled, true, but I made sure to provide

Grace with a good home and a nanny who she adores. She and Tia have become quite close in the time they've been together, and I think it would harm her if you took that away from her. A child needs to know she has someone she can rely on, and she has that in her nanny."

Now I sounded like Tia, but for the first time since Grace came to live with me, I liked saying something like that. I may not have been the best choice for that kid, but I wasn't the only person in the house who had grown attached to the nanny.

"As much as I can appreciate her affinity for her nanny, Mr. Allen, it's out of my hands. The law is clear. As her father, Mr. Groves has a right to his daughter."

I jumped out of my office chair and began pacing across the room. "You make it sound like she's an expensive European car or a piece of furniture. Grace is a person, a child who's become attached to someone here. I won't let you simply quote me some ridiculous law that the men and women in Albany haven't gotten around to changing. You'll be hearing from my lawyers."

Before she had a chance to say anything else that might make me want to get truly nasty, I ended the call and immediately dialed Andrew Rochester, my lawyer for my business. He likely wouldn't be an expert on this type of thing since he preferred to keep to the corporate side of the law, but he could point me in the direction of an attorney who could help.

When he answered, I immediately began relaying my problem. "Andrew, I need your help. I've got a

DIRTY BOSS

situation with my niece I need a good lawyer for. Her father wants to show up out of the blue, probably fresh off some nationwide tour of all the open air festivals in the United States, and he wants to take my sister's kid away. I want to stop him, so who do we know who can help me do that?"

"Nico? You have a niece? Since when do you have a niece?" he asked, frustrating me with how slowly he seemed to be catching on this morning.

"Five years. My sister got in trouble and is spending the next eighteen months upstate for insider trading. You know Fiona. She always has believed she's got some special talent, but this time it got her sent to prison. But that's not the point, really. The point is this guy named Groves wants to swoop in and take the little girl away. I don't think he's ever even met the kid, and trust me, she's just settled down and stopped crying after being here for a few weeks, and that's only because of the nanny I hired. I don't want him coming in and taking her, so direct me to whoever you know in the child custody business who can help me prevent that."

He didn't answer for a long moment before finally saying, "I don't know, Nico. Parental rights are a tricky thing to get around. Even absent parents have more rights than most people would prefer them to have."

This wasn't helping.

"Fine. Then I'm going to need a first rate lawyer, so who do you suggest? Money is no object."

"Well, if money's no object, then Jeff Handelman.

He's the best in the business, but I wouldn't get your hopes up. You can throw as much money as you want at a problem like this, but parental rights — "

Before he repeated himself, I cut him off. "Yeah, yeah. They're tricky. Got it. Okay, thanks again, Andrew."

I wasn't above throwing my name and reputation around, and as I listened to the phone ring at Jeff Handelman's office, I remembered meeting him a few years back. He was dating a friend's sister or something like that, and they were considering a home in my neighborhood. That would be a good enough introduction and then we could get down to the business of stopping whoever this damn Groves guy was who suddenly came to love the idea of fatherhood.

"Hello, Handelman, Murphy, and Murphy. How may I direct your call?" a soft voice asked.

"I need to speak to Jeff Handelman."

"I'm sorry. Attorney Handelman isn't available right now. I can take your name and number and he'll get back to you."

All the times I avoided answering my calls instantly came back to haunt me. I gave her my information and impressed upon her that the situation was urgent, but if Handelman was anything like me, that would mean very little.

I'd give it a few hours and then decide what to do if he didn't return my call. In the meantime, I needed to decide if I should tell Tia about this or put that discussion off until tomorrow.

As much as I hoped whoever this guy who claimed

to be Grace's father would disappear, I doubted that would happen. Any man who stepped up to take a five year old was likely not going to just walk away any time soon.

TIA BLUSHED WHEN I WALKED INTO THE KITCHEN, and for a moment, I forgot what I was there for in the first place. I would have preferred telling her how much I enjoyed last night. Instead, I needed to break bad news after my call from Jeff Handelman.

"Where's Grace?" I asked and then remembered she took a nap every day in the afternoon.

"She's gone for her nap. We spent a lot of time outside. She really loves leaf hunting, Nico. I can't decide if she's a budding artist or a budding scientist," Tia said with a sweet smile.

God, I hated what I had to say right now. She truly cared about Grace, and it was going to crush her to see her leave.

I nodded like I was listening to anything about what leaf picking meant and pulled out the chair from the table to sit down. After I took a deep breath, I let it out slowly. Christ, I didn't want to do this. I needed to, though. She deserved to know what was going on.

Better to just say what I had to say and get it out.

"The woman from child services called today. Grace's father wants to take her while her mother is in jail. It looks like it's a done deal because he has parental rights."

Tia's eyes filled with tears and she shook her head. "No! Don't let them do that to her, Nico. She's had a hard time being separated from her mother and then coming here to a place filled with people she didn't know. Tell them she cried for a week straight. Tell them she's just now getting used to the idea that she's safe and can be happy."

"I told the lawyer that. The courts don't care. Parental rights seems to be some impenetrable suit of goddamned armor."

"Don't let them send her off with her father. She's never even met him, has she? She's never said a single word about her father to me, and trust me, she talks about her mother all the time so if she knew about her father, she would have said something in all the time I've been here."

Seeing her so upset made me feel like a complete failure. I wanted to do exactly what she was telling me to do, but ridiculous laws made that impossible.

"I can't do anything about it. I have no real rights in this situation, unfortunately."

She continued to shake her head as tears rolled down her cheeks. "No, Nico. Don't let this happen. Use that money you told me you'd use to make any problem disappear. She doesn't even know her father. Rights mean nothing when a little girl is in danger of feeling like she's just a football to be passed around from house to house. She's happy now. She even thinks you like her."

"I do like her, Tia, and not because she's blood.

She's a cute kid. You've really brought out the best in her."

Tia reached across the table and grabbed my hand. Staring up into my eyes, she pleaded, "Then tell them that. Tell them whatever you have to so she doesn't have to leave. I'm afraid if you let them take her away that she's going to be the saddest little girl in the world."

"His rights as her father are too much to overcome. There's nothing I can do."

"Then force them to do it slowly, like he can come to visit for an hour at first and then build up to earning her trust. It's not right to just shuttle a little girl around from person to person and expect her to not feel anything. Nico, please! At least give her some time to get to know this man she's never met. You have no idea about this man. He could be a pedophile or worse. Don't let this happen. Please don't."

I hung my head and slowly nodded. "I'll see what I can do."

"Thank you. It's only right. Grace deserves some sense of permanence in her life. I mean, I know she won't be living here forever, but she should be able to be around people she trusts."

"She trusts you, Tia. I think if child services could see you two together they'd understand. I feel like I'm talking to a wall when I try to convince anyone to let her stay here."

"Then bring them all here!" she said excitedly. "Let them watch us playing outside in the leaves or making arts and crafts while we drink hot cocoa. She's happy here, Nico. That should count for something, right?"

"I'll do what I can, Tia. I promise."

"Thank you, Nico. It will mean the world to her. You watch."

As I walked out of the kitchen, I looked back and saw Tia looking at me like she had all the confidence in the world that I'd be able to fix this problem. I didn't have that level of confidence at all, sadly.

ia

WHILE GRACE AND I COLORED PAGES IN HER alphabet coloring book, I kept watching for Nico to come tell me everything would be okay. I imagined the nasty attitude he'd be giving to anyone who got in his way. Having seen it firsthand, I had a feeling it would sway some minds, for sure.

"Look, Tia. I finished my F. Isn't it nice?"

I turned to look at her and saw a wonderful blue F wearing a smiley face. "I love it. It's a happy F. Do you know what the word is at the top?"

She shook her head and frowned. "No."

"It says F is for friend. Like you and I are friends."

Grace looked down at her picture and smiled. "F is for friend."

K.M. SCOTT

"Do you know what people call their close friends? They call them best friends. Can we be best friends?"

She eagerly nodded. "Yes, I want to be best friends."

"BFF. Best friends forever. Can you draw a B and an F and another F on the page right here?" I asked, pointing to the blank spot in the upper right hand corner.

Carefully, she set the coloring book on the white carpet and began to draw the three letters with her cornflower blue crayon. They came out perfectly, and I leaned over to hug her.

"You do such an incredible job with your letters, Grace. You're going to do so great in kindergarten next year."

A big smile lit up her round little face. "I can't wait!"

As I started to tell her about my first day in kindergarten when I drank my milk too fast and it came shooting out of my nose and got all over my yellow dress, Nico appeared in the doorway. I knew by his expression he had bad news.

"Hey, girls. What's going on?"

Grace proudly held up her coloring book to the F page. "I made an F. F is for friend. Tia and I are best friends. Right, Tia?"

"Right," I said, forcing a smile so she didn't know how torn up I felt inside. "Best friends forever."

"Grace, I need to speak to Tia for a minute. She'll be back in two shakes of a lamb's tail."

The confused look on her face told me she had no

idea what he meant, so I gently tapped her on the nose and said, "I'll be back soon. You move on to your next letter. I'll come back when your uncle and I finish talking, okay?"

As always, she followed my instructions and moved on to the letter G as I stood up and walked over to where Nico stood in the doorway. With every step, my heart sank more and more as I stared at his face and knew things hadn't worked out.

He didn't say anything at first, but then he simply shook his head and frowned. I needed to hear what really happened, though.

"What? They didn't wholesale say no to everything you asked for, did they?" I asked, barely able to hold back the tears.

Nico focused his attention on the floor and sighed. "I did everything I could, Tia. The law is the law. It's not right, but there's very little grey area when it comes to parents' rights."

"Well, it's not right!" I said loudly and then quickly looked into the room to see if Grace had heard anything.

She sat there happily coloring the letter G's page in a beautiful hot pink color, oblivious to the fact that the adults in her world were busy talking about what was going to happen next to her. I hated the idea of her being taken away. I hated it so much I wanted to scream. She didn't even know this father of hers, and now she'd have to get used to him and another strange place.

Nico took my hand in his and I turned back to

focus on him. "I did everything I could. I hope you know that."

As tears filled my eyes, I tried to keep calm but I couldn't. I was angry and sad and scared, and I didn't know what to do with any of those emotions.

"It's not right. She's going to be so frightened. She's going to cry, and what if he doesn't know how to handle a little girl crying and he hits her or tries some other way to discipline her?"

"I won't let that happen. I promise. I'll make sure to keep an eye on him and her. They're only going to be in the city since it seems he has wealthy parents and that's how he gets to devote his life to the dream of finding the perfect wave."

I wiped the tears from my face as what he said filtered through my brain. "What does that mean? Is he some kind of surfer guy? He isn't going to want to stay here for long then. He's going to want to take her to wherever waves are. California? They have waves there, right? Australia! They have beaches and waves there too. I saw it on a nature special I watched one night. Nico, he's going to take her halfway around the world!"

He pulled me to him, probably because I was unraveling like a cheap suit right there in the hallway, and whispered, "It's not going to be like that. I promise. He says he plans to stay in the city until my sister gets out, so Grace will be right nearby."

All I wanted to do was bawl my eyes out, even if he was telling the truth and Grace wasn't going to be whisked away to another continent. I couldn't do that, though, or she'd know something was terribly wrong. She didn't need the adult she trusted most in the world falling apart.

"He better not because I'll find a way to get to Australia or wherever he takes her," I whispered into the shoulder of Nico's suit coat.

Both of us knew it was nothing but an empty threat, but I didn't care.

"Tia, I finished G. Want to see?" Grace called out.

I quickly wiped under my eyes and took a deep breath. She couldn't see me upset. I didn't want the last few times she saw me to be anything but wonderful.

"Of course I want to see it," I said in my best pretend happy voice. "I'll be right in!"

"He's coming tonight, Tia."

My heart sank at those words. "Tonight? So soon? What's the hurry? Did he suddenly come into a stash of car seats or a warehouse of dresses for little girls?"

Nico simply shrugged. What could he say that would make this any better?

"I don't know how I'm going to tell her. She's going to be so scared. I don't know what to say."

For the first time, he smiled. "You'll do what you always do. You'll make her see she's loved and it'll be fine."

All I wanted to do was cry. This wouldn't be fine. Nothing would be, and I had no idea how to make it better for her.

He kissed me once more and I walked back into Grace's bedroom that would soon be just another guest room in Nico's house. She smiled up at me and pointed at the letter G she'd colored.

"I'm onto H now. How do you spell H, Tia?"

I shook my head and forced a smile. "Honestly, I don't know. I think it might have an a in it. Your letters look really great, you know that? You're going to be the smartest girl in kindergarten when you go next year."

She beamed her happiness and nodded, like she instinctively knew she would be the best in her class. I hoped she'd keep that confidence for the rest of her life.

Fighting back tears, I cleared my throat and said, "Grace, guess what? Your father is coming to get you and take you to his house in the city. How does that sound?"

Surprisingly, she didn't even bother to look up at me, like what I said didn't register in her brain. "Are you coming?"

For a second, I thought this might be easier than I had built it up to be, but as soon as she asked me that, I knew all my worry was right.

"No, I can't. I'm sure your daddy will want to spend as much time as he can with you, so he doesn't need me."

That made her lift her head, and in her eyes, I saw fear begin to grow. "But I want you there. Why can't you come to where I'm going?"

"I wish I could, Grace. I do. But that's not my decision to make. I'm sure you're going to love your new house."

None of those words sounded sincere to my ears. I didn't know what her father's house would be like. He was a stranger who'd suddenly decided to take an interest in his daughter after five years. That's all I knew about him. I didn't even know his first name.

She slammed her crayon down onto the coloring book and jumped up to her feet. Tears began to stream down her cheeks as she frantically shook her head. Before my eyes, she morphed into that terrified little girl I'd met that first day I arrived at this house.

"No! I want you to be with me, Tia! Don't let them take me. I want you there!"

Grace ran from the room crying into the bathroom and slammed the door. My heart ached for her, but all I could do was try to make her see things would be okay.

Even if I didn't trust that they would.

Rushing over to the door, I jiggled the doorknob and found she'd locked it. "Grace, listen to me. It's going to be good. You'll see. Autumn in the city is a beautiful time. You can take all your leaves so they can get to see what it's like to live in the city. Honey, say something. Please."

I listened for her to speak, but all I heard was crying. Her tears made mine come easier, and I slumped down against the bathroom door as my heart broke for her. She'd just gotten used to living in this house with her uncle, and now she had to get used to a new home and a brand new father she'd never met before.

Worst of all, she had to do it all alone.

The injustice of what had happened to this little girl who loved the outdoors and leaves and making cards for others tore me apart. None of it was fair, and I hated that I couldn't do a damn thing about it.

SOMEONE SHAKING MY SHOULDER ROUSED ME FROM sleep, and I opened my eyes to see Nico standing over me. "Tia, it's time. He's going to be here soon."

"What time is it?"

"Five. The woman from child services just called to tell me they're on their way."

I jumped up and got my bearings, remembering Grace had been in the bathroom for all this time. I must have fallen asleep talking to her. She probably thought I gave up on her. Oh, God!

"Grace, honey, it's Tia. I'm right here, sweetheart. I just fell asleep. Talk to me. It's okay."

All I heard was silence.

Turning to Nico, I clutched at his arm, feeling like if I didn't hold onto something that I'd spin out of control. "She locked herself in there right after I told her. She's been in there for over four hours! We have to do something before he shows up and the last thing she thinks of before leaving is being trapped in a bathroom all this time."

Nico tried to turn the handle but found it locked like I had hours before. "I'll have to get someone up here to open the door. That'll give you a little more time to talk to her, but that's the best I can do."

He left to call whoever he needed to, so I pressed

my mouth against the door and said in a soft voice, "Please, Grace. Just come out and we can spend some time together. I don't want you to leave without giving me a hug."

"Don't make me leave," she answered in a teary voice. "I don't want to go, Tia. Make it so I can stay here."

"I wish I could, honey. I do. I want you to stay here and we can go for walks and I can teach you all about your letters and numbers so you're ready for school next year. I really do. But your father wants you to live with him, Grace, so you have to go there. But you can send me cards you make at his house. I'll give you my address and you can send me as many cards as you want. Please come out, honey."

She said nothing in return. I heard her whisper something, but then she fell silent.

Exhausted from how sad I felt, I stumbled back against the wall and let myself cry like I'd never cried before. With my head in my hands, I sobbed at how much I was going to miss her, how afraid I was for what she'd go through when she left here, and how hard I knew it was for her to understand all these decisions the adults in her life were making.

In the midst of feeling worse than I ever had before in my life, I felt someone touch my arm, and I dropped my hands to see Grace standing in front of me. She looked up at me with kindness in her eyes, as if she was the one who should be comforting me.

Without saying a word, I opened my arms and she stepped into them so I could hug her. She wrapped her little arms around my waist and sighed against me like she had the weight of the world on her five year old shoulders.

I brushed her blond hair off her face and whispered, "I'm sorry you saw me crying. I was just sad that I might not get to see you before you left."

"Why won't they let you come with me, Tia?" she asked in a voice that threatened to make me cry again.

"Your dad has his own things he wants to do, and he probably has someone just like me at his house, so he doesn't need me. But it's going to be okay because you're going to send me lots of cards, right?"

Grace sighed again and tilted her head to look up at me. "I'll send you one every week just like I send one to mommy. Don't cry. I promise."

I had no idea where this strength in her came from, but somehow, she'd found a way to handle all that was happening to her better than I could. I'd only known her for a couple weeks, but I knew I'd never forget her.

CHAPTER 11

 *ico*

As I waited for Joshua Groves to arrive, my phone rang. I recognized the number immediately. Louis DeVille from DeVille Staffing. Suddenly, I remembered I was supposed to return his call from earlier.

"Mr. DeVille, how are you today?"

"Mr. Allen, I had hoped you would have returned my phone call. Since you didn't, this is going to be slightly awkward. I am sorry if this causes you any grief."

Just what I needed. More grief in my home. I hadn't gotten a shred of work done all day.

"Why would anything you do cause me grief? Tia has worked out wonderfully as my niece's nanny. I can't thank you enough for choosing her for this job."

"Well, unfortunately, that job is ending, isn't it? That's what I called to speak to you about this morning. I'll be at your house in a few minutes to pick her up for her next assignment. I hate that I have to inform you of this now, but again, I had hoped you'd call back before this afternoon. She starts her new job tonight."

I sat there in my office in shock. Tia leaving? I knew she wouldn't stay around for long after Grace left, but I thought we'd have a few days to enjoy one another's company and make plans for the future.

"She can't leave yet, Mr. DeVille. My niece is still here, so she needs to stay until she's gone."

"As much as I wish that could happen, I'm afraid it simply isn't possible. Tia has to start her new nanny job tonight. The man she's going to be working for insists upon it. There really is no other choice, unfortunately."

"Tonight? Why? What's the hurry? She can't start tomorrow? This is ridiculous. Tell him I need her here until the morning, so he'll have to deal with whatever he needs her for himself."

Why did everyone in the world suddenly need to do things this very fucking day? What happened to red tape? Didn't that exist anymore to slow things down?

"I'm sorry. That's not possible. Mr. Groves requires her services immediately."

Groves? Did Grace's father somehow arrange to have Tia go with his daughter tonight? How was that possible?

"Mr. Groves? Is Tia's new boss named Joshua Groves? That's my niece's father. How in the hell did he hire her and I didn't know?" I asked, incensed that I wasn't informed.

"As I said, Mr. Allen, I called you earlier to let you know about the new arrangements. How Mr. Groves and I met and arranged for Tia to be his daughter's nanny is, unfortunately, private information I cannot share with you, but I'm sure you're happy to know the little girl is going to get to stay with Tia. From what I understand from her, they really do care about one another. That must make you happy."

My heart clenched at the thought that Tia would be able to stay with Grace. She wouldn't be heartbroken about having to miss the little girl, and my niece was going to be thrilled to know her favorite person in the world would be able to stay with her.

But that would mean she and I couldn't be together. I had planned on asking Tia to stay with me here. She wouldn't have to work as anyone's nanny ever again because I'd take care of her. Anything she could want I'd give her.

Now that plan seemed impossible. How could I ask her to let Grace go when I knew it would devastate her?

I swallowed hard to push my emotions down before I answered DeVille. "Yes, of course it makes me happy. I know Tia and Grace are going to be ecstatic."

"Good. Well, I'll be there in just a few minutes to pick up Tia. Mr. Groves thought it would be best if he and his daughter met alone, without the nanny, and then he's going to surprise her later tonight."

No doubt Grace would love that. I imagined her little face when she saw Tia walk through the door at her new house in the city. I could see the two of them doing that squealing thing they did when they're happy, like when they ran around the yard chasing leaves.

But if Tia knew about this, why didn't she tell me and why did she look so torn up about Grace leaving?

"Wait, Mr. DeVille. When did you tell Tia about her new assignment?" I asked, feeling utterly betrayed by everyone at that moment.

"I haven't," he said with a laugh. "Mr. Groves thought it would be a nice surprise for her too, so I must insist that you don't say a word to her about it."

My heart sank. I couldn't even give her the good news myself. Even that had been taken away from me.

"That Mr. Groves is really a kid at heart, don't you think? When I heard he was planning to take his daughter, I immediately put out the word that I wanted to speak to him since Tia had told me about how close she and the little girl are. As soon as he heard his daughter loved her nanny, he told me he wanted to hire her permanently. I know Tia is going to be over the moon about having a full time position with a child she adores. Don't you agree?"

Unable to say much of anything as the reality of all I was losing settled in, I mumbled, "I'm sure. Well, I need to get things in order for all the changes that will be happening. I hope you understand I won't be here when you arrive, but my staff will be happy to help you and Tia take her things. Thank you for everything, Mr. DeVille."

"You're more than welcome, Mr. Allen. I'm so happy Tia turned out to be exactly what you needed."

As I ended the call, that truth hit me hard. She had been just what I needed. Tia was everything I needed, and now I had no choice but to give her up so Grace could be happy.

I had to get out of this house before he arrived because there was no way in hell I wanted to watch her walk out the door and leave my life forever.

CHAPTER 12

I PACKED THE LAST OF GRACE'S CLOTHES IN HER suitcase and heard a knock on the door behind us. When I turned around, I saw Mr. DeVille, of all people. Surprised he would be standing there in the hallway, I smiled as I zipped up the bag.

"Mr. DeVille? What are you doing here?"

With a charming smile, he said, "I'm here to take you to your next assignment. It's time to go, Tia."

Panic tore through me. I hadn't gotten to talk to Nico since I'd been so busy getting Grace ready for her father's arrival. I couldn't leave yet. I needed to speak to him. We had so many things we needed to discuss.

"I can't yet. I need to have a final meeting with Mr.

Allen before I go. It seems only right and the professional thing to do."

Mr. DeVille held up his hand to stop me. "No need. I've told him all about you having to leave now, and I believe he said he was leaving before I arrived."

"But I need to talk to him. And Grace isn't ready to go yet. Her father isn't here. I can't leave her alone."

With a smile, he stepped into the bedroom and nodded. "I saw someone coming up the drive as I pulled in, so I think he just arrived. She's going to be leaving too."

"Are you saying she doesn't get a chance to say goodbye to her uncle?" I asked in horror.

So the two of us were just going to leave without even a word to him? Is that how Nico wanted it? He must have if he left the house.

But why? I thought he cared about me. After the last few days, I was sure he did. And I thought he had grown to care about his niece too. It seemed like he had. Was it all an act? Why?

I knew why. I didn't need to ask such a stupid question. God, I was such a fool. I thought we had something special.

It had all been nothing but sex to him.

"It's time to go, Tia. I'll give you a few minutes to say goodbye to Grace," Mr. DeVille said.

When he walked out into the hallway, she tugged on my hand and smiled up at me. "He's a weird guy."

Out of the mouths of babes. She wasn't wrong. Mr. DeVille did have a weird thing going for him. I didn't notice it that day in his office because I was too busy noticing his jet black hair and sparkling blue eyes, but now that I thought about it, he had an almost otherworldly feel to him.

"He's my boss. He's taking me to my next assignment. I have to meet another little girl or boy and be their nanny. But I'm going to miss you, Grace."

"Me too. I promise I'll send cards just like I said I would. Should I send one to Uncle Nico too because I can't tell him goodbye?" she asked innocently.

I pushed aside the hurt growing inside me over what I knew to be the truth of our relationship and smiled. "That would be nice. I bet he'd like it. I think he got to really like having you around, so I think he's going to miss you."

Grace threw her arms around my waist and hugged me tightly. "I love you, Tia. Promise you'll send cards to me too?"

Fighting back the tears, I hugged her and answered, "I promise. Lots of cards."

I knew every moment we stood there together made the next one harder to leave, so I crouched down in front of her and smiled. "Now promise me something."

Her blue eyes grew big. "What?"

With a wink, I said, "Promise me you're going to be happy and you're always going to remember how smart you are."

A smile lit up her beautiful face, and she nodded in that way that told me she believed in herself as much as I did. "I promise, Tia."

"Okay then. We have places to go and people to

see, so I guess we better get moving. Your father is probably so nervous and excited to meet his little girl. You ready?"

"I think so."

I had no idea who was going to be there with Grace when she met her father for the first time since Nico had abandoned the two of us and Mr. DeVille insisted I leave now. God, I hoped it wouldn't be Agatha. That women couldn't find an ounce of warmth inside her if she was on fire.

"Best to wait here in your room. You've got your coloring book and crayons, so just pick a letter, okay?"

Grace opened up to the page she wanted to color and held it up to show me. "I'm going to do T because you told me that's what Tia starts with. T for Tia."

"Very good. Okay, I have to go now, so give me a kiss and wish me luck that I don't get stuck with a rotten kid who likes to eat dirt or tries to pull my hair all the time."

She giggled and kissed me before throwing her arms around me once more. "I love you, Tia."

I couldn't stop the tears this time. As they rolled down my cheeks, I whispered in her ear, "I love you too, Grace."

When she sat down to color the letter T, I walked over toward the door. I took one last look at her before I left so I could have that memory of her happily coloring the first letter in my name.

T for Tia.

I found Mr. DeVille standing in the main foyer near the front door staring up at the crystal chandelier above his head. With a smile as I thought about Grace saying she thought he was weird, I walked over to him to leave.

"She shouldn't be alone, you know. I would have preferred to have waited with her. With her uncle gone, she should have someone who cares with her when she meets her father."

I didn't give a damn if I sounded out of line. This wasn't right, and no matter what Mr. DeVille said, I'd never change my mind on that.

"Interesting thing this chandelier. Years ago, they had crystals that created prisms of light. Nowadays, they don't have all of those little pieces and have lights instead. I think I prefer the more intricate crystals. I'm not a fan of simple things. Believe it or not, the most beautiful things in this world are the complicated ones."

Definitely weird.

Tilting my head back, I looked up at the light and tried to find the feeling of amazement he seemed to have for it. To me, it was just another thing in this house that cost a fortune but meant nothing.

Like everything else in Nico's life. Items he collected that mean nothing to him.

"Did you see Grace's father? I had hoped to tell him a few things about her. You know, just to bring him up to speed."

Mr. DeVille finally looked away from that chandelier and smiled at me. "That won't be necessary. It seems Mr. Groves had a change of heart. I suspect the reality of dealing with a five year old finally dawned on him. He just called Mr. Allen to say he won't be coming."

I looked around to see if Nico was nearby. If Grace wasn't going with her father, did that mean she was staying here?

"With all due respect, Mr. DeVille, if Grace is staying with her uncle, then I should continue working here. Is it possible you can find another person to fill my new position?"

A slow smile spread across his mouth. "You must be reading my mind. I think you should stay here. As for the other position, not to worry. It's taken care of. But the final decision isn't up to me. It's up to Mr. Allen. If he wants you to stay, then that works for me, but if not, then I'm afraid I can't do anything about that. Why don't you see what he wants to do while I wait here and admire this interesting chandelier?"

I dropped my suitcase, letting it hit the fine marble floor with a thud, and ran toward Nico's office. "I'll be right back, Mr. DeVille!"

By the time I reached the end of the hallway, I needed to catch my breath. No matter what Nico thought of me, he had to admit I was the one person who should be with Grace. If he intended on being petty and cruel, then I'd give it right back to him and let him know I wasn't leaving without a fight.

I marched into his office to find him sitting behind his desk very much like that day when Grace and I brought him that picture she made him. He looked about as miserable too.

My heart started racing, but I took a deep breath

and said, "If Grace isn't going, then I don't want to go either. She and I should stay together. She's had a hard enough time with what happened to her mother. To take away her closest friend in the world would just be cruel, and as much as I think you're a son of a bitch, Nico, I don't think you're someone who wants to be intentionally cruel to a five year old girl anymore."

He looked up at me with shock written all over his face. "Why am I a son of a bitch?"

"I don't really want to talk about that now. I'm here to tell you I think if you send me away from that little girl because you don't give a damn about me and only wanted sex from me, then you're an ass."

Nico stood from his chair and walked over to me, still looking surprised I was saying any of this at all. I bet he thought I'd just be some pathetic lay who would beg him to stay with her.

Well, he needed to erase that thought from his head right now. I only wanted to stay because of Grace. Nothing else. The fact that I still cared for him and could barely stand in this room without wanting to kiss him didn't matter.

All that mattered was Grace.

"Is that what you think? That I only wanted you for sex and I don't care about you?" he asked in a voice full of hurt.

"Well, you left without even saying goodbye. That sounds like you don't care, which logically leads me to believe you just used me for sex. Not that I care, because I don't. I only care about Grace. So are you going to be a decent human being and let me stay with her now that her father has decided not to bother actually being her father? By the way, I have to tell you this poor child has the worst people in the world related to her. Her mother is in prison for stealing from people, probably elderly people on a fixed income who couldn't afford to lose a penny, much less their life savings. Her father is a flake who turned this house upside down and a little girl's life with it and then decided to just go catch a wave or something. Hang ten, douchebag. And you, well, you thought it was okay to leave the two of us without even letting us say goodbye. You people are a piece of work."

By the time I finished, Nico's dark eyes stared down at me, wide open and full of what looked like anger. Well, he better be prepared to defend himself with all his anger if he planned on sending me away and bringing in another nanny.

God, I hated that idea. What if Grace didn't like her? What if she was like Agatha?

Or what if Nico liked her and the new nanny and he ended up together, happily ever after?

"Are you finished?" he asked brusquely.

I set my jaw defiantly and nodded. If he was going to send me away, I planned to look him dead in the eyes when he did it. He'd get to see my judgment of him being an asshole with every word he spoke.

For a long moment, he remained silent, but then he pulled me to him in a kiss that took my breath away. I felt like my head was spinning, and when he finally released me, I didn't know if my legs would hold me up.

"So does that mean I get to stay as Grace's nanny?"

For the first time since I walked into this office, he smiled. "Yes. I can't believe you thought I'd let you go."

"Well, Mr. DeVille told me it was up to you, and since you basically just walked out without saying goodbye to Grace or me, I figured you didn't want me here anymore."

I lowered my gaze to the floor and added, "Because you didn't care about me and all we were was sex."

Nico said nothing, and as the seconds ticked by, I struggled to keep myself from crying. Why wasn't he saying anything? He really didn't care about me at all? Then why the hell did he just kiss me like that?

Finally, in a low voice, he said, "I left because I couldn't face losing you and Grace. I love you, Tia. It was so much more than sex between us. You made me want to be a better man. No one has ever accomplished that with me. I never want to let you go."

Did he mean that? He loved me?

I looked up at him and saw he was serious. "You love me?"

He smiled and sighed. "Yes. I'm hoping you feel something like that for me, because if you don't, I'm just going to have to work harder to make you fall in love with me."

Thrilled to hear those words, I threw my arms

around him and kissed that beautiful mouth. "I love you too, Nico."

As we stood there in each other's arms, I knew I'd never been happier than at that moment. I'd get to continue living with my two favorite people in the world. I loved Nico, my job, and most of all, I loved being Grace's nanny.

"So what happened with Grace's father?"

Nico shrugged. "Not sure. The person from child services called a little while ago to say he wouldn't be coming. I guess he changed his mind. I told her she and he would be in for the legal fight of the century if he tried this again. I don't plan to have some surfer dude think he can simply cruise into my niece's life any damn time he wants."

"You sound like you like Grace. How did that happen?"

With a smile, he nodded. "It turns out she reminds me a lot of me when I was young. You were right. She's a smart kid. I like that."

"Let's go tell her we're all staying here together. She's going to be so happy," I said, pulling him toward the hallway.

"Okay. I need to deal with Louis DeVille first, so I'll meet you in her room."

All of a sudden, I remembered she expected her father to show up tonight. How would she feel when she heard he didn't?

"What are we going to tell her, Nico? I don't want her to feel like her own father didn't want to be bothered to come get her."

He thought for a moment and kissed me. "Tell her I didn't want to lose my two favorite girls. Don't worry. She's going to be so happy you're staying with her that she won't care anything about him. Now go tell her the good news."

"Okay! Don't be long. I'm thinking we should have a tea party, and you're invited!"

I ran down the hallway, past Mr. DeVille still staring up at that silly chandelier. "I'm staying, Mr. DeVille!" I called out as I ran to the other side of the house. "Thank you!"

Grace sat in the middle of the floor coloring her letters and looked up in shock when she saw me run into the room. "Guess what? We're both staying. Your uncle didn't want to lose his two favorite girls, and your father said he'd wait, so you and I are staying right here! Let's unpack your things."

She dropped her crayon on the beautiful picture of the letter T and ran over to her suitcase. "We're staying! Yay!"

We were all staying together. Grace, Nico, and me. And he loved me.

Everything about the three of us was complicated. Just like Mr. DeVille said, the most beautiful things in this life were just that.

Complicated.

NICO ALLEN CARED ABOUT NOTHING BUT MONEY AND HIS comfort when he came to me looking for a nanny for his niece.

For one of the few times in my career, I actually gave a client what he wanted.

But he needed something much more.

That's where Tia came in. Sweet and caring, she showed him there was more to life than just business and whatever selfish things he wanted for himself. She offered him a different way, one that let him see all work and no love made Nico a miserable man.

A way that combined her love of Grace and her youthful love of life.

Human beings get so lost in possessions that they forget what really matters is love. Tia showed Nico that lesson through her caring for little Grace. But he didn't fully understand how much he cared for either of them until the little girl's father threatened to take them both away.

I often find that men need a little push in the right direction, so I made sure Nico got that push. As for Joshua Groves, he's more than happy being a single, childless man.

Maybe if he comes to me looking for help someday, I can give him the happiness he hasn't found yet. That's what I do, after all.

The person who impressed me most in all of this was little Grace. Normally, people get frightened when I suddenly appear in front of them, but not her. She simply looked up at me and asked if I was an angel come to help her. With a smile, I shook my head. She's too young to understand the particulars of who I am.

But she never cried the whole time I stood in that bathroom and told her everything would be all right and that she just had to trust me. I believe that little girl has a strength the world will have to reckon with in the years to come.

I wonder how long it will take before Nico and Tia have a baby of their own. I think they'd be wonderful parents. Don't you?

KEEP READING FOR MORE ABOUT K.M.'S BOOKS!

SNEAK PEEK

Have you started the NeXt series yet? The couples from the Club X series had kids, and now they're getting their stories told! Start it today and see why readers love the NeXt series!

NOTORIOUS (NeXt #1)

Cade March loves his life. Free to do as he likes and wealthy enough to afford whatever his heart desires, he's all about having fun.

As the only son of Stefan March, he's the spitting image of his father in every way.

And that's the problem. At least for everyone else.

Hailey Canton lives a very different life. Still recovering from a betrayal that's left her shaken and no longer believing in love, she only has the desserts she makes for her parents' small restaurant to make her feel like she can do anything.

The cakes and cookies she lovingly creates are

works of art, but to her, they're simply a lifeline so she doesn't give up.

What happens when the very thing she's feared comes into her life in the form of a gorgeous man with no idea that life has any limits and who fears nothing?

START THE NeXt SERIES TODAY!

ABOUT THE AUTHOR

K.M. Scott writes contemporary romance stories of sexy, intense, and unforgettable love. A New York Times and USA Today bestselling author, she's been in love with romance since reading her first romance novel in junior high (she was a very curious girl!). Under her Gabrielle Bisset name, she write paranormal and historical romance. She lives in Pennsylvania with a herd of animals and when she's not writing can be found reading or feeding her TV addiction.

Be sure to visit K.M.'s Facebook page at **https://www.facebook.com/kmscottauthor** for all the latest on her books, along with giveaways and other goodies! And to hear all the news on K.M. Scott books first, sign up for her newsletter today and be sure to visit her website at **http://www.kmscottbooks.com**

BOOKS BY K.M. SCOTT:

Crash Into Me (Heart of Stone #1)

Fall Into Me (Heart of Stone #2)

Give In To Me (Heart of Stone #3)

Heart of Stone Volume One

Ever After (Heart of Stone #4)

A Heart of Stone Christmas (Heart of Stone #5)

Return To Me (Heart of Stone #6)

Forever With Me (Heart of Stone #7)

Heart of Stone Volume Two

Hard As Stone (Heart of Stone #8)

Set In Stone (Heart of Stone #9)

Silent As A Stone (Heart of Stone #10)

Heart of Stone Volume Three

All of Me (Heart of Stone #11)

Temptation (Club X #1)

Surrender (Club X #2)

Possession (Club X #3)

Satisfaction (Club X #4)

Acceptance (Club X #5)

Complete Club X Series Box Set

Dirty Boss Volume One (contains all three Dirty Boss series books)

K.M.'S BOOKS ARE IN AUDIOBOOK TOO!